THE THINARA KING

REBECCA LOCHLANN

ERINYES PRESS

The Thinara King
Copyright Rebecca Lochlann 2012: All rights reserved
Internal design Rebecca Lochlann

Trade Paperback:
ISBN-13: 978-0-9838277-2-6
ISBN-10: 0-9838-2772-9
Library of Congress Control Number 2012931397

Published in the United States by Erinyes Press

Also available as an eBook:
ISBN-13: 978-0-9838277-3-3
ISBN-10: 0-9838-2773-7

Praise for The Child of the Erinyes

"Lochlann has a great flair for sensory detail and fills her novel with such a wealth of sights, sounds, smells and flavors that the reader feels absolutely immersed in the world of ancient Crete from the first page."
Historical Novel Review

"The depth of historical information in this novel will delight fans of the genre. A surprising amount of history and archaeology has been slipped unobtrusively into the narrative. Lochlann has clearly done an astounding amount of research into her historical setting and culture, yet she never overwhelms the reader with specifics, nor does she lecture. The conveyance of historical facts and archaeological tidbits feels very natural, woven deftly into the dialogs and thoughts of her intriguing cast of characters."
Libbie Hawker, author of *The Ragged Edge of Night*, published by Lake Union

"There is, quite simply, nothing about this book which is not superb. You have translated words, ideas, poetry, character, myth into an alchemic wonder, a dazzling novel of the ancient world, and are a fit heir to the great mantle of such writers as Mary Renault, Scott O'Dell and Robert Graves, and even, dare I say it, the goddess herself."
M.M. Bennetts, author of *May, 1812* and *Of Honest Fame*

"A collision of destiny and passion from the pen of a true bard."
Sulari Gentill, author of The Rowland Sinclair series and *Crossing the Lines,* 2018 Winner of the Ned Kelly Award for Best Crime Fiction, published by Poisoned Pen Press

"The Year-God's Daughter succeeds in bringing to life a very distant world and capturing a heady blend of archaeology, legend, myth and fantasy."
Judith Starkston, author of *Hand of Fire,* published by Bronze Age Books

"A difficult subject risen to with an imagination at the height of its powers. I have a vivid memory of my trip to Mycenae and Lochlann gave back to those broken stones all their lost life and colour."
Violet Wells, author and translator

Of *The Sixth Labyrinth*: "Lochlann evokes the world of Victorian times as effortlessly as she did when she conjured the ancient world."
Elisabeth Storrs, author of *The Wedding Shroud, The Golden Dice,* and *Call to Juno: A Tale of Ancient Rome,* published by Lake Union

"Passion, love, ancient rituals, and a world that truly comes alive every time you turn a page. A spell-binding story."
History and Women

"Lochlann's over-arching narrative, switching from character to character, is deftly composed, making for many surprises without deviating from the backdrop with its elaborate history-rich trappings. A tale of ancient kingdoms, of love promised and lost, heralded victory and hopeless defeat."
Chanticleer Book Reviews

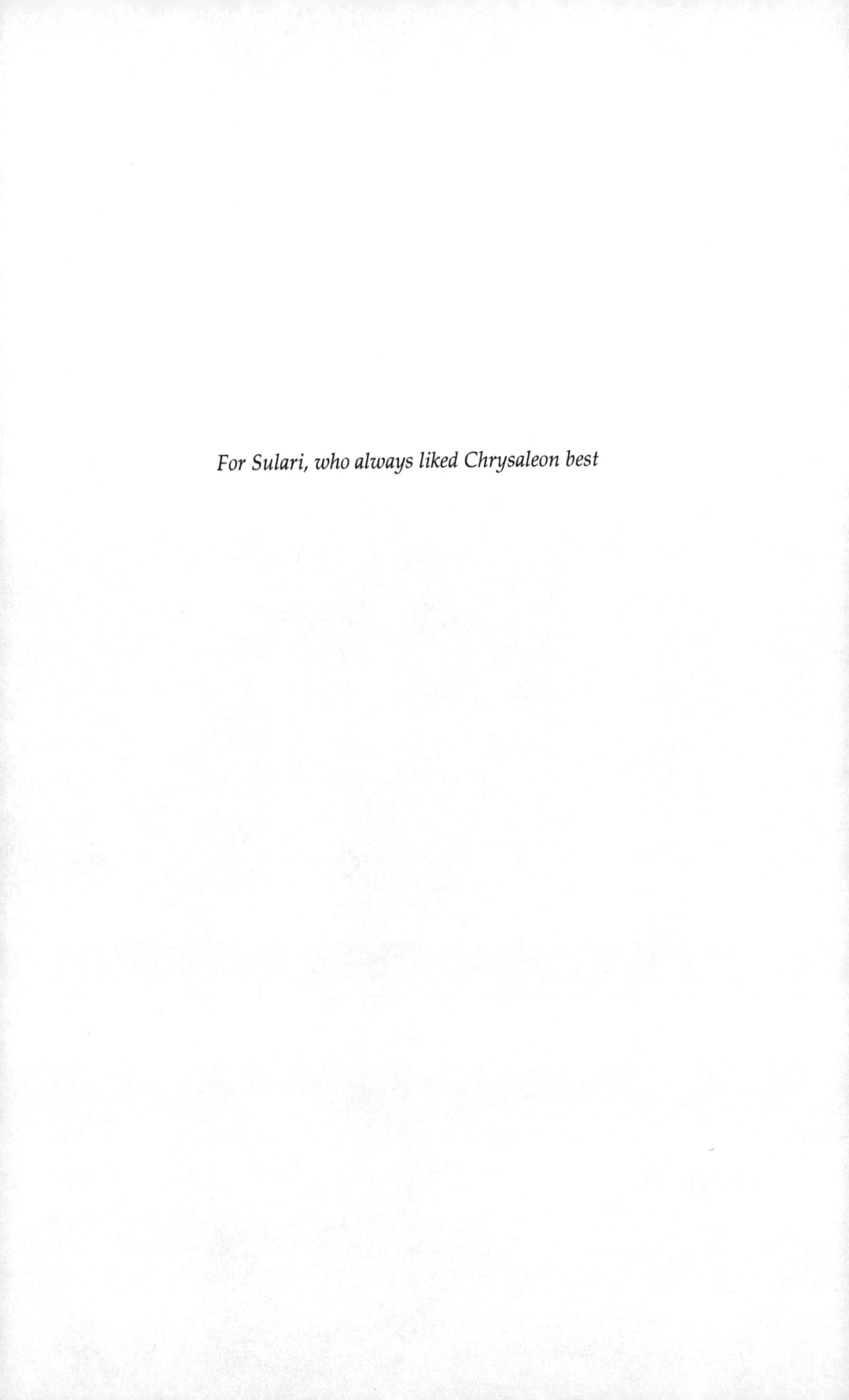

For Sulari, who always liked Chrysaleon best

THE THINARA KING

REBECCA LOCHLANN

ERINYES
PRESS

Book Two

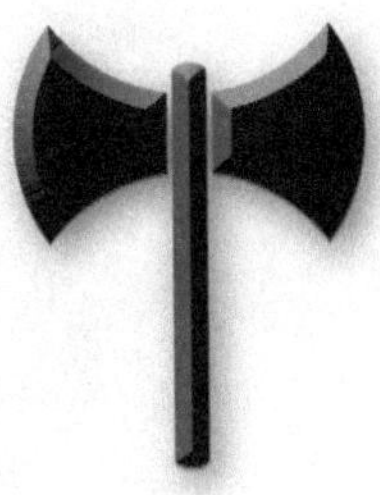

The Child of the Erinyes Series

Maiden

"Now came the dust, though still thinly. I look back: a dense cloud looms behind us, following us like a flood poured across the land. "Let us turn aside while we can still see, lest we be knocked over in the street and crushed by the crowd of our companions." We had scarcely sat down when a darkness came that was not like a moonless or cloudy night, but more like the black of closed and unlighted rooms. You could hear women lamenting, children crying, men shouting. Some were calling for parents, others for children or spouses; they could only recognize them by their voices. Some bemoaned their own lot, others that of their near and dear. There were some so afraid of death that they prayed for death. Many raised their hands to the gods, and even more believed that there were no gods any longer and that this was one last unending night for the world."

~~Pliny the Younger

PART I

The Abyss

Moon of Figs and Acorns

FIRE. A BLINDING SHOCK OF GREEN LIGHTNING THAT COULD ONLY BE hurled from the mind of a god. Smoke. Blizzards of crystallized grey snow that didn't melt but collected in his eyelashes, around his nose, and in his throat. No, it was not snow. It was ash.

Discomfort woke Alexiare abruptly. Fighting for breath, covered in sweat, he sipped from a pitcher of watered wine, restoring calm and freshening his tongue before returning his concentration to the dream, undoubtedly one of the most vivid he had ever experienced.

The very ground had shifted and moved like water. The air scorched the inside of his nose and deeper, in his lungs. He was reminded of the night, six years gone now, when he attended a feast of celebration on the isle of Crete. High-ranking refugees from the northern outpost of Callisti had terrified everyone with horrifying tales of fiery stones shooting from the heavens, the earth's heavy yaw, poisoned air, and once-pristine lakes transforming to boiling black sludge.

He examined every detail he could recall of the dream, lingering on images of Chrysaleon, Mycenae's prince and his master. Arrogant, handsome Chrysaleon, who turned his head up to the heavens and shouted defiance at a shower of sparks.

You won't have me!

Who did he bellow at so furiously? Who was up there, just out of sight, hidden in darkness and streams of fire? Whatever god brought Alexiare the dream veiled that part.

Chrysaleon gripped the hand of a young woman. Alexiare knew who she was, though six years had passed since he had last seen her—years that had taken her from innocent child to beautiful woman. She was Princess Aridela, second of Queen Helice's royal daughters. He remembered how that rash, headstrong child had entered the bullring and, of course, been promptly gored. Later, when she sneaked away from her nurses and her wound broke open, it was Menoetius, Chrysaleon's bastard half brother, who rescued her from a cold, lonely death in the temple labyrinth.

A shiver crept down his spine. Was this dream a premonition? Was it something that had already happened, or was going to happen?

Alexiare gave dreams serious regard. Omens, he called them. They could direct a mortal's life for good or ill. Many times they offered warning, and were ignored or dismissed at the dreamer's peril.

It was possible, though, that the dream was simply born from the terrible ache of longing he'd suffered since Chrysaleon and Menoetius left Mycenae on a ship bound for Crete. Nearly a month had passed since that day. He had waited patiently at the water's edge, hoping Chrysaleon would gift him with a smile at least, perhaps a word or two, but he didn't. It was Menoetius who grinned and cuffed him on the shoulder.

A few nights after, the first of the dreams descended. Nightmares. Anxiety troubled his days as well. There was no way to know what mischief Chrysaleon was getting into, no way to intervene. Not for an instant did Alexiare consider Menoetius a trustworthy guardian, though the king apparently did.

Idómeneus, High King of Mycenae and father to both Chrysaleon and Menoetius, wanted Crete. He had sent his sons there, charging them with the task of finding weaknesses that would allow his armies a way in—a trick that would give him the edge he needed to overthrow the island, steal its wealth, and make its people his slaves. Yet another bauble for his own glory. Yes, he had extracted a vow from Chrysaleon to keep his head down, to avoid danger or risk. Alexiare rose from his pallet, fists clenched, muscles itching with frustration. The king was a simpleton if he thought some hastily coerced promise would stop Chrysaleon from throwing himself into the midst of disaster.

If only the impetuous warrior-prince would relinquish his stubborn love of danger, rebellion, and adventure. But asking for such a thing was like screaming at the heavens to stop the sun from rising.

If Idómeneus had been wise enough to send Alexiare along, he could have watched over Chrysaleon, kept him from harm. Alexiare would do anything to protect the heir to Mycenae's crown—the youth he loved in tortured silence, knowing he would be banished or slaughtered if Chrysaleon ever suspected his true feelings.

Should he risk the king's unpredictable temper with a request for ships and a squadron or two of warriors? Suggesting that Idómeneus's eldest trueborn son might be in some nebulous danger could earn Alexiare a beating. Hearing that Alexiare's fear was birthed from a dream would make himself the subject of ridicule.

Alexiare longed to journey to the coast. If he could stand on the cliffs and gaze southward, over the vast fathomless seas, perhaps his mind could conjure a way to help. But his aged bones creaked painfully at the mere thought of overland travel, and he was a slave. He couldn't go where he wished, when he wished.

Perhaps he should once again delve into the ancient mysteries. It was dangerous, to be sure, and he was still haunted by the last time he'd done so. Wicked Sorcha, Menoetius's dead mother, had punished him for his arrogance. Just thinking of it brought back the stench of the poor puppy he had burned in the hearth fire.

But when a man couldn't find practical answers to a dilemma, the power of blood and enchantment could often provide one.

For his beloved Chrysaleon, he would brave any peril—the anger of his master, the derision of the council, even the dangerous attention of the Immortals.

Moon of Figs and Acorns

ON THEIR THIRD DAY AT PHAISTOS, QUEEN HELICE'S SOUTHERN PALACE ON the isle of Crete, Chrysaleon and Aridela went along with a team of bull leapers to watch the capture of a wild bull.

All too soon, they would return to Knossos. Chrysaleon would take up the mantle of bull-king and consort to Aridela's boring sister, Iphiboë. The thought was intolerable. He had overheard the Phrygian woman, Selene, make a prediction that Aridela, not Iphiboë, would be queen of Kaphtor. On that nebulous foretelling, he had fought and nearly died to become Crete's king. But what if she was dreaming, or mistaken? The possibility made his guts grind.

The troupe painted themselves with stripes of green dye to help them blend into the foliage. They tethered a cow near the bull they hoped to attract then hid downwind and waited.

Chrysaleon and Aridela set up a picnic on a slope beneath the shady branches of a poplar, where they could view the scene without disturbing it. Aridela's attendants and the litter-bearers sat nearby, within sight but out of earshot.

"She is ready to mate," Aridela said. "Her scent entices the bull. He will mount her and the team will hobble his back legs. When he finishes, they net him."

"Cruel sport for the bull." Chrysaleon popped an olive in his mouth.

"Dancing with the bulls helps us keep peace with the Lady. For time beyond measure, she has harnessed her Earth Bull in our mountains, beneath the rocks where no mortal can reach. When she is angered, he roars and the land heaves. No matter what stone we use nor how thick we cut our pillars, everything we have built crumbles as though made of twigs, balanced one upon the next without any mortar." Her voice lowered. "Once, long ago, Potnia ordered her bull to topple all of Kaphtor. Multitudes were killed. Our palaces and cities were destroyed."

"How did your people anger her?"

"Some say we changed, and believed we were as strong as she, or as wise. Others claim the queen allowed one of her consorts to live beyond his time. Athene did send warning through one of our oracles. Some escaped onto the sea in boats. We rebuilt, as you have seen."

She twined her arms over her head, stretched, and turned her face to the sun. Golden light bathed her cheeks, glinted through her eyes and lashes like a lover's touch, sparking more colors than Chrysaleon knew existed.

"Look." She scooped a handful of ivy from the trunk of the tree and placed her hand on one of the leaves, spreading her fingers over its surface. "Each leaf has five fingers, honoring the hand of Athene. Artisans fill their homes with vases of ivy to spur imagination and creativity."

He could well believe Aridela a goddess in her own right, with her black eyes, the delicate yet defined bone structure she'd inherited from Helice, and a mouth that made his groin ache. He could almost picture giving up everything for her, even his life, without regret. Perhaps the old saying was indeed truth—that Athene planted the desire to die within the heart of every bull-king.

The image of Aridela's triumphant leap in the bullring would never grow dull—that and the first time he had seen her, swimming naked in the forest pool on Mount Ida. On the heels of those memories came more, of their coupling in the cave, of her erotic desire and fierce response. Yet something else nagged him, something harder to define. He hadn't expected wisdom, or such reckless courage, or the trust she had so quickly and loyally granted him. He felt dazzled, as though he stood in the path of a star, and feared she could fast become a compulsion.

Below them, the cow flicked her tail at flies and grazed, untroubled.

Heat made the wound on his forearm itch. He rubbed the dressing absently. Eleven days had passed since his struggle for the crown in the labyrinth at Knossos. Lycus, Kaphtor's foremost bull leaper, had managed to inflict several wounds upon him, which he still found unbelievable and annoying. Besides the large slice in Chrysaleon's forearm, there was also a deep puncturing cut in his thigh and a tender, half-healed gash on the side of his head. But Lycus had fared much worse. He couldn't even walk yet, and suffered from blood fever.

"I cannot bear this," he said quietly.

Aridela continued to watch the cow, but the muscles in her jaw tightened and a shadow formed between her brows.

"It is you I want, you I fought for. Not your sister."

She met his gaze. "Do you understand what you have done? Your father—is he truly willing to give you up?"

Chrysaleon considered. He didn't want to lie to this girl with the obsidian eyes, not completely, anyway. He would take a chance and see where it carried him.

"He wants our countries united. Yet he respects your mother, and ruled out any talk of invasion or war."

"So you competed to strengthen this alliance."

"He forbade me the competition. I defied him because, when you entered the ring, when you leaped the bull, a god's noose slipped around my neck and bound me to Kaphtor—to you. I have known from that day to this I will never leave."

She tucked her lower lip under her teeth.

"Before I saw you," he went on, "I railed at my fate, ordered to travel so far to watch other men fight for some dust-dry princess. How was I to know that here, in the bullring at Labyrinthos, I would discover my perfect mate?"

Shock passed over her face. "I felt Athene's hands pushing me into the bullring that day. Since I was small I knew she wanted me to dance with a bull. I knew it would change something, but was never sure what. Now I see. It changed you. She wanted you to enter the Games, so you would win and become our Zagreus. The bull dance was how she spurred you to it." She frowned as she squinted at the ivy resting on her palm. "I don't think—no, I am certain. I have not had the dream of leaping a bull since that day. Not once."

Her acceptance of deliberate divine intervention reminded him of a child. He started to smile, to tell her she shouldn't give deities too much importance, but the scene below called for their attention.

The underbrush shook and a colossal brown bull crashed into sight.

The cow stopped grazing. With a gruff snort, the bull pawed the earth and trotted to her, smelling the air.

Chrysaleon offered the scene a cursory glance before turning back to Aridela. He sensed the advantage he'd created and didn't want to lose it. "How could I have known," he said, "before I came here, that your waist would fit my hands like it was made for them? That your body would mold into mine and mine into yours as though we were fashioned within the same womb?"

Appreciation flickered across her face, but the frown returned. Someone had warned her against him—he saw it in her eyes.

Receiving acquiescence from the cow's uplifted tail, the grunting bull mounted her hindquarters.

Chrysaleon plucked one of the leaves off the vine and traced it from Aridela's shoulder to her wrist. "The bull cares for nothing but his brief pleasure, and when it is done won't remember the cow. But that is not the way for us. Whether I want to or not, I love you. Have I not proved it through the battle I waged in the labyrinth? By these wounds I suffer for your sake?"

His argument formed without planning or preparation, and for the first time he wasn't sure if he was still telling lies.

Her deep black gaze softened. "Goddess Athene paired you to my sister. You will ascend Kaphtor's throne at her side. The council made the decision."

"Your decision holds me, not the council's. If they forbid our union, we can leave. Your home will be the citadel of Mycenae. We have mountains in plenty to remind you of Kaphtor, but I will never leave you alone long enough to miss it. Our palace, though not as magnificent as yours, is the finest on the Argolid. I have seen how much you love honey. I will pack our storerooms with jars and serve you honey-cakes three times a day. You will know honor and respect as my wife, as Mycenae's queen. Would you not rather come with me than waste your life buried in caves praying and breathing smoke?"

"And what of Iros of Tiryns, who is already your wife?"

Ah. Her doubts came from Harpalycus, his oldest, most hated rival. He should have known. "That means nothing to me. It was arranged without my knowledge or consent. I will send her back to her father."

"And in doing so, make me the cause of war between Mycenae and Tiryns."

He shrugged. "I would gladly flatten Tiryns if you would agree to join me at Mycenae."

"You ask me to abandon my people, betray my mother and sister, defy Lady Athene. Do you imagine we would be allowed a single day of happiness?"

The painted team crept out of hiding and roped the hobble around the bull's hind legs. His furious bellow reverberated up the slope.

"Do you want that to be my fate?" Chrysaleon nodded toward the bull. "Hobbled, cheated, helpless?"

"You would take me from all I was born to do and leave Kaphtor in turmoil." Aridela shuddered. "My mother would never stop hunting you until you were dead."

The dancers fell back, laughing, and allowed the bull to finish his business. Afterward there was some thrashing, but the strong nets eventually won out. The bull gave up and sprawled on his side, exhausted.

"I am restless," Aridela said. She started to take his hand in her own but, glancing at the attendants, brushed off her tunic instead and rose. "There is no purpose in debating things that will never be. Why don't we hunt or explore?"

He bit his lip to hold back angry demands. Seldom was he forced to wait for what he wanted, whether it be a pomegranate, a well-crafted spear, or a virgin. When had he ever bothered to speak so many flowered words to a woman? And why did he offer marriage? She was right; it would mean war, not only between Mycenae and Tiryns but Mycenae and Crete. He had declared his willingness to fight for her, but was he willing to send thousands to their death for the sake of this unreasonable lust?

Litter-bearers carried them back to the palace. She went off to exchange her gown for a sturdier tunic while Chrysaleon wandered the terraces on the hillside and stretched his leg, which had stiffened from sitting beneath the tree. He saw his half brother, Menoetius, and Aridela's friend, Selene, walking along a low rock wall. Selene laughed up at him, and Menoetius bent to kiss her.

Aridela reappeared, clad in muted brown and a plain leather belt. She carried two bows but warned him that the hills around Phaistos had little game to offer, as the farmers did their best to keep animals away from the crops.

"My friend is taken with your guard." She nodded toward the unaware couple. "She called his lovemaking a pleasure beyond belief, and blushed as though he was her first."

Even as Chrysaleon gave a skeptical snort, he was struck by a transient expression on Aridela's face. Sadness? Nostalgia?

He saw again in memory how Menoetius had reddened when it was revealed that he and Aridela knew each other.

"Perhaps she was dreaming or drunk," he said. "He spares little time for women. I cannot believe him accomplished in such matters."

Aridela dismissed her attendants in a tone that brooked no argument, something she had been specifically forbidden from doing by both her mother and the oracle, Themiste. His hopes leaped. She had put him off so far, citing his wounds and all those who watched them so carefully. Perhaps she had finally realized he was perfectly capable of making love to her.

In answer to their timid protests, she said she was taking Chrysaleon for a short walk along the road, pointed where she meant, and promised to remain in sight. They reluctantly agreed. Wasting no time, she led him south along the well-worn road. At first they passed fishermen, women carrying baskets of laundry, litters, and oxen, but the farther they walked, the fewer people they encountered. Eventually, trees and rolling hills hid them from the palace altogether.

Chrysaleon's hopes crept upward again.

"Tell me about the first time you met Menoetius," he said. The request stuck in his throat like bad cheese; he hated the idea of his brother sharing secrets with this woman, no matter how innocent the circumstances. He needed Aridela's side of things.

"He didn't tell you?" Aridela's gaze turned up to his and he was freshly astonished at her eyes, which seemed to consume half her face, and never displayed any hint of trickery or deceit. He wanted badly to rip off that tunic, to feel her beneath him, and he suspected she had arranged this walk so he could, but it would wait for the right place, the right time. Then he would have her, again and again, and forge her to him as a sword blade forged to its hilt, leaving no room for Menoetius, Lycus, or any other man.

"No." Now that they were out of sight of the palace, he clasped her hand. "I learned of it the day of the Games, from your brother, Isandros."

Her mouth turned up in a wistful smile. Apparently, his question sparked fond memories. He struggled to maintain an unconcerned air and tightened his grip.

"It doesn't surprise me," she said. "Even then, he was quiet. Shy. He saved my life. I confess I loved him, as a child will love an older, brave, and handsome man. I am sure he thought me quite silly. I remember weeping for days when he left, and thinking death preferable to losing him."

Chrysaleon unclenched his teeth with effort and forcibly swallowed resentment and jealousy. "What happened?"

"I tried once before to dance with a bull." She laughed. "I was ten and very stupid. I thought the bull was no match for me. Of course I was gored. You have seen the scar."

"Yes."

"Isandros helped me sneak into the ring. He was under sentence of death for that. So I went to the shrine to pray for mercy, and my wound broke open. I would have bled to death but for Carmanor. That was the name he used; I don't know why. It is hard to think of him now as 'Menoetius.' He was there, praying. He carried me to the courtyard. He told you nothing of this?"

Chrysaleon shrugged. "He was praying?"

"Yes." With a glance backward, she pulled him off the road, beneath the overhanging branches of a plane tree, and into a verdant, deserted meadow. "I loved his reverence. It was not idle habit or show, but real, and meant much to me, for I had heard all mainland barbarians were crude and impious."

"Menoetius, devout?" Chrysaleon laughed coarsely. "Not anymore, my lady. He no longer has any use for such things."

Surprise passed over her face then she looked sad, saying only, "He is much changed."

Good. If he could damage, even raze those tender memories, so much the better. "What happened after?"

"It was not clear at first if he had tried to help or hurt me. My mother was suspicious. She confined him until I could verify his story. Then of course, we feasted him and gave him many gifts."

"So I am in my blood brother's debt." He brought her hand to his mouth and kissed it. "I must thank him."

A strong wind lifted from the west; it was hot, dry, and made them thirsty. Darkness fell earlier than usual, leaving vaults of purple in the heavens and the scent of wild thyme flowing on swift currents of air.

They came upon an old ruin of a wall that offered protection at their backs, and built a fire with bits of wood and debris they found.

"All my life I have heard of Kaphtor," Chrysaleon said as they settled beside it. He put one arm around her and made a sweeping gesture with the other. "Rich land of ships, palaces, mountains, caves, and fertile plains. I thought these must be fanciful lies. Women, owning the land, passing it to their daughters? Such a thing could never happen in my country. Yet my slave, Alexiare, explained how well your people managed, and for how many long ages—since before any of Argolis was tilled or any citadel built. My ancestors brought powerful gods to help them crush and conquer, but when we came to the edge of land and looked out for more places to vanquish, Crete's mighty ships forced us to stop."

"Where do your people come from?"

"Our bards sing of vast plains of grass, high mountains on every side, of snow and ice that can freeze a man solid in a single night. It is said our ancestors journeyed four entire seasons to reach the lands we now call home."

"And your gods? I have only learned a little about them."

"They reside in the sky, the ocean, on mountaintops. They control everything, from sunlight to earthshaking, and have jealous tempers. Foremost among them is King Poseidon, Hippos, Father of horses, Lord of the earth, sea, and heavens. He gave us the horse, a beast more precious to us than any other. One of his palaces lies beneath the sea, where he keeps stables of coral and white stallions with manes of gold. He sinks our ships when angered, and destroys our coasts with waves as tall as thunderclouds. He visits us in the form of a bull, and in the heavens, we see him in the sun and the moon."

"My tutors told me about Lord Poseidon, but they never made him sound as glorious as you do."

"Every village my ancestors conquered worshipped Lady Athene, White-Armed Hera, and she the farmers call Dark Hecate. We merged these mistresses into our own beliefs, for we saw their worth and knew we would have an easier time with the people if we honored their deities."

Wind swooped as though wanting attention. The fire leaped in response, swirling, lifting blue-edged tendrils of flame and brilliant sparks.

"Kaphtor," Chrysaleon continued, "where the path of moon and stars is as familiar as the change of seasons, and the smallest lump of gold can be measured. Palaces sprawl like cities, marvels of comfort and elegance. In truth, Alexiare reminds me how Labyrinthos stood established and civilized when my own people were naked savages living in caves." He bowed his head in exaggerated homage. "A commanding yet generous lady—that is Kaphtor, lying in perfect conjunction along the best trade-routes from Egypt and Isy. She brings us the tin we crave, purple dye to impress our rivals, and all the comforts we can no longer live without. She forges ties with everyone and leads all in prosperity."

"Do you mock us?" She looked wary.

"Perhaps I would like to," Chrysaleon said with a shrug. "But Alexiare spoke the truth. I always thought his claims mere lies, the overblown boasting or false memories of an old man. But now I see they were not."

"Lady Athene showed favor to my people when she sent her daughter to lead us here from our homeland."

"Where is the land of your ancestors?"

"To the south. It is a country so vast it takes years to get from one end to the other. The sun burns everything; no snow ever falls but on the highest mountains. There is a beast, I am told, which towers as high as our highest walls. It eats leaves from the very tips of trees, and I have heard tales of another, so big it can crush a man with one foot. It has a nose like the body of a serpent! And lions, my lord." Lifting her hand, she touched his hair then rested her palm on his cheek, her mouth curving into a slow smile. "You are like a lion. Your father named you truly."

The need to kiss her threatened to blot out Chrysaleon's argument. His mind fell into blankness, but he fought his way back. "You say Athene showed your people favor. Yet it seems to me she has shown you no favor at all."

"Why?" Aridela's smile faded into startled surprise.

His wounded leg ached; he rolled onto his side so he could stretch it and cupped her knee in one hand. "If you were a peasant or a farmer's child, you could leave Crete and be with me."

"Athene sees all, from beginning to end. She does not plan things according to the fleeting wishes of mortals."

"You accept your lot without question or protest." He sat up and seized her shoulders. "Does it never weigh upon you?"

"It has," she said in a small voice. He felt her tremble.

"And now?" He shook her, more roughly than he intended.

"If I were a peasant, you would not want me."

He bit back the urge to shout, to strike, to cut something with his sword. "Can you not see this is beyond any duty? Curse my father, my brothers, and the child who believes herself my wife. I would have you no matter what your station, or mine. You alone separate us. I would abandon my vows, betray my father and my country to have you."

"No, you wouldn't. You would not do that."

Wind zipped over the wall and set upon them, pulling Aridela's hair free of its knot and sending it flying about her head.

Chrysaleon's gaze followed the flight of her hair as he recalled his purpose. To find a way to overthrow these people. To end the king-sacrifice. He realized how hard he was gripping her and saw pain reflected in her eyes. With a deep, calming breath, he relaxed and massaged her shoulders. "Perhaps not," he said, "but I would perform my duty like a man whose soul had been stripped from him and cast into the shadowlands." Uneasy truth laced his words. Could he over-throw Kaphtor and subjugate Aridela, make her and her kin his slaves? No longer certain, he pulled her against him, closing his eyes and mind as he kissed her.

When he did at last release her, she sighed and rested her cheek against his collarbone. He felt her resistance dissolve, yet he experienced no sense of victory.

She fit against him like song to a lyre, like a dolphin's greeting to scarlet dawn.

"I wish I were common," she whispered. Her voice broke. "And no one cared what I did."

"Were I truly a man of honor, I would leave. But I will not. I have desired one thing since I arrived and now I have it. You long for me as I do for you, and what does it accomplish? I will be consort to your sister and you will live far from me in the mountain caves. We will be as lost to each other as if we never met. And in a year...."

He felt her stiffen.

Another gust of wind smacked them. The fire jumped in response and sparks fanned out in a whirlwind. "A storm is coming," Chrysa-leon said. "We should return to the palace." But he didn't move.

She ran a finger down his temple and through his beard. "The fire-light makes jewels of your eyes."

Lust seethed, yet he forced himself to remain still. "I saw you, before the cave. Before I came to Labyrinthos."

She waited, relaxed, her face mirroring the love he felt running hot through his veins.

"When we landed, Menoetius and I set out to explore. I wanted to see your country. I wanted to learn everything I could, to determine if my father's army could invade and overthrow you."

For one endless instant she seemed frozen, then she broke free and scrambled away. She crouched on the other side of the fire, staring at him, so many emotions streaming across her face he couldn't separate them.

"No, Aridela," he said, stretching out a hand, but she backed farther away.

"How could you think to plan our destruction then woo me as you have?" Her voice dropped. "They were right about you."

"I tell you this truth so no secrets remain between us. I would not invade Kaphtor now, not if it contained all the riches of the world. Kaphtor is precious to me because it holds you. I would die to defend it."

She covered her face with her hands.

He breathed in and out slowly. "I thought if I couldn't win the Games, and if Kaphtor seemed ripe, I could convince my father to attack. It would be bad, Aridela, if your island fell into the hands of Gla, Pylos, or Tiryns, or any of the mainland kingdoms. Especially Tiryns. It would be the end of us."

She uncovered her face and glared at him. "You and your Kindred think you can fight over us like dogs with a bone. You think us easy prey."

"It was foolish arrogance."

She watched him, silent, narrow-eyed, all hint of trust vanished.

"We heard gossip that you and Iphiboë were hunting on Mount Ida. We went there, hoping to catch a glimpse of Kaphtor's princesses. We searched and spent the night. We had almost given up when we came upon a path in the forest and heard laughter. There you were— you, Iphiboë, Selene, and your cousin, swimming in a pond. That was the first time I saw you."

He waited, but she said nothing. Her chest rose and fell, giving away her shallow breathing.

Chrysaleon peered into the sky, his eyes tracking the fire's wild, darting sparks. "That was my end." He hesitated as his mind worked out what words would convince her. "Our bards sing of tribes who live on hidden isles in these seas. Amazons, we call them. Moon-women. It is said they shoot as well as any man and are joined to their horses. Proud as the proudest king, they fight to the death rather than suffer dishonor."

"Selene comes from those tribes."

"She taught you their ways?"

"Yes. My mother brought her to Kaphtor to teach us the skills of her people. She stays now because she is our friend, and Kaphtor is her home."

"They are legendary in my country. When I looked down on that pool, I thought I had discovered a cache of those women. Your weapons lay on the ground. You swam without fear, never suspecting you were being watched. I know you and your council wonder why I competed in your Games when there is so much for me to lose. This is the reason. Since that day in the forest, I have been yours, Aridela, though I have tried to deny it."

He thought he discerned an almost imperceptible relaxation in the bow-strung tenseness of her body. "I had ideas of climbing down for an afternoon of pleasure. Menoetius held me back. Then I heard Selene call you 'Princess,' thank Black-Horned Poseidon, and I realized who you were." He gave a wry shake of his head. "Queen Helice would have diced us into fish food if I had done what I intended."

His brief amusement died away. "I watched you step from the pool and wring water from your hair. I couldn't breathe. I knew what it would feel like, to die."

He added, low, "You are the woman my father promised I would find someday. The one who would bind me, make me a willing slave. All my doubts vanished when you entered the bullring and danced with that bull."

She still made him wait an interminable length of time, suspended, not knowing what to expect. Then she crawled back, her eyes wet with tears. He enclosed her, not only with his arms but his legs, trapping her against his body. He felt her heart quicken, swift and fluttery as a bird's. She was strong, but she could never escape her ancestry. Her bones were fragile. She was a small woman, and ever would be.

"Princess of Kaphtor." He rolled on top of her, holding himself up to keep from crushing this bird. "For longer than can be dreamed, I am yours. Even death will never break our bond."

He saw her startle, her eyes widen.

Propping his elbows on the ground, he took her face in his hands. "Even in death, Aridela. I am yours."

He kissed her a long time to keep her from speaking. When he felt all resistance evaporate, he raised his head. "We return to Labyrinthos in two days. Is this the last for us?"

"I don't know."

He pressed his mouth and tongue to her neck, wanting to taste her, to blot out every memory of her insipid sister.

The unguents she used intoxicated him. "If this be the last time—"

"Yes...yes," she whispered.

He pushed up her tunic, struggling to hold back, for in truth, his body needed satiation and had no concern for gentler emotions. But this was Princess Aridela of Kaphtor, not a defeated female in a conquered province. Her thighs crept around his hips; he sank into her, and fought to control his basest instincts.

"Aridela," he whispered. "Aridela." *Mother of kings.*

Unbearable pressure blazed, turning his body to a rampage of fire.

He heard her cry out, but faintly; his need deafened any other concern. Fulfillment shot from mere pleasure into divine ecstasy. He pierced like an arrow, seeking her very core. "Aridela," he choked, clutching, thrusting, driving into a void of unconsciousness.

"Chrysaleon, stop!" She shoved him, hard enough to push his upper body off hers.

He opened his eyes and rolled onto his side, gasping. Awareness was slow to return.

She grabbed his injured forearm as she stared into the sky, her face rigid with concentration.

The pain her grip caused brought him back to the windy night. "Did I hurt you?" he asked, fighting to catch his breath and calm his blood.

Then he heard what she had heard, felt it through his bones. A guttural vibration emanating from the ground.

With a grating clash, the earth beneath them split, sucking them into a fissure. Chrysaleon, flailing as he fell, caught a protruding root in his right hand and Aridela's wrist in the left. He strained to hold her, groaning beneath shooting agony in his injured arm and thigh as she climbed his body, gripping his thighs then his waist, and finally his shoulders. There they hung, choking in a cloud of dust and an avalanche of dirt and stones, suspended by one tough root and Chrysaleon's ability to disregard his injuries. Outside the trench, he heard blasts and roaring. The crack of wood. The earth splitting open in a thousand wounds.

The world was being unmade.

BLOOD RAN DOWN CHRYSALEON'S FOREARM AS HE HOISTED ARIDELA TO the summit of the chasm. She pulled herself out and turned, grabbing him, helping him over the crumbling lip and back onto the earth's welcoming surface.

But what he had always considered solid and imperishable was dissolving. Dirt and sand erupted in fountains on every side. A nearby grove of black oak and junipers thrashed as though a titan stamped through them, yanking them out as he came.

Blood dripped off the ends of his fingers. He tucked his arm behind his back and tried to ignore the burn of the wound being torn open.

Distant susurration echoed like the faraway roar of lions, and built until the air itself seemed to throb.

Aridela reached out to him. Chrysaleon took her hand and pulled her, first one direction then another, as gashes split the earth and barred their way.

Above them, the heavens fractured.

Neither could do anything but press their hands to their ears and wait for death to end the terror. The detonation of the sky ripped through Chrysaleon's head with such force he feared his skull would shatter. The ground heaved.

"Goddess, forgive me!" Aridela shrieked as she stumbled on land turned to maelstrom. "Forgive us!"

She thought Lady Athene was punishing them for what they had done. Shivers arced through Chrysaleon's spine as he peered into the sky, convinced she was right. A dirty red glow, sparked by eerie rapid-fire flashes of lightning, marred the northern horizon.

Aridela dropped to her knees. "Velchanos." She stared into the sky at the lightning. "He comes for us...."

Another rift opened, so close that she lost her balance and started to fall, but Chrysaleon grabbed her shoulders and steadied her.

Something else, a boiling blackness, ringed with molten haze like clouds of fire, obliterated the heavens in the same direction as the lightning. He stared, stiff with horror, seeing Great Poseidon rise from the sea, and knew this blood-soaked shadow brought their deaths. "Come! Run!" He half-dragged Aridela past freshly uprooted trees.

"There is a place—" Aridela took the lead, pulling Chrysaleon to the west, into a wood untouched by damage. She found an indentation at the base of a tree-covered slope, where erosion, root-growth, and the digging of animals had created a hole in the earth. They knelt and wormed past the roots only to realize it was too shallow to cover them completely.

"Fill it in," Chrysaleon shouted over the roar of an approaching gale.

They scooped everything they could, earth, rocks, and leaves into the opening of their refuge as the world around them transformed into a white rage of heat and fire.

Murderous wind snapped tree trunks like twigs. The air grew hot and stank of sulfur. Branches burst into flames. Chrysaleon made sure Aridela pressed her face to her knees and he did the same. He covered his head and hers with his arms, but there was no escape, no choice between breathing and not. His lungs and mouth seared like meat on a spit. Aridela whimpered.

The wind died, leaving a crackle of burning wood, branches collapsing, the tortured shrieking of animals. They saw nothing through the gaps but a smoky-red haze.

"Are you hurt?" The words scraped against Chrysaleon's scorched, swollen throat.

She whispered, "I am burned."

He scrambled from the depression, holding out his hand to help her. She followed more slowly.

The smoky gloom was unbroken but for the fire-glow. The nearest reflected in her eyes. At least they weren't incinerated, but he was shocked to see that her glorious cascades of black hair had melted away, leaving only singed tufts no longer than his fingers.

Her teeth chattered. Chrysaleon felt his own flesh prickle in angry, offended waves. He wanted to comfort her, but knew that touching her would only add to her pain.

"Are you thirsty?" He tried to sound calm and reasonable even as he felt the ground scald his feet through the soles of his sandals. He had never experienced such thirst, and fought a childish urge to beg the gods for a drink. "Let's search for water."

Her voice was small and feeble as she struggled to speak through hoarse coughing. "The palace. We must go back."

They stumbled through a ruinous tangle of wood and debris. Trees lay on the ground, naked and vulnerable, all bark burned away. Jagged remnants of trunks appeared suddenly from the smoke, barring their way.

Blood began seeping between the stitches on Chrysaleon's thigh. Putting weight on the leg sent keen-edged misery streaking clear into his jaw and temple. His limp grew more pronounced as they forged on.

The earth groaned. Thunder reverberated. Aridela startled again and again at the abrupt echoing shatter of collapsing limbs, but she didn't speak and hardly lifted her gaze from the ground.

Chrysaleon suspected by her stiffened, precise movements and the set of her jaw that she was suffering, and he longed to hold her. He, too, felt involuntary shivers run deep through his skin. The pain would soon become unbearable. But for now, his burned flesh remained like his mind, shocked into numbness.

They topped the last rise on the road above Phaistos and looked down.

There was no music. No light. No graceful terraces, pristine fountains, flagged courtyards, or stately pillars. If anything remained, it was hidden beneath a noxious black cloud, broken only by branches of fire that shot through it in spiraling columns.

Faint ghastly screams emanated from the depths. The stench made Chrysaleon gag.

"Selene. Halia." Aridela started toward the city at a run, but Chrysaleon grabbed her hand and held firm.

Menoetius, he thought, startled by fleeting amazement, a sense that he had far less control over matters than he had arrogantly believed.

He seized her other hand and pulled her back. "We don't dare go down there."

"Goddess," Aridela whispered. She dropped to her knees, clutching at handfuls of dirt. "We meant no harm."

She peered up at Chrysaleon, tears streaking through the dust on her cheeks. "I have dreamed of this. Athene showed it to me."

Chrysaleon knelt, keeping a tight grip on her hand.

The air grew blacker. Thicker. Intermittent bolts of lightning traced like blood vessels across the sky. A mutter ran through the heavens as though, somewhere far away, gods were battling.

And then the screams died away, leaving a terrible silence.

Chrysaleon could tell by the pungent sulfuric scent flowing on the wind that a conflagration greater than anything he could imagine was burning somewhere. The only place on Crete that could generate such a fire was surely Knossos, which lay in the direction from which the cloud had come. He glanced at Aridela, hoping she hadn't worked this through.

"Please," she begged. "I cannot wait any longer. We must see if anyone is alive. They need us."

"Patience," he said. "Soon."

They sat without speaking. Every now and then he heard the faintest release of a sob, though for the most part his young lover remained silent, slumped, and still.

In an effort to distract her, he said, "Tell me your dream."

"What you see." She didn't lift her head. "The world destroyed. The earth heaving. The lightning of Velchanos cleaving the sky. Our oracle ordered me to remain untouched. I thought I knew the Lady's mind better than she did." She drew in a ragged breath. "You and I lay together that first time. Nothing happened. There was no sign of anger. I grew even more defiant. Now see where my insolence has brought Kaphtor. What of the babies? Their mothers? Our brave men?" She gestured toward the ruined city. "What do they suffer because of us?"

He opened his mouth but found no words. What could he say? He, too, believed they were to blame.

If Athene was punishing Aridela, what would she do to him? It was he who had enticed Helice's daughter to her defiance. He hadn't known the restrictions placed on her the first time, but the second? Knowledge had not stopped him.

He pushed tangles of damp hair off his face and realized for the first time that it hadn't burned. Though Aridela's was singed almost to her scalp and he had squatted at her side in the shallow earth cave, the tawny mane for which he was famous remained, incomprehensibly, as it was before the searing heat.

At last he relented. The crimson tendrils of fire gorging on Phaistos seemed to have drifted to the south. Holding Aridela's hand, Chrysaleon led the way down the hill to discover what was left.

3

Moon of Figs and Acorns

Come with me, said the woman wearing a crown of silver and ivory. *It is time for you to learn Our Lady's plan.* She held out her hand and Themiste took it, shivering at the surge of wellbeing that flowed from the woman's touch.

She followed Athene's servant down a slope to the edge of the sea. There they sat on damp sand, observed by a lone crab and a snowy-white crane wading in the shallow water.

The sun, the moon, and the star Iakchos were all shining in the heavens at the same time, suggesting a dream. Yet the murmur of water, the call of a dove, and the hint of a breeze against Themiste's cheek made her wonder.

The holy triad is joined, the handmaid said. *It begins here, but its finish is farther than you can conceive, and many shadows must be pierced before the end.*

The holy triad. Themiste shivered again. These words had weighed heavily upon her ever since Sidero, one of her oldest acolytes, had succumbed to a puzzling, incurable ailment that left her unaware of her surroundings. The woman spoke the phrase constantly, sleeping and awake.

The handmaid again spoke. *You will see it as mere mortal passion, but that is no more than its outward shape. These three are formed from one thread. They are connected, now and forever. Athene has unraveled their bond so they may follow separate purposes, which will, in the end, return them to each other and either make whole or destroy your world.*

Themiste ventured to ask, "Who is the holy triad, lady?"

The daughter of Queen Helice...the gold lion of Mycenae...and one other. The bull marked by his fate.

Themiste surmised the daughter was Aridela rather than Iphiboë; the prophecies had long ago convinced her of the younger princess's divine purpose. The gold lion was, of course, Chrysaleon. But why would Potnia Athene unite Aridela to a barbarian, a crude foreigner with vastly different obligations and beliefs? How could such a union influence the world? She resisted the idea and her mind searched for ways to thwart it, but the handmaid interrupted.

The eyes of Kaphtor's child will be darkened, her mind filled with clamor. She must forget the ways of your world and follow the call of the lion, for she is the wounded woman, and will carry within her the suffering of all my Lady's children.

"But why?" Themiste asked, startled and dismayed.

In order to gain the trust of the lost, she must be one with them. She will struggle without deliverance, as they do. Her eyes will be put out. She must find her way through seven labyrinths to learn what she must learn.

Themiste pictured Aridela stumbling without sight through black tunnels, her arms outstretched, alone and frightened. Horror constricted her throat. But she was familiar with the serpentine language of prophecy, and hoped this prediction was like the dream itself—not to be taken literally. Seven labyrinths. Why seven? What could it mean?

The way of the Lady was incomprehensible, even to oracles.

"You speak of Aridela and of Chrysaleon, the lion of Mycenae. But this marked bull. Who is that?"

If I told you, you would try to change his fate. Remember this when the time comes, Minos of Kaphtor—what seems the end is only the beginning.

The handmaid held out her palm; the crab crawled onto it and she stroked its shell.

After some time of bewildered silence as Themiste fought with her own conviction of failure and stupidity, she asked, "Can you tell me Chrysaleon's purpose?"

The lion's purpose is to fulfill his obligation.

"What is it? Will he know? Will I know?"

You yourself did conceive it.

Filled with an oppressive sense of defeat, Themiste pondered everything she knew about the prince of Mycenae, but couldn't produce any insight. Raw frustration expanded; how could she have formed the duty of a man she did not know? She put the question aside until she could think more calmly. "Aridela has always understood that she would live a profound fate. She claimed it many times. I always dismissed her...."

A loom weight, suspended upon thread, will swing from one side to the other before settling into the middle.

Themiste peered into the sky at the hazy sun, the creamy moon, and the glittering star. Guilt and sadness weighted her down. She wanted to weep, but fought against it.

Behold. Athene's maiden swept out her hand. Through some divine power, a stage of sorts formed in the air above the water, and a scene upon it. Themiste watched women carrying baskets, catches of fish, and armfuls of cloth. In the shade beneath leafy trees, men lounged, holding cups, and odd devices from which they drew smoke into their mouths and blew it out again. One of the men called to a passing woman. Head bowed in a servile attitude, she crossed to them. Her clothing was ripped. The men amused themselves upon her, inflicting many blows and lacerations. They ignored her stifled cries and when they were done, sent her creeping away with a slap to the rump.

This is the future as it now stands, the handmaid said. *Will you remember? Will you do what is necessary to help these three fulfill their design? For it can be changed. You can help change it.*

Screams woke her. Her bed quaked as though it rode upon an angry sea. Crockery fell from the shelves. She staggered to the door and into the corridor.

"Lady!" One of her serving women ran toward her, covering her head as chunks of rock fell. "The earth is shaking!" She grabbed Themiste's hand and dragged her to the steps.

They emerged from the underground as the ornate latticework built around the cave entrance collapsed. Stones crumbled and blinding dust rose. The earth groaned. People ran in every direction, shrieking.

"Look, look, my lady!" Her maid pointed at the sky to the north.

Deeper than the deepest black, shot through with bloodstained lightning, came the cloud.

A few still lived. Some sat listlessly. Some lay, twitching. Some crawled. Most had lost their hair, leaving naked, blistered skulls. Clothing was seared into skin that hung off bone in gruesome sheets.

Chrysaleon stepped in front of Aridela when a hideously charred object rose from the ground and fell again, only to realize it was all that heat and fire had left of a living man. Flames engulfed a woman next to him, feeding eagerly on her skirts.

"Can we help them?" Aridela whispered.

Chrysaleon could only shake his head. Most expired as they stared.

Swallowing the urge to be sick, Chrysaleon picked up a torch from the ground. He lit it in one of the numerous fires that consumed the once-gracious, elegant palace.

Heavy snow began to fall, slowly at first then furiously thick, yet it was not cold or wet. Chrysaleon scooped up a handful from the ground. "It is gritty," he said, rubbing it between his fingertips. "Like sand." He looked up, blinking against the onslaught. "It smudges like ash." It piled on the ground, covered their heads and shoulders, caked around their noses and mouths, and burned their eyes. It sucked moisture from the air, making it hurt to breathe. Chrysaleon had been thirsty since they had crawled from their makeshift shelter, but now it was almost impossible to think of anything but water.

Pale stones now fell through the ash. Some were tiny, some as big as pomegranates. They were pitted with holes, weightless, bouncing as they struck the earth. Chrysaleon and Aridela ran from one dangerous overhang to another to avoid them.

The sandy, ashy substance stuck to his raw burns. Both succumbed to helpless coughing as they breathed it in. Every time Chrysaleon coughed, his seared lungs stabbed him with hot spear-points of agony.

Before long, they were coughing up blood.

"I am so thirsty." Aridela's eyes were red, streaming. Chrysaleon felt the ash grate against his own eyes, and had to willfully stop himself from scouring at them.

The ruins offered one atrocity after another. Motionless carnage. Thick pools of congealing blood. Limbs protruding from beneath splintered wood and stone, or lying piecemeal, burned to charcoal. One corner revealed piles of burning flesh, while in another, a dog quivered in final torment.

The hair on Chrysaleon's neck rose as he stared at something more monstrous than any nightmare could conjure.

It was a human body—that much was evident. Hair and clothing gone. Features burned away. As he stared, the torso swelled like a blowfish. The stomach ruptured; scarlet entrails squirmed like a mass of living serpents then blackened and stilled. He stumbled away from Aridela, helplessly retching.

All around them was the sickening sound of other bodies swelling. Bursting.

He forced himself to his feet, muttering, "Cruel Poseidon." Aridela too, had fallen, and retched upon the ground.

His throat was as dry as a stone. He was dizzy, disoriented, barely able to hear Aridela moaning through the buzzing in his ears. She compressed into a ball, hiding her head beneath her burned arms.

Part of a nearby wall crumbled. Dust clouds mushroomed. Pillars hung fragmented, topless. Debris and silent corpses covered the flagstones.

Breathless and awestruck, Chrysaleon gazed, holding himself stiff, still, and blank.

He stood in the presence of malevolent gods, witnessing a depraved power he had secretly dismissed as fantasy born in weak minds.

"I want to go home," Aridela cried, sobbing. "I need my mother...."

"We will go at sunrise," he whispered.

If we are still alive.

4

Moon of Figs and Acorns

ARIDELA AND HER LOVER FLED FROM THE HORRORS OF THE DEAD AND
dying but could not bring themselves to abandon Phaistos until they
had searched for survivors. They wandered listlessly through the
ruins.

After some wearisome length of time, they discerned faint shouting
and followed the sound. They cleared a rubble-choked entrance
leading to the underground, and there discovered a cache of people
who had escaped the poison clouds.

Seventeen climbed from the hole. Each one stared aghast at the ruin
and death.

Then no more came. Aridela pictured beautiful flaxen-haired
Selene, her cherished nurse, Halia, and Carmanor, the boy she had
loved so much as a child. Emptiness engulfed her, more painful in
some ways than the burns, which were already swelling into massive
blisters on her arms, neck, and shoulders. She saw blank disbelief in
Chrysaleon's eyes, though he said nothing of his blood brother, the
only link to his home and his old life.

Never again would she listen to Halia's elaborate stories or hunt in
the mountains with Selene. She could never mend things with
Carmanor, who seemed so different, his heart as angry and sullen as
the scars carved into his flesh.

But Chrysaleon and three other men were descending again into

28

the hiding place. She heard one say there were more survivors, too injured to climb out on their own.

They carried up three more victims and laid them underneath an overhang that offered protection from drifting ash and falling stones.

"Aridela!" Chrysaleon's voice held a note of excitement, but when she started to climb down, he said, "No, stay there. I will bring them."

He lifted a half-conscious Selene out of the hole into the arms of another man. Once she was safely removed, Menoetius followed. His face was bloody and his left hand frighteningly swollen, but he was able to walk.

Racked by sobs, Aridela toppled to her knees, but such was the moaning, coughing, and despair around her that she quickly stifled the luxury of relief. Wiping away her tears, she tried to give comfort and reassurances to the other survivors, keeping to herself the horrors she had seen.

As the men returned to the underground one more time to carry out the last two living victims, Aridela knelt next to Selene.

In a weak, slightly slurred voice, Selene said, "You're alive," and touched Aridela's hand. "I am so happy to see you."

Her hair was clotted with blood. Aridela feared a head injury, but didn't know what to do. "And you, Selene," she whispered. "I was sure you were dead."

"What happened? Do you know?" The dark soot and ash that caked Selene's face made her sea-green eyes glow bright, like stars.

Aridela couldn't meet that beautiful gaze. She stared at the ground. "Goddess Athene punished all for the sins I alone committed. Themiste commanded me to remain untouched. I ignored her. I brought this death, this suffering, when I lay with Chrysaleon—not once but twice, the second time tonight, just before the cloud of fire and wind killed so many, and nearly took you from me."

Selene remained silent. Aridela finally forced herself to meet her friend's gaze.

Selene opened her mouth but still said nothing, only bit her lower lip and frowned.

"Rest," Aridela said. "Forgive me for burdening you with my crimes and regrets."

"Aridela, your hair. Your skin. Your eyes."

She had tried not to think about her burns since she and Chrysaleon entered the ruined palace. Her head seemed oddly light. Yesterday her hair fell well past the small of her back. Now, coated with gritty ash, stinking of smoke, the short, brittle ends broke off in her hands. She glanced at her arms. The only light came from a few torches, but the red blotches, blisters, and wave upon wave of shuddering warned of profound injury. She was dizzy as well, nauseated, and desperately thirsty. Sharp, piercing misery accompanied every helpless cough. Her eyes burned so relentlessly, she almost wanted to gouge them out.

"Sleep, my sister," she said softly. "I am in no pain."

Selene obeyed, though tears seeped from under her lashes. Aridela held her hand until Selene's breathing evened and her fingers relaxed.

Chrysaleon and others who were able fanned out through the destruction, searching for water.

Aridela made another round among the injured. She blotted blood with strips of cloth, gave a smile or kiss where it seemed to help, then returned to Selene's side, where she sat, hugging her knees, and tried to force herself to be calm.

She felt Menoetius watching her for a long time before she finally looked up, catching a frown that left her stricken with fresh guilt.

His eyes, too, were red and swollen, his scarred face smeared with dried blood and ash. Aridela couldn't help picturing Carmanor, the beautiful youth from the mainland, who laughed as he told her she was "still little," and that princesses in his country could never get into mischief the way she did.

This ruin of a man, this 'Menoetius,' somehow mirrored everything she had seen tonight. The destruction of all she had believed inde-structible.

She kept her voice low so she wouldn't disturb Selene, but the words escaped as if they had a will of their own. "You believe it as well. Athene is angry at what your prince and I did. This is her punishment."

His gaze faltered, betraying him. "I do not claim to know the mind of the Goddess."

She turned her gaze to the south, where the killing cloud had gone, and clenched her hands. "I love Chrysaleon. Surely that is not such an odious crime."

"If what you say is true, would you not now be dead instead of all these others?"

"If I died, I would be released from pain. The suffering of others would no longer touch me."

Leaning across Selene, Menoetius extended his hand as though to touch her cheek, but then he didn't, and dropped his hand back to his side.

Her throat blocked with tears.

Those who had gone exploring returned with incredulous tales of how heat melted everything, even tin and bronze, in one chamber, while leaving feathers and wax tablets unharmed in others. They had found a few jars of water. Aridela sprinkled a little over her burns and drank sparingly. Never had anything tasted so delicious as this tepid, stale water that carried a flavor of smoke.

Unable to rest, she watched fires lick across the fields and hills. She sensed Menoetius's gaze upon her several times through that endless night, but whenever she looked at him, his eyes were closed.

Scarcely any change came with morning. Thunder rumbled. Crimson lightning sliced wounds in the sky. If there was still a sun, its light could not penetrate the murk.

Some wanted to travel north to Labyrinthos. Others were willing to stay behind with the more severely wounded.

Aridela was determined to reach the palace or die in the attempt. Chrysaleon would not be separated from her.

They journeyed north, knowing not what to expect.

5

Moon of Figs and Acorns

THE NORTH AND EAST WINGS OF LABYRINTHOS COLLAPSED, INCLUDING THE family bedchambers and baths. Gaping cracks split walls and pillars, yet more of that palace withstood the rage of Athene than at Phaistos in the southern provinces.

Shortly after the initial firestorms, Queen Helice ordered a ceremony. Without knowing Aridela's fate, grief-stricken over the deaths of those near to her, terrified of what might happen next, the queen stood before her surviving people, holding Iphiboë's hand, and spoke hollow reassurances. Why would the Lady spare so much of the great palace-temple dedicated to her unless she still felt love for it? Lamentations, prayers, and the sacrifice of twenty precious oxen completed the pleas for forgiveness. All who lived turned frightened eyes to the ash filled, blistered sky.

Their reward came in a blanketing sulfur stench and another precipitous blast, nearly as deafening and startling as the first. Pottery shattered. Unstable walls crumbled. The ground wallowed and churned.

Messengers from the harbor at Amnisos informed the queen that the sea had vanished, sucked down the throat, perhaps, of the barbarian god Poseidon. Nothing remained but mud, shells, writhing sea creatures, and beached ships. Helice wanted to inspect this phenomenon, but the counselors forbade her from taking such reckless action.

While they argued, the sea returned.

A lone, broken boy reported before he died that it came in a wave so tall he could not see the summit. This mountain of water crushed every building, pier, and ship at Amnisos and the west precincts at Tamara. Its murderous tentacles stretched halfway into the town of Knossos. Subsequent waves completed the destruction. Corpses of fish, sheep, fowl, and human littered the coast and mingled in the sea among debris and vast suffocating mats of floating stones.

THE SURVIVORS OF PHAISTOS LIMPED INTO KNOSSOS THREE DAYS AFTER surviving the death-clouds. They joined a desperate influx from every corner of the island.

Aridela listened to appalling tales of monstrous waves and observed with heavy sorrow the ruin of so much of her home and the great city where she had spent her childhood.

Rhené smoothed unguents into her skin and sheared off the charred ends of her hair. "You resemble the soldiers on the mainland," the healer said, attempting a smile.

At one time, Aridela would have agonized over this loss, but now she hardly glanced in the mirror at a reflection she no longer recognized.

Rhené's touch, and her balms, caused such pain that Aridela had to clench her jaw to keep from sobbing. Because she had mostly kept her face pressed against her knees during the onslaught of fire-wind, it had escaped serious burns, but swollen, unspeakably painful blisters covered her arms, shoulders, and back.

If only she could rest in her own bed…but her chamber was buried in wreckage. Her dog, Taya, her cat, and her little lovebirds were dead. All dead.

Dead also were Halia, Aridela's nurse, who served as her day-to-day mother, and Isandros, Aridela's beloved half brother, who taught her how to dance with bulls. A prince in his own right, he and Aridela shared the same father, Damasen, and unassailable loyalty. Neoma, Aridela's cousin, lay senseless after a rock shot out of the sky with the force of a driven spear and struck her in the forehead. Neoma's sister, eleven-year-old Phanaë, succumbed to the ash and suffocated in her own blood. Aridela found some comfort in the company of her sister and mother, who had, through the grace of the Goddess, both survived. Helice was convinced that the dream she'd had prompting her to send Aridela to Phaistos with Chrysaleon had saved her daughter's life.

The storms of ash gradually subsided but fine clouds continued to drift across everything, clinging to hair, faces, and clothing. Thick brown haze lay between sun and earth so that each day dawned drearier than the last and the warmth of summer evaporated.

Prince Kios, whose wife was killed when a wall collapsed upon her, spent much time in grieving solitude on the northern cliffs. "Beyond our sight, the earth burns," he told Helice. "I can tell by the smell and clouds of black smoke in the distance. It must be the disaster we have long expected on Callisti."

This conjecture quickly spread. Refugees from that island leaned upon their comrades and wept.

Helice sought comfort from her daughters. "Goddess Athene seeks a hideous vengeance," she said in a private moment.

"We must find a way to appease her," Aridela said.

"What did we do? How did we anger her?" Helice shook her head and wandered aimlessly away.

The rumors began slowly, quietly, and when Aridela first heard them, icy threads of fear tightened her stomach. The people were eying the barbarian from Mycenae. Some said Chrysaleon, by winning the Games and killing the bull-king, ignited this ruin. Yet the conjectures remained soft. No one was brave enough to shout accusations; they were all too fearful of enraging the Goddess further.

The permeating ash caused nosebleeds and inflamed eyes. Countless children and old ones died, blood seeping from their mouths and noses. Artisans claimed the ash was actually fine particles of obsidian.

The people clamored day and night. *Help us. Save us, Queen Helice. Avert the Lady's anger.*

A messenger sent from the sacred caves reported that Kaphtor's oracle lived. Themiste was uninjured. But she did not journey to Labyrinthos, nor did she make any statements or predictions. Day after day, the silence continued until the people demanded to know where she was. Why did she say nothing? It was the oracle's duty to read the signs, to enter vision, to determine what should be done.

"If she will not come to us, we shall go to her," Helice said. "Let us seek answers from Themiste at her shrine."

FROM THE ORACLE LOGS
Themiste

NEWS OF KAPHTOR'S FATE COMES SLOWLY. THE HARBOR AT AMNISOS IS *gone as though it never was. Winds of fire ripped down buildings, toppled trees, and burned people alive. The queen and Iphiboë were nearly crushed in the partial collapse of Labyrinthos, but thankfully, loyal slaves pulled them into an underground corridor. All were later found and rescued.*

Powdery dust poured from the heavens, at times warm as though it carried a memory of the fire from which it came. It covers the ground and hangs like fine-spun veils in the sky, blocking the sunlight. Some call it ash, but to me it seems more like sand. It scratches and burns, and makes us cough. Many who breathe in too much drown in their own blood. Those of us who remain are now keeping our faces covered with wet linen.

As if fires, poison, and dust are not enough, we suffer downpours of rain like none we have ever seen. Farmers tell of annihilating mudslides. Day has forsaken us, and bitter, clammy cold creeps across the land. Thunder gives warning, all day, all night. Lightning—not white but crimson, sometimes blue—flickers in the clouds, always to the north, displaying the continuing anger of Velchanos. Insects and birds drop from the sky, dead. Emboldened rats swarm, killing cats and dogs. Some have even killed small children.

When I was named Minos, the safety of the Oracle Logs became my sacred charge. Written upon these tablets is our entire history, our prophecies and traditions. Now they are buried beneath stone, ash, and debris. Perhaps they can be recovered, but what of the papyrus scrolls? Our library at Phaistos, filled with writings from the countries we have befriended, was destroyed as well.

I am sickened by all we have lost.

It is time to plant life-sustaining grain. Our nuts and figs should be harvested, and soon the grapes, but the crops that were not destroyed outright now wither. So many farmers are dead, and the land is flooded with mud or poisoned by dust. Hunks of stone fell out of the sky like weapons from an angry god's hand, devastating both plants and livestock.

What of the olive groves, nurtured since the time of Kaphtor's first settlers? Have any survived, or is our whole island laid waste? I do not yet know.

The razing of Kaphtor began three days before Iphiboë was to take the barbarian, the foreigner who is called 'Gold Lion,' as her consort.

Lion of gold from over the sea
Destroy the black bull, shake the earth free
Curse the god, crush the fold,
pull down the stars as seers foretold.
Isle of cloud, Moon's stronghold, see your death come
in spears of gold.

Six years ago, in a near faint, Aridela spoke this prophecy. I should say more correctly that Potnia Athene spoke through her.

It cannot be chance. The Gold Lion came to destroy Kaphtor. With the help of his barbarian gods, I fear he may have succeeded.

No one has ever killed a sacred king out of his time. The murder of the bull-king before his time would be a crime so outrageous that the murderer would be hunted, hounded, tortured without mercy. Still I would not hesitate if I thought it would cool Goddess Athene's rage.

But I have seen that she requires more than a king's death.

Helice and her daughters journey to my shrine. The people are desperate and she does not know what to do. I must provide answers. Can I? Am I strong enough?

For I have seen what is to be done.

The time of payment, which was shown to me in vision so long ago, has arrived.

HELICE, IPHIBOË, AND ARIDELA SET OUT FOR THEMISTE'S MOUNTAIN shrine.

Ash lifted in clouds around the litter-bearers' feet. It invaded every crease and pore, defying all methods of holding it at bay, provoking everyone to cough and rub their eyes, which only made things worse.

Aridela tried to shut out the irritating sound as she sank more deeply into a spiraling well of guilt. With one breath she believed she no longer deserved to live, and in the next demanded to know why her crime was so much worse than her mother's. Damasen competed, won, and became Kaphtor's bull-king. He and Helice were lovers long before he entered the Games. Nothing happened. There was no punishment.

Why were the actions of Helice's daughter so different?

She didn't really need the Goddess to appear before her and explain. The answer was simple. Chrysaleon was meant for Iphiboë. Queen Helice had not defied holy commands in order to be with Damasen. The two events could not be compared.

Aridela had never feared Kaphtor's high priestess, but now she did. Themiste had no doubt seen her blatant defiance in vision or by some other means. If she revealed it, the whole island would know the queen's daughter had caused this devastation and death through self-ish, petty lust and arrogance.

Why could you not have punished me alone, Mother, not these others? They did nothing. The question remained a never-ending, never-answered litany.

Though they had sent no messenger ahead, Themiste was waiting for them outside the shrine.

Helice stepped from the litter. "You know why we have come. Is there hope? What can we do?"

Themiste clasped Helice's hands, saying only, "Rest now, Queen Helice. Later, we will talk."

"There is no time for rest. Tell me what I must do to quell Athene's anger, to bring peace again."

Themiste beckoned to her attendant. "Wine then," she said. "You must be thirsty."

Helice agreed she was. Two priests hurried to assist Iphiboë but she waved them away, descending from her litter and walking on her own into the shrine.

Aridela accepted a cup of wine. It helped wash away the dry, lingering taste of gritty ash and sulfur.

The Holy Minos stood to one side and waited.

Before long, her mother's head drooped. Her eyes fluttered and closed. No doubt she hadn't allowed herself to sleep since the first explosion fractured their island.

"Lay her on the pallet," Themiste ordered.

"What's happened to her?" Aridela asked as the priestesses made Helice comfortable.

"I put poppy in the wine. When she wakes, after she has rested, I will tell her what I have seen."

Themiste instructed a priestess to bring stools and the three of them sat close together. She dismissed the maids and when they were alone, carefully examined Aridela's arms. "Are the balms helping?"

"Yes, Minos. It is nothing."

Themiste gave Iphiboë's knee the same scrutiny. "I see no bruising now," she said. "Is there any pain?"

"No, my lady," Iphiboë replied. "I am fully healed. It's been a month."

"A knee thrown out of joint is a small price to pay, I suppose," Themiste said, "for the way you two have defied me."

Her words were chastising, but she didn't look angry. Perhaps she didn't know everything about that prophetic night when Aridela went with her sister to the Cave of Velchanos, against Themiste's orders, and joined with Chrysaleon—also against Themiste's orders.

Maybe Aridela's secret was safe—for now.

Themiste leaned back. She pressed her palms together and regarded the sisters. After a long moment of heavy silence, she said, "You are goddess beloved."

Tears spilled from Iphiboë's eyes. She only half-succeeded in stifling a sob.

Themiste's considered words made Aridela's throat close up too; her heart started to pound.

She suspected a measure of poppy might have found its way into all their wine cups.

"True love brings unforeseen strength." The high priestess's voice, though low, reverberated through Aridela's skull. "When we make sacrifices for the sake of love, miracles happen. Do you understand?"

"Yes," Aridela said, though she didn't. Her pampered life had not included many sacrifices and certainly none of consequence until now, but Themiste appeared agitated; her hands repeatedly clenched and Aridela saw her jaw clench too. If she could offer respite, she would.

"In Hesperia," Themiste said, very softly, "the great orchard on the far side of Okeanos, fruit hangs ripe upon the vine. Spring blooms every day. Those who reside there drink happiness from rivers. They absorb joy from sunlight. Kaphtor's heroes are taken to Hesperia when they give their blood to the crops. Earthly cares and sorrows are forgotten."

"It must be beautiful." Iphiboë's tears had stopped. She watched Themiste, her eyes wide, intent.

"Everlasting renown comes to those who give all they have." Themiste caressed Iphiboë's cheek then leaned in close and kissed her on the forehead. "The greatest kings know this. It is why they meet death unafraid. They know it is but one of many labyrinths on their path of immortality."

"'There is never new life without death,'" Iphiboë said. "'No new god without annihilation. Acceptance brings unimaginable glory.'"

Themiste drew back. Tears ran freely down her face.

"Why do you weep over me, Minos?" Iphiboë asked.

Themiste knelt on the floor so she could kiss Iphiboë's foot. She rose, drew Iphiboë up from the stool, and embraced her. Aridela stood as well so she could hear what Themiste might say.

"Athene will have retribution. The greatest payment we can give. A god did say this to me. '*Iphiboë must open the path.*'"

Shock spread from Aridela's scalp to her toes. "No," she whispered.

Iphiboë gazed beyond Themiste into the darkness of the shrine. "I can avert the anger?"

"Truly," said Themiste, "out of all our long line of queens, you are the greatest. You are your vision-chosen name, 'Strength of Oxen.'"

Swallowing hard and clenching her hands, Aridela fought for control. "No," she cried, her voice suddenly hoarse. "It was my crime. I must be the one. It must be me!"

Themiste didn't ask what crime she had committed. She simply shook her head and repeated, "A god did tell me, long ago, what must be done."

"Be quiet, Aridela," Iphiboë said without looking at her.

"You don't understand—only my suffering can soothe Athene's anger."

Iphiboë turned her gaze upon her sister. "Would you take this from me as you have taken everything else?"

Aridela opened her mouth but whatever protest she might have made died unsaid at the bitterness in Iphiboë's eyes.

Iphiboë crossed to her sleeping mother. She bent and kissed her lightly, so as not to wake her. "Give me your blessing, Minos," she said.

Themiste touched Iphiboë's forehead. "Great princess of Kaphtor, you have my blessing. You have my gratitude." Her voice broke. "May you live at the side of the Lady in joy eternal, as beloved by her as you are by your people."

Iphiboë crossed her arms over her breasts and lowered her head.

"I will go with her," Aridela said forcefully. If Themiste forbade it, she would—

But Themiste nodded. "It will not anger the Lady. But Aridela, you too have tasks to complete." Her eyes said the rest. *Return to me. Do not think to take her place.*

Iphiboë held out her hand. Aridela clasped it and walked with her from the cave.

6

Moon of Figs and Acorns

Iphiboë's hand trembled in Aridela's like a newborn bird. Her breathing was choppy. Yet she half-ran, half-stumbled up the steep narrow path to the cliffs.

"Stop," Aridela cried. "Iphiboë...."

Twelve more steps at most would bring them to the edge. Aridela knew without looking what they would see. Water edged in grey foam, pinnacles, boulders, and, since the destruction, massive ugly reefs of rocks so light they would not sink but clogged every cove, every niche along the shore.

Iphiboë paused. She stared at the edge, breathing hard, before leaning on her sister.

"Please, for my sake," Aridela said.

But Iphiboë stumbled on, half-falling over slippery scree. "If I stop the fear will catch me."

Thundering spray shot high, as though striving to reach them. After the destruction, the water had transformed into thick brown sludge. It seemed to Aridela a hungry beast, eager to devour whatever it could seize. She turned her back on it and grabbed her sister's hands.

"Iphiboë. Don't do it."

Iphiboë looked up from the fury, her eyes haunted with fear.

For the first time Aridela noticed Themiste. The oracle waited some distance away, hands clasped, head lowered, yet she seemed alert and wary. Aridela tightened her grip on Iphiboë's hands, fighting rage.

Iphiboë freed one hand and stroked Aridela's hair. "Now you can be queen, Aridela."

"It is you Athene chose. Not me."

"A mistake, somehow. A mistake of birth. And you can be with Chrysaleon. Do you think I have not seen how you look at each other?" She smiled. "A cow could see."

"Have I hurt you? If he had found you in the cave instead of me...."

"He would have been miserable." With a brief, faraway smile, Iphiboë added, "I would not have liked him either. Everything about him is too big. Too bold. He is terrifying. You have not hurt me, Aridela. You and he...seem a perfect match." She touched the puckered burn above her sister's left ear. "I cannot decide which one of you I would wager on in a fight."

Iphiboë returned her gaze to the surf. Aridela embraced her, ignoring the sting from her half-healed burns, agonized more by the unceasing tremble rippling through her sister's body.

Iphiboë pressed her forehead to Aridela's and closed her eyes. "I dreamed of this," she said. "I have always known this was my purpose. It is why I could not love a man. Love might make me cling to this life. Now I can make my offering freely, with my whole heart."

"You—dreamed of—doing—*this?*"

"Many times. Potnia Athene was preparing me, I think. She planned it this way from the beginning. She has plans for you, too, Aridela." Tucking Aridela's cropped hair behind her ears, she added softly, "We go about our lives in ignorance, but the Goddess has every shade and texture perfectly woven into a magnificent tapestry. I feared ruling. I only wanted to serve her." Her shoulders lifted. "Now I can."

"But what if Themiste is wrong?" Aridela glanced at the oracle, who remained motionless and silent, giving no indication she could hear them.

"You know she is not." Iphiboë shook her head. "Listen to the Lady. Pay attention to the signs. You will see. I have seen, and it is so clear. You are meant to be queen. You will bring recovery to Kaphtor and our people. That is *your* purpose." She kissed Aridela's cheek and with determination, pried herself from her sister's grip. She backed away. "I could not have made him happy. Consorts deserve to be happy. Their lives are so short. I go to Hesperia, where I will ask Athene for mercy. I will heal the land, and you will bring the world of the barbarian closer.

You will forge peace among those who worship the Lady and those who follow angry gods."

One more step brought Iphiboë to the precipice. Aridela couldn't breathe. *This cannot be happening. It must be a dream.*

Somehow, she rallied. She swallowed useless fear and managed to speak in a fairly steady voice. "Your name will live in our hearts until the earth grows old and brittle," she said. "I love you, Iphiboë."

Iphiboë smiled. "Yes. That is the one thing I always knew was real."

Even as Aridela stretched out her arms to pull her back, Iphiboë stepped into space, her smile fading.

Aridela started forward, but strong hands clamped down on her shoulders, preventing it. Themiste had come forward at last.

Misery crept up her feet and legs, through her belly and into her brain, turning her stiff and rigid as a shaft of bronze.

Then, without warning, she dissolved. Her cheek struck the earth. Dust filled her nose. The sting of sharp stones burned her skin.

Far beneath her, the water roared its triumph.

7

Moon of Figs and Acorns

FROM THE ORACLE LOGS
   Themiste

I TOOK CARA. I BREATHED THE SMOKE AND GOADED MY SERPENT SO SHE *would bite me. I gave myself to the vision and prayed for true sight.*

YEARS AGO, OUR NORTHERN SETTLEMENT OF CALLISTI WAS ABANDONED BUT *for a colony of priestesses whose only duty has been to appease the mountain's anger. All this time these women have tried to quiet the earth, but if what I have seen is true, Lady Athene was angered beyond the ability of any mortal to placate.*

As Prince Kios surmised, Callisti was the root of Athene's fury, but so staggering was this rage that Kaphtor was nearly destroyed as well, and who knows how many other lands? Perhaps the whole world lies dying or dead beneath burning ash.

I was sent into the mind of one of those women. I saw through her eyes. Unbalanced by fear and loneliness, by the poison she constantly breathed, she did welcome and lie with a man during the time dedicated to chastity. Not only that; she took him to the shrine, where he turned on her. He beat and bound her. This warrior's men found the high priestess, asleep in her chamber.

They dragged her to the altar and outraged her there, she whose body was dedicated to the Goddess alone.

This warrior and his soldiers pulled over the sacred statues and hacked them to pieces.

Blurred impressions came to me: people screaming as they were cut down, steam rising from pots, concoctions, black prayers, and blood. The outline of this man seemed familiar. There was a beard that proclaimed him an Achaean or some other barbarian, mighty shoulders, battle scars, but his face remained hidden, smeared like wet paint. He stood before the priestesses and declared himself lord and king of the islands, even of Kaphtor. He proclaimed an end to the holy king-sacrifice and promised he would rule for the length of his natural life—which he claimed was unending.

Laodámeia tells me I shrieked during the trance and tried to throw myself into the pit. Horror lies like the weight of the ocean upon my soul.

I see such a length of deep shadow that our children's distant unborn descendants will be blinded by its darkness.

If we can show we are still Goddess Athene's, completely, utterly, that we will give whatever we must, whatever she wants, to prove our devotion, we have a chance. It begins with Iphiboë. I think we must also seek out and kill this murderous barbarian. Only then can we hope for forgiveness.

At first Helice did not believe me. When she realized I was not lying, she dropped to the shrine floor, gouging at her eyes. "Why could Athene not take me?" she cried. "I would have given myself. I have lived. Iphiboë. My child...."

With much poppy, she fell asleep in my arms, whispering her daughter's name. I hate myself for the grief I have caused this poor woman.

When did she become so thin and fragile? Holding her, I realized for the first time that Queen Helice of Kaphtor is lost to her people. The imperious ruler who cowed would-be invaders and brought warriors to their knees, she who commanded the respect of all surrounding countries—that singular leader is gone. She slipped away and I did not even notice. All that remains is a tired old woman, crushed by illness and desolation.

She is not the one who will lead us back to prosperity.

NONE THOUGHT IPHIBOË POSSESSED MORE THAN A GLIMMER OF THE fascination that draws everyone to Aridela like flame to oil. Shy and timid, she became almost invisible in her sister's presence.

Yet she kissed Aridela and leaped from the cliffs with determination and courage. Iphiboë made this sacrifice with a willing heart, to save Kaphtor.

For the first time in many days, the earth did not shake. Today it rained— real, fresh rain, which seemed to bury some of the ash. After, the sun came out, still hazy, but bringing rainbows that stretched from horizon to horizon.

I CANNOT DESCRIBE THE BRILLIANCE OF THE HEAVENS. IT IS LIKE BEING LIFTED in the hand of a god, swimming through color, breathing every hue ever imagined until one becomes color itself. It is like being washed clean in a vast sea of fragrant paint.

The waning moon is as red as blood.

CHRYSALEON FOUND MENOETIUS AFTER A LONG DAY OF CLEARING RUBBLE. His brother looked tired. Not surprising, as he had spent his day collecting corpses. Chrysaleon was tired too, but not enough to seek slumber. Though his burns and other injuries didn't hurt so much anymore, gruesome nightmares made the nights difficult, and lying in bed made the longing for Aridela almost unbearable. Nine days he had waited for her to return from the oracle's shrine. She had promised him it would only be two or three.

"Knucklebones?" he asked. Menoetius hesitated then gave a weary nod.

They'd hardly begun their game before messengers came through announcing the royal family's return. Exchanging a glance, the two ran to the south gate.

Helice stepped out of her litter, drew her fur close around her face, and walked away without responding to anyone who bowed and greeted her.

Chrysaleon frowned after the queen. "Aridela? What has happened?"

"My sister is dead." The gaze she leveled on him was opaque. Emotionless. "She offered herself in the hope that Athene's rage might cool."

Shock bolted through him like a fist blow. He sensed more than saw Menoetius straighten sharply. He started to speak then didn't, not knowing what to say.

Murmurs rose from those who overheard. Aridela glanced at them and released a pent-up breath. "Athene's anger is great," she said. "Our oracle understood that we must make a sacrifice beyond any other. I only pray, if ever I am called, that I can equal my sister's courage." Her voice trembled and she fell silent, breathing hard.

Only later, when Chrysaleon lay alone and sleepless in the undamaged west wing of Labyrinthos, did realization wash over him.

He no longer faced union with a woman he had scorned.

Aridela was now Queen Helice's oldest daughter.

Selene's vision on the mountain had come true. Aridela would take Kaphtor's throne.

Helice closeted herself and refused to see anyone. Aridela sank into despair so dark Chrysaleon could see no way of breaking through. The intensity of her grief was foreign to him. He found himself dwelling morosely on the uninhibited passion she had offered in the cave, her incandescent laughter when she leaped the wild bull, her unselfconscious exuberance as she played with her companions in the forest pool. Was that woman lost forever? Could she possibly come back after this?

Iphiboë. Half the country ridiculed her when she was alive. In death, she became Crete's greatest hero.

Chrysaleon walked with his brother to the razed port of Amnisos. Wreckage and carcasses still littered the beach and clotted the bay, giving rise to a rotting stench. Every ship at anchor that day succumbed to the tremendous wave. Now Crete's people were cut off from the rest of the world. Worse was the annihilation of the island's master shipbuilders, who had made their homes in the ports. Only a few survived, and to those fell the gigantic task of reconstruction.

His thoughts turned to his father, his brother, and his sister. What of Iros, his child-wife? Had those lethal clouds of fire reached Mycenae? He and Menoetius were prisoners of this destruction. How long would it be before they could find out what had happened elsewhere?

Grief and shock had numbed the rulers of this once invincible country into listless apathy. In one night, Kaphtor had been rendered weak and vulnerable.

He half-hoped the kingdoms of Argolis had suffered as much damage to their ships and harbors, for if they hadn't, they would soon arrive to take advantage of this newly helpless land.

"What is out there, beyond our sight?" he asked. "Isy. Kos. Rhodes. Does anything live, anywhere?"

"Truly, Goddess Athene's anger is terrible, that she would destroy her own faithful lands." Menoetius made the sign against evil.

"What caused this anger? What did these people do?"

"Some say you brought it."

Chrysaleon faced his brother. "Why?" He'd felt the growing chill directed towards him, glimpsed it in averted faces.

"You have heard the rumors. Their oracle claims one of us desecrated the shrine on Callisti. She says this man raped and murdered the holy priestess. You and I are the same to them, barbarians who give allegiance to Poseidon, not Athene."

"If Lady Athene did not want me as Iphiboë's consort, why did I win the Games? Aridela's father was a warrior of Gla. He was heaped with honor and glory. Why did they not kill me, instead of Iphiboë, if they think I am the reason for all this?"

Shrugging, Menoetius said, "I merely repeat the gossip. I have no answers. The people are afraid, and want to blame someone. Anyone."

"I must diffuse this suspicion."

"How?"

"I will find a way."

8

Moon of Field Poppies

Survivors from the eastern provinces claimed they walked through ash so deep it covered their anklebones. Fire and the heave of the earth obliterated Elasa, the palace-temple in the northeast, and Phaistos in the south.

Messengers from the western provinces, however, offered better news. Only a smattering of ash fell west of the Ida mountains, and no one saw any poison clouds. The ground suffered nothing more than minor quivers as the Earth Bull cleared his throat. Crops in the west might survive, unless this unseasonable frost continued.

A lethargic Helice followed her council's advice and relocated her court while repairs commenced on Labyrinthos and the port of Amnisos. After hearing from every precinct, she chose as her temporary refuge an inconspicuous hamlet in the southwest province called Natho. Though it lay on the coast, the murderous waves ravaged no more than its harbor and ships; the village, tucked into the cliffs and hills above, suffered no damage.

Though death and injury had diminished her entourage, the royal train still stretched in a seemingly endless serpentine line. Aridela, reclining in a litter just behind Helice's, peered backward at refugees and litters, oxen and sheep, carts and goats, and wondered how a negligible spot like Natho could possibly feed and shelter them all. Not only would this influx of people need to be fed, but food and other essentials must also be found and sent back to those who worked in

49

the ruined areas. Her mother should have picked Kydonia, a major city center in the northwest that also escaped the worst of the destruction, but Helice confessed to a shrinking horror of the entire northern coast, and wanted to be as far from it as possible.

Ash polluted the snowfall on the eastern slopes of Mount Ida. All the way through the pass, bouts of thunder and lightning threatened; cold darkness made day and night nearly indistinguishable and the earth shuddered as though recoiling from a mortal wound. Every time thunder muttered or a blood-red moon rose in the heavens, Aridela had to fight off streams of fear, guilt, memories, and grief.

Yet as the procession emerged onto the west side of the mountain, sunlight pierced the clouds, glinting against drifts of pure snow. There was no discernable ash. The air was clean and fresh. The land continued to improve the farther south and west they traveled. Dusty green olive groves stretched across the foothills. Cypresses remained tall, unbent. It felt as though the queen's court had abandoned Kaphtor altogether and journeyed to a distant, undisturbed country.

The people of Natho emerged in welcome, yet none cheered or threw flowers as they would have normally. They kept their heads lowered; swollen-eyed women offered sympathy as the royal family passed, and touched the edges of Helice's litter. Aridela heard the words *our beloved queen* repeated until it merged into a sorrowful chant.

They surrounded Chrysaleon too, recognizing him as the mysterious foreign bull-king by the crown he wore, along with the fact that he and Menoetius were the only ones riding horses.

No one here knew Iphiboë had dreaded taking him as consort, or that Chrysaleon and Aridela were lovers. They didn't know the affectionate title of 'Gold Lion' used on the mainland, nor had they heard any gossip suggesting he might be the cause of the destruction. They believed him an honorable king, cheated through no fault of his own out of his kingdom, queen, and country, and generously extended their sympathy.

Do you think I have not seen how you look at each other? A cow could see.

Tears welled, blurring Aridela's first glimpse of her new home. Iphiboë had blessed Aridela's union with Chrysaleon. She had never suggested he might have secret motives when he lay with Aridela or sought to win the kingship.

We go about our lives in ignorance, but the Goddess has every shade and texture perfectly woven into a magnificent tapestry.

Iphiboë had known, perhaps for years, how she would die. Yet she never said a word. She embraced her death with faith and courage even as she shrank from coupling with a man. While Aridela complained about her own small dissatisfactions, Iphiboë held close this heavy secret. How long had Aridela felt superior to her sister, only to discover, when it was too late, that her sister was not what she seemed?

The road made sharp switchbacks through the village and up a steep hill. At its apex, the travelers beheld the sea, sparkling, peaceful, and blue as always, giving no hint of the open-jawed hunger for destruction it had manifested in the north. Only distant piles of trash and the lack of ships in the harbor offered any suggestion of loss.

Their guides brought them to a spacious villa, offered for their use by the merchant who had built it.

Aridela drew in a deep breath.

She felt isolated and alone in a land of strangers.

Once, in happier times, Aridela and Iphiboë whisked a visiting emissary's daughter away from her nurses. It was, of course, Aridela who conceived the prank and bullied her sister into going along. They took the five-year-old to a waterfall where they often swam, and talked her into jumping off the summit to the pool beneath. Through Athene's grace, the child came to no harm. When Helice and her guest discovered his daughter missing and the Cretan nurses came crying about losing the princesses, an alarm was called. Searchers found the three girls beside the pond. Aridela had placed a crown of moss and leaves on the naked child's brow and was teaching her to commune with the spirits of the water.

Helice's daughters were sent to their chambers with nothing to eat but stale bread for three days, and forced to apologize to the foreigner for their bad manners.

Eight days after the move to Natho, Aridela dreamed of that event, but this time it was Iphiboë who leaped from the top of the waterfall. The grassy hill transformed into the high, dangerous summits overlooking the sea. The face she lifted toward Aridela as she dropped to her death was contorted with fear and accusation. Rocks at the bottom shattered her body and silenced her screams.

"Where is our prince this morning?" Helice murmured. "It grows late. I fear Lycus may come and there will be more unpleasantness."

Neither the Destruction nor the passage of time had cooled Lycus's hatred for the foreign prince from Mycenae. Since the night Chrysaleon nearly killed him in the labyrinth, Lycus's rage had only escalated.

The petulance in her mother's voice startled Aridela back to the present, to the airy chamber where they were being served breakfast.

"Then why invite him?" Selene asked. "It only aggravates Lycus's jealousy."

Aridela looked down at her untouched figs and barley bread. A maid poured her a cup of goat's milk. Once a favorite, today the smell of it gave her a headache.

"I feel as Lycus does," Selene said. "Look what came of a barbarian winning the Games. It would be better for Kaphtor if he were to leave on the first ship strong enough to carry him home."

"Would you send Menoetius away so easily?" Aridela asked, her voice sharper than she intended.

Selene's gaze faltered.

Helice dismissed the tension with an impatient sigh. "We must find a way for these western precincts to feed the entire island. Surplus stores from the palaces will help. But the workers tell me most of the grain and honey jars at Labyrinthos were crushed. Aridela, I am meeting today with local farmers. Go with me. Put your mind to work —brooding helps nothing." She leaned over to touch her daughter's hand. "I worry about you."

Aridela avoided her mother's tender gaze. She could not confess the depth of her grief and guilt to Helice, who remained ignorant of all that had transpired between her daughter and the foreign prince.

She felt closer to Chrysaleon than ever. His actions during the cataclysm had replaced her girlish infatuation with admiration and trust. He had offered his body in defense of hers, when rifts in the earth sought to swallow them. It must have been agonizing for him when she'd climbed up his chest and over his injuries. He had placed his arm over her head and shoulders in an effort to protect her during the blaze of wind-fire, and later, at Phaistos, he tried to shelter her from the horrors. He never left her side except when he descended into the underground to rescue survivors and to search for water.

She didn't want to add to her mother's despair, either. Helice was no longer the proud queen of legend and bard song. Iphiboë's death had completed the ruin of that monarch, much like the poison gases, ashfall, and earthshakings ruined Kaphtor. The queen had little interest in anything now, and spent most of every day in her darkened bedchamber, alone with her grief.

"Don't worry about me, Mother," she said. "I am simply tired."

Themiste's visionary recounting of the barbarian overthrow on Callisti hadn't dampened Aridela's bond to the prince from Mycenae. Thankfully, Helice disagreed that Chrysaleon should be held to blame for the actions of others simply because they hailed from his area of the world.

When Helice's expression remained distressed, she added, "I dream of Iphiboë…often."

"Messengers from Labyrinthos tell us there have been no convulsions of the earth since her sacrifice," Selene said. "They say the sky is beginning to clear. Her intercession has softened the Lady's anger—I know it. Iphiboë proved herself worthy and courageous, yet, Aridela, even so, you know taking the throne would have been difficult, if not impossible, for her."

The Natho merchant's ubiquitous servants opened the far doors, saving Aridela from finding a reply. They bowed as Chrysaleon and his guard entered the room. Silence fell as people throughout the chamber nudged each other.

The prince was clean-shaven. The sight of his bare young face resurrected in startling detail Aridela's dream on Mount Juktas.

For longer than you can imagine, I will be with you, in you, of you. Together, we bring forth a new world, and nothing can ever part us.

She had nearly forgotten that warm, honeyed night and seductive voice. Thinking of it now left her aching for lost sunny days, when she had nothing to do but plot a romance with Lycus, dream of golden gods, bicker with Iphiboë, and complain about tutors she thought were too strict.

He approached the queen's table and bowed. "My lady," he said.

Helice stood, inclining her head as formally as he. "What has happened to your beard, my lord?"

"Kaphtor is my home now. I want to adopt your customs and traditions."

"You show us great honor. I can only apologize to you for the poor showing you have been given so far." She paused then briskly gestured to the cushions beside her. "I have not yet had a chance to ask after your father. All Kaphtor joins me in hope that your country escaped these troubles. Sit here with me. Have something to eat."

"First, my lady, I crave your indulgence." Chrysaleon's voice carried through the room.

Silence, thickened by curiosity, infused the chamber.

"All we possess is yours, Zagreus." Helice inclined her head again.

"Yes, I am Zagreus, bull-king of Kaphtor. I performed every rite you asked of me and was chosen to win by Lady Athene. But it is a title without meaning. I am unaccustomed to such idleness, my lady, and have given the dilemma much consideration. Since I can never be consort to Iphiboë, I propose that you join Princess Aridela to me in her stead."

Helice stared, clearly shocked. The rest of the room echoed with the scandalized whispering of those who overheard.

"I won the Games," he continued. "I strengthened my claim through the killing of the old Zagreus. I am here, ready to make the thirteen sacrifices and fulfill my obligation. I want to lead our people back into Athene's grace."

An odd ringing in Aridela's ears almost drowned out his voice. She clenched her hands to stop their quivering. *No, not now. Not yet. You belittle Iphiboë with this haste.*

Chrysaleon cut through the rising wave of gossip. "Queen Helice, I offer myself without condition, though more than a month of my rightful time as consort has been stolen from me—"

"You go too far, barbarian."

Lycus, assisted by two women, entered just in time to hear the last part of Chrysaleon's speech.

Helice sighed and nodded to her guards. They advanced, one on either side; pushing the women away, they seized Lycus's arms.

He struggled, staring with white-rimmed eyes from Chrysaleon to Helice to Aridela. "You restrain *me?* He is the one. He fools you all. Are you thick-headed, or blind?"

"Take him to his chamber," Helice said. "He needs rest." Her lips tightened as the guards dragged him from the room. She motioned to a handmaid. "Send Rhené to him with poppy." Turning back to Chrysaleon, she smiled and bowed. "Patience, my lord. As you know, Lycus has not yet recovered from his wounds."

His angry frown smoothed. "I understand the suspicion your people feel. I am a foreigner, a barbarian, as some say. But Queen Helice, I ask you to understand why I make this offer." He paused, half turning as if to include the onlookers in his speech. "Never in my life have I known any woman comparable to the royal daughters of Kaphtor. Iphiboë possessed the courage of the wild lions that rule my homeland's mountains. I see the same courage in her sister. I saw it when she stepped into the bullring, and again the night Phaistos burned. The acceptance Lady Aridela has shown me recalls my mother, whose nobility never failed her in any circumstance. She was famed throughout Argolis for her spirit and generosity." He met Helice's gaze and added, his voice betraying nothing but steady confidence, "Love for the princess of Kaphtor has overtaken all other ambitions. I offer my life in her service. Surely Lady Athene herself instilled this desire in me."

The carved ivory disks and onyx beads hanging from the circlet around Helice's head trembled. So did her voice, very slightly, as she replied. "Prince Chrysaleon, you show us great honor. My daughter feels as I do."

Aridela nodded, but she knew by Helice's set mouth, shuttered eyes, and the deliberate use of his real name, what she was thinking. *It is too soon.* Menoetius, standing to the side, scowled as though he, too, disapproved. If only she were still friends with the man she had known as Carmanor. She could advise him and he could in turn advise his master. Tears filled her eyes. She seemed incapable of finishing half a day without self-indulgent weeping over one thing or another.

"These matters cannot be undertaken lightly," Helice continued. "They deserve the most serious consideration."

Chrysaleon nodded.

"You have in truth made the great sacrifice, as our traditions demand. You have honored every requirement we set before the man who would be consort and bull-king."

He sent a quick glance towards Aridela.

"I must discuss your request with my council. Nothing is as it was, my lord."

"I understand," he said with the slightest of bows.

With unreadable eyes and an impassive face, Helice motioned to Aridela to accompany her, and left the chamber.

THEMISTE COULD NOT BE FOUND, SO HELICE'S TWELVE ADVISORS CONVENED without her. Oneaea, the queen's sister and chief counselor, drummed her fingers on the table and leveled a narrowed glare upon Aridela. "Did you have knowledge of this beforehand?"

"No." Aridela spoke the truth, yet her lover's character should have warned her. He was not a man to wait for things to happen. He was a man who made things happen. The fact that his life would end in one year if he remained on Kaphtor as bull-king must have spurred him to disregard the inauspicious timing and make this preemptive move. What brought beads of sweat to her scalp and uncomfortable heat to her face now was the fear of his actions leading to their secret being exposed. The humiliation would be worse than any physical punishment.

"It is most grave," Oneaea continued. "There is much to be decided and the path we tread is dangerous. But I tell you: I will never condone such a union, even if we were to put aside Themiste's choice for your future. An Achaean—the same breed as Callisti's destroyer. Everyone knows by now of the Minos's vision. All the mainland clans are cursed. Were it up to me, I would banish the prince and his men to some out-of-the-way corner until a ship can carry them away." Oneaea sent the queen a stern, openly blaming gaze.

"True, everything has changed," said Prince Kios before Helice could react. Aridela's uncle was a thoughtful man with a reputation for wisdom; as soon as he spoke, all those at the table turned to him and offered courteous attention.

He looks tired. His grief has not yet abated. The thought only served to bring back images of Iphiboë. Aridela lowered her head beneath a new barrage of sadness.

"It is hard to know what to do," Kios said, rubbing his eyes, "but my instincts tell me that we dare not accept this man as our king, despite the outcome of the Games." Drawing in a deep breath, he added, "We must be rid of him, somehow."

Oneaea returned her accusatory stare to Helice. "You have given him an excessive sense of himself with your doting and attentions. How could he otherwise be unaware of the arrogance he displayed today? Most did not trust him before, including me. He has no humility. That he dare come before us publicly and demand Aridela, like she is one of his mainland slaves—to be given for the price of a beard!"

Helice frowned. She crossed her arms over her chest and ran her palms over her shoulders as though to warm herself.

"It could be as he says." Aridela tried to appear casual. "Perhaps he is willing to love me in Iphiboë's stead."

"What does that matter? His own countrymen caused the near-annihilation of our entire world—perhaps with his knowledge." Oneaea struck the table with her fist. "You may not know this, but some suspect he staged the horrors on Callisti while remaining here, courting Iphiboë and cloaking himself in innocence. I agree with Kios. The violence of that night, all we have suffered, and most of all, your sister's death; these events have destroyed established relations with the mainland. We are weakened and must be extra vigilant. There can be no sacred king now unless it is one of Kaphtor's own, a man we can fully trust."

"Does he deserve this judgment?" Aridela rose from her chair and paced, fighting to quiet her scattered nerves and keep her voice even. "I feel as Mother does—there is no evidence linking him to what happened, and without that, we cannot blame him for what other men may or may not have done. Kaphtor's women have long taken Achaean men as husbands. You did so yourself, Mother. There is nothing new about it. Chrysaleon is my equal in rank and he won the Games. Where has he transgressed us? He has made every effort to show us respect and honor, and he denied any knowledge of whatever evil may have transpired on Callisti. We have not yet received news from there, anyway, only Themiste's vision. None of us can pretend her visions have always been accurate." Locking her gaze to her mother's, she added, "Chrysaleon could have abandoned me multiple times on the night of the poison fires and death. When the earth split open, he could have let me fall. He could have left me to burn. But instead he used his body as a shield to protect me. He risked his own life to preserve mine."

Helice's reply shocked her. "Apparently you have developed feelings for him as he has for you."

Aridela felt her face betray her with hot color. She had given away more than she intended. "I try, as you taught me, to be impartial. I do not believe the prince to be underhanded. I have conversed with him many times, more than any of you. There is no deception in his face or manner. It was clear to me that night that he would sacrifice himself in order to save me." She placed her hands flat on the table. "My aunt says he has no humility, but Chrysaleon came to you and asked your permission. He shaved his beard, which we know is never done, and vowed to submit to our ways. How can this be called arrogance? What more could he do to win your approval?"

"You are right, Aridela." Helice gave a brief nod. "We cannot allow emotion to sway our judgment. I have given much thought to the prince, and though your words are eloquent, I will share my concerns. Chrysaleon expends considerable effort to achieve brief kingship and his own death, when he could have Mycenae's crown and live until unknowable fate severs the thread of his life. I have learned he has a wife there and has fathered children. Does he mean to die at the next rising of Iakchos, or does he have other plans, plans designed to benefit Mycenae rather than Kaphtor?"

"He is subject to our laws, now more than ever. He cannot think that has changed." Even as Aridela spoke in her lover's defense, she remembered him asking her to abandon her country for his. He had dismissed with scorn the wife who waited for him there. Confusion and fear sharpened her voice. "Do we or do we not believe the Lady chooses our sacred kings? If we believe it, as we have always claimed, our direction is clear. Chrysaleon descended into the labyrinth and killed the Zagreus. He won the Games. Athene chose him. To send him away now…it is this sort of defiance that risks more divine anger."

Oneaea fingered a crystal in her necklace. Her clenched jaw and stony expression remained unrepentant. "He does not and never has seemed to me a man who would walk willingly into certain death. At Mycenae, he is heir to kingship over all the Kindred. He will inherit riches, power, and glory, if any remain. He has fought in his father's name to increase Mycenae's wealth and expand its borders."

"We have discussed this many times." Aridela no longer tried to hide her impatience. "We asked him repeatedly if he wanted this, if he was willing to honor our laws. He agreed, time and time again."

"Yes," Helice said. "We are not arguing that fact. We wonder if his agreement was sincere, or if other motives hide beneath his spoken words."

Oneaea rose from her chair. She leaned forward, fists pressed against the table. "Mycenae offers but shallow honor to Potnia Athene. I have heard they call Poseidon her uncle, and give him authority over her." She sneered, making clear her disdain. "If he were anyone other than the son of Idómeneus, High King of Mycenae, I might consider this union—if, indeed, Themiste would relinquish her claim upon you, Aridela. I wish she were here to consult. That aside…." She banged her fist on the marble tabletop. "I do not trust him. I vote to refuse and banish him."

"The ship being built in the harbor is almost finished," Kios said. "It will be ready to sail in a few days."

Helice nodded. "In many ways I admire the prince, and I will always be grateful for the protection he offered you, but in this matter I agree with my sister and brother."

Aridela bowed her head. Again, her sight melted into a haze of tears, but these burned with fury, not grief. Her teeth clenched. Here at this momentous crossroads, she was being dismissed, her years of training, education, and preparation given no weight. The council obviously did not think she should have any say, though every one of these decisions concerned her. Even so, her mind, trained to look at things from all sides, forced her to concede. "Chrysaleon is a proud man from a race of warriors where the male reigns supreme," she said. "I have to admit there is a chance he may not understand, or might plan to thwart the ways of our people. A sliver of a chance."

"The barbarian profanes us." Triumph glittered in Oneaea's dark eyes. "Before more punishment falls, we will show the Goddess and her son that we shall never bend to the ways of foreigners. Themiste must go into trance—false if need be, to speak Athene's wishes. Then Chrysaleon will not be able to accuse us of prejudice."

"A false trance?" Aridela stared at her aunt. "Is that what we now stoop to? Cheap trickery? Is that what you think of our oracle?"

"Aridela," Helice began.

Aridela threw up her hand in angry challenge. "Why do you think you can speak for Themiste? Intolerance has clouded your judgment, aunt. I want to know what Minos Themiste's true opinion would be if she were here, not what you foist upon her."

"Silence!" Helice rose from her chair, her skin mottling from forehead to chest. "You will not speak in such a manner to my council. Go to your chamber and wait there for me."

When Aridela opened her mouth to argue, her mother stopped her with a pointed finger and flashing eyes. For an instant, she resembled the Helice of old. "Do you think to defy me?"

"Follow your mother's wishes, child," Prince Kios said, giving her an understanding smile.

Aridela ran from the room. Tears flowed so hotly she could scarcely see where she stepped. She longed to run to Iphiboë, to scream, weep, and allow her anger its just release. But Iphiboë was dead. Neoma would be her next choice, but her cousin still lay near death from her head wound. Isandros, who shared so many of her childhood adventures and helped her defy the restrictions placed by birth, was dead as well.

There was only one person in whom she could confide. One person, who should have been at this meeting, and to whom she must now bare every secret.

9

Moon of Field Poppies

CHRYSALEON WAS SUMMONED TO THE QUEEN'S MAKESHIFT COUNCIL chamber the following morning.

Helice sat upon her throne, which had been hauled over the mountains from Knossos to Natho on an ox-drawn cart. At her right stood Aridela, wearing a stunning necklace of golden ivy that had been recovered from the collapsed storerooms at Labyrinthos. Themiste stood on the queen's left, her face and thoughts hidden behind the ominous bull's mask marking her station.

"We must choose our words with care," Helice said to Aridela. "Kaphtor is unprepared to engage in war. Anything we can do to preserve the ties we have forged must be done."

"Except giving Chrysaleon what he wants. What he fought for, nearly died for, and has every right to expect."

Helice made no verbal reply, but her measured stare and pointed frown demanded obedience.

Bystanders gossiped. Lycus reclined on a litter in the corner, scowling. Four beautiful and attentive women knelt beside him. But his angry gaze kept returning to the dais and Aridela.

Helice's steward escorted the Mycenaean prince and his guard into the room. Chrysaleon strode through the press, watching the three at the throne as though he might discern his fate from their expressions, but only Aridela's gaze faltered. The others were too experienced to give anything away.

Helice rose and lifted her scepter, a gold and ivory labrys, to command silence. With a polite inclination of her head, she began. "Prince Chrysaleon, heir to the kingdom of Mycenae, son of High King Idómeneus. You fought for my daughter Iphiboë, who gave her life in supreme sacrifice to save her people. You have stated your willingness to accept my younger daughter in Iphiboë's stead. My council has discussed the matter with care and consideration."

Chrysaleon's gaze never wavered. His brows lowered. Aridela saw his jaw clench as though he had somehow discerned what the queen was about to say.

The air felt charged, as though invisible lightning was shooting between the two. The crowded chamber grew quiet and hot.

Aridela could hardly breathe. She sensed Athene's eyes staring down upon the scene.

"My lord," Helice said, "you have proved yourself as powerful a warrior as Aridela's father, my beloved Damasen, who gave his life bravely, and who now watches over those he loves from Lady Potnia's land of honey and nectar."

Chrysaleon inclined his head, accepting the praise, but his demeanor warned that he was losing patience.

Helice seemed to decide she'd made enough conciliatory statements. Lifting her chin, she said strongly, "Kaphtor's council refuses your request, though we recognize your worth and all we owe you. Our gratitude is measureless, Prince Chrysaleon."

She offered her most gracious smile, but Chrysaleon's frown intensified.

With a quick, disappointed sigh, she continued. "We cannot continue as though nothing is changed when everything has. I urge you to return to the mainland, my lord, to your wife, and a long, respected reign as High—"

"You disregard your own laws?" Chrysaleon's voice rang off the walls. "Aridela will be queen. I won the Games. I am bull-king, and have won the right to be consort, either to her or to you."

Briefly, Helice's eyes narrowed in a way Aridela knew and respected. The queen of Kaphtor was not accustomed to being confronted in such a manner. "My lord, you are not privy to every circumstance surrounding my youngest daughter." Her voice was studiously patient now, as though she was hanging on to the last shreds of control. "On the night she was born, a bolt of lightning struck the summit of our holy mountain and she herself was marked with its burn. Long have we considered the portents of this event. Aridela added to her own mystery by speaking prophecy when she was but a child. Because of what we have suffered, of what our oracle has seen, because of the written prophecies—of which you know nothing—the council has decided to initiate new traditions. Aridela was promised to Minos Themiste, and dedicated to oracle training; the prophecy she spoke showed this to be her calling. We will now combine the queenship with her original purpose."

Aridela stared at her mother. No one had informed her of this plan. Helice and the council must have come up with it after ejecting her. She noticed smug satisfaction on her aunt Oneaea's face.

The way Chrysaleon jerked his chin and released a sharp breath clearly demonstrated his growing impatience.

Helice hurried on. "Aridela will take no yearly consort. She shall rule according to the Great Marriage. The children she bears will be the fruit of the grove. We hope this will please Goddess Athene and bring us back into her favor."

Aridela's breathing shortened. Her heart sped up unpleasantly.

Chrysaleon's gaze broke its hold on Helice's at last, shooting first to Aridela, then Menoetius.

"The Great Marriage," he repeated.

"This is no reflection upon you," Helice said. "It is merely our attempt to correct a certain laxness, an indifference, that has crept into our lives and angered our Mistress."

From the corner, Lycus gave a snort of laughter. "At last," he said, loud enough to be overheard.

Eyes narrowed, Chrysaleon pivoted, his muscles tensing. Aridela feared a brawl. Menoetius stepped closer to his prince.

But Chrysaleon surprised her by turning back to the queen with a dismissive snort. The anger on his face vanished, leaving determination. "It is too late for that." His voice snapped like a whip over the assemblage. "Mortal man has already coupled with Princess Aridela, outside the grove. I was that man. She may in fact carry my child in her womb."

Gasps and protests erupted. Aridela closed her eyes, swaying under a deluge of lightheadedness. She gripped the backrest on her mother's throne. If only Helice had warned her of this excuse they meant to foist off on him. She would have confessed her crime. This public humiliation would have been avoided. She sensed Themiste staring at her and tried desperately to control her expression and her reaction.

"My lord," Menoetius said in a tone of warning. His hand wandered to his hip, where his sword would be if weapons were allowed in this room.

"Barbarian filth," Lycus shouted. Chrysaleon smiled, lifting his brow as he glanced at the wounded bull dancer. Aridela could not help but admire his triumph and confidence, when, if he but knew it, his very life hung by a single strand of seaweed.

Themiste stepped forward. Such was her dominance from behind the mask that silence fell instantly. Her voice, neither male nor female but reflecting the Divine, echoed off ceiling and walls. "You dare blaspheme us? Aridela was dedicated to Athene when she was born. At my decree, she has given herself to no man, in or out of the grove."

Chrysaleon faced Aridela, his eyes demanding. "Tell them."

Helice seized Aridela's arm. "Is this true?" she asked, fear and anger in her eyes.

Before Helice finished her question, the pottery in the wall niches started to rattle as though a herd of oxen were stampeding on the other side of the wall.

Themiste's hand stretched to Helice's.

Murmurs grew swift, loud, and frightened. Those who had come to see what might happen with the foreigner milled like trapped beasts.

A lamp fell and shattered on the tiles. From the stones, from deep within the earth's dark, secret places, a low, throbbing bellow oozed.

Panic exploded. "The Earth Bull," someone cried.

"Goddess is again angry!"

Several women screamed. It was deafening in the small chamber.

The moan of the earth caused the walls to reverberate. Vases shattered. Water splashed over the edge of the purifying basin.

Themiste dropped to her knees. She pressed her fists to her breasts and lowered her head.

Helice and Aridela did the same.

"Isoke," Helice whispered.

Aridela opened her eyes. Chrysaleon stood before them, feet planted firm and wide, arms crossed. He scowled down at them as though he wasn't aware of the rumble of the earth, the broken pottery, or the frantic people who fought to escape through the single narrow door.

"Pray, my queen," Themiste cried. "Pray for forgiveness."

"You have betrayed the wishes of Athene, not I." Chrysaleon seized Aridela's arm and yanked her to her feet. "I won't leave her here," he said to Helice's startled protest. "What if the ceiling falls? Stay if you wish, Queen Helice." He shoved through the crowd, knocking people out of his way, dragging Aridela with him. Menoetius followed close behind.

The heave of the earth was short. By the time they emerged into the courtyard, all had stilled, leaving giant cracks in the brilliant blue paint on the entrance pillars. Broken pottery and overturned flowerpots littered the ground. The threshold stone bore an ugly ragged fracture.

"Did you do this?" Aridela asked, trembling and terrified.

"I cannot make the earth shake," Chrysaleon said with the faintest of smiles. "But in truth, had I that ability, I would have used it." He clasped her upper arms so hard she gasped and nearly cried out. "By the Father of Horses, I will have you." His lips whitened and the tips of his fingers dug into her flesh. "I will rip that woman's head off."

"No," Aridela cried, not knowing if he spoke of her mother or Themiste.

"Menoetius." Chrysaleon kept his narrowed, furious gaze fixed on Aridela. "Find a ship, a boat, or a plank of wood, and we will leave this cursed island."

"No," Aridela and Menoetius shouted in unison. Menoetius shoved Chrysaleon in the chest, forcing him to release Aridela and driving him backward until the courtyard wall stopped them both. Aridela remained still, gasping, bracing for the next shudder of the earth.

Surprise passed over Chrysaleon's face when Menoetius pinned his arms then drove the breath from his lungs with a hard thrust. Every time Chrysaleon attempted to free himself, Menoetius's grip changed to keep him trapped.

At last, only a sneer betrayed Chrysaleon's impotent rage.

"Does the queen speak for you?" Chrysaleon asked Aridela.

"I am bound to follow the council's decision."

"You will lie with a man only at the Festival of Velchanos—a man wearing a mask. You will never know the name or face of he who plants his seed within you. That is what you want?"

Once more he strained to free himself, but Menoetius held him firm. "Curse you and every bastard you ever sire," Chrysaleon said. "You have lied to me about far too many things."

The way they stared into each other's eyes sent an uneasy tremor down Aridela's spine.

"You make my duty seem a poor fate," she said, hoping to divert this hostility between them.

"Why did the council reject me? The true reason."

Aridela searched for duplicity in Chrysaleon's eyes, but saw only anger and frustration. "They believe Mycenae will use our weakened condition to subjugate us. The truth is they have never trusted you. They remember the history of your people. Did the ancestors of your Kindred Kings not overthrow all Argolis?"

Menoetius frowned at her, his expression indecipherable, but Chrysaleon laughed bitterly. "Is there a Mycenae? Does it have ships or warriors? My father might be dead. Our citadel may lie in ruins like so many of yours. I asked to remain here because living my old life, without you, is worse than death. Worse than defeat."

Menoetius's stare, as it shot back to the prince, was naked with surprise. That more than anything else convinced Aridela of Chrysaleon's sincerity.

"Release me," Chrysaleon said, "before I order my *loyal* men to throw you into the deepest hole on Crete."

Menoetius stepped away and Chrysaleon straightened. Aridela approached him and leaned against his chest, closing her eyes. He put his arm around her.

"I know you grieve for your sister," he said. "I grieve with you. But her death does make you Kaphtor's heir. You won't be given to the priestesses nor will they abandon the sacred kings. It is me they don't want. They have lost their faith. That is why the earth shakes, and why it will go on shaking."

Lycus emerged from the villa on his litter with his female attendants and began screaming curses and threats as soon as he spotted Chrysaleon. The bearers took him the other direction, down the steep road toward the village.

Aridela touched Chrysaleon's temple. She grasped a lock of his hair and pulled gently.

His expression of rage faded as he looked down at her. His love was so clear, so clean and honest. Why could no one else see it?

"I have not lost my faith," she said. "Goddess Athene holds me in her hand and has since my birth. If the Lady wants this union, she will give me a sign."

Chrysaleon's eyes narrowed. "Are you saying there is still a chance?"

Aridela nodded. "Give me a little time."

He returned her nod. "So be it. I await your decision."

Though no messenger came to summon her, Aridela knew Themiste was waiting to hear her confession.

She cloaked herself in heavy wool, for even here on the southern coast, persistent haze blocked the sun's warmth. Every day dawned clammy cold, chilly enough to bring snow to this fishing village whose inhabitants had never seen such a thing except from a distance, on the highest mountain summits behind them.

Day faded into evening before she found the oracle. Themiste was sitting on the ground inside a cave shrine overlooking the sea. A statue of the Goddess stood next to her; one marble hand rested upon a loom fashioned from grapevines and the other held an olive branch. Yet Themiste didn't seem to be praying or making offerings. Her distant, meditative expression was turned away from the statue towards the sea, the sound of which echoed eerily against the cavern walls.

"Minos." Aridela stepped around an offering basket of bread and honey.

Themiste looked almost relieved at the interruption. "Aridela. I pray for answers, but...." She shrugged. "I felt so helpless when the earth shook today. Small and useless. As though, for all the power and rank I have been given, I could do nothing to protect you or the queen. Never again can we assume our world is solid and safe."

Aridela ran her hand over the olive branch in the hand of the statue. "Unfamiliar sounds send me into cowardly shivering. Sometimes, when I go to sleep, I feel uncommon gratitude for a day without earthshakings."

"And this cold...." Themiste stood. "If it does not subside, any crops that survived the Destruction will die." She paused, her stare perceptive, but instead of the accusations Aridela feared, she said, "Let me see your burns."

Glad for a distraction from her purpose, Aridela pushed up the wool covering her arms. "They are better."

Themiste inspected her skin. "You will have scars."

Aridela shrugged. "I am alive. Many are not."

"Have you come to pray?"

"I have come to confess."

Themiste's brows rose. "Walk with me."

They left the shrine and followed a narrow path through the hills. Wintry breezes eddied around them. A conflagration of pinks, purples, blues, and greens swaddled the heavens, creating mirrored reflections across the surface of the sea, where dark blue succumbed to every imaginable tint of fire.

"Never could I dream of such displays of color and light," Themiste said. "I wonder sometimes if your sister sends this beauty from Hesperia, so that we do not forget her."

"Perhaps." Aridela swallowed the sudden knot that formed in her throat.

"You worry about Chrysaleon's lies."

Again Aridela swallowed as she sought courage. "Do you remember last Moon of Mead-making, when we took Iphiboë to the holy mountain to prepare her for dedication?" She kept her gaze locked on the sea, watching it lap against the rocks far below.

"Yes."

"That night, I had a dream—or a vision. Velchanos left his statue. He came to me. He spoke."

Themiste stopped walking. There was silence, until Aridela gathered her courage and met the oracle's expressionless but intent gaze.

"I remember," Themiste said quietly.

"The first time I met the prince of Mycenae, I believed he was the god of that vision. Many times since I have told myself I was wrong, but when he came to us yesterday, clean-shaven, I was certain. Chrysaleon is the god as he appeared to me that night. His hair, his eyes, even his voice. Surely this means something."

Themiste's gaze narrowed almost imperceptibly.

Aridela rushed on, too afraid now to pause. "Minos, on the night of Iphiboë's dedication, I sneaked out of my bedchamber and went with her to the cave of Velchanos."

Themiste's lips parted.

Aridela backed away from the Minos's unfathomable expression and unnerving silence. "Chrysaleon found me. How could he have done that if Athene had not directed him? We told no one where we would be except my mother, and not even she knew I was going. My intent was only to offer Iphiboë strength and encouragement—I did not mean to defy you. I meant to hide nearby if a man found us. How could I have known she would fall and injure her knee, or that she would charge me with fulfilling the dedication in her stead?"

"An omen of what was to come," Themiste said slowly, as if to herself.

"Chrysaleon told the truth. We lay with each other. Nothing happened to suggest we had angered Athene. Until the night of the Destruction, I believed we had done no more than follow the Lady's wishes." Aridela's muscles relaxed as she concluded her confession, though an ache lingered along her shoulder blades. "Minos, in the dream-vision, the god, or Chrysaleon, said he would be with me for longer than I could imagine. He promised nothing would ever separate us. It made me feel safe, like when I was small, and you kissed me, and helped me brave the nightmares. Oh, I make no sense, but I swear to you. We never meant harm to anyone."

Themiste turned her face down and closed her eyes.

Flooded with guilt, Aridela cried, "I beg your forgiveness. I never meant harm, least of all to the innocent people of Kaphtor or Callisti."

Lifting her face, Themiste clasped the sides of Aridela's head. "In the vision on the mountain, it was the Achaean? There must be no doubt."

Aridela's gaze faltered. "Not at first. When he crossed the clearing he was a god of the night, of darkness and moonlight, but then he transformed and became Chrysaleon in every detail."

Her voice shook as she stammered out the second crime. "Minos, the prince and I lay together again, just before the fire and rocks fell from the sky. He repeated what the god said on Mount Juktas, and this time I was fully awake. 'I am yours,' he said. 'Even death will never break our bond.' And he said, 'for longer than can be dreamed.' I felt I knew Athene's mind. I believed she approved our union, but now it is clear we angered her. You commanded me to remain untouched, and I defied you. My crime was more than child's mischief—look what has come of it. Chrysaleon and I...we caused the destruction of Kaphtor, and of Callisti." Aridela rubbed so violently at her tears that she left red streaks on her skin. "I caused Iphiboë's death."

"You gave yourself to him again, outside the rites? You defied me not once but twice?" Themiste covered her mouth with one hand and clasped Aridela's shoulder with the other.

"We were going home the next day," Aridela whispered. "Chrysaleon to wed Iphiboë. I, to enter the mountain shrine. We intended to honor our obligations. I beg your forgiveness...."

"You cannot be oracle now," Themiste said. "You cannot take my place."

Aridela looked out over the steep hills, across the vast wash of water. If she jumped, she would join her sister in the cold dark sea. Perhaps that would quell Potnia Athene's anger. She looked down, where sea met land, and pictured herself falling, but Themiste, still holding onto her shoulder, pulled her away from the edge.

Themiste placed the fingertips of one hand to the frown between Aridela's eyebrows and cradled the back of her head with the other. Aridela felt a queer inner pull. Themiste was initiating the ancient oracle art of *subliquara* to see into her mind.

"True," the Minos whispered, her eyes closed. "Pure. Your thoughts flow like a mountain stream."

Aridela tried to jerk free but the mind link had a way of freezing the body. She hated it. As a child, she had enjoyed their 'game' and how Themiste could speak her thoughts. Now she wanted to hold onto her privacy.

Themiste's hand dropped to Aridela's stomach. She pressed her palm there for some time. At last she opened her eyes. They held shadows of some emotion Aridela could not name. "There is no child. For that I am grateful. Your vision remains clear. I heard the words he spoke to you. Velchanos took the form of Chrysaleon during the rites. That seems certain. And the fact that he found you in the cave…I wonder if he will ever understand the blessing he received? I saw the prince's guard too. He was grieving and afraid. Somehow…lost."

"Menoetius?" Aridela thought back. At the beginning Velchanos hadn't resembled Chrysaleon. He was darker. Yes, very much the opposite of Chrysaleon. Something had snapped. When the ring of sound and blinding light faded, Velchanos had changed. It took effort to recall that in the beginning, she had recognized the god as Carmanor, her childhood love. She had even named him, and he had not denied it. In the months since that night, she'd forgotten how at first, the statue bore the likeness of Menoetius. Golden Chrysaleon, with his vivid, bold personality, had smothered the rest.

Themiste turned away. "Oh Athene," she said, "I want to do as you wish. Do you hate these barbarians or love them? Do you want Chrysaleon punished or rewarded?"

She walked away, leaving Aridela on the edge of the cliff.

Then she stopped and swung around. "Come." She held out her hand and beckoned sharply. Aridela hesitated, but couldn't disobey. She placed her hand in Themiste's. The oracle pulled her charge down the hill, back to the villa, leaving the sea's hunger unquenched.

10

Moon of Field Poppies

THEMISTE SPENT HER FREE TIME HUNCHED OVER TWO LARGE TABLES IN HER chamber, transcribing from memory Kaphtor's lost prophecies onto new clay tablets.

She worked at this task until her mind blurred, her fingers numbed, and she no longer trusted the phrases and symbols she pressed into wet clay. Was it Melpomene who wrote *the holy child will follow a path of deep shadow,* or Pelopia?

Hundreds of prophecies, some on clay tablets, others on fragile papyrus, had survived, safely preserved, even through other earth-shakings, for thousands of years....

Until now.

Themiste tried to suppress the fear that she was sending Kaphtor into a future built on hazy, unsound recollections. Laodámeia, her most trusted handmaid, did her best to help, but she had never been allowed to study the logs thoroughly. All she knew of them came from forbidden, secret readings deep in the night when she was unlikely to be discovered, and from transcribing Themiste's oracle visions.

Themiste had left instructions at the ruin of Labyrinthos, and a crude map. As laborers cleared and opened the labyrinth, they were to search specific areas. The first time a messenger came to Natho holding a recovered tablet, Themiste snatched it from him and smiled. The act felt foreign, awkward, as if she had nearly forgotten how to form such an expression.

Though the recovery of a tablet was cause for celebration, she knew she couldn't rely on the hope that more would be found. She must create replicas as best she could, from memory.

After the confrontation with Aridela, she returned to her chamber and settled at one of the tables, a lamp by her side. She knew which reconstructed tablet she wanted and quickly found it—the prophecy Aridela herself spoke when she was ten.

Lion of gold from over the sea
Destroy the black bull, shake the earth free
Curse the god, crush the fold,
pull down the stars as seers foretold.
Isle of cloud, Moon's stronghold, see your death come
in spears of gold.

For years, this prophecy had defied her attempts to understand it or winnow out its hidden message. But what had started to make sense when she first learned the meaning of the name 'Chrysaleon' was now completely clear. The prince of Mycenae, he who was known as 'Gold Lion,' had not only appeared from across the sea; he had gone farther. He had lodged himself like a fishhook in Aridela's heart.

Aridela always gave her affections fully, and this was no different. Themiste remembered how the child had once loved Carmanor, who, as it happened, was the prince's personal guard. Carmanor was Aridela's first love, but now she hardly noticed him, such was her obsession with Chrysaleon.

It might be amusing, were there not so much at stake.

The scent of damp clay and hot oil hung in heavy stagnant layers, making her room oppressive. She longed for the clean, cold air at the cliff shrine, but there was no help for it. Aridela's revelations changed everything. Themiste would have to rearrange the future, yet again.

She searched through her newly created tablets until she'd gathered all that mentioned the lion. If she could connect the pieces from the different prophecies, she might be given insight into what must be done.

The first was Melpomene's.

He of one father but two mothers will grow to dominion in a foreign
land—one split into two, gold and obsidian. The universal egg will

crack. All that is sacred will spill and be lost. Lion and bull, they are forged.

How could a child be born of two mothers, split into two yet at the same time remain forged? The lion must be Chrysaleon of Mycenae, but who or what was the bull? A memory sparked—she dug out a papyrus on which she'd recorded her dream from just before the Destruction.

One of Athene's handmaids had shared what was to come. The great design. But that dream left many questions unanswered. Themiste remembered asking for the identity of the bull, but the handmaid had refused to say. *If I told you, you would try to change his fate*, was all she would give.

She had added a puzzling statement. *What seems the end is only the beginning.*

Could he be Xanthus, the bull-king Chrysaleon killed in his quest for the title? If so, Kaphtor was already overcome, for how could a dead bull defeat a living lion?

Minos Timandra also mentioned a lion.

This lion must bare his throat and consent to his destruction. The bull must consume the lion. The moon and stars will return to the egg and the bull will repair the egg with his divine seed. If three become two, all the world will be reborn to the bountiful Mistress of Many Names, and the vine will again bear fruit.

She read two more of Timandra's prophecies, though they didn't talk about the lion. They did mention the child—the child she was certain was Aridela.

One more completes the triad. A child will spring from the loins of Velchanos, god of lightning, her celestial brother. Without her, all will fail.

The child must rise up from the intoxication in which she willingly drowns. If she becomes pure, utterly clear, the thinara king and his disciples will give her their allegiance. If she does not, every living thing will languish and the end will come.

Before she could pick apart these words, she was distracted from her purpose by another prophecy, which captured the lamplight and drew her eye.

Women are bartered for land, titles, and gold. Their songs are silenced. They are brought as low as fleas on the pelt of a dog, and the mysteries they have always guarded are lost. The days are set to come when earth withers and women forget their divinity. Then will they embrace their own slavery.

Themiste leaned back in her chair and stared at the hearth fire.

Since coming to Natho, she'd hardly slept or eaten. Rewriting the tablets took all her concentration. She was so tired. But there was no time to rest. She must do something, even though she felt as fragile and weak as a poorly forged clay jar. Rubbing her temples, she left her work area and delved into coffers containing her visionary aids—the cara mushroom, the laurel leaves, and her preserved vials of serpent venom.

No amount of pondering had brought her any closer to a solution. Perhaps, if she opened her mind to the sacred pathways and prayed for guidance, Athene might finally grant her true sight and wisdom.

THEMISTE SENT FOR HELICE AND ARIDELA.

Dressed in her most formal open bodice and heavy layered skirts, she waited beside the lustral basin, wherein the water remained perfectly calm.

She had not completely thrown off the aftereffects of the powerful aids she'd used to open her mind. Inside, she reeled from the revelations she had experienced; outside, she hoped she displayed a veneer of poise and confidence. Closing her eyes, she concentrated on what to say and what to leave unsaid.

A priestess stood close on either side, ready to support her if needed. Behind them, two lines of priests, bare-chested, in flounced skirts, stood with arms crossed. Kaphtor's council members congregated nearby, half-hidden by drifting smoke from the incense.

She drew in a deep breath as the queen and her daughter entered the chamber, noting Aridela's nervousness in the way the young princess glanced back and forth between all those gathered. It irritated her, and she used that to strengthen her resolve.

None of these people could know that behind the expressionless bull's mask, Themiste's mind went beyond the smoky chamber, back to the night Aridela played proxy for the injured Iphiboë. The entire act was preserved in Aridela's memories, and revealed to Themiste when she'd used the craft of *subliquara*.

The memory, coupled with the hallucinatory strength of the potions, threw Themiste's exhausted will into the experience as though she were Aridela. Chrysaleon's mouth, his hands between her legs, the scrape of his beard against her thighs and face, the final culmination—each sensation reenacted with such immediacy that Themiste's body livened from scalp to toes. Her breath shortened. She was aware of the surreptitious glances of the two priestesses who shored her up, and wondered if they could hear the erratic thudding of her heart.

She swayed; the women grasped her arms and pushed against her. Her hand shook as she raised it to command silence.

"We have read the omens," she said, pleased that her voice sounded steady. "Seldom do the entrails and visions give such clarity." She stopped and waited, drawing to herself perfect silence, rapt attention. "Aridela must be joined to the barbarian."

"After what you saw his countrymen do?" Helice cried. "No."

Themiste feared the sense of suffocation caused by the mask might overcome her. She must finish before it could. "Lightning struck our holy shrine at Aridela's birth," she said. "This was the lightning of Velchanos, promising transformation. Yet another sign came when Aridela was a child. Divine prophecy spoke through her. Do you remember, Queen Helice? I translated it for you. *Lion of Gold, from over the sea. Destroy the black bull, shake the earth free.* Years later, on Mount Juktas, Aridela was given a dream of power. The statue of Velchanos stepped off his pedestal and came to her—to Aridela, not to you, not Iphiboë, not to any of the others who were there."

Everything melted and swam; Themiste's knees gave way. The priestesses pressed firmly against her and put their arms around her shoulders. Using the last of her will, she forced herself to finish, hurrying now. "He blessed her and vowed to always be with her. But he was not Velchanos alone. Goddess Athene placed upon him the foreign prince's face, so that Aridela would know him when he came to Kaphtor in truth. Chrysaleon of Mycenae and Velchanos merged.

The meaning of Chrysaleon's name is 'Gold Lion.' His coming was prophesied by the child, Aridela. And now he is here in truth, the man upon our land. If he is indeed a man, and not a god."

Helice turned a shocked, bewildered gaze to her daughter.

"When Chrysaleon shaved his beard I was certain," Aridela ventured. "In the mountain vision, Velchanos had no beard, and Chrysaleon's eyes. It was him—the prince of Mycenae."

Themiste welcomed the impatience she felt at the sound of Aridela's voice. It helped her shove the imagery of Chrysaleon's love-making to the back of her mind and concentrate on the present dilemma. "If Aridela had told us the truth long ago," she said coldly, "many mistakes could have been avoided. Now I must go before the foreigner and reverse the council's decision. I must ask him to accept *us*. He will believe we are acting out of fear."

Aridela's lips tightened and her brows lowered ominously, but Themiste felt no remorse. The girl had brought much trouble upon them with her defiance and lies. Only the fleetest prick of guilt made her wonder if there was another reason for this anger, but as her mind reacquired control over her emotions, over the physical needs she had long submerged, she forcefully dismissed the suspicion.

"The barbarian came here by design, not chance. Athene's design." Themiste's voice trailed off as disjointed images disrupted her concentration. She rallied, fighting to stay clearheaded. "Remember—the earth remained calm after Iphiboë's offering until we refused the foreigner. Runners from Tarrha tell me the earthshaking was felt there; it may have traveled much farther. Do you not see? The lightning of Velchanos has marked Aridela twice now. It has marked our entire world. Unless we marry Aridela to Chrysaleon, the Earth Bull will again roar. The lightning will come. Will we survive a second scourge? Whether or not Chrysaleon had any part in it, this is what Athene wants."

Themiste slumped and the priestesses caught her. Her legs shuddered; she could barely speak now. "When the waxing crescent begins its second phase and we harvest the surviving grapes, then we must give the prince of Mycenae our greatest treasure. We must make a spectacle like none have ever seen—a celebration that will be remembered for eternity. If we defy prophecy, every blade of grass on Kaphtor will be destroyed. Chrysaleon wants Aridela. He battled for her. We have no choice."

Her ears rang; faintly, she heard Helice say, "So soon?"

The last thing she remembered was motioning. One of the priests came forward, cradled her in his arms, and carried her away. In the instant before she descended into the fog of sleep, she allowed herself to imagine she was being held in the arms of another.

11

Moon of Field Poppies

From the Oracle Logs
   Themiste

THREE SHIPS HAVE RETURNED—THREE OF OUR OWN THAT SAILED TO EGYPT *before the Destruction! They entered the bay near the ruin of Phaistos and were sent on to us here at Natho. Not only do they bring living men and desperately needed supplies but also stories of what they saw and experienced. While on the seas south of Kaphtor, they witnessed the boiling black clouds and lightning—fearful lightning of many colors, far in the north then expanding, reaching out for them. The ash that buried our crops fell on their ships; the men scooped it off as fast as they could, yet still one sank beneath the weight. Terrified, they fled back to Egypt, and only now have dared attempt the voyage home. As far as high waves, they say the turbulence they encountered was insignificant, no more than gentle surf. It seems the crushing mountains of water that destroyed so much of our coast dispersed harmlessly on the open sea.*

We welcomed these men and made offerings of gratitude. The wives and children of the sailors we thought dead now rejoice.

They bring gifts from Pharaoh—barley, cloth, oil, and most importantly, shipbuilders. The Egyptian traders used to provide perfumes and trained monkeys for our entertainment. Now we weep in gratitude for barley seed. Such are the changes brought upon us.

Ships from other ports are venturing forth with their own tales. On the isle of Isy, only one city, Salamis, escaped destruction. These travelers tell us the storm of ash fell there to the depth of a tall man's thigh, and that it was so hot it engulfed those it struck in fireballs.

One shipload of curious sailors braved the waters around Callisti. It is gone but for a single curved black ridge, which sends up plumes of smoke and a burning stench. The sailors sensed a divine presence in the utter silence, watching them. Knowing they were in danger, these men sailed away as fast as they could, making sacrifices and uttering prayers for mercy.

There is but one thing to be glad about: the evil faceless man who murdered, raped, and pulled down the sacred statues could not have escaped, nor any of his followers. At least they are dead.

Callisti's disappearance confirms my vision. No longer do any doubt me or my power.

Pervasive cold continues, along with more snow than we have ever seen, and dismal, overcast skies. How I long for sunlight, for the warmth we once took for granted.

No news has come from Chrysaleon's homeland. We would not stop him if he wanted to go, yet he lingers. Nothing, it seems, will induce him to leave Aridela.

Now I come to that which I dislike admitting, though I must. Full and complete truth is required in the Oracle Logs. I see why Aridela finds him mesmerizing. He is handsome, and can be charming when he wants. His presence has the power to quicken my heartbeat. I am drawn to him, though I do not wish to be. Whenever Chrysaleon's attention turns to me, I feel my skin blush and hear my tongue stammer—I, who have never lain with any man and never thought I wanted to.

ARIDELA STARED INTO THE SKY, AWESTRUCK BY WHAT HAD BECOME THE rarest of events—a clear, cloudless morning.

As the sun lifted above the mountain summits, vivid color splashed the heavens like a vow of forgiveness—a promise that the union between Aridela and Chrysaleon, scheduled for two days hence, would bring renewed prosperity.

Villagers left their work and turned their faces up to the sky. Laughter rose spontaneously with the sun.

In preparation for the ceremony, garlands had been draped on every post and pillar. Pennants, embroidered with olive trees, fluttered above the doorways of all the villages up and down the coast. Chattering bounced off mountain crags to merge with the echoing drum of hammers, the grating saw of wood, and the resinous perfume of sawdust.

Runners and merchants left Natho to spread the word of Themiste's edict and collect goods from various precincts. Priestesses lit new altar fires. Gifts piled high in caves and temples, ranging from gold rings and necklaces to seashells, jars of honey, clay statues, and woven baskets. Near the ruined harbor of Amnisos, crowds of women entered fertile Eleuthia's cave to pray and make offerings. The common people quickly embraced this new, oracle-blessed union, believing it would bring good fortune.

For a moment, Aridela joined in the villagers' happiness. *We no longer have to lie or hide how we feel. Chrysaleon will be my consort, openly.*

Yet it was hard to feel joy without guilt. Iphiboë was dead. How could she be happy? How could she let go of her sister?

You and he seem a perfect match. You have not hurt me, Aridela.

Iphiboë's last words did bring some measure of peace, as did the wash of golden sunlight and laughter from below.

Besides, Athene herself wanted this union. It was blessed, even prophesied.

Helice joined her on the balcony. Aridela had been so busy making arrangements that she'd hardly seen her mother since Themiste's astounding announcement. She smiled, sure that Helice would feel bolstered by this beautiful dawn. But the queen stared listlessly, seemingly oblivious to the transfiguration of the heavens. Her eyes were red-rimmed and puffy. She was thin, her cheeks sunken, her hands trembling. The grey pastiness of her skin was frightening.

After a long silence, she said, "The prophecy of your childhood is at last made clear. Chrysaleon of Mycenae is the 'lion of gold from over the sea.'"

Goose bumps shivered across the back of Aridela's neck. "Goddess Athene wanted to prepare us for his coming; that is what I think."

"There is nothing good for Kaphtor in that prophecy, Aridela." Helice's frown matched her words. "And, I fear, nothing good for you."

"Only if we refuse to follow Athene's wishes. Chrysaleon will protect us from the warnings in the prophecy. Yes, the earth shook and fire rained from the sky. But look." She gestured. "Now the sun shines.

The sea is calm. And there are still grapes to harvest. How can you doubt Athene's blessing? Renewal flows from Chrysaleon."

"If renewal is indeed returning, it comes from Iphiboë, not Chrysaleon. The prophecy says nothing about the Gold Lion protecting Kaphtor. Only his destruction of it."

"Athene wants this union. Themiste made that clear. Everything will be fine, now that we understand."

Helice's head tilted and she sighed, a sound both despondent and impatient. "You blind yourself, Aridela. You see only what you want to see. I, too, am guilty—I believed the gossip about you, that you are wiser, older than your years. Yet here you stand, spouting nonsense like any common love-struck peasant."

Aridela's hands clenched, but the discipline her mother had just denied she possessed kept her from speaking in anger.

Helice turned her face away. "This is what comes of keeping you overly sheltered. It was the same when you were ten, with Carmanor. You are easily impressed by anything different."

Aridela gritted her teeth. She set her posset cup on the balustrade and gripped the wood. "All my life I have received praise for my ability to see through lies to truth. Yet in this matter, you and many others continue to doubt. Well, I have none. Chrysaleon won the Games because Goddess Athene wanted him to win. She gave him the strength he needed. You will see, Mother."

The queen's gaze dropped from Aridela's eyes then moved onward to the sea. "Lycus weighs on my mind as well. Pain and injury have broken his reason."

Aridela's fragile, guilt-edged happiness disintegrated. Yet what could she do? She couldn't force herself to love Lycus over Chrysaleon. Love possessed its own cadence and will, and went whatever way it chose, dragging the physical body behind. Didn't it?

She sensed that her mother, and others, blamed her for this trouble. How many thought her a selfish, empty-headed fool? Perhaps some, like her aunt Oneaea, believed she should have given Lycus her backing instead of Chrysaleon, no matter what she felt. If she had, would Lycus have triumphed?

Keeping those thoughts private, she said merely, "His outlook is much changed. Is there not something else we can try?"

Helice shrugged. "Every day, admirers visit him—women mostly, but he refuses their offers of romance." With a discerning glance, she added, "His suffering is not caused solely by you, isoke. It is mostly jealousy, hatred of Chrysaleon, and being prevented from seeking vengeance. What angers him is his perceived humiliation. These are the reactions of a spoiled child."

Tears stung Aridela's eyes. Helice would never recover from the loss of Iphiboë, nor was she reconciled to the union of her younger daughter to the foreigner. Long, debilitating illness, too many deaths, and the ruin of all she had known had dealt a mortal wound, yet she still tried to offer what comfort she could. The hurtful criticism was forgotten in a rush of love.

Perhaps she could divert Helice's sadness into happier thoughts, if only briefly. "Isn't Natho lovely? The air is fresh. Summer flowers bloom. What a difference from the east, where everything is poisoned and dead." She pointed at the sky, where the burgeoning moon glowed as it bid farewell to the rising sun. "We are told the land there is without feature, like the face of the white mother's orb. Thank you, Mother, for bringing us to this place, where recovery and hope are clear to see. It was an inspired choice."

"Yes, at least this much was spared, and your union does create an opportunity to take our minds off all we have lost." She turned an intense gaze upon her daughter. "Have you given care to the plans? Are you overseeing the arrangements?"

Aridela rubbed Helice's cold hand. "It will be wondrous."

"It must inspire songs and tales, and exceed any festival or celebration we have ever held. It is up to us, Aridela, to return hope and dignity to our country. I am certain that was Themiste's intent. I am not reconciled to this coupling, but I do see the wisdom of her advice."

"All will be done. I promise."

"Were it not for my fears, I would be happy to hand you the titles. I am so tired."

Though this statement seemed at odds with Helice's earlier criticism, Aridela accepted it with gratitude. "The time has come to rest, to enjoy your freedom." She tried to speak with confidence, but her mother's sallow skin and the ever-deepening darkness around her eyes and mouth made it difficult.

"It is hard for a queen to love, isoke. This is something for which I cannot prepare you."

Aridela could think of no response other than the pat answer that Helice's consorts were resurrected in the beautiful gardens of Hesperia —that their eternal lives were filled with joy.

Her memories took her back to the day a sweaty, panting Chrysaleon seized her hands after winning the footrace. Fear and guilt had forced her to hide her feelings, that day and for many days after. She was glad to leave secrecy behind. Now she could spend all the time she wanted with him, openly, as she preferred…until the end.

Helice was watching her. Abruptly, she realized her mother had broached the one subject she'd always before avoided. "Mother," she asked, "is it true that you loved my father more than any other consort, as you have said, or was this something you thought you should tell me?"

"No," Helice replied after a slight pause. "No, Aridela, I meant it. Damasen gave me something no other consort ever did. They all have unique gifts and I loved many of them. But Damasen and I shared everything, all the mysteries within us. I have never felt as close to anyone."

"Then…how could you allow him to be killed?" She knew this question would hurt her mother. But in two days, she would take on Helice's role as leader of the people. She must know what lay beneath the words, *It is hard for a queen to love.*

Helice's pause stretched into lengthy silence. She appeared to shrink somehow. Aridela forced herself to wait, to refrain from saying, *Let us talk of other things.*

Finally Helice said, "You love Chrysaleon very much, I think."

"I know you and many others distrust him, but Chrysaleon and I share a bond that is hard to explain. He will never betray me. When Iakchos rises, he will offer himself as Damasen did, if for no other reason than to prove his love."

Tears filled Helice's eyes and spilled over. "Then Chrysaleon is like your father."

With a deep breath for courage, Aridela asked the question she knew every queen who had ever loved a consort had pondered. "Would you…would you have changed anything, if you could?"

Helice faced her straight on, tears bringing a shimmer to her eyes. "Yes."

There were those on the council who would consider such words treason. Aridela realized she was holding her breath and let it out on a sigh.

"I would gladly have died in his place," Helice said. "But he would not allow me to change the laws or appeal for more time." She brought up her hand and touched the necklace at Aridela's throat. "Be careful, isoke. Yours is an impulsive nature. You will be forced to curb it, again and again. Damasen's most loving gift to me was his refusal to allow me to change things. It showed his love more than any other act could." She gazed into Aridela's eyes. "When Iakchos rises, that is when Chrysaleon's truth will emerge."

"You will see. He will honor his vows."

Misgivings shadowed Helice's faint smile. She turned and motioned to her handmaid. Leaning on the woman's arm, she said, "Come to me later. We will watch the sun set over the sea."

When she was alone, Aridela tried again to admire the landscape, but anger and uneasiness eclipsed the view. *He will honor his vows,* she'd declared. But the truth she didn't dare examine was that she didn't want him to. A year was such a short time.

In two nights he would be her husband. She would not squander an instant of this gift from Athene. Iphiboë wouldn't want that, and neither did she.

12

Moon of Field Poppies

MEMORIES OF EARTHSHAKINGS AND DEATHS, IPHIBOË'S SACRIFICE, AND fears of what winter might bring were put aside to celebrate two monumental events—Kaphtor's royal union and the crushing of precious grapes.

Themiste had determined that the ceremony must take place during the second phase of the waxing moon. The augurs chose the day after for blowing the conch shell to the four winds and dancing upon the grapes.

The prayers and sacrifices begging for sunlight and warmth were many, but the morning of the event dawned cold and overcast, with bouts of splattering, dirty rain.

In the old days at Knossos, the couple would have descended into the labyrinth to be blood-cleansed. At Natho, they had to substitute caves. There, deep in the earth, in echoing, dripping, torchlit chambers, each underwent somber rituals meant to free them of unconfessed crimes and purify their hearts.

While they prepared, multitudes from across Kaphtor collected outside the villa and throughout the village. Heads bobbed, elbows stabbed, and bodies collided in fierce jostling for the best position; all wanted a clear view of the royal parade as it made its way down to the sea.

They were not disappointed. Two lines of warriors marched, outfitted in shining leather and polished bronze armor. Behind them pranced Chrysaleon's black chariot-stallions, white-eyed and snorting, their manes plaited with ribbons. Over their hindquarters fluttered tapestries embroidered with Poseidon's image, holding a trident, and Athene, wearing a crown of poppies.

It was not Chrysaleon but Menoetius who handled the beasts, while Queen Helice waved and smiled at his side.

"Obsidian to his master's gold," one woman shouted from a windowsill, but she received no more than a brief frown for her poetry.

Litters came next, decorated with ivy-wound poles at each corner. Reclining upon cushions, the ranking women of Kaphtor displayed themselves like living frescoes as they tossed wreaths and garlands into the crowd.

Robed priests followed, their pennants depicting Mycenae's lions and the bulls of Crete.

The crowd sent up a huge cheer at the sight of a gilded, pine-draped cart drawn by two white oxen.

His hair wreathed in holly and grapevines, face painted with swirls of royal crimson, Chrysaleon held the oxen's reins. Beside him, Aridela wore skirts in a multitude of layers. Her hair boasted a wreath of golden ivy woven through with clover. She waved and tossed flowers to those who crowded against the cart, calling to her for blessings.

People hung out of the windows above the lane. They pelted the cart with leaves, making it seem the very heavens rained greenery.

The procession swept past. Those trapped in the narrow wynds fought to avoid being crushed.

"She is beautiful...I caught a flower...."

"He is the most handsome to ever win the Games."

"Their glory pleases the Lady."

"All will be as it was...."

The onlookers, cheering, dancing, and leaping, flowed after the couple down to the strand by the sea.

HUNDREDS CONGREGATED ON THE SAND TO WATCH AS THE PROPHESIED bull-king was joined to Kaphtor's last remaining princess.

The shrine was a marvel. Sheer white draperies rippled between carvings of sacral knots and double-headed axes designed by master woodcarvers. Greenery and holly berries festooned the ceiling and eleven columns carried the power of indestructible life.

The care and effort put into the structure brought tears to Aridela's eyes. With the survival of such gifted artisans, Kaphtor would surely follow suit and regain its former glory. Lined up on one side, the master builder and his men shuffled, pleased and embarrassed when she sent them her most dazzling smile.

She and Chrysaleon climbed three steps to join Helice, Themiste, and two priestesses. Aridela tried to fill her mind with the familiar image of Athene, the grey-eyed Goddess who had resided within her for as long as she could remember.

Grant me strength and wisdom, Mistress. Show me how to earn your forgiveness.

She knew she'd changed. The spoiled, overconfident child seemed a stranger now—a distant memory. Since the Destruction, she could seldom relax; whenever she began to slip into carefree enjoyment or happiness, guilt jerked her backward. Sometimes she caught Chrysaleon studying her, and fancied his expression was brooding. Perhaps he was sorry for the promises he'd made to a woman who no longer existed.

Besides the ache for Iphiboë, she missed her half brother, Isandros, her nurse, Halia, and her cousins, Neoma and Phanaë. Neoma had awakened only to fall back into senselessness where she continued to languish. The rest, and too many others, rotted in mass graves.

Helice was known as a fair and devout queen, but that had not protected Kaphtor from fire, poison, and stones raining from the sky.

Themiste, however, often stated that Athene had tempered her anger. After all, Kaphtor still rode the waves of the dark blue sea, and given enough time, could recover, unlike the vanished isle of Callisti.

At Helice's nod, Aridela and Chrysaleon knelt side by side on a smooth limestone block. The fitful splatter of rain subsided as the queen looped a strip of fine white cloth around their wrists and Themiste placed triton shells in a circle around them. Sunlight broke through the clouds.

Helice was impressive in her tall ceremonial hat, wide belt, and full panoply of layered skirts and high-backed bodice. Crossing two ceremonial axes over her breasts, she projected her voice outward to the throng crowded as close as they were allowed. "Though this day brings feasting and celebration, it is also a solemn event." She passed the axes to one of her attendants and took from Themiste the ancient Labrys, the wood and stone double-headed axe that had come with their ancestors from the homeland, and which, for more years than anyone could reckon, had spilled the blood of kings. "Forged through holy sacrifice, the bond between our queen and consort is sacrosanct. None may sever it until the rise of Iakchos, and all upon this island will give their lives in defense of our bull-king."

She leveled a grave countenance upon the couple. "Chrysaleon of Mycenae has given his oath to honor our great sacrifice, to make the land fertile with his blood and body. He has sworn to go consenting, to surrender his life so that all may live."

Wanting to show her gratitude, Aridela faced him, but he wasn't looking at either her or the queen. Following the direction of his gaze, she found Menoetius, who returned his brother's stare with an expression she could only call incredulous.

The prince bowed his head and made the proper response. "I am Zagreus. My life and my death belong to Kaphtor."

A shiver ran over her. She looked again at Menoetius. From the corner of her eye she saw Themiste's arms lift towards the heavens.

"Wondrous Athene of Many Names," the oracle said, "enter into the soul of thy servant, he who kneels before thee. Fill the chalice with thy fire. His blood shall flow to the rhythm of thy design, and he shall walk the remainder of his days in the footsteps of every king before him, holding thy hand and adoring thee."

A blanketing mist rolled in from the sea; the caress of water against sand gave off a hushed, tranquil susurration. Themiste's voice faded beneath the heightened sound of Aridela's breathing. It filled her ears, punctuated by the steady thrum of her heartbeat.

Menoetius's gaze shifted from Chrysaleon to her. As they stared at each other, shocked surprise replaced the frown on his face.

She had never felt so strange, as if she were no longer a part of the ceremony. Her mind soared, becoming part of the mist, and she saw Menoetius as he used to be, his youthful beauty restored—Carmanor as she remembered him.

Through some divine visionary gift, Aridela was allowed to see through his eyes everything that happened the morning he carried her out of the shrine, bleeding and near death. She felt his need to save her, the tenderness with which he held her, the kiss he placed on her forehead. She startled along with him when the doves in their cages began their terrified fluttering and the dim torches abruptly blazed. She felt her soul slip away as he raced up the steps, shouting, and saw the beautiful, shining handmaid smiling at her.

A voice broke into the memory. Gentle and melodious, it merged with the whisper of the sea. She couldn't distinguish if it was male or female.

I have lived many lives since the beginning, and so shalt thou. I have been given many names and many faces. So shalt thou, and thou wilt follow me from reverence and worship into obscurity. In an unbroken line wilt thou return, my daughter. Thou shalt be called Eamhair of the sea, who brings them closer, and Shashi, sacrificed to deify man. Thy names are Caparina, Lilith, and the sorrowful Morrigan, who drives them far apart. Thou wilt step upon the earth seven times, far into the veiled future. Seven labyrinths shalt thou wander, lost, and thou too wilt forget me. Suffering and despair shall be thy nourishment. Misery shall poison thy blood. Thou wilt breathe the air of slavery for as long as thou art blinded. For thou art the earth, blessed and eternal, yet thou shalt be pierced, defiled, broken, and wounded, even as I have been. Thou wilt generate inexhaustible adoration and contempt. Until these opposites are united, all will strangle within the void.

Aridela couldn't move. She couldn't even blink. As she stared at Menoetius, his body disintegrated and remolded into his blood brother, with Chrysaleon's green eyes and honeyed hair, but the cruel expression worn by this phantasm immersed her in dread and anguish.

The voice spoke again.

I have split one into two. Mortal men have burned my shrines and pulled down my statues. Their arrogance has upended the holy ways. I decree that men will resurrect me or the earth will die.

The mist lifted and rainbows shot through the sky. Aridela heard the innocent wash of water. Freed from whatever had drawn her out of her body and filled her with holy vision, she turned towards Chrysaleon then her mother. Nothing had changed; Helice placed one hand upon Chrysaleon's shoulder as she spoke to him of his duties as bull-king. Themiste knelt to refresh the patterns of red dye on his face, which had melted in the rain.

Aridela shivered. Almost afraid, she turned her head to find Menoetius, wondering if she had imagined it all. He no longer wore that macabre guise of Chrysaleon, but was himself again. He stared at the sand, his hands fisted, white-knuckled.

As much as she had loved and trusted him in the visionary interlude, joined almost as one, she now welcomed the anger that surged through her.

Every day since he had stepped upon Kaphtor's shore at Chrysaleon's side, she'd felt nothing from him but judgment and censure. This man was now the stranger, 'Menoetius.' Her beloved Carmanor was worse than dead; he had never existed. Her cherished memories were lies.

Menoetius raised his head and leveled his dark, unsmiling gaze upon her. Her anger sharpened and she turned away, hoping he recognized her disdain.

As she set her gaze upon Chrysaleon's profile, sudden insight into Helice's long unhappiness shocked her into stillness. Even Iphiboë understood Kaphtor's ways better than she. Numerous men would join with Aridela after Chrysaleon. She couldn't possibly love them all with this intensity. Some might be disgusting or repellent. Dizziness and grief flooded her; she gripped Chrysaleon's hand as though that alone could prevent what must happen in one year.

Her stricken awareness caused her to glance once more at her consort's blood brother. She was freshly shocked to see him stalking away, his back stiff. Menoetius was abandoning the sacred ceremony.

Why did Selene love him so? He never made any effort to be charming. He seldom smiled, and his morose frown was all too often directed her way.

He hated her—no doubt because she hadn't recognized him. That must have hurt his pride. But he had changed so much.

Yet Selene had known him. Selene had remembered.

Another wave of dizziness washed over her. Her eyesight blurred, making Chrysaleon's features indistinct; for the briefest instant, she glimpsed Menoetius's scar and the tawny hair darkened. Treasured words floated through her mind like a soothing balm.

For longer than you can imagine, I will be with you, in you, of you. Together, we bring forth a new world, and nothing can ever part us.

How she had loved that handsome youth. His pure, unmarred skin, blue eyes bright as stars, the thick fall of dark hair and easy laughter. The wonderful smell of him, like clouds and fallen leaves. She'd felt such overpowering sorrow when he left.

Divine intuition told her that something greater fused these two than the mingling of blood between the mauled, dying Menoetius and the prince who had saved him. She imagined the bindings that lashed them together. They were frayed, nearly worn through, but there nevertheless.

"O Athene," Themiste was saying, "in the heavens thy face is crowned by eternal stars, and upon this soil thou art robed in the glorious green of life.

"Thy servant has from birth carried the name Chrysaleon, but now he rises, naked and unarmed, crowned in thy holly, and becomes for the remainder of his days Zagreus, as he follows in the steps of every hero before him."

Chrysaleon's hand tightened around Aridela's.

The bull, securely harnessed on a low sacrificial table, struggled and moaned, but the priestess expertly ended its fear with a swift deep slice to the throat. Its blood flowed through a grooved channel into a bowl, which Helice turned onto the ground. She scooped wine from one of three tripods and poured it on the earth over the blood.

Themiste mixed a few drops of the bull's blood into the wine in the tripod and stirred it with a silver ladle. Aridela and Chrysaleon dipped in the ceremonial cup, made of purest gold and carved with scenes of the bull rite. They drank of the potion, their arms entwined.

The priestesses rang small silver bells, which signaled an end to the rite.

Now, when all should be pleasure and celebration, Aridela found a corner of her mind recoiling over this union with a foreigner, a male of different beliefs and traditions. Chrysaleon had assured the council he would honor Crete's laws and customs, yet how could he and still fulfill the expectations of his own people? Would he again try to convince her to flee to Mycenae, where she would live as royalty but relinquish her hereditary titles of Goddess-of-Life-in-Death and Goddess-of-Death-in-Life? She couldn't even imagine the repercussions.

Thinking he must feel the gravity of the rite as she did, must have heard the same warning revealed to her in the murmur of the sea, she stole a sideways glance at him.

Triumph gleamed in his expression, from narrowed eyes to the uplifted curve of his lips. Without hesitation or stumbling, he spoke the ancient words they had taught him, vowing to uphold the laws and give his life in defense of Kaphtor. He seized a rhyton and poured a libation in appeasement to the shade of the recently dead Zagreus.

Aridela remained thoughtful as they left the shore and returned to the village. The price she and her lover paid for their year together was great. She relived the night the earth split, the suffocating ash and screams of mothers who lost their children, the gruesome swelling of the burned at Phaistos. Iphiboë's grave face. *You will forge peace among those who worship the Lady and those who follow angry gods.*

Beyond those sorrows, winter would soon descend. Everyone believed it would be severe. Many were afraid their losses and suffering had only begun.

As rain again coursed from dreary clouds, Aridela sensed the full spectrum of foreboding in the words carried to her mind from the sea.

Thou shalt be pierced, defiled, broken, and wounded, even as I have been.

Before the ceremony, Helice had overseen the sacrifice, prayers, and offerings. Now the dead bulls were set to roast for feasting. Aridela had tried to dissuade her mother from this custom since food was so scarce. It made more sense to nurture the animals for the coming winter, but Helice cited her faith that honoring the old ways would inspire the people and draw Athene's good will. The only concession she made was to drastically reduce the number of bulls she sacrificed from a hundred to fifteen.

Chrysaleon lounged at the head of the queen's table, his hair bright and wavy, his brown chest richly oiled. Helice herself served him the finest cuts of meat, the plumpest dates and figs. Aridela held a goblet to his lips when he wished to drink, giggling at the faces he made to amuse her.

Dancers swayed to beating drums and airy flutes. A Thessalonian harpist, trapped on the island after the Destruction, played the lyre and sang ancient songs of Athene, praising her priceless gifts of weaving and the olive.

Chrysaleon was presented with a jug the height and breadth of a man, picturing his battle with Xanthus. The hero in the painting wrestled a gigantic bull-man, whose tail and horns coiled round and round before disappearing into the neck of the container.

One of the eastern region's judges beckoned to his men and they brought in a wooden cask filled with black stones. Pitted with sharp edges and holes, they gave off a pungent, scorched odor. Mixed with them were the same white clumps of rock that pummeled Phaistos the night of the Destruction, and which now choked the seas.

"These fell from the sky the night Elasa was destroyed," he claimed. "We find them half-buried in the earth. Can you smell the fire that lives still inside them?"

Chrysaleon rose and came closer. He picked up one of the black ones. "This is like no rock I have ever seen."

"Evidence of Our Lady's anger," Helice said quietly. "That we may never forget. Take them to the shrine and place them upon the altar with the jars of ash."

Bowing, the judge signaled and his men removed the cask.

Chrysaleon returned to Aridela's side. "These rocks trouble you."

"Athene has never shown such rage in all our history. Was it because of the priestess who defiled her vows? Was it the barbarian's sack of all within the shrine? Or something else? I fear we, too, will be swept from the world and forgotten." She glanced at the crisscrossed scars on her arms, shivering.

"The ways of Immortals are beyond understanding." Chrysaleon ran a soothing fingertip over the outer rim of her ear and along her jaw before shrugging. "It is difficult to care about things I cannot change or control. Pray, if it eases your mind." He sent his gaze over the noisy crowd. "Let us walk in the moonlight, my lady. Let me spend time alone with you, before the coupling. I want to see you smile again, like you used to."

She clasped his hands. Emotion ran through her like a fierce drumbeat. "Promise nothing will come between us. Promise me, Chrysaleon."

"Nothing," he murmured, with the faintest smile. "I vow it."

Until the rise of Iakchos hung between them like the misty veil of rain. Aridela saw his eyes darken, but he turned away to drink from his cup and the words dissipated beneath the chatter and ring of laughter echoing through the feasting hall.

A HOST OF PRIESTESSES SPUN A DANCE ON THE SAND, HOLDING BANNERS sewn with polished silver disks designed to catch and reflect light from the red-tinted half-moon.

The nearby sea muttered like a vast invisible beast, black but for starlight sparkling on the countless tips of its rough-hewn back. Mist drifted, a sign of good fortune.

"Mist is moonlight, drawn to earth by the dancers," Aridela said.

"Why must the people watch us mate?" Chrysaleon asked, though he'd asked the same question twice before. "You said it mirrors the sowing of the barley and rebirth of the land, but in my country, these are private matters."

Aridela heard his annoyance. It was confusing. She had grown up with the public consummation of queen and consort. Without it, no one would recognize the marriage. Longing for his full approval, she tried a new interpretation. "Athene once fell in love with a fisherman who sang to the seals. She appeared to him disguised in the body of a seal and set fifty of her handmaids to dance for him. Then she showed him her true self and they lay together in the sacred cave of Eleuthia. Athene loved this mortal. She wanted to do something for him. He had sung to the seals since he was a boy. They were his only friends. To please him, Athene gave these beasts the ability to become human whenever they wished, and she caused Kaphtor to bear fine and healthy crops for the length of his life. The coupling of consort and queen places the seeds of new beginnings in the minds of the people, and shows our recognition of the blessings we are given. When a queen joins with her new consort here, at the edge of the sea, we honor the Goddess. The people witness this union of earth with the Goddess, and the act is mirrored in the land's bounty. Tonight holds more importance than ever before. Look how we have suffered. Frost blights the crops, yet Themiste has seen that rebirth will come if we show reverence to Lady Potnia."

"What we do will help?"

Aridela leaned against him and closed her eyes. "I know it will. The cara makes my blood burn. Why did you refuse it? It would have blinded you to those who watch, and heated your lust."

He scowled. "I have no trust for those concoctions. I will do what I must under my own power."

Themiste approached, followed by two priestesses. The mysterious reddish moonlight made all three seem more wraith than human. "It is time, Aridela," Themiste said, bowing.

The priestesses led Chrysaleon away.

Aridela followed the oracle down a path to the sand, hushed and awed by the ethereal light. The soft sough of waves made its endless lament, prompting shivers along the back of her neck. Creeping mist created a diffused, dreamlike stage.

Themiste draped the traditional sealskin around Aridela's shoulders, covering her hair with the seal's head and fastening it at the throat with silver clasps. To complete the preparations, she painted a blue crescent moon on the princess's forehead.

"You never saw yourself as a priestess or oracle," she said. "Somehow, I think you always knew you would be queen. But every time I look at you with Chrysaleon, my worry intensifies. I feel a strong urge to help him, yet also this fear I cannot dispel. Promise you will be careful."

"I promise," Aridela said, but her mind and body, livened by cara and the beginning notes from a lyre, carried her from nebulous warnings into the pulsing joy of mist, moon, and love, leaving little room for doubts and suspicion.

Taking up a banner in each hand, Aridela placed herself at the center of the dancers. The priestesses sang and danced, their pennants reflecting captured moonlight.

Chrysaleon stepped out of the shadows. The nearest priestess cried in mock fear and broke away from her place in the dance.

Priestesses ran in every direction. Chrysaleon leaped among them, clutching one then another. Each slipped away until only one, the one they'd circled, remained.

Aridela was acutely aware of every grain of sand that caressed the soles of her feet and the night chill pricking her skin.

She lifted her arms. "Mother, you who have always been, enter into me, your vessel. Use me as I lay my body upon yours. Plant seeds within me and within your earth. Bring life and growth to your blessed isle, a child from my womb, barley golden and full, and grapes upon the vine. Weigh down the olive limbs with fruit."

Helice and Themiste approached and stood on either side of the new queen.

Helice held up a rhyton of bull's blood. "Lower your eyes from the Goddess before you," she ordered Chrysaleon. "Kneel, Zagreus, and when you rise, stand reborn, worthy of what you are given." She drew him up from the ground and bowed before him. She and Themiste striped blood on Chrysaleon's chest and shoulders then backed away as drums began beating.

Chrysaleon picked Aridela up in his arms. He gazed into her eyes somberly and lowered her to the sand.

Priestesses chanted. Drums vibrated like the underlying beat of many hearts. Aridela remembered her mother performing this duty and drew strength from the memory.

Moonlight crept over the boulder's edge, showering them in translucence, and with the light came the Lady.

Chrysaleon pressed closer.

The drumbeat quickened. Aridela was replenished in communion, her thirst quenched. The pitch and sway of her lover's body brought images of barley, high and ripe, ready to feed her people.

She ascended in delight and joy, taking her lover with her, until both found the divine release promised by Eleuthia, goddess of love and childbearing.

She peered through the delicate lacing of mist towards Crete's cheering populace. Menoetius stood apart from the rest, his isolation making him seem forlorn. Instead of the guilt and resentment she usually experienced at the sight of him, benevolence flowed through her. After a priestess wrapped her in a robe, she held out a hand and beckoned, inviting him closer.

He approached, but would not meet her gaze, return her smile, or take her offered hand. His rejection left her burning with humiliation.

She would demand that Chrysaleon send him to Mycenae so the lovers could enjoy their year free of his censure.

Turning away pointedly, she took Chrysaleon's hand and held it high.

The people cheered for some time before Aridela motioned for silence. "It is done," she announced. "We have honored Goddess Athene."

Renewed cheering echoed. At last it grew quiet but for the sound of the sea. She lifted her head so her voice would carry. "As your queen, I give my first command." She paused, feeling the earth pause with her.

"Bring wine for my people!"

The cheering continued long after she and Chrysaleon left the beach.

13

Moon of Field Poppies

THE FIRE IN THE ROUND HEARTH COULDN'T QUITE EXPUNGE THE CHILL from the bedchamber. Aridela rubbed her arms, noticing how the fire-light gleamed against her scars. Some were circular, some straight, as though carved by a vengeful whip. The worst were still raised, red, and tender, while others had faded to white. She knew from mirrors that a few marred her upper back, and two, still pinkish, disfigured her face—one wove snake-like along her hairline above the left ear, and the other followed the line of her jaw. She remembered how curiosity had briefly won out over terror the night of the Destruction. She lifted her head and peered through the makeshift barrier she and Chrysaleon had constructed. At that very instant, a burning object flew in and struck her, bouncing from her jaw to her temple and searing her skin.

Most of the burns no longer hurt. Rhené promised time would diminish even the worst. But her flesh would never again be without flaw.

She couldn't help thinking of Menoetius. Did he rub his scars as she did in a fruitless wish to erase them? Did the ruin of her once-perfect skin soften his resentment toward her or strengthen it? He never gave his thoughts away, except for that churlish frown that left her alternately furious and ridden with guilt.

Movement in the air caused the lamps to flicker, taking her back to the prophetic night in the Cave of Velchanos. Two men, one disguised as a bull and the other a lion, had dropped off the ledge. Each had stalked towards her, outlined in wind-blown lamplight, and from that night on, her life was forever changed.

When would Chrysaleon come? She snuggled deeper into her fox-skin cocoon, not wanting to feel introspective. She wanted to see her husband's smile and warm her skin against his, to curl next to him and know it was the first of many nights they would sleep together, their breath and limbs mingling.

Bringing a creeping sense of doom, the divine words of prophecy returned in an uneasy blend of names and troubling predictions.

Eamhair, Shashi, Caparina, Lilith, Morrigan. Where could such names be common? Her tongue stumbled over them.

Menoetius had heard something too. She'd seen it in his expression. Yet it changed nothing. He still avoided her, still leveled judgment upon her. She longed to speak to him of the experience, to learn what he'd heard, and what he thought it might mean. But his demeanor would not allow it. He deliberately kept her at arm's length, and his obvious disgust made her too angry to attempt reconciliation.

Laughter, singing, and the stutter of footsteps broke off her somber thoughts.

The door flew open and men crowded in, bathing the bed with light from the lamps they held.

Someone cried, "We have brought him to you, Queen Aridela. Be gentle; he is as shy as an untried boy."

Chrysaleon's attendants betrayed varied stages of intoxication. Two had their arms draped around each other's shoulders and struggled to hold each other up. Almost without realizing it, she scanned the group for Menoetius, but he was missing. It was too bad. Chrysaleon should have the support of his blood brother tonight, instead of men he hardly knew.

The bull-king wore nothing but a white loincloth, and his garland hung askew around his head. Only traces of royal paint remained. He staggered—his shoulder struck the partition set up to make the room easier to heat. He grinned as it crashed to the floor.

More men shoved through the doorway, craning their necks to catch a glimpse of her.

"Move. Out of my way." Old Laodámeia's sour voice shot over the press of bodies. Themiste's most trusted handmaid shoved through the horde. She placed a tray holding two bowls of wine on the bed.

"Your health," she said, "and the health of your womb." Her bow was perfunctory; Laodámeia scraped to no one.

She turned, clapping her hands. "Out. Leave them alone." She shooed at Chrysaleon's attendants like an impatient mother chasing away misbehaving children.

With much grumbling, the men offered lewd advice as Laodámeia herded them from the chamber.

The door closed. The hearth-fire crackled. Someone somewhere plucked at a lyre, a pretty yet haunting tune.

Chrysaleon's grin lingered, but he remained where he was, swaying a little.

Aridela shrugged off the fox-skin blanket, stepped from the bed, and crossed to him, returning his smile.

He stopped her at arm's length. Gripping her shoulder with one hand, he grasped her hair in the other, drawing her head backward so her face was illuminated by firelight.

"Do you love me, Aridela? For myself, not because I won your Games."

Shadows leaped behind him, making him seem tall, though the prince of Mycenae was in truth more hefty than tall. Aridela traced the scar on his left bicep where Harpalycus had stabbed him that night in Velchanos's cave. "I loved you before you even came to Kaphtor," she said, so startled and shy of the truth beneath her words that she tried to turn her face away, but his grip remained unyielding. "We are united by divine will. I have waited for you, Chrysaleon. Waited for you to come to me."

He studied her, squinting. She felt him probing her expression. Then he leaned forward and kissed her, hard.

"You and I will be together…forever," he said. When he added 'forever,' he blinked and his brows lifted as though his own words surprised him. "For as long as the pyramids stand in Egypt," he said more firmly.

He picked her up and carried her to the bed. She wove her arms around his neck and fought back tears. Why did he say that? He knew his future. When Iakchos next rose, he would die, and she would take the man who killed him into her bed.

How…where would she find the strength?

As he joined her in the cushion of fox-skins and brought her close, the bright flicker of the hearth fire reached out and seized her gaze.

It seemed, just for an instant before she blinked, that Immortal Athene's face was there, in the reddish yellow flames, staring at her. Tears of fire fell from her eyes, hissing as they struck the embers.

Thou art the earth, blessed and eternal, yet thou shalt be pierced, defiled, broken and wounded, even as I have been. Thou wilt generate inexhaustible adoration and contempt. Until these opposites are united, all will strangle within the void.

Aridela closed her eyes and feverishly returned her lover's kisses, locking away tomorrow and its many unendurable possibilities. She would embrace every instant of happiness. She would fill the bull-king's days and nights with joy. Chrysaleon would never regret accepting the title and the doom of Zagreus. This she vowed as the daughter of the god of lightning, *Shariheid, Velchanos Calesienda,* even as the face in the fire whispered the question she could not shut out and could not answer.

Will you fulfill your obligation to me?

Aridela blinked sleepily into the dark. Next to her, Chrysaleon released a broken, muffled snore. That must have been what woke her.

She stretched, careful not to disturb him, smiling a little at how he'd thrown off the fox skins though the chamber was chilly. He lay on his side, his back to her, his hair, his cheek, and his shoulder illuminated by the faintest of light from the dying embers.

Her mind wandered ahead. The celebration of the grapes, the dancing, offerings, and pleas for abundance would consume the day. It would be her first grape festival as queen. No doubt she would be tired, as much of this night had been spent in lovemaking rather than sleep, but that didn't matter. She would head the procession to the clearing beside the vines and stand upon a boulder covered with sheepskin. She would blow the conch shell as her mother and every queen had done before her. Girls would climb into the vats and crush the grapes while couples vanished into the hills in search of privacy. She dared hope that sunlight and warmth might grace the day.

The hearth fire was a mesmerizing, radiant bed of embers, the heat glowing black, red, orange, and yellow, all in perfect silence.

Faint luminescence played over Chrysaleon's shoulder like fingers of light. Opening one hand, she held it above the curve of his cheekbone, not touching, not wanting to wake him. She slipped her hand down, careful not to touch but close enough to feel the warmth from his skin. She followed the contours of his shoulder, his waist, his hip and thigh.

Beauty and tranquility were scattered by the memory of Athene's face in the fire.

Will you fulfill your obligation to me?

Of course she would. She had always followed Athene's wishes. But she could not bear to think of it.

Red circles of light flickered across the wall. The embers were far too low to cause such a reflection. Just as her tired mind began to wonder on the cause, a piercing scream echoed through the room from outside, jerking her upright.

She sniffed. *Smoke.*

Leaping from bed, she threw open the wooden doors at the balcony and stared, dumbfounded. Frozen.

Every building along the cliffs below the balcony was on fire. As she watched, a roof disintegrated in an avalanche of sparks. Flames glowed in the window openings of the nearest villa. Far below in the harbor, fire reflections shimmered across the surface of the water as two ships burned. She heard more screaming and the crash of collapsing structures.

"Chrysaleon!" Backing into the chamber, she found that her voice refused her command. The name she meant to scream escaped in an inaudible squeak. She lit a lamp, her fingers shaking so violently that it took several tries to achieve a spark.

He shifted with an incoherent mutter.

"Chrysaleon!" This time she uttered his name with purpose. For added measure, she ran to the bed and shook him.

He heaved onto his elbows, squinting.

"Fire!" Aridela swiped at a cascade of bitter tears. More punishment. More suffering. Nothing they'd done had appeased Athene's rage.

"Fire?"

She shook him again. "Natho burns," she cried. "The village is on fire. The ships in the harbor. Everything."

His eyes widened. He leaped out of bed, shrugged on his discarded kilt, and ran past her to the balcony.

She heard him curse as she plucked her sleeping tunic from the floor and pulled it on. Hesitating only an instant, she belted a dagger around her waist.

Chrysaleon returned. They gazed at each other. There was no sound of alarm. No beating drums.

Aridela shivered. "Why is it so quiet?"

"Come," Chrysaleon said. "Perhaps a storm blew through and lightning ignited these fires. We will sound the warning." He held out his hand.

As their fingers touched, the chamber door crashed against the wall. Aridela cringed away from the cacophony of stamping feet, clink of metal, and glare of torchlight.

Chrysaleon shoved her behind him. There he forced her to remain with a relentless grip on both her forearms.

"No. This will not do," a familiar voice said. "You have had her long enough, my brother-in-law. Far too long."

Aridela leaned to the side and peered around Chrysaleon's arm.

"Take her from me if you can." Chrysaleon's grip tightened.

"You offer your life for this girl?" Harpalycus rubbed his palms together. He wore the fancy wolf's head breastplate she remembered, and his cloak sported a magnificent crest of crimson-dyed hawk feathers across the shoulders. In every detail, he embodied a powerful, ruthless monarch. "Surely that is not part of your father's plot to conquer Crete. But it makes no difference to me whether you die now or later. I have no need of you, and my sister might thank me for freeing her."

The soldiers in the doorway moved aside to allow another man to enter. He hesitated, glancing from Harpalycus to Chrysaleon.

"No," Aridela cried. "No...."

Lycus tilted his head and grinned. "Long days have passed since I have seen you, my lady. I feel neglected. I had to invite myself into your bedchamber so I could offer congratulations to you and your new consort."

Harpalycus laughed.

Chrysaleon backed up, moving Aridela with him, but the chamber wall stopped their retreat. Aridela slipped her dagger into his hand.

He lunged, slitting the nearest warrior's throat before the man could raise his guard.

Lycus took a hasty step back and Harpalycus scrambled behind one of his men.

The terror and grief coursing through Aridela's limbs heated into rage. Harpalycus. The evil prince, returned.

And somehow, Lycus was part of it. He had helped Harpalycus start these fires, and no doubt they had already killed many.

Yet another betrayal by one of Athene's own.

The warriors surged forward. Chrysaleon stabbed at one as another aimed a sword toward the vulnerable flesh beneath his ribs. Aridela leaped against the warrior's arm, throwing him off balance. He pulled her down with him as he fell and she sprawled across his torso, wincing as his bronze-inlaid armor bit into her.

Her forehead struck the side of the stone hearth and she nearly blacked out in a scatter of sparks.

"No. Don't kill him yet," she heard Harpalycus say.

One of the men yanked her to her feet. A splinter caught the delicate chain at her neck, snapping it; the charm she'd worn since she was a baby dropped to the floor.

She searched for Chrysaleon. He lay on his stomach, unmoving. Blood ran in a widening circle from an unseen wound.

Athene had guided the Gold Lion from over the sea. She had given him victory in the Games. Was it only to see him killed on the first night of his long-delayed triumph?

Do not take him from me. Not yet, my Mother. I beg you.

She turned her gaze upon Lycus and seared him with loathing. Fear and guilt passed across his face. Then he lifted his chin and smiled.

Harpalycus motioned; two of his warriors pulled her from the chamber.

PART II

Shadows

1

Moon of Field Poppies

THE MEN BOUND ARIDELA'S WRISTS SO TIGHTLY HER HANDS LOST ALL feeling. They pushed her along narrow corridors and down many stone steps until they came to the underground storerooms, and shoved her into one of them. She stumbled and fell, landing on her shoulder. Overwhelmed by pain and despair, she made no effort to rise.

Moonlight crept through cracks in the wall, creating slices of pale radiance across the floor. Other than that, only the faintest glow from the wall sconce in the corridor managed to enter through slits in the door.

The air was close and fetid, smelling of mold, dirt, damp wood, and underneath, hints of wine.

A voice came out of the dark. "Aridela."

"Mo-Mother?" Aridela struggled upright and stared into the shadows. An indistinct figure in a torn nightdress crept forward.

Aridela fought back tears. "Have they hurt you?"

"My arm is broken, I think. It does not matter. What of you?"

"They attacked us in our chamber. Chrysaleon was bleeding...."

With her good hand, Helice worked at the knots around Aridela's wrists. "Themiste is confined nearby, in another cell."

"Themiste, too? Is she—?"

"I am unharmed." Themiste's voice floated through the dark. "Did they hurt you, Aridela?"

The knots loosened. Aridela flexed her hands to help return the flow of blood. "No, Minos," she said, though the bruises on her chest and stomach made breathing painful. "Harpalycus. Lycus. Did you see them? What could make Lycus do this? What will become of us?"

Helice got to her feet and limped the breadth of their cell, passing between rows of enormous clay jars and wooden coffers before slumping back to the cold dirt floor. "It is my doing. I brought Kaphtor to this." She closed her eyes and keened, scratching at her cheeks.

"My lady," Themiste cried from the other room.

Helice pressed her face to the wall. "I am undone."

"They cannot triumph," Themiste said softly. "As soon as your brothers hear of this, they will come with armies. This is only a little village. These men could not have conquered all of Kaphtor. Their invasion is futile."

Aridela crossed to her mother and knelt beside her. "Why do you blame yourself? How could you have caused this?"

"The night you defied me and accompanied your sister to the cave of Velchanos, I saw you and Iphiboë speaking to Harpalycus at the feast. You confessed you found him handsome. I thought that, as always, what you admired, so would your sister." She drew in a ragged breath. "Memories of Damasen were strong within me that night. I fancied him at the edge of my sight, nodding his approval. He was a foreigner, yet he gave himself to Kaphtor. I had other notions, absurd ones, I know now. I had an idea that if Harpalycus and Iphiboë loved each other, it could strengthen ties with his father's kingdom, and help protect us in these violent times."

"Mother, what are you saying?"

"May the Goddess forgive me, I sent him to the cave, thinking he might please Iphiboë. I thought his difference from all she was accustomed to might spark her passion."

"You sent him...."

"Iphiboë was so frightened of men. He was handsome. Charming. Why would Athene begrudge Iphiboë this insignificant pleasure, if afterward she gave her life to her duty? And Damasen—"

"But the Goddess makes the choice."

"Oh, Aridela. Are you still such a child? Have you not yet realized that rulers cannot leave their countries and people to function on whim and prayer? I have manipulated many rites during my reign. I always felt I did so with the blessing of Athene, but it seems I finally went too far. I have brought Kaphtor to ruin."

Aridela had believed chance brought Harpalycus to the cave. But chance had been Helice. In truth, the rites were outraged, not only by herself and Chrysaleon, but Helice as well. "Chrysaleon and I completed the rite before he got there."

"I didn't know that until the day we told Chrysaleon you would be dedicated to the Great Marriage. Perhaps that was the true reason for Harpalycus's rage, but if so, he said nothing to me. When he returned to the palace, he shouted curses and vowed revenge upon Chrysaleon. He accused me of sending Chrysaleon to the cave as well, and I couldn't convince him I had not. He believed I sent them both there hoping they would kill each other."

Aridela placed a hand on her mother's shoulder. "How could you have known?"

"There is more." Helice rubbed her knuckles over her eyes. "My crimes are many."

"No, Mother. You have given your best. Always. You must know that."

"When Chrysaleon won the footrace, I could not accept that Idómeneus's son, the crown prince of Mycenae, might become Iphiboë's consort. I was certain trickery was involved. Athene forgive me, I defied her wishes. Surely it is time for me to die."

"Stop!" Aridela seized Helice's hands. "Never say such things."

"I had poppy put into his wine. I wanted Lycus to kill Chrysaleon in the labyrinth. Idómeneus could not have blamed us."

"Mother, no."

"When Themiste told us she wanted you to remain untouched, I was pleased. It is hard, my child, to put consorts to death, men you have loved. It is so hard. I wanted to spare you."

The heavy door at the top of the corridor steps squealed as it opened. Helice stiffened. "What now?" she whispered.

They heard the distinctive high voice of a eunuch. "Your father will be pleased that you captured the oracle, my lord. He has often expressed his desire to see her, such is her renown."

Footsteps passed by their cell and stopped some distance beyond.

"Who is it?" Helice whispered. Aridela didn't answer, but rose and went to the door. She leaned against it, listening.

"She wasn't defiled, thank black-horned Poseidon," the same man said. "I have never seen hair that color. And her eyes, my lord. So mysterious. The rumors were not exaggerated."

Aridela's heart pounded. Her hands closed into fists.

The scent of smoldering ashes drifted through the slits in the door. Harpalycus.

The usurper finally spoke. "Are you well, priestess? Have the guards fed you?"

Themiste remained silent.

"Come, lady," the eunuch said. "Do not be angry. You must realize how your rich island tempted us. We will rebuild. All will be returned to its former greatness. This island will become a wondrous shrine, wholly dedicated to Lord Poseidon."

"You will all die," Themiste said flatly.

There was a space of silence. Themiste's words seemed to cling to the invisible layers of air, heralding some inescapable destiny.

"I will have you," Harpalycus said. "I don't care what my father wants. Why should he reap every benefit when I have taken all the risks?"

"Your meddling takes you to realms you cannot imagine," Themiste said. Her voice dropped so that Aridela strained to catch her next words. "Do you believe you are in control?"

The eunuch's laughter was high and shrill. "If we wish, we can open this door and allow every warrior in the city to take his pleasure on you until there is nothing left but bloody pulp. Now who do you think has control, oracle?"

"You could do that. But you will not."

Another long pause. Aridela pressed her ear closer to the slits in the door. *Athene, my Mother, don't let them harm Themiste.*

"Pray, priestess," Harpalycus said. "Perhaps your goddess will save you, but I doubt it. My father wants a redheaded concubine. That is the only reason you remain untouched. The oracles you speak from now on will glorify your conquerors."

The sound of footsteps returned to the cell holding Aridela and Helice, and there they paused. Aridela braced. When the door opened, she would fly out. She would shred his face from his skull before anyone could stop her.

She heard quiet breathing.

That smell grew stronger. What was it? Why did it adhere to him like flesh itself?

Neither man spoke. The footsteps continued along the corridor and up the steps. The portal squeaked then slammed.

Helice put her mouth close to the slits. "Themiste?"

"He did not touch me." Themiste laughed. "I frighten him."

Aridela sank down to the packed dirt floor, trembling. Helice joined her and held her hand. "Harpalycus boasted to me," she said. "I can hardly believe how his evil gods assisted him; that is why I think Athene must back his scheme."

"What do you mean? What did he say?"

"When he left Kaphtor after the Games, he did not return to his home. He sent for his father's army and waited for them on Callisti. Themiste's vision was true. It was Harpalycus who seduced one of the priestesses. He did not tell me her name, but from what he said, I think it must have been Leiriope."

"She betrayed us?"

"I think it must be as Themiste saw, that she was maddened. So many years too close to the heat and fire of Lady Athene's rage. We were wrong to leave those women there with no companion but that poison. How differently I would do things, if I had Athene's divine sight."

"Leiriope's decisions, nor her madness, can be your fault. Tell me what Harpalycus did."

"He convinced Leiriope that he was Velchanos, and that the Goddess sent him to quiet the mountain. She took him to the hidden shrines in the caves. There he discovered Orseis."

"The high priestess?"

Helice nodded. "He raped her upon the altar in deliberate insult. He and his men pulled down the statues and set fire to everything. He murdered Orseis and the others, all but Leiriope. He bragged that as he and his men climbed down to their ships, he looked back and saw her throw herself into one of the fire pools."

Aridela pictured it with nauseating clarity. Harpalycus would have laughed. He would have enjoyed watching the flames shoot up in a blazing caress then subside as they consumed her.

"One day," Helice said, "the pain Harpalycus has caused will revisit him, but many, I fear, will fall before then."

"How did he escape the wall of water, the poison clouds, the heaving of the earth? How did he survive? Did he tell you?"

"A divine hand sheltered him, Aridela. That is the only explanation. I know he and his army sailed west from Callisti. He claims he lost two ships. Remember our sailors who returned. They, too, were on the open sea."

"What part did Lycus have in all this?"

"Lycus killed the watchman at the harbor. Harpalycus and his warriors entered the bay without raising an alarm."

"But how did Harpalycus know where we were?"

Helice shrugged then winced and rubbed her shoulder above the break in her arm. "He did not tell me. They must have planned this after Lycus was wounded in the labyrinth. Hatred of Chrysaleon is at the heart of this attack. Harpalycus has hated Chrysaleon for a long time, I know not why." She paused, her breath hitching. "If only none of these foreigners had come here. How different everything would be."

Aridela could think of nothing to say. There were no reassurances left, and she was so cold she could hardly even shiver.

"He waited for the day of your union," Helice said, "when everyone would be distracted with celebration. He claims he has overthrown all our ports, and tells me that his men have spread through every precinct, killing and burning as they go." She dug her fingernails into her face, leaving angry welts. "Could he have so many warriors? If only I knew. I feel my people crying out to me to help them."

"I don't understand why these barbarians must vanquish and destroy everything they see," Aridela said.

Helice put her good arm around Aridela's shoulders. "If I could somehow go back to the days before all of this, I would sit in the gardens and spend more time on the mountaintops. I would walk in the rain. I would mingle more with my people and worry less about the crops." She tousled Aridela's hair. "What I would do is spend more time with my children. Why do we think of these things when it is too late?"

It seemed her hand moved absently through Aridela's hair, but then she said, "I know you must grow out your hair. But I confess I like it this way."

Tears trailed down Aridela's face.

"We have been overly concerned with shallow things," Helice said. "Things that don't matter. Polished armbands, the tassels on our sunshades, bright jewels, and pretty dyes. Since we left our wars behind and embraced peace, we have cared more about beauty than anything; we forgot how to look beneath it for the substance that matters. Harpalycus is a handsome man. So is Lycus. Yet see what lies beneath."

Aridela rested her head against her mother's shoulder and closed her eyes. Her throat tightened and she wondered if indeed, Helice could be partly to blame for Goddess Athene's anger.

"My meddling has brought Kaphtor's downfall," Helice said quietly. "I deserve whatever punishment Areia Athene sends. Remember that, isoke. But you must survive. Do whatever you have to do. Will you promise?"

"We will both survive. We will fight and win back Kaphtor. That is what I promise."

2

Moon of Field Poppies

"Does she please you, my lord?" the eunuch asked.

"I haven't decided." Harpalycus slanted his head one way then the other, scowling as he looked down upon her.

Aridela gave all her effort to hiding any sign of pain or fear.

Two of Harpalycus's men had torn her from her mother. They'd bound her wrists again and dragged her to this lavish bedchamber in the merchant's villa.

Blood trickled through her hair from a cut where Harpalycus struck her after she spat at him. One shoulder lay bare, as he had ripped her tunic when he'd thrown her to the floor. The eunuch he called Proitos stared down at her as though she were a sheep and he was judging the merit of her wool. Harpalycus had a different expression.

"A prize, indeed," Proitos said. "We shall take her to Tiryns and put her on display. All will praise your cunning strategy, your merciless strength. Harpalycus of Tiryns, the only man in the world with enough wit and skill to overthrow mighty Crete."

"Yes." Harpalycus's lips stretched into a grin. "And finally, my father might take measure of my accomplishments." His gaze traveled over her, lingering on the bare shoulder. Those watery-blue eyes were unnerving, fish-like in their coldness. Aridela bit the inside of her cheek, setting her resolve to die with courage, no matter what he did.

But she was afraid.

Proitos said, "We will look down from the walls of Tiryns upon the old queen as she beats our dirty linens in the river. And we have the oracle. There is no doubt you will enjoy your father's highest favor when you present her to him."

Screams and the echoing din of violent carnage floated in from the village. The stench of burning buildings was heavy.

Pouring himself a cup of wine, Proitos added, "Though Crete has suffered much adversity, there remains no land so coveted. Under your rule, it will bring you everything you have ever wanted."

Harpalycus continued to stare at Aridela. He squatted and ran his fingers along her hairline. "These scars are new," he said with surprisingly little spite. "Too bad. You are not the beauty you once were."

"If only Chrysaleon had killed you." Her voice was hoarse from the cold damp storeroom. "You are to blame for all of this, for everything."

"Me?" Harpalycus frowned. "No, my lady. Chrysaleon brought these afflictions upon you. Do not blame me. I merely seek vengeance as any man would."

"Vengeance. For what?"

Harpalycus stood. He took a hunk of meat from the platter held by his man and gnawed at it. His face hardened as he chewed; his eyes grew colder. "I remember Chrysaleon never bothered to tell you about Iros, his wife. My sister. She was insignificant to him." Grimacing, he returned the meat to the platter and licked grease from his fingers. "She was not insignificant to me. You will come to understand. She was more important to me than anything."

Uneasiness crept into Aridela's fear. "What does she have to do with this attack upon us?"

Harpalycus lifted his gaze from her. He squinted at something beyond her sight and sighed.

Proitos took up the story with a toadying bow. "The royal Princess Iros was given to Chrysaleon by my lord's father. She was young, a mere girl, but so jealous were Chrysaleon's citadel whores, that they had her murdered, though she was quickened with child."

Harpalycus's hands clenched. The skin whitened over his knuckles as he said softly, "My child."

Aridela kept her face expressionless, seeing how closely he watched her. On Kaphtor, such things were frowned upon, but elsewhere, as in Egypt, common among royals.

"I have already taken my vengeance on the priest who betrayed us, and one day, my father too will regret his choices." Harpalycus fell silent as his throat worked. "But first," he said through lips as tense as his fists, "Chrysaleon, and everything Chrysaleon loves."

Ah, of course. He meant to make her suffer. He would not stop until she screamed. Perhaps not even then. She saw it in his eyes.

Many heartbeats passed. Harpalycus's jaw relaxed as he stared at her. Some of the rage seemed to fade.

"Were you witness to what happened on Callisti?" she asked.

"Cursed island." His anger flared again; she forced herself not to shrink away.

"Nothing remains but a sliver, my lady," Proitos said. "Charybdis swallowed the rest at Lord Poseidon's command. We were fortunate to escape. Poseidon holds my master in his hand. There is no safer place to be than at his side."

"For a time I believed the entire earth and sky would be engulfed," Harpalycus said. "I do not know who or what caused such fury. I feared it was me, but if so, why do I still live? Some of my men abandoned my cause, thinking your death goddess would slaughter any who served me. But Poseidon stayed her hand. We sailed west, hard and fast. Two of my father's ships fell behind and disappeared." He stared blankly at the far end of the room. "Pillars of fire rose out of the sea. A most fearsome cloud, hurtling flames and lightning, spread across the heavens. We sailed on, knowing if we hesitated, we would die. The cloud overtook us. We nearly sank beneath the weight of ash and stones piling upon the decks. In time we came to an island and harbored on the far side. We prayed and made sacrifices. Poseidon must have heard us and accepted our gifts, for the destruction turned away. It went east, I think, and here, to Crete."

He returned his gaze to her and smiled, leaving her even more apprehensive. "Aridela." He knelt again, smoothed her hair and stroked her throat. His fingertips lingered. "Your heart beats like a bird's. There is no need to be afraid. This day has been long in coming, but everything has happened as I wanted. Soon, I will announce my kingship—king in truth, not one of your sacrificial goats. Those days are gone. There will be no more sacrifices of men."

He bent, putting his mouth close to her cheek. "You, Aridela, will bear my children. My father does not know it, but I intend to marry Themiste as well, and I will have her title. Minos. You are surprised I've heard of this. But Lycus holds much knowledge, and he has been generous. My son will rule when I die. The sons I make on you will mate with our daughters, who will be declared high priestesses. Do you understand? The ways of Egypt suit me. My line will grow strong. Poseidon will be glorified and your goddess will be lost. Great Labyrinthos will be a monument to the Lord of Horses." He paused and his eyes narrowed. "Know that I will kill any child you bear too soon. Chrysaleon's bastard will not taint my line."

Rage overtook fear. She spat at him again.

He closed his fist and struck her. His seal ring tore her cheek. Stars shot through her head and her ears rang. Her neck, jarred to one side, burned.

Seizing the rope around her wrists, he rose, yanking her up with him, and brought her face close. "You still think yourself a queen? You are my possession. I choose the method and time of your death. You could have ruled at my side had you not been so smitten with Chrysaleon. Aridela, my slave, you chose the wrong man."

He threw her down. Her skull cracked against the tiles, causing her to fade in and out of consciousness. Flashes of color, lightning bolts, and pain made her barely aware when Harpalycus straddled her. He ripped her tunic down the front. "You will learn what it means to cross Harpalycus, King of Tiryns, of Crete, and soon, of Mycenae."

Holding her wrists above her head with one hand, he stretched over her, pushing her legs apart. "I swore you would suffer when you stood in the cave and chose Chrysaleon instead of me."

She tried to clamp her legs together and squirm onto her side but he merely laughed. He thrust into her dry, unwilling flesh and she knew for the first time what unbearable pain the act of sex could cause. She bit her lip to keep from sobbing, and tasted blood.

"Queen of Crete," he whispered. He shoved harder, deeper, panting against her face, until she thought she would die. She longed for death, or at least unconsciousness. No matter how she twisted, his mouth, his wine-saturated breath, followed. He shuddered then lay still and heavy, breathing hard.

Her empty stomach retched. Bile burned her throat.

"Commander." Proitos's amused voice echoed through waves of revulsion. "Look. They have brought a new pitcher of wine. Are you thirsty?"

Harpalycus rose and rearranged his tunic. "Take her to my chamber," he said to his guards. "Your lives are the penalty if she escapes. I might give her to you if she does not."

They saluted, pulled Aridela to her feet, and dragged her from the room.

"I HAVE NO STOMACH FOR THIS," ONE SAID.

"Nor I," said the other. "I feel the wrath of the Lady in my bones." His voice lowered. "What if the—the—"

"Don't say it."

"But—"

"I would rather face the Solemn Ones than Harpalycus. You have seen how he enjoys making men scream."

They spoke freely, in the tongue of the mainland. Maybe they thought Aridela couldn't understand. She pretended to swoon, hoping they would reveal more.

The second guard almost dropped her in his zeal to make the sign against evil. They didn't know what to fear more; Harpalycus or the Erinyes, the three fearsome crones older than the earth itself, who would torture them, drive them insane for crimes committed against priestesses of Athene, against mothers and daughters.

The first guard changed the subject. "I heard something tonight from one of the villa guards. He told me he eavesdropped on Harpalycus and his generals. King Eurysthenes has promised Harpalycus sixty ships. Eighteen hundred men."

"Your news is old. I heard that rumor days ago. Have you heard that Eurysthenes has been fashioning delays? That he is demanding more treasure? He knows we don't have enough men. I wager he knows if he does not send his ships before winter closes the sea, Harpalycus's invasion will fail. Harpalycus will lose everything, either to the Cretans or to Eurysthenes. You know what I think? I think our master will be a rotting corpse by this time next year."

As they yanked Aridela up a set of stairs, the other hissed, "You will get us both killed with talk like that. Eurysthenes knows the more time these Cretans have to rally, the bigger the chances are they will find a way to defeat us. If he has any sense, he will take what he can get, as soon as he can get it."

Aridela welcomed the gossip. It gave her something to concentrate on besides what Harpalycus had done. She went over what she knew of mainland families and politics. Eurysthenes was the king of Pylos, one of the most powerful citadels after Mycenae. His son, Nyctimus, had once visited Kaphtor on behalf of his father, and had brought Helice many fine gifts. An educated, witty youth, he'd been popular, and had stayed for over a month making many friends, including Isandros. But before she could sort through the implications of what she had heard, the guards stopped and rapped on a door.

It was opened by a mainland priest who gave her a single indifferent glance before ordering the guards to prop her on the edge of the bed.

"What are you going to do?" the first guard asked.

"Prepare her for her coming union." The priest dipped a sponge into a bowl of water and dabbed at the blood on her cheek. "King Harpalycus wants to stand before the people as her husband at daybreak. The entrails warn against delay."

The guards fell back to the corridor as another priest came forward.

Tearing off the remnants of her shift, the priest dropped it on the floor and laid out a flounced ceremonial skirt covered with gold disks. Beside it he placed a bodice heavy with gold and fancy embroidery.

"She is young," he said.

The other shrugged. "She is queen, and soon will be a wife."

"I am already a wife." Aridela spoke dully, staring at the floor.

Both priests regarded her with surprise, but continued their tasks without pause, one only clucking disapprovingly.

They arrayed her in the skirts and a belt studded with lapis and miniature ivory elephant tusks. One searched through dishes on the table until he found a pot of crimson dye. He rouged her palms, feet, and the tips of her breasts.

When Aridela fought him, the guards were called back in to restrain her. Her strength faded. The dizziness was unrelenting. Her wounds throbbed. She could not center her mind.

"She is ready," the first priest said. "Take her to the shrine."

The guards dragged her through corridors, down stairways, and into the courtyard, where she looked up at an ice-blue dawn, studded with pink and yellow clouds. The heavens reflected nothing of Kaphtor's continuing misfortunes.

More warriors joined in, forming an impenetrable armed escort to the cave shrine at the west edge of the village.

Harpalycus was waiting at the lustral basin in the center of the chamber, holding an unsheathed dagger. "At last," he said irritably. "Can she stand?"

An image formed, one so strong that for an instant Aridela's surroundings vanished. She saw herself stumble into the shrine at Labyrinthos and fall before the statue of Athene. Gentle arms picked her up and she peered into incandescent blue eyes.

At first she'd believed they were Athene's, but it was Menoetius who saved her. Where was he now? Was he alive?

Her legs crumpled like decayed papyrus when the guards released her. Someone caught her around the waist as she fell; she gasped as she met Lycus's frowning gaze. He returned her to the guards and stepped back.

Hatred burned through her limbs. "Lycus," she said. "In the name of my mother, I curse you."

He would not look up, the coward.

Heaving an impatient sigh, Harpalycus spat out, "Hold her," and strode to the altar.

Aridela blinked, trying to free her eyes of the acrid smoke in the cave. Harpalycus gestured, and two of his warriors prodded a woman forward—a woman who held her head high, though her dress was ripped and filthy, her face smudged with dirt. It was Helice.

Now Aridela saw a line of women in the shadows—priestesses of Kaphtor, constrained by several of Harpalycus's men.

Harpalycus seized a handful of the queen mother's hair and jerked her against his chest. He pressed the edge of his knife to her throat. "Poseidon is lord and master over Athene," he said. "He will take her to wife even as I take you, Aridela. He will see my devotion, my loyalty, and he will reward me. All I do is in his honor."

"No," Aridela whispered. Ice crept through her blood.

There was no fear on her mother's face. "Isoke," she mouthed.

"Let her go!" Aridela struggled, twisting one way then another to escape the grip on her arms. "You said she would be a slave!"

"Bring her," Harpalycus said, and the guards dragged Aridela closer. Harpalycus pulled Helice's head backward. "A queen so reverenced is too much of a danger. Better to be rid of her." Never taking his gaze from Aridela, he slashed Helice's throat, one side to the other.

Blood splattered across Aridela's chest. She reeled against the guard's implacable armor. "No!" she screamed.

The priestesses moaned. Several tore their hair and scratched their faces.

Harpalycus dropped Helice's body onto the altar. She choked, convulsed, then lay still.

Lycus strode forward, his hand pressed against the partially healed sword wound in his side. "What have you done? You will make everything harder."

Harpalycus still wore a faint smile. He motioned; two of his men seized Lycus and pulled him away. "Peace, my friend," he said. "I know what I am doing."

"Mother...." There was a deafening roar in Aridela's head. Stars spilled through her eyes, blinding her. She couldn't feel her legs.

"I am the daughter of Helice," she intoned. "She called me isoke, which means 'Beloved Gift.' Helice was born from the womb of Admete, who was the daughter of Selene, who was the daughter of Evadne, who was the daughter of Zoë. Before her came Thandiwe, Mawiyah, and Chausiku, from the line of Niachero most holy."

Harpalycus motioned. The next woman was yanked forward— Laodámeia, Themiste's beloved maidservant, the one person trusted to stay with the oracle during her holy visions.

"For you, Blue-skinned Poseidon," he said, and lifted his bloody blade.

She screamed and tried to shrink away. He grabbed her, jerked her, and punched her in the nose with his balled fist. Then he slit her throat. Her cries faltered into a sickening gurgle and her body fell on top of Helice's.

Aridela staggered and retched, and would have fallen but for the guards preventing it. Blood from the murdered women flowed into the lustral basin, swirling, eddying, thickening the water.

"I am the daughter of Helice," she whispered, "the daughter of Admete, the daughter of Selene, the daughter of Evadne, the daughter of Zoë, and before her Thandiwe, Mawiyah, and Chausiku, from the line of Niachero most holy." White-hot fury brought her limbs to shivering life; she lifted her face and screamed, "Demon Women. I call upon you. Hound him!"

Harpalycus's eyes glittered with killing lust. "No one can hear your threats in here. I will sacrifice many, many more. Enough to satisfy my master. He craves blood now, for Crete's years of neglect."

He signaled to the guard holding Aridela, and she was pulled to the basin and forced to kneel. "Come," Harpalycus told the priests. "Let us be finished."

Next to her lay the bodies of her mother and Laodámeia. Helice's face was turned down, but Laodámeia's eyes stared blankly into hers.

Aridela no longer felt the sting in her wrists or the throb of her bruises. Watery rainbows danced wherever she looked.

"I am the daughter of Helice, who was the daughter of Admete, who was the daughter of Selene, who was the daughter of Evadne, who was the daughter of Zoë, and before her Thandiwe, Mawiyah, and Chausiku, from the line of Niachero most holy. My mother called me isoke, her beloved gift."

Dropping to his knees, Harpalycus forced her head back as he had her mother's, and pressed the edge of his knife against her throat. He held her face close to his, half-turned toward him.

Her gaze locked on a pulse beating in the side of his neck and gradually, the roaring in her ears began throbbing in concert with the pulse, obliterating the words of the ceremony taking place above her. She knew the barbarian priests spoke words that were sacred to them. Wine was sprinkled and strong incense inflamed her nose, but she heard nothing.

Someone held the ritual goblet of wine and bull's blood to her mouth. She pressed her lips tightly together so that none could enter her mouth. It ran over her chin and dripped to the cave floor.

Harpalycus yanked her to her feet. For the first time she saw Kaphtor's council, herded into a tight group between several armed warriors.

They stared at her. Some wept. Kios looked old and broken. Her aunt Oneaea was stony-eyed, her expression defiant.

Aridela searched out Lycus. Still restrained by two guards, he stood near the cave opening.

"My Mother," she said clearly as she met his cold yet anguished gaze. "Bring your son's fire and lightning. Sweep us away as you did Callisti, and free your world of this evil. Let us all die here, together."

As the sun followed its upward path, Harpalycus stood before the people of Natho and made his decrees. Aridela was forced to stand at his side, her wrists bound behind her. A soldier pricked her in the small of her back with his knifepoint to keep her quiet.

"I am your king," he finished. "You will show me the same honor and obedience you gave your queen."

The people muttered, but as a phalanx of warriors lowered their spears and readied their shields, they grew quiet, cowed, perhaps, by what they had already endured. Aridela knew Harpalycus's men had spent the night burning, slaughtering, and raping at will.

"My ships have sailed into every one of Crete's ports," Harpalycus announced. "I now hold Tamara, Damerto, Phaistos, Aptara, Tarrha,

Knossos, and Kydonia. Your queen is my slave. Her mother is dead. Your famed oracle starves in my prison."

Was he blustering? Could he have achieved such an incredible thing? Between the mighty waves, poisoned air, fires, and earthshakings, the long, intoxicated marriage celebration, and help from Lycus, she could not be sure.

"No land escapes change," Harpalycus said. "Now change has come to Crete. Follow my laws, obey me, and you will live in peace."

Seizing Aridela's arm, he pulled her under the arch towards the villa, which still boasted garlands and pennants from the wedding celebration of the night before.

"Fight!" Aridela struggled and managed to twist free. She ran back towards her people. "Fight them!"

The crowd's mutter expanded into a low, threatening rumble. They began to mill.

The man with the knife grabbed her. Harpalycus swung her around and struck her so hard she could neither hear nor see.

"Curse you, Harpalycus," Lycus shouted. "You promised—"

"You are growing very tiresome, bull leaper," Harpalycus said. "You helped me achieve this. Your pathetic quibbling wears on my patience. All this blood is as much on your hands as mine. Stop sniveling and become the warrior you wish to be. Did you think these people would invite us in and give us their land without protest?"

Motioning to his men, he said, "Remove my young friend if he has no stomach for war."

He turned back to Aridela. "Tie her to the bed in my chamber," he said to the soldier. Twisting his fist in her hair, he drew her chin up and kissed her.

She did not twist or struggle. She did nothing.

He raised his head, one brow lifting, the hint of a smile at the corner of his mouth. "You don't fight me, Aridela?"

"For you to remember," she said, returning his smile, "when the Erinyes come."

3

Moon of Winemaking

CHRYSALEON WAS SHOVED INTO AN OXCART. HIS ARMS AND LEGS WERE bound with rope. Another rope was wrapped around his neck, nearly strangling him, and anchored to the front of the cart. One of the warriors mockingly placed a crown of grapevines on his head and sent the oxen trudging through the village of Natho.

The newly vanquished stood on either side of the lanes. Many wept. Some wore expressions of sympathy while others seemed apathetic or angry. The slaughtered lay where they had fallen. Chrysaleon's guards had to kick a few out of the way.

High on the cliffs gleamed the white villa where Chrysaleon had so recently made love to his young bride. Sunlight reflecting off the walls sent his mind to another day, when the hot midday sun had glared against the walls of Labyrinthos. Jumping from his chariot, he had admired the massive horns adorning the entry into the palace, and the enormous fresco of a black bull, stylized yet still realistic. Aridela, her mother, cousins, and aunts had come forth to greet him in their colorful gowns. It was the first time he had seen his lover from the cave in her royal setting.

The memory dissipated as the oxcart bounced over a stone, jerking him off balance, returning him to the chafe and scratch of the rope around his neck and wrists, to his humiliation.

He was taken before Harpalycus.

The usurper had wasted no time stealing Crete's riches. Gold bands adorned his arms and wrists. An embossed belt cinched his clean white kilt. He wore Chrysaleon's jeweled crown, his sword, and the king's bright gold seal ring.

Thoroughly immersed in the role of conqueror, he stood with his feet planted wide, fists resting on his hips. Behind him were his priests and personal guard, and to one side Proitos, his slavish lackey.

Cold breezes tinged with the scent of the sea teased the priests' robes and the purple-dyed edges of Harpalycus's tunic.

Soldiers dragged Chrysaleon from the cart and pushed him to his knees before his enemy. He knew he would be gutted. He also knew Harpalycus would toy with him first.

"Behold, crown prince of Mycenae, bull-king of Crete. I offer news of home—of your father. If you hope he will rescue you, I fear you will be disappointed." Stepping closer, Harpalycus said, "For months he has been fed infusions of the helleborus root. He dies, and when I send you after him to the land of shades, I will be High King, not only of Crete, but Mycenae and all the great Houses. Every one of your kin, even to the lowest bastard you have sired, will perish on my sword."

Chrysaleon tried to show nothing but contempt, though he reeled inside with shock and despair. "No one trusts you," he said. "None will forget your treacheries."

Rage whitened Harpalycus's lips then he threw back his head and laughed. "Chrysaleon. Heir to the crown of Mycenae, but you wanted Crete's as well. You already had a wife, but that didn't stop you from taking another. Have you thought of Iros once since you came here?"

"No."

"No." Harpalycus's eyes narrowed and his fists clenched. "You have been obsessed with Aridela. My sister is forgotten."

"I had no wish to marry her. I was forced into it."

"Yes, by our fathers. Do you know why it happened so quickly? My father arranged it because Iros was carrying my child and he was afraid of what might happen. The people were already grumbling about me for other things. He saw a way to prevent judgment against him and to foist his grandchild off upon the House of Mycenae at the same time."

"There is no honor among your kin. If I ever did feel any debt to her, it is gone."

"She will never know," Harpalycus said softly, his eyes now mere slits and his lips twitching, "because she is dead."

Chrysaleon pictured that small, pale girl, weary in her bridal finery then later, weeping in his bed. He experienced a surprising instant of pity before he began to wonder how she'd died. He couldn't stop himself from asking, "You have found out what happened there?"

"You will wonder for the rest of your short life. But know this. Your whore, Theanô, wasn't it? She killed my sister, and you will pay the price for that." His face moved from anger to triumph. "The queen of Crete lies in my bed. She is chained for now. Soon she will be more willing."

Chrysaleon strained at the ropes, but they withstood his efforts. Sword points inched closer—one so close it pricked the flesh over his ribcage.

Harpalycus's smile widened. "I will use her," he said. "And then I will give her to my men. Everything I do to her will avenge Iros, and bring suffering to Chrysaleon, the spoiled prince. You will burn because you cannot save her from me."

"You think the Kindred will allow you to live after murdering the High King? Your body will be torn to pieces and left to putrefy. Not even jackals will eat you." Chrysaleon lifted his head and sent his words echoing off the surrounding walls. "Hear me, Daughters of the Night. Formidable Erinyes! I call for vengeance in the name of my mother, Clematia. Gnaw his heels, chase him across the earth. Send him madness and death."

"They won't come," Harpalycus muttered. Yet he peered at the wooden-faced warriors who overheard the curse. Straightening to his full height, he strode from one to the next, clasping a shoulder here, a forearm there. "Not even the goddesses of dread can harm my warriors. You are the finest in the world, the only men strong enough to overthrow legendary Crete."

His men cheered.

Returning to Chrysaleon with a satisfied smile, Harpalycus said, "I am sending you and Themiste to Labyrinthos. I want you to die in the bowels of the citadel where you sought to be king. But you will see me once more before that day. I will bring Aridela. I want you to look upon her belly when she is about to give birth to my child."

Chrysaleon tried to suppress his rage. Perhaps, if Harpalycus believed he didn't care what happened to Aridela, things would go more easily for her. But he couldn't stop his teeth from gritting or his breath from growing shallow.

Harpalycus watched him. Then he laughed. He gestured to the guards, who yanked Chrysaleon to his feet. He started to turn then swiveled sharply and punched Chrysaleon in the stomach, leaving him doubled over and gasping.

"Take him." Harpalycus's smile lingered as the guards dragged his hated enemy away.

WATER TRICKLED DOWN ONE OF THE CELL WALLS. LABYRINTHOS'S ingenious interlocking water pipes must be leaking.

At least his prison offered hazy light during the day, and a bit of fresh air, something that would rankle Harpalycus if he knew. There were three holes high in the walls; it appeared rocks had punched through during the Destruction. Several black, pitted stones lay on the floor.

Pacing across the packed dirt, Chrysaleon tested every crack for a means of escape. He slept, woke, and slept again. At first a guard brought food and water, then, nothing. Chrysaleon lost track of how many days and nights passed.

Help me.

He started awake, hearing Aridela's voice in his head. Sweat stung his eyes.

"Harpalycus holds me prisoner," he whispered, and beat the walls until blood spattered from his knuckles.

Chrysaleon's last glimpse of her had been in their chamber as warriors surrounded him.

You would have happily tricked her, if Harpalycus hadn't beaten you to it. Do not think you have more honor than he.

His thoughts assaulted him with unfamiliar guilt. He didn't know if his starving mind was torturing him in his last days with brutal honesty or if the voice belonged to someone, a god, perhaps, wanting to humble him. He daydreamed about starting his time on Crete from the beginning and making no mistakes. His favorite vision was of killing Harpalycus during the wrestling.

If you had another chance, would you become bull-king and end your life in Crete's sacrifice?

It was easier to allow his thoughts to spin in useless circles than to contemplate what Harpalycus might be doing to Aridela.

Death from starvation was painful. But at least the leaking pipe provided water, though never enough to truly slake his thirst.

At some point, as his stomach chewed at his bones, he thought he heard voices. He hoisted onto his elbows, unable to tell if the sound was real or another dream. Gradually he discerned words. Women were speaking somewhere above him. Their conversation floated through a clay pipe that entered his cell at the ceiling and ran down one of the walls, ending at the floor. Somehow it concentrated the sound at its source and sent it to Chrysaleon quite clearly, almost as if the women were standing in the same room. He inched closer, his nose wrinkling at the sour smell of rat droppings.

"Our spies say he's become a drunkard. How does he manage to keep us enslaved? Potnia must want him to succeed."

"Just be grateful you are not the queen."

"Can you hear me?" Chrysaleon cupped his hands around the ragged opening. "Are you there?"

No answer. The hole's occupant squeaked and shuffled.

He still heard the voices, but they grew fainter. Soon there was only silence.

The next day he heard the same two, speaking their disgruntlement. And the next. And the next. Sometimes the voices came and went swiftly, as though the women walked past without pausing. At others, they stopped to gossip. But no matter how loudly he shouted into the hole, they never heard him.

At last they said something so strange he didn't even try to get their attention.

"Harpalycus has learned of the thinara king," said the one with the raspy voice.

"Who would have told him?" This one sounded younger, and had a tendency to giggle or weep with equal frequency. "He is male and uninitiated. And our enemy."

There was a brief silence. The first woman said, "He probably tortured Minos Themiste."

The voices faded then returned.

"—the entire prophecy?"

"Everyone will believe him Goddess-blessed. The king-sacrifice will be defeated."

"Is it not already?"

The voices faded again, making Chrysaleon grit his teeth in frustration.

"—make the council believe that a god gave him his triumph."

"If he convinces them he is the great-year-king...."

"No one but Minos would hold more power."

"How can he do it, though? He murders our people, rapes the priestesses."

"No one ever said the council had any brains."

"But—"

"His commands will be accepted, no matter how outrageous. And you know what his first decree will be."

"Hsst—someone is coming."

He heard faint sounds. Scuffling. A male voice.

"What are you doing hiding in here? Lazy whores."

A scream. Then the unmistakable keening women always made when someone died. It cut off abruptly, and there was only the same empty silence that usually filled his days and nights.

Great-year-king. What else had she called it? Thinara king. He had never heard either of these titles.

Everyone will believe him Goddess-blessed.

The king-sacrifice will be defeated.

He pondered until awareness ebbed into sleep.

His belly crept past hunger. Thirst made his throat swell. He sucked the ends of his hair and licked water off the wall. Day by day, it grew colder until he was constantly shivering.

A girl stood beside him, looking at him with an expression of serene curiosity. How long had she been there? Her black hair fell long and straight over naked shoulders. Around her forehead ran a crown of blood-red anemones.

Her voice was like soothing cricket-song and cool misty air. "You are the fountainhead."

She ruptured into a scatter of ivory light as another form walked through her. A dark hood disguised the features but she lifted her hands and pushed it back, revealing herself.

"Selene?" he whispered.

For some time she just looked at him. Then she bent, grasped his left hand, and wrapped something around his wrist. He was too weak to protest or struggle.

She straightened. "I could save you," she said. "But it would be better, I think, if you died."

He bit the inside of his lip in an effort to remain conscious. How he hated this bitch. If only whatever was being done to Aridela could instead be done to Selene.

She backed away. "I have brought you Aridela's token. Now die in peace."

"No—stop. Help me." He was sure he said the words, but she melted into the shadows and vanished.

Dying made his dreams exquisitely vivid. No doubt this was another. Selene couldn't enter his cell and leave again. Hadn't he inspected every crack, every flaw for a means to escape?

He was so thirsty. Yet now when he tried to lick moisture off the cell wall, he tasted only stone dust. The leaking water pipe, his only salvation, must have dried up or frozen. Death would come quickly now.

The king-sacrifice will be defeated.

Aridela reclined on a bed of soft grass and pine needles. Menoetius knelt before her. He clasped her hand and she made no protest. He kissed her. She put her arm around his neck and pulled him closer. Golden light infused them. *I will be with you…in you…of you.* She didn't seem to mind the scars. The colors surrounding them were bright and fluid, like water formed of rainbows.

Was Menoetius alive? What of Aridela? Harpalycus wouldn't kill her or give her to another man. He would keep her for torture and rape, for his sadistic pleasure. He would force her to bear his unholy offspring.

Gasping, his heart fluttering and skipping, Chrysaleon inched, digging his fingertips in the cold dirt, to the wall of his cell. He pounded with his fist before falling, drifting from vision to vision.

He and Menoetius dropped off the ledge in the cave of Velchanos. There was Aridela on the sheepskin. Seductive. Willing.

But Menoetius was in his way. He yanked on his brother's arm. Menoetius turned, too slowly to be real. His mask disintegrated then reformed into the head of a real bull. His body elongated; he dropped on all fours. A heavy, dangerous hoof scraped the dirt.

Before Chrysaleon could react the bull charged. One of the horns splintered his ribs and pierced his heart. His life ebbed in a hot flow, not unlike the unstoppable fall of water over a cliff. The bull stood over him, snorting.

Aridela came forward. She rested her hand on the bull's neck and looked down at him indifferently.

"No," he whispered. "Menoetius won't defeat me."

The air felt thick, silent, and black. It must be night. He thought he heard breathing. He listened, no longer caring if the death maidens came.

"Chrysaleon?"

He opened his mouth but his voice caught against the back of his throat like old, corroded bronze, and he gave up the effort.

Cool fingers caressed his forearm then slipped around his neck, lifting his head. The rim of a cup touched his lips.

Water. Wondrous, delicious, life-giving water flowed over his tongue. He choked. The cup waited, ready to give him another chance when he recovered.

Just enough moonlight pierced the holes in the wall to chase away shadows from the center of the floor.

A figure knelt beside him. He felt the swell of a woman's breast against his arm. Gradually, as he caught a hint of the crescent moon on her forehead and the perfect symmetry of her bone structure, he realized she was Themiste, Crete's famed oracle. A warm smell, like dusty sunlight and blooming mountain wildflowers, surrounded him. He tried again to speak but couldn't.

She helped him to his feet. He was surprised at how nimbly he rose. Glancing down, he saw with a start his own body, thin and filthy, on the dirt floor.

He held up his hands. Gauzy as a veil of cloud, they merely softened his view of Themiste's form as he peered through them.

Yet every muscle and sinew, even his skin, throbbed with pain. He couldn't straighten. Every step hurt. Shifting his gaze from his dream-like hand to Themiste hurt.

She waited. Of course there was no hurry. Just the journey to the land of shadows. No doubt she, too, had been killed by Harpalycus, and now served as one of Goddess Athene's handmaids. She would lead him to the House of the Dead, make him ready for crossing the Acheron, for surely, since he hadn't given his blood to the holy axe, he would never be allowed to enter that happy place the Cretans called Hesperia.

She made a sweeping gesture as though outlining an arch on the wall. The rocks melted into a cavernous black hole. "Come," she said, lighting a small clay lamp, and stepped through the opening.

Her long loose hair moved as though it had life of its own. What he'd thought a necklace was really a snake coiled around her neck like an ornament.

She sealed the stones behind him so perfectly that Chrysaleon couldn't tell where the doorway had been.

There were glowing lamps set at intervals into the walls, lifting the rock corridor from complete blackness. As they walked, slowly, because every step sent arrows of pain shooting through Chrysaleon's legs, he began to notice painted images. Some were faded, crumbled, while others seemed newly composed. He paused to examine the nearest. Two stylistic men stood on either side of a crowned, bare-breasted woman, who held in one hand a staff topped with the labrys axe. One of the men saluted her; the other reached out in supplication. The artist had added a crouching lion and a bull, head lowered. Behind them was a gnarled tree with spiraling, serpentine roots.

"What are these?" he asked.

"The paintings tell Kaphtor's story, from its beginning and beyond, to its end."

The wall displayed illustrations of flowers, sheaves of barley, women weaving baskets and boys knocking olives from trees with sticks. Doves and swallows swooped around pillars. Men and women turned somersaults over the backs of bulls. Time and again he saw crescent moons, similar to the one tattooed in blue on Themiste's forehead. Next to every moon representation stood a youth in a loincloth, sword in hand.

The path wound downward, causing Chrysaleon's gossamer shins to burn. He stopped to rest many times. He didn't understand how he could suffer physical pain when he was dead. Themiste waited whenever he stopped, watching him from tranquil, long-lashed eyes. She had been one of the most beautiful women he'd ever seen in life. In death, she left him breathless. He tried not to stare.

"Where are you taking me?" he asked.

"To Velchanos."

Shock bolted through his body. At last he managed, "The god lives here?"

"We travel his pathway. This is the true labyrinth. It exists in secret, beneath the layers of cities that have come and gone with the life and demise of civilizations. Our Lady created it when her people fled the wars and crossed the sea to Kaphtor. Now it is the way to Velchanos, the Keeper of the River of Light, he who gave his blood for the sake of mortals." Her voice was soothing, melodious. It held no hurry or strain.

"What wars?"

"They happened long before any record-keeping, in another land. Many of my ancestors died, for the greed of our enemies was strong."

"Who were they?"

She tucked his arm through hers and they walked again, ever

downward. "No one knew them, or from where they came, but they were well armed and ruthless. At the end, in the desperation brought by loss of hope, my people's leaders used holy, ancient rites to bring Athene's son. By that time only a few remained. If they had called him sooner, perhaps the ruin would not have been so complete. But fear held them back. It was believed that to summon the Velchanos would bring unforeseen consequences that might never be reversed." Themiste's doe eyes were full of indecipherable entreaty. For what, he could not comprehend, but a powerful urge rose within to fulfill it, whatever it was.

"And so what happened?" he asked. "The enemy was defeated?"

"Velchanos destroyed the invaders," she said simply. "Then he scattered the survivors to every corner of the world. In these underground corridors, he placed the beasts of old, the basilisk, the sphinx, the dragon, and gryphon. He gave the Above World to mortals: to women and men. That entire time is now lost, as is the thread of kinship. The dispersed tribes developed their own customs and beliefs. They composed their own languages. Some fight their neighbors and some seek peace. Some have pale skin, like the face of the moon, and some are obsidian, like moonless night. But all were once one. One kin, one people."

"Your tale is like nothing I have ever heard. Is it true? Did it really happen?"

Themiste's shrug and the tilt of her head suggested she had considered the same question. "No one knows. It has come down through time. It is legend, or perhaps an enchantment."

"An enchantment?" Chrysaleon wanted to scoff. But he was dead, walking arm in arm with a ghost. Everything he had ever believed was upended.

Themiste nodded. "The Moerae weave enchantments through the skeins of our fate, my lord; they can turn our course when we think of other things, change our destinies and we won't ever know. Magic runs alongside every action we take. Best to remember, and tread carefully."

The walkway emerged into a cavern. She held her lamp high as they felt their way, but the light made only the faintest pool of illumination at their feet.

There were no paintings here. Their footsteps echoed into unfathomable space. Water dripped from unseen stalactites. Yet, surprisingly, the air was warm, carrying the faint scent of spices.

"We will continue to an underground sea," Themiste said. "You can rest there."

Chrysaleon tensed when he heard a rumbling growl ooze from the darkness.

"Many creatures live here," Themiste said. "We must be quiet."

They walked on, pausing once as a lizard, big as a man, crossed their path. It was red, scaled, with slitted eyes and a crest of bone around its neck. It hissed at them, revealing rows of wicked teeth.

Chrysaleon itched for his sword, or at least a knife. Themiste gripped his forearm and put her finger to her lips. They waited, and soon the lizard went off into the darkness.

They walked on. The encounter sparked a memory of his younger brother, Gelanor, who had given him a dagger on his last birthday. Gelanor…the babe who slipped from his mother's womb making a sound she'd insisted was a giggle, though the king maintained it was more likely distress. She'd waved away his cynical comments and demanded the child be named accordingly. Gelanor. 'Laughter.'

If the boy still lived, he would be sixteen, the same age as Aridela. Grief and remorse weighted Chrysaleon's limbs as he trudged the path. The last he'd seen of his brother had been on the pier as he and Menoetius were setting sail for Crete. Chrysaleon had been dismissive, impatient to be away. He'd brushed off the youth's requests for trinkets, and his complaints that he never got to do anything exciting. Now Chrysaleon would give much for an afternoon of hunting, a fistfight or wrestling match. Time was what he wished for now. Time with his brother. Guilt and worry proving too much to bear, he stopped again, panting. His heart pounded.

Themiste missed nothing. "Yours is a long journey and a heavy responsibility," she said, her expression unfathomable. "You have more power than you know, Zagreus, and choices to make which will determine the future of generations. I wonder what you will do—will you reunite the queen with her throne? Or will you choose another path?"

Chrysaleon fought to catch his breath. He felt old and tired, but Themiste's words ignited dazzling hope. "Aridela is alive?"

"For now." A frown formed between her brows. "Our kings are the blood of Kaphtor, and our queens the earth that drinks it. If death claims the queen, our civilization will vanish from history, from all human knowledge, as Callisti has done." Gently gripping his elbow, she began walking again, and he followed.

"The marrow of Callisti fell from the skies upon Kaphtor,"

Themiste said quietly. "By the time the Lady's anger burned out, nothing remained. Athene, when angered, is swift in exacting vengeance."

Chrysaleon's joy at hearing of Aridela's survival faded into the horror of that night when fire, ash, and wind nearly destroyed Crete. If Themiste spoke the truth, Athene was a goddess so powerful, so merciless, no mortal could dare cross her; from such a deity no mere man could keep secrets. Yet if that were so, why would she seek to help him, knowing as she must his true designs? And why had Harpalycus, the instrument of Callisti's obliteration, escaped without injury while so many innocents perished?

Surely none of this mattered. He was dead and could no longer make any difference. Why did the oracle imply that he could reunite Aridela with her throne? Perhaps there was a way to do it from beyond the grave.

A greenish glow, like sunlight shining through ferns, pierced the darkness ahead. Themiste said, "We are through the cave."

The light seemed to have no source, but surrounded them softly. It rippled and shimmered as though diffused through water. As they rounded a bend in the path, the view before them opened up. The smell of saltwater filled the air and Chrysaleon looked upon a vast underground sea, stretching into blackness.

Two creatures stood on the shore. They had the bodies of lions, but with feathered, birdlike wings tucked into their shoulders, and the heads and faces of eagles. He recognized them immediately from many children's tales. Gryphons.

"Yes, my lord." Themiste nodded, though he'd said nothing. "They will carry us the rest of the way."

Chrysaleon lifted her onto the back of one and mounted the other, moving slowly and avoiding the enormous hooked beaks. The feathers unfurled into huge, diaphanous wings that carried them into the air soundlessly and gracefully.

Now he knew beyond doubt he was dead.

The sea below changed. At first, Chrysaleon thought Themiste's lamp had weakened. As they flew on, the greenish tinge at the seashore took on a violet glow, like a vivid twilight.

"See the difference?" She laughed. "We rise from the land of Darkness into Calesienda's orchard. The world of Light. Can you feel it?"

Tingling energy flowed through his extremities, diminishing the earlier pain. His thirst lessened and he felt, for the first time since beginning this journey, closer to life than death.

Even as she spoke, the air around them lightened to the tender blush of the summer flower his people called 'mother's tears' for their drooping, tear-shaped petals. The gryphons turned their heads up and made a sound similar to the cry of hunting hawks.

Far above, the ceiling of the underground cavern became visible. It was covered with enormous hanging blooms, drifting from side to side in a breeze he felt against his face.

The beasts they rode sped toward a gigantic cliff. Just as it seemed they would slam into it they tilted and skimmed into a narrow crevasse then dove through a sheer wall of foaming blue-green seawater.

Themiste smiled, her red hair flowing in currents made by the swimming gryphons. Light and shadow filtered through the water, transforming the aspect of this new world, making everything more vivid.

I can breathe. Chrysaleon realized it even as he realized he didn't feel cold or wet.

The light shining through the water brightened as the cliffs fell behind. The gryphons followed the edge of an underwater bluff into a valley; as suddenly as they had been submerged into water, they broke through the other side and were again on solid ground. The beasts landed lightly, like cats. Themiste's shook its back as if to say, *I have carried you long enough.*

Chrysaleon slid off, careful of his creature's wings, and helped Themiste dismount.

"Are you surprised, my lord?" The ends of her hair still drifted like seaweed in shallow currents, though, as far as he could tell, they were no longer underwater.

He had no words for what he felt. To all appearances everything was the same as at home, though the air was different. It carried an invisible sensation, like a living thing. It seemed to move, soft as kisses against his skin. "Am I dead or dreaming?"

"That is for the Goddess to decide. This is Hesperia, Athene's paradise."

"Already? That was not such a long journey. You exaggerated, Themiste."

"I was not speaking of this journey," she said, "but of learning all you must learn, suffering all you must suffer, in the name of she you claim to love."

Her gaze was level, unsmiling, but she allowed him no time to ask more questions. "I have brought you, as I was instructed." She plucked the serpent from around her neck. "Now you must forge your own way. There are many paths for you to choose, Prince. Or you might construct a new one." Placing her companion upon the grass, she watched as it zipped away to a tumble of rocks.

He began to feel uneasy. What were these choices? What would happen if he made the wrong one?

The gryphons shook their heads and padded down to the stream.

To a man raised among the Argolid's dusty rock-strewn mountains and plains, this landscape proved almost beyond comprehension. He and Themiste stood on the summit of a gentle knoll. Forest surrounded them on three sides. The evergreens and spruces made all greens he had known in the land of men grey by comparison. Beeches swayed and rustled. Glossy dark leaves and bunches of acorns weighted mighty oak branches. Damp, springy grass covered the ground, spotted with poppies and other wildflowers. To the south of the knoll, a stream spewed, bubbling over stones that glittered like stars. Movement caught his eye. He stared, squinting, and finally discerned young women, dressed in what appeared to be leaves, their hair unbound. Some sat upon branches, half-hidden in the foliage like birds or lazing cats, while others peered at him from behind the trunks of oaks.

Themiste laughed. Her eyes had changed from the deep brown he remembered to the predominant color of this strange land—green, flashed through with gold. Sunlight brightened her hair from auburn to copper. He blinked, awed by such beauty, struck speechless by the way she was looking at him.

Delight trembled through his spine and fingers. He knew the change he saw in Themiste had affected him as well, that he was more vivid, more alive. The haze of the mortal world had been washed away. He could taste as well as feel the air here. It was sweet as honey.

"Come," she cried, touching his hand. Lifting the hem of her gown in both fists, she ran down the hill. He followed eagerly.

These surroundings, so different from the ash-choked land they'd left, enthralled his mind. Blue-purple hills swept away to the south; bright color spotted the ground where every manner of flower thrived. Fleecy clouds scudded on breezes, high above in cobalt heavens. Sunlight shimmered through the cascades of water that had served as a gateway into this paradise. He wasn't quite certain if what he felt against his face was air or water.

The grass was soft and pliable. Birds covered in jewel-like plumage flashed among the branches in the forest. A full-antlered stag observed him, while nearby, a fox licked its bushy russet tail.

Themiste had left him behind. Speeding up, feeling as though he could run forever, he caught her and grabbed her waist. They lost their balance and fell, rolling in a tangle down a short slope, and came to rest at the edge of the stream. Themiste, landing on top, immediately kissed him, demanding he return a passion he'd assumed she couldn't feel. He submitted willingly, laughing. Seizing her arms, he pushed her tunic off her shoulders, threw her over so she lay on her back in the grass, and proceeded to cover her with kisses as he plunged inside her with his fingers and found her ready.

Her hands slipped beneath his tunic. They were soon naked and coupling with unreserved lust.

When it was finished he lay upon her, one cheek against her breast, sunlight warm upon the other, listening to her heart slow into steady beats.

He'd nearly fallen asleep when she pushed him. Unprepared, he tumbled inelegantly into the stream, gasping at its icy bite. The cold shock evaporated whatever anger ran through him at her unexpected dismissal. Remembering his thirst, he gulped the clean liquid and let it wash over his face before stumbling out and falling onto the grass, panting, laughing.

Themiste, shrugging into her tunic, laughed too. "You snore." She made a face.

"Only when I am uncommonly content," he replied, pulling his tunic over his head.

A flock of geese drew his attention with their honking as they flew over. "By the black thundering waves of Poseidon," he said, shading his eyes with one hand against the glitter of the sun. "This is a wondrous place."

She instantly sobered. "Do not insult Athene. Not here."

"I cannot speak the name of Poseidon, the god of my father's father?"

"Athene's roused temper is not a thing to test. Don't you know that by now? And we no longer stand in the world of mortals, where thick air and noise protects the irreverent."

"Where is she?"

"Everywhere. Listen, Prince. Who gave birth to your dream of Poseidon? Gaia, who gave birth also to the queen of the wild things, our Lady Athene. This is the unsullied land of Gaia, and here you must show fealty. She was the beginning and will be the end. Can you not feel her in your mind? Did you not just quench your thirst upon her breast?"

Chrysaleon leaped to his feet, fighting a rush of anger. "I feel nothing but pleasure and awe as I look upon a beautiful landscape. How can this help Crete or Aridela? Answer me, Themiste. Am I dead?"

"The bull-king of Kaphtor...."

It wasn't Themiste who spoke. The voice was male. Chrysaleon pivoted, habit balling his hands into fists.

A man stepped out from the forest's edge. Rather, a youth, with curly black hair, a fine, firm mouth, and slender body robed in a sleeveless white tunic woven of some delicate, glossy material. Braids of fine, thin silver circled his head, half-hidden by his black locks. A partridge scurried about his feet and two of the girls Chrysaleon had seen earlier giggled behind him.

There was such a likeness in his face to Aridela that it left Chrysaleon squinting.

"Welcome," said the youth.

Glancing at Themiste, Chrysaleon asked, "Is this—"

"I am Damasen," the lad said. He gazed beyond Chrysaleon. "Welcome, Themiste." He held out his arms.

She knelt, covering her face with her hands.

"Rise, child," he said.

Child? Damasen didn't look as if he'd lived seventeen years.

Chrysaleon remembered the evening Aridela made the bull leap. Before she'd slipped away, she showed him her necklace, two crescent moons cupping a bead of blue lapis. She said her long-dead father, Damasen, had given it to her mother. Now here he stood, not a spear's throw away.

Themiste rose and Damasen clasped her hands. "Thou art well," he said. "The barbarian could not harm thee nor even hold thee in his prison."

"Of course not, my lord. He has no knowledge of the secret corridors. But I was unable to save Queen Helice, and Aridela is his captive."

His smile faded. He rested his forehead against hers. "Why have you brought the prince of Mycenae to my orchard?"

"He made the holy vow. He protected Aridela the night of the Destruction, and he has been tortured near to death by his own countrymen. Vision revealed to me that he must reunite the queen with her land if we are ever to recover. Did I see truly?"

Damasen contemplated Chrysaleon, his expression giving nothing away.

"Leave us, Themiste," he said at last.

4

Moon of Winemaking

No outside sound penetrated the dim, airless chamber in which Aridela was kept. From time to time she feared the entire island of Kaphtor had been sucked into her nightmares and no longer existed except in memory.

With both ankles and wrists bound, she could do nothing but lie upon the moldy, insect-ridden bedding thrown upon the stone floor. But after a few days, the nameless eunuch who attended her cut the binding around her ankles and left it off. There was no danger of her escaping, as the leather strap around her wrists was secured to the bottom of a pillar, making it impossible to take more than one step away from the bedding, and that could only be managed doubled over. Testing the leather tightened it and strangled the flow of blood to her hands. This annoyed the eunuch, who, as he rearranged the bonds, would mutter mainland curses and cuff her on the head, where her hair would hide the bruises. Beyond that miserly kindness, he did nothing but toss down a bowl of thin broth twice a day, letting her struggle on her own to reach, lift, and drink, and, not nearly often enough, he carried the chamber pot away to be emptied.

At first she worried about the passing of time. There was nothing to do as she languished except fret, grieve, and rage. She tried to mark the days but couldn't keep up. For a miserable blurry interlude she lay on the filthy bed, scratching those fleabites she could reach, and wondering if Harpalycus had forgotten her, for he never came and the eunuch shared no information.

The nightmares worsened to the point where she dreaded falling asleep. She was so hungry she dreamed of eating the straw beneath her. She dreamed repeatedly of Harpalycus's rape, of his heaviness, his hot, suffocating breath, his painful invasion. She dreamed of swelling, bloating with child, not knowing if it was Chrysaleon's or his. The larger she grew the louder and more echoing grew Harpalycus's laughter.

Her dreams of Chrysaleon's death were perhaps the most agonizing. She saw herself struggling free of her captors and approaching her fallen husband. Walking across the bedchamber seemed to take all night. Sometimes she never reached him. When she did and turned him over, maggots swarmed from his eyes.

Sometimes, weaving beneath horror and anguish, she dreamed the promise of the god: *For longer than you can imagine, I will be with you, in you, of you. Together we bring forth a new world, and nothing can ever part us.*

Kaphtor would have slipped out of the Moon of Field Poppies and into the Moon of Winemaking by now. No sound of the traditional grape festival seeped through the walls, nor any hint of the rich call of conch shells to the four winds. Aridela felt in her tendons, her belly and bones, the cry of abandoned grapes as they rotted on the vines. She experienced through every layer of her soul the sundering of the ancient bond between her people and the sanctified crops.

Every now and then she caught a whiff of fresh air clinging to the eunuch's robes or sneaking beneath the door, and this helped her pinpoint where they were in the wheel of the year. The faint scent of grapes melted into a sweet hint of apples. One of Kaphtor's most vibrant months, the cool nights and warm days of the Moon of Winemaking brought apples as well as grapes to ripe fruition. She couldn't help inhaling with desperate desire and a plummeting sense of helplessness and fury. Before the rain of fire and ash, this month kept everyone busy crushing grapes and beginning the fermentation process, bringing out last year's wine, planting new grains, and picking the ripe apples. Cider was made through the laborious process of grinding apples with stones then pressing the mush. There were sweet apple cakes oozing mouth-watering juices. The Moon of Winemaking gave way each year to brisk winds and the excitement of the olive harvest, but who would knock down the fruit this year? Who would care for the surviving olive trees? Who would press the rich dark oil and contain it in clay jars, ready for export to the many countries that craved it?

She wept for all Kaphtor had lost and wondered how long she could continue living tied to this pillar, in an eternal silent gloom as the forgotten prisoner of Harpalycus.

Athene, am I still your daughter? Do you listen anymore?

Harpalycus finally came. Awakened by some sound, she peered up groggily and there was his face, staring down at her with an expression of triumph and satisfaction.

Without a word, he shoved her onto her back with his foot and fell upon her, slaking his monstrous urge almost immediately. Aridela pressed her legs together as he rose, feeling sticky wetness on her thighs that might either be his semen or blood. She screamed until she was hoarse and kicked at him, inadvertently twisting the thongs around her wrists and causing them to squeeze without mercy. He stepped back, laughing at her attempts to harm him then raped her again, more slowly. When she struggled and spat and called to the Erinyes for vengeance, he raped her a third time, smiling, never closing his eyes but observing her furious helplessness with obvious pleasure. He only lost interest and stopped when she bit her lip, turned her head away, and lay without movement, in silence.

After that day, Harpalycus sent a messenger regularly to the storeroom in which she was kept. Upon receiving the summons, the eunuch would sponge her from her hair to her toes. He cuffed her so hard when she struggled or kicked that she would often lose consciousness, only waking to find herself either being carried to the bedchamber she'd once shared with Chrysaleon and which now housed Harpalycus, or already in the bed, bound to the bedposts. Sometimes Harpalycus would be sitting in a chair, drunkenly watching her, or he would enter the room at some point after she woke, giving her time to dread his arrival.

He loved to brag about his campaign. Everything, according to him, was proceeding smoothly, without resistance. He told her how much he enjoyed it when she fought him, and encouraged her to struggle, often slapping her in an attempt to spark her anger. Lycus, who had apparently fallen in his own fortunes from accomplice to prisoner, was sometimes brought in and forced to watch, such was the usurper's perversion. On those occasions Harpalycus delighted in doing whatever it took to elicit cries of agony from the queen of Kaphtor.

When his needs were exhausted, he had her carried back to her cramped bare cell, where the air and stones grew steadily colder.

"It is a fine, sunny day, my queen." Harpalycus flung open the bedchamber door and strode in, bringing with him streams of cold, fresh air. He motioned to the eunuch. The man knelt to remove the prince's greaves then lifted the gold crown from his master's forehead and placed it on a table. It was a crown worn on ceremonial occasions by Kaphtor's bull-kings, and was heavy with gold, shining stones, and carvings.

Aridela, bound as usual to the ornate bed, made no reply.

"Bring Lycus," The slave bowed and backed out, closing the door behind him. Soon Lycus was dragged in, his wrists and ankles shackled. A leather strap covered his mouth. He was bruised and filthy.

Aridela barely glanced at him.

She encouraged random images to form in her mind. It was her method of blocking out Harpalycus's attacks and helping her remain still and silent, which discouraged him—sometimes to the point where he couldn't keep an erection.

There was the day Selene stepped off the ship from Phrygia. Aridela and Iphiboë had clutched each other, speechless with awe at this tall, flaxen-haired girl who had come so far to instruct them. Stern in the beginning, Selene was a hard teacher who left many a bruise with her wooden sword, especially if she thought they weren't paying attention or not trying their best. There was Helice on her high-backed stone throne, surrounded by her council and judges, preparing to hear suppliants from the various provinces. Motioning to a younger Aridela, she pointed to a spot where her daughter could listen and learn about justice. There were days of summer, saturated with the soft wing-hum of bees and thick scent of hyacinths and rosemary, Aridela hitching up her tunic and nimbly climbing trees, dismissive of the long white scratches the bark left on her legs, equally dismissive of the swarming bees. Using a smoker, she lulled them and stole their dripping honeycombs, seldom suffering any stings. Neoma, Aridela's partner in most of her wayward adventures, would usually stay on the ground, keeping an eye out for the nurses. "Come down," she would hiss. "It's not fair. Save some for me."

"Come and get some if you want it so much," Aridela always replied.

And there was the rush of air as she vaulted over the mighty back of the aurochs.

The god-lover spoke his vow. *I will always be with you, in you, of you. Know me, Aridela. See me. I am with you, even now. My Mother and I are by your side.*

Many memories to choose from, all of them cherished.

The acrid smell of ashes and violent shaking forced her awareness back to Harpalycus. He leaned over her, a scowl marring his handsome face.

"Wake up. You cannot sleep in your master's presence." He crossed to the table and poured wine. "I have had a satisfying day. Eurysthenes of Pylos and I have come to an agreement that benefits us both. His armies will soon be here. Your people cower in their hovels, trying in vain to hide their daughters from my men." He returned to the bedside. Aridela smelled the wine on his breath as he bent over her. She tried to swallow, but her throat was so parched she couldn't. "Did we really think Crete invincible?" he said. "You, your country, and everything within it are mine, and always will be."

"Never."

He didn't respond. She must not have spoken out loud. She was so intolerably weary, so weak from hunger and thirst she could hardly tell truth from fantasy. The last time she'd truly slept had been the night of her wedding. Tears trailed from her eyes. "Chrysaleon...."

Harpalycus straightened with an impatient sigh. "Still calling your feeble lover? I expected more of you. When I finish here, I will move my court to Knossos. I mean to bury his skull beneath the road into the palace and take my place as king." He drank off his wine, shattering the finely crafted, elegant bowl against the wall. Tilting his head as he sat next to her, he ran a hand so lightly along her arm it caused a shiver. "This is the way it should be, for all women, everywhere. You have no honor. We on the mainland have always known this. You claim to be blessed with divinity, but you are nothing. Necessary vessels, soil in which to grow our offspring. I am the one with true power. One day, all people, all civilizations, will worship me." He pressed two fingers over the pulse in her throat. "It took me many years to find the secret of life and bend it to my will." His smile widened. "But I succeeded. I cannot die. Do you understand?" He stood, stretching, scratching his scalp. "Is it time yet to untie you?" She watched his eyes narrow as he slit the ropes that bound her ankles and trailed his hands along her calves to her thighs, pushing down between them and forcing them apart.

Aridela inhaled and released her breath. Part of her longed to twist, scream, and kick, but she couldn't muster the strength, and something, something she couldn't quite remember, advised her to ignore his taunts.

"You don't struggle." He lowered himself upon her, parting her thighs again with his knee. "Is the fight at last leaving you?"

His weight crushed her bound arms. One shoulder felt close to coming out of joint. Though she bit her lip until the coppery taste of blood seeped into her mouth, a miserable groan formed in her throat.

He grinned. It was all he needed. Soon he collapsed, heavy and sated, over her body. His breathing rasped in her ear.

Kissing her earlobe like an ardent lover, he said, "Sweet Aridela. I swear by Poseidon I never tire of you. You lie there without protest but I see the hatred in your eyes. You cannot hide it from me. I hope you never lose your hatred. It's so much more exciting than the sniveling acquiescence other women offer. One day, when you hold my son in your arms, I think you might give yourself to me willingly. I'm not sure that is what I want at all."

"I will kill any child you make on me."

He laughed, instantly reinvigorated. It was true, what he said. Her defiance did nothing but add to his strange erotic fulfillment. Many times she'd told herself to say nothing, to close her eyes and lie as though dead when he tormented her. Yet sometimes the old spark, the 'cauldron of fire' that used to simmer within her, blazed and would not be silenced.

There was movement at the corner of her eye. She glanced at Lycus. His shoulders were hunched, his face streaked with tears. The eunuch was there too, staring without expression over their heads.

Say nothing. Do nothing. As she grew hungrier and weaker, it became easier to follow the internal command.

She turned her head away, lying still and silent until Harpalycus lost patience and struck her in the face.

"Wash her," he said to the eunuch. "Put new bedding in her cell. I'm sick of these ugly fleabites." He sat on the edge of the bed and ran his fingers over her thigh. "If she can ever learn humility," he said almost gently, "and how best to please me, she will find her life much easier. She will be the mother of a line of kings. If she does not, I will hand her over to my men and see how she likes that."

He motioned to his guards. They grabbed Lycus and pulled him from the room. The once-famed and adored bull leaper stared at her as he was dragged away. She returned his gaze, her eyes slitted with venom.

If only she could die.

But wishes for death were cowardly. As long as there remained the slightest chance she could free her people, she would suffer any agony to that end.

"Aridela? wake up."

She started as a hand gripped her shoulder. She felt the close presence of another being, but in the dark, she saw nothing.

"Aridela," he said again, low, and she recognized the voice. She hadn't seen Lycus in days, not since the last time Harpalycus had made him watch while he raped her. How could Lycus, as much a prisoner as she, be here, unbound, alone, in what must be the middle of the night?

"Is Harpalycus with you, traitor?" she said. "Are you here to watch again?"

His grip tightened. He made choked sounds.

"I don't blame you," he whispered. "I—I was mistaken in my trust." He fumbled with the knots at her wrists.

"Mistaken in your trust?" She laughed, infusing it with all the contempt she'd been harboring. "What are you doing?"

"Helping you escape."

"Get away from me."

"I promise you. I have planned this since the day he imprisoned me. I dug my way out. I have a knife. I took it off a soldier while he slept. These mainlanders are lazy and careless, and always drunk."

Aridela felt herself growing more alert. For the first time since she'd been captured she felt a spark of hope. She feared it.

"You're lying. Where is Harpalycus? He's watching, isn't he?"

"No." Lycus shook her. "If we're caught he'll kill us both, and we'll suffer before we die, do you understand? This is our only chance. I could have gone by myself, but I won't, not without you. Do you want to come with me or stay here?"

She tried to judge his honesty but without any light, unable to discern his expression, she couldn't.

He freed her wrists and rubbed her cold hands.

"We must hurry," he said. "Your guard will return. I've been waiting for him to leave. He won't be gone long."

She struggled through exhaustion to sit up.

He kept talking as he rubbed her arms and calves.

"He lied to me. He promised neither you nor your mother would be harmed. I only wanted to see Chrysaleon ousted."

"Idiot."

He helped her rise. Weakness forced her to lean against him. Not since the bull gored her, nearly seven years ago, had she felt so helpless.

"How did you do it?" she asked. "Tell me that at least. I want to know how you and Harpalycus overthrew us."

He sighed twice as if trying to build his courage. "We planned it before he left Kaphtor. After the Destruction, I thought he must be dead. But two of his men came to Kydonia on a tender and learned where we were. They rowed around to Natho and found me. We made arrangements. I slit the throat of the watchman the night of the celebration. Harpalycus did the rest. His father's armies overthrew every major harbor in just a few days."

She gritted her teeth to keep from spitting on him. "What did he offer to make it worthwhile? Gold? Were you not wealthy enough already?"

"What I told you," he mumbled. "He promised to rid Kaphtor of Chrysaleon." His voice lowered further. "He promised me your hand."

She could only hiss her disgust.

"Listen to me," he said. "You must know, if we—if we are caught. Has he said anything about what he can do? Things no mortal should dare?"

She fought to keep from collapsing as they made their way across the room. "He claims he cannot die. He is a madman."

"He may be mad, but he does possess power. Proitos taught it to him."

He kept his arm around her waist to keep her on her feet. Aridela clenched her teeth, both to stop their chattering and to keep from cursing him.

Keeping his mouth close to her ear, Lycus said, "I have heard that

Proitos learned his craft from a master. I tried to find out his name, but I only know he is close to Chrysaleon."

They stopped at the doorway. Lycus listened, looking both directions, before helping Aridela into the corridor. "Hurry."

They stumbled along, trying to be quiet. "You don't know anything," she said. "You lie to serve your own ends, to discredit my consort."

She began to feel a little stronger, and shoved free of Lycus's supporting arm.

"No, Aridela." Lycus caught her hand and led the way down a set of steps. "I'm not lying. It troubles me that I couldn't learn this man's name. He could be here right now with Harpalycus. This man is someone to fear. He possesses an unholy power."

They entered another corridor and slipped along the wall. Aridela was groggy from exhaustion and furious at Lycus's insinuations. Instead of these back stabbings and accusations, they should find the fastest way to escape. She stared into shadows, trying to identify their location even as her mind leaped ahead to the gathering of an army that would bring down Harpalycus.

"I hated you." Lycus's grip tightened around her hand. "You can't know how much, for giving yourself to him."

She twisted until she freed her hand from his.

"And such a love," he continued. "So consuming. You forgot about everyone else. Chrysaleon was all that mattered. By the Lady, I hated you."

"Why are you helping me then?"

Lycus guided her to a door. She shook her head. "That isn't the way out."

"Yes, it is. I've mapped it. Trust me."

She shrugged and they passed through. Blackness encased them. They felt along the walls. Finally Lycus stopped, searching until he found what he was looking for.

"Here it is," he said, throwing open another door.

Aridela heard the wash of the sea as they stepped onto a pillared terrace. She and her mother had breakfasted here in better days. Tears blinded her as she breathed the air of freedom. Never again would she take such a thing for granted.

Snow covered the flagstones, drifting in the corners to knee height. Icy wind howled against them. "How long have I been in that room?"

she asked, remembering the fine warmth and sunlight she had reveled in the day before the ceremony that made her Chrysaleon's wife.

"A month. Winter came early, as we feared it would. Eurysthenes will use it as another excuse to delay sending the armies he promised. Hurry." Lycus seized her hand again. "I found a set of stairs. It leads both into the hills and down to the sea. Only a little farther." He turned as he pulled her forward. Faint moonlight revealed a hesitant smile. "Remember how it used to be? Do you remember that day in your mother's arboretum?"

"I wish not to remember it."

His smile faded. "I am not evil; I know that now. Harpalycus is evil. I have only been stupid."

"The dead cry for vengeance because of your stupidity."

"And they will have it," said another voice, a voice Aridela recognized, coming from behind them.

Terror sent Aridela onto her toes as Harpalycus emerged from the open doorway.

"Quick—" Lycus hissed. "Down the stairs. Hide in the rocks. Find the caves—"

They backed toward the stairs. Harpalycus walked towards them, smiling. "I knew you had escaped, my old friend," he said. "You think yourself clever, but you always do exactly what I predict. I've won my wager with Proitos, who believed you too cowardly to try."

Lycus pushed her away from him then faced Harpalycus. He held up his stolen dagger.

Aridela watched as Harpalycus took three long, quick strides, raising his sword. Lycus threw his dagger but the blade flew wide and sank into the snow. Still smiling, Harpalycus took one more step and thrust his sword into the renowned bull leaper's stomach.

Lycus doubled over. Aridela glimpsed his wide-eyed shock.

Turning, she raced for the steps, hearing Harpalycus shout through the strangled screams in her head.

Arrows struck around her. One grazed her thigh. She descended, slipping on ice, gasping, clutching the stones on either side. Blood ran down her leg, leaving black streaks in the snow.

Warriors blocked her way forward. The high stone wall surrounding the steps prevented any escape to the side. She turned and fled back the way she'd come.

They caught her at the top. Her arms were seized. Sword blades pressed against her chest and the back of her neck. She could hardly breathe, much less move.

"Take her to my chamber," Harpalycus said. "Tie her tightly." He stepped closer. She smelled blood and that other scent she had grown to associate with him. The caustic stench of smoldering ashes.

"Killing makes me lusty," he called as his soldiers pulled her away. "What happy fortune that I've a whore in my bed."

5

Moon of the Olive Harvest

From the Oracle Logs
  Themiste

Prince Chrysaleon has at last awakened, and is hungry. Neoma *brought him a hot strengthening brew made of ox bones. She feeds him with the patience of a mother tending a sick child, which shows how different she is since her own visit into the shadowlands.*

When we took him from his prison cell, his flesh was grey and sunken; he hardly breathed. Two men carried him here, to the holy cave of Velchanos, where I believed he would soon expire. I admit I'm surprised he didn't.

I cannot help but gloat over Harpalycus losing not just me but his most hated enemy as well. I sense the rage behind his promises of extravagant rewards if we are returned. His warriors came to the cave yesterday and stumbled around the outer cavern while we laughed in the back chambers. Does he think we don't know how to conceal ourselves?

All we must do now is free Aridela.

Though he is skeletal and weak as a newborn, Chrysaleon's eyes shine. His mouth is tranquil. He looks as he did the first time I took notice of him, dusty and elated after winning the footrace at the initial trials. On that day I learned the meaning of his name. I knew he had come to Kaphtor by sacred design.

When I explained where he was, he gave me a smile of such brilliance it almost stopped my breathing.

"This is where Aridela and I...." He didn't finish. I knew he was remembering the first time he lay with her.

Then he added, frowning, "She needs me."

His voice sounds younger. His face, too, is different, perhaps because he came so near to death and defeated it. He seems changed from what he was, more thoughtful, maybe a little less reckless.

Every time I look upon our handsome Zagreus, Aridela's vivid memories of their mating return. I should let these recollections go. They do not belong to me. But I haven't. I confess they leave me desirous for that which I cannot have.

Before Chrysaleon came to Kaphtor, I used to dream of the vision in which Damasen appeared. He lay upon me, gazing into my face as we merged, flesh to flesh, soul to soul. The memory is sweet yet amorous, and roused passions that were difficult to quench, but they were always touched by divinity, somehow removed from this world.

Chrysaleon has intensified those longings but in a mortal, earthy fashion that heats my skin. I turn away from him and try to feign indifference. I am afraid of betraying myself.

He dwells upon his death-experience. I understand. There have been times I have awakened from vision certain it was truth and this world false. I recognize the questioning confusion in his face. He asks if there are hidden corridors beneath Labyrinthos, under the prisons. My denials agitate him. He claims Kaphtor was embroiled in an ancient war, and creatures such as dragons, lizards, and gryphons live in a world beneath our feet. He insists I am the one who revealed these legends to him.

I hope his journey to death and back hasn't damaged his mind.

THEMISTE WATCHED CHRYSALEON SLEEP. SHE COULDN'T HELP IT. HER GAZE roamed over him, and in her imagination, her hands followed.

She lost track of time, which was easy to do in the cave, where all light came from clay lamps. When he woke with a sharply indrawn breath, his arms flailing, she didn't know how long she'd been there, but her back was stiff and her neck hurt.

"My lord," she said soothingly. "You are with friends."

"Themiste." His voice hadn't yet regained its old strength. His weakness made her feel protective; his use of her name made her smile.

She brought her stool closer. "I have broth. It's still warm."

"I don't want any." He frowned.

"Just a sip," she said, hoping to tempt him as she brought the bowl closer.

His frown deepened. Clasping her wrist, he pushed the bowl away but kept hold of her. "No. But I am happy you're here, my lady. I have questions."

"I hope I have answers." She tried to ignore the flicker of desire that ran up her arm from his hand.

He released her. She put the bowl on the floor and folded her hands on her lap.

He hoisted himself into a sitting position with a sigh. Shadows lingered beneath his eyes. The flesh over his cheekbones was tight and pale and his hands weren't completely steady, but she resisted the urge to coddle him and simply waited.

The frown remained as he began. "I walked with a god called Damasen, in an amazing country; Hesperia, you called it. Athene's paradise."

Shock ran through Themiste. She straightened. "Damasen? Aridela's father?"

"Yes." He fell into thoughtful silence. Themiste, needing to absorb this amazing information, picked up her spinning and busied her hands, saying only, "That is very peculiar."

"How do you tell the months?" he asked suddenly.

Thinking a simple answer would suffice, Themiste said, "Long ago, our stargazers mapped the heavens and calculated the passage of time into the calendar we use today."

He shook his head. "I want to know more. Describe the process you use, how it is different from Mycenae's."

"We follow the moon, my lord, as it disappears then grows to round and fertile fullness. When this cycle repeats thirteen times, one of our years has passed. Each of our months lasts twenty-eight days, a consecrated number matching the cycles of women. As you know, our year begins at the rise of the star Iakchos. Kaphtor's new consort must triumph against the old bull-king on the day before, the one day that lies out of time, between the old year and the new. This day is our holiest. It forms the passage into paradise for the dead consort and crowns the living man."

Chrysaleon's intent scrutiny caused a spark of uneasiness to creep up Themiste's spine. It felt as though he was trying to see inside her. Sensing some secret purpose, she sought to distract him. "In our most ancient times," she said, putting on a disarming smile, "sacred kings gave their lives twice a year, in winter, at the solstice, and at the height of summer. That one was most important, for the land was thirstiest in the dry heat, and we suffered much destructive pestilence. Long ago, we started our new year in winter; the summer solstice was known as the seventh moon. Some old people still calculate time this way, so you might sometimes hear our first month also called the seventh."

"Why did you change?"

"History tells of a queen who wanted more time with a consort she loved. She changed the custom." Only after she spoke the words did Themiste realize that perhaps she shouldn't have. She quickly added, "It was only accepted because we had left the homeland by then and settled on Kaphtor, which doesn't have the same destructive heat. The twice-yearly sacrifice was no longer needed."

For a while he was quiet, but then asked the question she had hoped to avoid. "And a great year?"

She wrapped several strands of wool around her spindle as she tried to form the right words. She didn't want to rouse his suspicions, but the calculation of the eight-year cycle was a secret, spoken of only within the mysteries. "It is a time of one hundred of the moon's rotations," she said. "Where have you heard of this?"

For a long while he didn't answer. At last he said, "Damasen named me the great-year-king."

The spindle fell from Themiste's numbed fingers. She rose from the stool, dropping her distaff as well. Her heart hammered as though he'd laid the point of a knife against her throat. "Are you lying to me?"

"No. I don't know what it means." He watched her, hoping, maybe, that she would explain. But with difficulty, Themiste backed away without betraying herself further. She bent to retrieve her tools, hiding her face and keeping her hands busy so he wouldn't see their trembling.

His frown returned but instead of pressing for an answer, he asked, "Can you bring one of my men to me here?"

Themiste called for one of his surviving Mycenaean guard and left them alone to talk.

Her thoughts spun like a whirlpool. Had Aridela's dead father gifted Chrysaleon of Mycenae with such a holy title? How could he have heard of it otherwise? She could think of no way. He must be telling the truth.

She sat down with her pens, ink, and papyrus, but didn't know what to write, and thoughtlessly sharpened her pen until she ruined it. The Oracle Logs spoke of the great-year-king—the ancient tongue called him the thinara king. Several of the prophecies claimed he would bring unimaginable change, not only to Kaphtor, but to the entire world, change that would affect future generations for more years than could be calculated.

Yet another prophecy coming to life in her time.

She readied a new pen and forced herself to record everything he had said, knowing there might come a day when she would need to remember their conversation exactly.

A messenger came for her later, saying the Zagreus would like to see her again. She composed her features into a pleasant smile, hoping it would disguise her unease.

He was still sitting up, but he looked exhausted.

"You should rest, my lord," she said. She remained standing some distance from his pallet.

"I wanted to tell you I am sending two of my men to Mycenae to ask my father for help. They'll join Harpalycus's soldiers and find a way onto a ship bound for the mainland." His eyes darkened. "Harpalycus claims to have poisoned my father, but we must try. I wish I could send Menoetius, but…has no one heard from him?"

She shook her head. "No, I'm sorry we have not, my lord."

"He must be dead," he said after a brief silence. "There's no help for it then."

She noticed him fingering a band of some kind on his wrist.

"What is that?" she asked. Strange that she hadn't noticed it before.

He lifted his arm. "It was there when I woke. I don't remember it. I don't know how it got there."

He plucked at it. It was no armband but a twine of silver, and as it unwound, a charm was revealed.

"Why, that is Aridela's necklace! Her father gave it to Queen Helice when Aridela was a baby. How do you come to have it?"

He held it up, staring at the crescent moons surrounding a lapis bead. "When I walked in the orchards of Hesperia, a partridge brought this necklace to Damasen and he gave it to me. He told me I must return it to Aridela. You say what I lived was no more than vision or dream, and didn't happen except in my mind. If that is so, how did this necklace come to be here, with me?"

There must be another reason. Perhaps Aridela had given it to him, and in his suffering he'd forgotten. But Themiste shrugged, unwilling to squelch his conviction. "There is always magic, my lord," she said, hoping to soothe him. "It weaves through our lives, guiding us onto paths we might never take otherwise."

He regarded her, his expression half-startled, but soon smiled, and nodded as though satisfied.

ARIDELA TRACKED THE SLIVER OF DAYLIGHT, SOMETIMES GOLDEN, sometimes grey, that crept down her cell wall each morning. She watched it twenty times after Lycus's failed rescue attempt. During those twenty days, Harpalycus had her brought to his bedchamber every evening and returned to her cell when he grew bored.

The band of light on the wall grew dimmer, greyer, as the days marched on towards winter. Harpalycus finally ordered that she be given a blanket as the cell turned frigid.

Day by day, her fear of him waned until one afternoon, when he gave her his tiresome leering grin, she felt nothing past old, stale hatred. She was always sore and bruised, often bleeding from cuffs she received, mostly from the eunuch. But as time passed, the blows seemed less intense, as though her skin had constructed a shell that allowed her to ignore them. Pain no longer frightened her. Harpalycus no longer frightened her. Hunger, too, ceased to torment her. She often saw a white boat in her mind's eye, sharply curved at stern and prow and surrounded by agitated water. The bust of Athene was carved into the prow—she was easy to recognize, and a young, unscarred Menoetius stood on the deck holding out his hand. Without any explanation, she understood that Menoetius, the boat, and Athene were offering her something. A release? If she accepted his outstretched hand, would all of this end?

But then she would wake, and know it as imagination or a dream. She could not climb onto the boat and sail away, and she wasn't sure she wanted to.

One fear did continue, resonating through every heartbeat. Day by day it worsened, perhaps because she had nothing to do while Harpalycus was occupied elsewhere but dwell on it.

Lying on the matted straw in her cold, dusky cell, Aridela imagined all she didn't know. What horrors were being inflicted upon the people and cities of Kaphtor? Within her soul lay unquestioning surety that Harpalycus enjoyed continued success solely because she was his prisoner. Her people were waiting for her to escape and join them. Until she did, there would be no recovery, no triumph, no return to grace and plenty. Like children, they wanted their mother to lead them. Through every weary muscle and shallow breath, through waking obsession and sleeping nightmares, Aridela knew she was the leavening of Kaphtor. She was the alchemist. She would cause the people to rise up in an unstoppable wave of rage. She alone could conjure victory.

Her continuing fear sprang from the possibility that she would never escape. She might die the prisoner of Harpalycus; she might grow so dulled and bitter that she would succumb to the temptation to sail away on that magical boat, especially if a child took root inside her.

She called herself a weakling, a coward, a fool. Every death, known and unknown, weighted her soul. She had allowed this to happen, by not watching Lycus more carefully. By thinking only of Chrysaleon. By occupying her days with decorations and parades when she should have been strengthening the outposts and coastal lookouts.

Her wrists were raw and bloody because she couldn't make herself stop testing the strength of the leather.

One morning, as she stared at the crescent of daylight work its way along the wall, she felt something on her forearm.

The snail's black shell spiraled into a perfect point. A glistening track of mucus dried on her flesh as it traversed the expanse of her arm toward her wrist.

Pausing at the leather strap, the tiny creature's translucent tentacles rocked back and forth. Though Aridela discerned no eyes or mouth, it seemed to rear up as though examining this barrier.

"Chew through it," Aridela encouraged softly, for the eunuch was snoring on the other side of the cell and it angered him to be awakened. "I must get free. The people need me. Can you help?"

The snail inched onto the strap. It stopped. Its shorter set of tentacles extended, gingerly exploring the leather.

"I must kill the eunuch while he sleeps. Otherwise he'll be too strong for me," she whispered. "Then I can escape. I'll slip through the villa like a shadow. Like you do, unnoticed."

A thought crept through her mind that a snail could never chew through anything like this tough leather. Or if it could, it would take years.

"Forgive me," she said. "It's unkind of me to belittle your abilities. I have faith, I vow it."

Another thought, passing beneath her fascination with this minuscule creature, suggested the elixir, the pith of Princess Aridela, was disintegrating into madness.

"I am of divine Athene. My course is set like the stars in the heavens. For as long as I am separated from my people, everything will wither—the land, the crops, our souls. Athene has turned her back on us. She will only return when I am free and fighting in her name. I am not mad. I'm not."

Yet her voice sounded unfamiliar, as though someone she'd never met used her mouth. Poisonous fear consumed another chunk of dwindling hope.

The snail's eye tentacles swiveled toward her face and waved as though in greeting.

She gave it a careful smile. "You want to know my plan? After I sneak past the guards, I'll go to someone in the village, a peasant or farmer. Someone who has suffered at the hands of the invaders. My people will hide me in some cranny until I find Chrysaleon and Themiste. Together we will make our way across the mountains to Knossos."

Knossos was the heart of her success. Aridela's imaginings always led to Knossos. There, she would gather her surviving warriors. She would find those of the royal court who had gone into hiding. There must be some. They could not all have been killed.

"First I will find Chrysaleon and Themiste."

But that annoying murmur spoke again. *Your plan is flawed. You don't know where Chrysaleon and Themiste are. It could take days upon days to discover. They could even be dead. If you escape, you won't have time to search for them. If you take the time, Harpalycus will find you and whoever helps you will be tortured and killed.*

"Are you questioning your queen?" she asked the snail. "Trust me. Someone will know where they are. Someone will know—"

"Be quiet, ugly shrew!" She'd forgotten the eunuch. Her musings and plots had awakened him. He struck her hard above the ear, but she felt only a dull throb and a ticklish trickle of blood in her hair.

When she looked back at her wrist, the snail was gone. It must have been knocked off when she tried to block the eunuch's blow. Though she searched frantically through the straw, she never found it.

She wept for three days over the loss of her friend.

Faint scuffling woke Aridela from fitful sleep. Unable to see anything in the blackness of night, she gradually picked out another sound from the first. It was rather sickening, as though someone fought to breathe through lungs filled with fluid. Perhaps the eunuch had fallen ill.

She felt hands upon her and stiffened. The eunuch had no interest in her. Harpalycus must have come to the cell in one of his drunken midnight fantasies. It had happened before.

But these hands tucked the blanket close and picked her up, cradling her like a child.

"What—" she began.

"Quiet." The command didn't come from Harpalycus. At least, she didn't think it did. But the voice was a man's.

"The guard?" someone else, a woman, asked.

"I cut his throat."

Dreaminess showered through the purple black, filling her mind with sparkles. She remembered this feeling from when she was small, when her mother enchanted her with stories, like the romance between Athene and the seal-man. She thought she saw a hint of milky paleness. It might be moonlight. Everyone knew the moon brought divinatory dreams. Lady Athene must be sending her one.

There came an interlude of movement and vertigo as whoever carried her left the cell. Her feet, protruding from the other end of the blanket, brushed now and then against cold stone walls. She made no protests, asked no questions. No one should question a dream from the Goddess.

Athene will show me what I need to see.

The sense of closed-in spaces evaporated. Icy breezes blew over her face. She heard wind hissing and soughing. Athene had taken her outside.

The person who cradled her made no sound as he walked. She felt like a cloud was carrying her. She couldn't hear breathing. He seemed to not find her much of a burden. Maybe it was one of Athene's holy serving-men.

He walked for so long she dozed and lost track of how much time passed before she heard the woman say, "We've gone far enough. Put her down here and rest."

Wind sighed through tall cypresses. She saw the black outline of their tightly packed branches against a starlit sky. It had been so long since she'd heard such a sound, or breathed anything other than the air emanating from stale, moldy straw. She inhaled, shivering, caring about nothing for one glorious instant but that fresh, free scent.

Water trickled over her lips, shocking her into wakefulness. She opened her mouth and sucked at it, trying to swallow as much as she could before it vanished.

Someone put an arm around her shoulders, supporting her while she drank. The blanket loosened and fell around her waist.

She stared at her wrists, at the raw raised welts. The leather straps were gone. Harpalycus's face leaped into her mind. After Lycus's attempt at rescue, he'd been angry...so angry. She couldn't think about what he'd done—

"Aridela," the woman said.

She turned toward the voice. The night was deep, but she saw and recognized the creamy whiteness of hair, and clutched at it. "Selene?"

"Yes. I am here."

Aridela burst into uncontrolled weeping as realization washed over her. This was no dream.

Selene pressed Aridela's face against her throat and held her tightly until the storm subsided.

"Where are we?" Aridela wiped at her eyes. "Where is Harpalycus?" She didn't know if it was the night wind or the hated name that lifted a fresh wash of goose bumps on her arms.

"He will never touch you again." Selene dried Aridela's face with a corner of the blanket. "I swear it."

"He's dead? You killed him?" Hope rose then crashed as Selene shook her head.

Wind caught at Selene's hair, tossing it about her head. She lifted her gaze from Aridela and beckoned to someone.

Another figure loomed above her then dropped to one knee. Even in the dark, she recognized him by the shadows around his form and face. "Menoetius." Aridela seized his arm. "You're alive. What of Chrysaleon?"

He didn't take her hand or smile. Agonizing conviction cascaded over her. It was her fault he and his blood brother had remained on Kaphtor—her interference that made Chrysaleon compete in the Games. Now Menoetius would tell her Chrysaleon was dead, and she couldn't bear to hear those words.

It wasn't he, but Selene who answered. "We know nothing of

Chrysaleon, other than Harpalycus had him taken to Labyrinthos. Themiste, too, was moved there. I have heard she escaped. I don't know if it's true, but I hope it is. You must go too, Aridela, to a hiding place, a cave in these mountains Menoetius and I found. We have stocked it with food and supplies. I will remain and do what I can. I'll try to find out if Themiste still lives. Menoetius will go with you. When it's safe, I will come for you."

Aridela stared at Menoetius. He returned her stare, the slight frown he always wore accented by night shadows, his eyes impenetrable black smudges. She shivered. "I've grown weary of being in the hands of foreigners," she said with a hint of her old swagger. "Take me with you, Selene. I won't hide like a coward while my people are slaughtered. You and I, together, will gather an army and defeat Harpalycus."

"Aridela, we can't argue about this now." Selene rose to her feet. "We killed two guards, and one of our own died to free you." She paced, clenching and unclenching her hands. "Harpalycus probably knows by now you're gone. He'll scour the coast and the mountains. Can you imagine what he will do to anyone he suspects of harboring you? If you won't go, many will die, many who must live to fight." She rubbed her eyes, and it seemed her fingers were shaking.

"For-forgive me," Aridela said. "I'll do whatever you say." She slipped the queen's seal ring off her left middle finger and pressed it into Selene's palm. "Keep this safe for my return."

Selene pulled Aridela up and embraced her. "May the Lady make it soon."

6

Moon of Flying Swans

AFTER ONLY TWO NIGHTS, MENOETIUS ENTERED THE CAVE WITH THE announcement, "I've found a better place."

Since he hadn't yet had time to acquire anything to cover her feet, he carried her on his back for the better part of the morning to his new hiding spot, so deep within this white, lifeless mountain range Aridela lost any sense of which direction the village of Natho lay.

The cave had two entrances, one at ground level, a low cleft disguised by the gnarled roots of a group of ancient cypress trees, and another on the summit of the knoll above, tucked within a tumble of rocks. Both led to a dank, frozen cavern spotted with animal droppings. Aridela was dismayed, both by the smell and the cramped quarters, which didn't even allow one to stand upright. Before she could protest, Menoetius led her to the back and a low dark hole, one they had to squeeze through on their stomachs. Only the dimmest glimmer of light followed them.

The second chamber felt deeper and bigger than the last, dryer and warmer. She inhaled, grateful for space enough to stand. Yet they still hadn't reached their final destination. Menoetius drew her to another orifice, at cross corners from the first and angling steeply downhill. It too had to be maneuvered, this time on hands and knees.

With a striker and flint, Menoetius lit a torch he'd left behind on his initial exploration.

Light reflected in dazzling rainbows off embedded crystals of selenite and quartz, shooting out an arc of ever-changing prisms as Menoetius lifted the torch.

This chamber had plenty of room to stand up straight—even to walk around. There were no animal droppings and nearly none of the chill in the two previous caverns.

Moreover, it was beautiful. Icicles of stalactites hung like decorative columns from a vaulted ceiling, some stretching clear to the floor. Crystals formed natural facets more intricate and perfect than any gem cutter's work. In comparison to the initial cave, which had been adequate, this seemed an exotic palace, eliciting a spontaneous laugh from Aridela and a rare grin from the man who had found it.

She breathed in the smell of earth, stone, minerals, and damp—the unique scent of a deep, undisturbed cave.

Menoetius left her there with the torch while he fetched their supplies and erased his footprints from the snow.

When he returned, Aridela set up house, using nooks and shelves in the cave walls for storage. As she put things away, she took inventory. There was a good amount of bread, nuts, raisins, dried figs and dates, plus flint and animal furs, along with arrows, bows, two spears, numerous knives, even a woodcutter's saw.

Another detail she couldn't help but notice was her protector's unusual relaxed confidence. He seemed more at ease than ever he had at the palace of Labyrinthos.

Still, even though the cavern was beautiful and comfortable, she chafed at the confinement. Menoetius, looking shamefaced, promised he would get her warm clothing and boots as soon as he could. Until then, she was forced to remain inside the chamber. To relieve herself, she had no choice but to borrow his boots and jerkin when he was there, or use a clay pot when he wasn't.

He built an ingenious charcoal pit that warmed the chamber and produced virtually no smoke. Next, with her help, he constructed a sleeping pallet padded with animal skins and raised off the floor on squat wood legs. She asked if they would make one for him, but he shrugged and said he preferred to sleep on the cave floor. He did, wrapped in that luxurious white fur cloak with the symmetrical black stripes he'd brought from Mycenae.

Through all of this, he managed to remain as aloof as ever. It made her ill at ease and tongue-tied. He seemed to share her reticence, so there was almost no conversation between them. He never touched her except by accident; whenever that happened he would start away, which caused many unhappy conjectures on her part. He hardly ever looked her in the eyes for more than an instant.

She studied him covertly one night as he stared at the embers in the fire pit. His expression was unguarded, as though he'd forgotten she was there. Worry lived in that frown, which she understood. But the way he drummed his fingers against one knee without appearing to know he was doing it, the way his jaw clenched, unclenched, and clenched again, suggested more.

Unkind intuition left her shrinking, breaking into a sweat as her mind recreated one of Harpalycus's more brutal rapes. He had gripped her chin and told her she had better show her fertility soon, before he tired of her.

Menoetius must feel trapped, but was caught up in his promise to Selene. Aridela was a nuisance, the 'whore,' ruined first by his prince then finished off by Harpalycus. He probably wondered, as she did, how soon her belly would swell.

She knew the beliefs of his people. Harpalycus had made it so clear, that long gone day in the palace garden at Labyrinthos, and many times since.

What had he said? *Duplicity poisons every woman's heart. All of Argolis knows this.*

Perhaps because of their unease with each other, they fell into a routine that allowed an excess of solitude. In the mornings, after consuming a fig or two, Menoetius would leave the cave to hunt. He hunted every day, but the Moon of Flying Swans was a cold, barren month even in favorable years. Here in these remote mountains, the weather never improved. Many days Aridela could hardly stand upright against the raging wind. The air was infused with a bitter, humid cold that burned her lungs. Snow lay as deep in places as her hips. Most of the wildlife had vanished, either hunted or gone to the lower foothills. Menoetius often returned at twilight without a single kill. They carefully rationed their food, which caused Aridela no hardship; she had lost her appetite while a prisoner of Harpalycus, and ate very little.

Seven days passed in this manner. Aridela spent the days alone, evenings and nights with her inarticulate guardian.

THE FIRST NIGHTMARE DESCENDED DEEP IN THE ABYSS OF THE SEVENTH night after they came to their cavern of icicles.

Comfortable on her soft pallet, mesmerized by the radiantly shifting glow of the embers in the fire pit, Aridela was slowly lulled to sleep. Her last sense was one of pure, selfish joy to be free of Harpalycus. She could close her eyes without fear, her body left in peace.

The dream took her back to the smothering cell. The eunuch was standing over her, holding the bowl of water and cloths that meant he was going to prepare her for her daily ordeal with Harpalycus. At first, these ministrations had sparked a firestorm of threats and protests, but by the time she was rescued, she no longer offered any reaction at all.

She heard Harpalycus's echoing drunken laughter. *I know you have quickened by now*, he said. *But I will kill it. You won't foist another man's get on me.*

Her stomach was swollen, heavy with her unborn child. Now she was in the bullring at Knossos; Harpalycus stood beside her, holding her hand high. A warrior, sword at ready, pressed close, hot sunlight licking the sharp edge of his blade.

Five other women were interspersed along the width of the ring, each under guard. Three slumped or wept quietly. Two stared, their faces naked with terror. All were pregnant. Six sets of stakes and ropes protruded from the sand.

Chrysaleon sat in the queen's royal seat, holding the crescent-topped staff. His gaze was expressionless.

Harpalycus sneered at his mainland rival and raised Aridela's arm higher, pulling her up on her toes.

An audience crowded the stands. There wasn't a child or female anywhere. Eerily silent, these men, too, stared at the women.

Soldiers poured into the ring from the entrances at either end. As they neared, Harpalycus released Aridela. Fear sent her racing with the other women toward the shadows at the far arch, but the soldiers quickly caught them. To a backdrop of sudden deafening cheers, the women were dragged to the stakes. Aridela struggled. She screamed. She even bit one man on the forearm. But no one came forth to help them. She was forced onto her back, her wrists and ankles roped.

Young males entered the bullring, dressed in loincloths and armed with knives. They spread out, one to each woman.

Now Aridela, in the way of dreams, knew what was going to happen. In an initiation meant to turn these boys into men, they would cut the babies from the wombs of the women. Male babies would elicit a celebration. Females would be thrown to the dogs.

Aridela and the other women would be left to bleed to death, spread-eagled on the sand beneath the burning sun.

She woke just as the first male, his eyes as hard and hungry as a jackal's, knelt beside her and lifted his knife.

Sitting straight up on the pallet, Aridela stared into the cave's depths. Ever-undulating shadows grew tall then shrank. Mouths opened, revealing teeth of crystal. Drenched in sweat, she gasped, long, painful breaths, pressing her hands against her throat.

Menoetius was coming around the fire pit. For one stifled instant she thought him the boy, coming to slice her open. She heard a blood-curdling scream and didn't at first realize it came from her own mouth. She stared into the corners, searching for the other women.

Shadows webbed his face as he knelt. She screamed again and fought as he tried to clasp her hands. She scrambled off the pallet and backed away.

"Aridela," he said. As he turned, the embers in the fire pit illuminated his face, sending the shadows into retreat. She knew him then, but still she burrowed into her dream to make certain he hadn't been there, hadn't held one of those knives. Only when she had recalled every face did she slump to the floor, hug her knees, and press her face against them.

Menoetius came to her and knelt again beside her. He didn't touch her. He said nothing as her heaving gasps and shuddering slowly diminished.

When she rose, she would not look at him. She ripped off the flounced skirts Harpalycus had forced her to wear and threw them on the embers. The tight linen bodice followed. She watched as the material blackened and crumpled.

"I won't wear this filth," she said. "I would rather be naked."

Menoetius fetched his cloak and placed it over her shoulders, keeping his gaze fixed on the clasp at the neck.

She tensed and shrank away, even as she remembered the night, so long ago, that she had envisioned wrapping herself in this sumptuous fur.

His hands dropped to his sides and he spoke carefully. "A merchant's concubine gave this to me. She called the beast it was taken from a 'tiger,' and claimed I could never live long enough to cross the distance between its homeland and Mycenae."

Clutching it around her, she returned to the pallet and lay on her side, curling her knees to her breasts, covering her head with the fur.

She didn't move until after she heard Menoetius leave the cavern in the morning.

Why do you linger here? You sit by this fire, warm and safe, while I die. Where is the woman who danced with a wild bull? Are you a coward now?

Aridela woke to the echo of Chrysaleon's voice. Goose bumps raced across her skin in a parody of chill, though she was covered in sweat. In the dream, he'd been thin, pale. Close to death.

Her head throbbed. Every bone felt the long expanse of time in which she hadn't truly slept. Menoetius squatted on the other side of the fire pit, watching her. Behind him, the shadows laughed and made obscene gestures toward the back of his head. He was oblivious. He couldn't see they were alive, malevolent, that they were just waiting to creep out and eat her.

She dropped her gaze.

"You've been dreaming," he said.

"We must leave this place. Avenge the deaths of those we love. I—I feel the Lady's anger at our inaction."

She said nothing of the white-hot terror that Harpalycus's offspring was growing inside her. Or could it be Chrysaleon's?

The blood of her *kaliara* hadn't come in a long time. She couldn't remember how long.

After a lengthy pause, he said, "Not yet."

"Have you had no word from Selene? Why hasn't she come for us? I want to go home, to fight Harpalycus, to find my consort."

A scowl sliced a sharp dent between his brows. "Selene no longer knows where we are. Harpalycus has offered cartloads of gold to anyone who returns you to him. Many search for you."

"You think Selene would betray us?" The possibility was so absurd she didn't wait for a reply. "I must know if Chrysaleon is alive—and Themiste. My life is slipping away and my dreams accuse me of cowardice while the people suffer and Harpalycus's hold grows stronger. I cannot bear it."

He said nothing, only sighed and pushed back his hair.

"We have to make our way to Labyrinthos before any more time passes. Do you not care about your blood brother?"

Menoetius rose and paced from one side of the cave to the other. "I didn't want to tell you. Chrysaleon is dead."

Shock jolted through her like a thunderbolt, though she'd been half-expecting this news. She'd thought it herself a hundred times. In a desperate attempt to ward off annihilating grief, she held onto logic. "Where did you hear this?"

"From a man in Araden. He heard it from others who claim to have mingled with the crowd when Harpalycus buried Chrysaleon's head under the north gate at Labyrinthos."

Aridela's eyes squeezed closed. Grief swelled from her stomach like vomit, choking her. She sensed the shadows crawl out of the corners and stretch toward her, and saw again the boat that offered escape. "Harpalycus uses Chrysaleon's courage to safeguard his own unworthy life. I curse him. I *curse* him. It might not be true. It's not true. It's not. I *curse* him."

"I grieve with you, Aridela. But those who watched said the warrior's hair was long and yellow, like a lion's." He bit the corner of his lip where the scar puckered it. "We should leave Crete. There is no safe place on this island for you anymore."

She grasped anger, feeling in its fire the dampening of pain, the slithering retreat of the shadows, and flung her rage like a spear at the person who had brought her such misery. Rising onto her knees, she shouted, "So that is your plan. You want me as your prisoner. Just like Harpalycus. Do you think to ransom me to him? You won't frighten me. You could never match what has already been done!"

"Aridela." He approached the pallet and seized her hands. "I only want you to regain your strength. Do you think I don't share your sorrow? But one day, because you are…wondrous Aridela…you will desire life again, peace, happiness. You're wounded, but you will heal. I know it. I will keep you safe until that day. I plan for that day."

"I…." Something made her pause. His whole face lay open in a way she had never before seen, not even when he was young and beautiful, and called himself Carmanor.

She'd been trained to read what people betrayed in their movements and expressions. Many had praised her abilities, including Helice.

But she must have lost the talent, for what she saw, in his eyes, the lift of his brows forming creases across his forehead, and that slight hesitation before he'd uttered *wondrous*—all this proclaimed something that couldn't be.

For months, his every glance had borne nothing beyond icy chill or blank reserve. She'd long ago concluded that her failure to recognize him when he returned with Chrysaleon had spoiled whatever tender feelings might linger from the past. No doubt she had bruised his pride by giving herself to his blood brother, though just six years ago it was Carmanor she had loved, Carmanor she had idealized with all the romantic fervor a ten-year-old girl could muster. Unwitting though it was, she had intensified the sense of ugliness his scars forced him to endure.

No. Menoetius couldn't care about her that way.

"Your life is in danger," he said, breaking into her astounded thoughts. He seemed to recover his usual reserve as he continued. "I haven't told Selene where we are because if Harpalycus captures her, he will torture her to find out what he wants. No one can know where you are, not because I distrust the people of Kaphtor, but because I know Harpalycus."

Aridela couldn't argue with his reason. She needed to think about what she had seen, what she had heard. Already she was half-convinced she'd imagined it, for his face now held no hint of anything but impatience.

"It was unfair to accuse you." She twisted her hands free. "I didn't mean what I said."

She ate a morsel of the bread he offered and accepted a sip of water.

"This is my fault," he said. "I will go to Araden tomorrow and find you clothing. When you have something to wear, you can help me hunt. You've been confined in here too long, without anything to do."

She gave a lethargic nod.

MENOETIUS WAS ALREADY GONE WHEN ARIDELA WOKE. SHE DRANK A little water but couldn't eat.

After stirring the fire, she examined the boots Menoetius was fashioning for her. They were like nothing she had ever seen, for nothing like this had ever before been needed on Kaphtor. He'd cut them high, to the knees, and insulated them with fox fur, inside and out. She couldn't imagine any chill or moisture cunning enough to penetrate them. Picking up the bone needle and tough intestinal cord, she attempted to finish the work but soon gave up, disgusted with her uneven stitches and leery of ruining his handiwork. She couldn't weave, much less sew. Working a loom had always been unbearably tedious, and she had never managed to produce anything worthy of hanging on a wall.

She returned to the pallet, pondering the riddle of Menoetius as she watched the flicker of embers in the fire pit.

The first thing that came to mind was the agonizing day he had sailed away from Kaphtor. Because she had fallen in love as only a ten-year-old female could, his absence left her inconsolable. It was so easy to fall in love with him, for Carmanor was flawless, his skin smooth, his blue eyes as reflective as these cave crystals, his nature affectionate and earnest, his devotion real. She remembered weeping that day until nightfall, and waking from sleep only to weep again. Her head throbbed and her eyes were swollen for many days. Helice came to her chamber with bowls of bread soaked in honey, hoping to renew her child's interest in eating.

In time, she had recovered. There came a day, though she couldn't remember it now, when she didn't think of him. His image grew vague and new adventures took his place. She had been, after all, ten years old.

He had returned, hidden inside this bearded, forbidding stranger with the disfiguring scars, his hair cropped and threaded with grey, lines etched around his mouth and at the corners of his eyes. Nothing remained of the god-like youth of her memories, not even his name. Carmanor eluded capture like one of these insidious shadows.

How had Selene recognized him so quickly? But that wasn't fair. Selene knew him because she hadn't forgotten. Because he had been important to her, and maybe because she had been older at the time.

Because they were lovers.

The day Chrysaleon descended into the labyrinth to fight Lycus, Selene had brought Menoetius to the queen's pavilion. *You goose,* she'd said. *You don't recognize the boy who saved your life?*

She protested. *I would know Carmanor in the blackest cave. I would know him if my eyes were put out.*

Apparently not, Selene replied.

She remembered staring into that scarred face, searching for a sign, some detail, hoping to prove Selene wrong.

But the opposite had happened. Horrified with embarrassment and regret, she embraced him, and in some terrible gift of moera from

Athene, she felt, for one awful instant, the claws of the lioness sink into her own flesh as they must have done into his.

Uncontrollable tears had flooded from her eyes, which even now made her cringe. He'd removed her arms from around his neck. Her pity must have hurt more than anything else she'd done or failed to do.

Waves of self-blame washed over her as she lay on the pallet in the cave. After that day in the pavilion, she hadn't improved things with her lover's blood brother. No doubt she'd made her revulsion clear in countless small ways.

Menoetius knew Aridela had encouraged his prince to compete in the Games. If Chrysaleon hadn't become bull-king, the two men would have returned to Mycenae. Chrysaleon might still be alive. Menoetius must blame her for that as well as everything else.

You asked him to stay and die in your name. Because of you, because of you….

He is dead because of you.

7

Moon of Flying Swans

Be careful, isoke. Helice leveled Aridela with her sternest gaze. *When Iakchos rises, Chrysaleon's truth will emerge.*

He will honor his vows, Aridela said. *You will see.*

Helice's smile was resigned. *Chrysaleon's child would remind you of him. His child would return him to you in some ways. It might even rekindle life in your heart.*

Or Harpalycus could be the father.

Which man's child sprouts in your womb?

Her mother rose from the lustral basin where her life had bled away. She stared at Aridela, her face and lips white, the skin around her eyes sagging. It was Helice, but she spoke with Chrysaleon's voice.

Why does this lowly bastard dictate to the queen of Kaphtor? You promised you would win back our country, yet you hide in caves. You shame me. You shame the Lady.

Aridela woke to discover she was crouched beside the fire pit, smashing one stone against another. She had no memory of rising from her bed. Her forearm ached as though she'd been striking stones for some time. While she was asleep, the cave shadows had crawled so close they were licking at her feet.

She dropped the rock and covered her face.

"My mother. Iphiboë. Isandros. Halia. Laodámeia. The priestesses. All dead. Perhaps Neoma, too, by now. I don't know about her. I don't know."

171

How many others had perished, slaughtered during Harpalycus's invasion? Was Themiste still a prisoner? Had she managed to escape, or was she dead?

She would not believe the gossips. Chrysaleon was alive.

Why wouldn't she bleed? Then she would know her womb wasn't growing the offspring of a traitor, a murderer. She stuck her fingers inside, tearing, gouging, trying to cause a rupture, reaching towards the baby in hopes of ripping it out.

Yet if she succeeded, it would also destroy any chance of bearing a child to Chrysaleon.

Harpalycus had bragged often enough that he left the Cretan dead to rot where they fell, without a proper burial.

Her anguish was so terrible she thought of walking to the back of the cave and letting the shadows swallow her, but the angry frown on her mother's face sent her instead to the pallet, where she sat cross-legged and watched the shadows stretch, slink closer, then retreat.

"Harpalycus steals Kaphtor's riches, defiles our women, murders and enslaves my people. How can Athene tolerate such crimes? Why does she not avenge us?"

They answered in their usual hiss. *She will do nothing until you rise out of the earth and fight for her.*

The embers in the fire pit subsided without any attention. Near darkness had engulfed the chamber by the time she heard a rustling echo against the walls in the adjoining cavern. Menoetius had returned.

He straightened as he entered. "It's snowing," he said, dropping his heavy quilted jerkin to the rock floor. Rapidly melting snow speckled his hair. He squatted near the fire pit and stirred the embers, bringing them back to life. "I've brought you a boy's jerkin and woolen leggings."

From the edge of her vision, she saw him glance at her. She hardly heard what he was saying. Earlier, as the embers dimmed, the shadows had crawled over her flesh, and she had breathed them in. Now they were inside her, forming a plank over the water to the boat.

She was so tired. It would take more strength than she had to reply.

"Look." From his hunter's satchel he pulled out the limp, white-furred body of a rabbit. "They were by the stream—three of them. Ice has melted, and water flows freely in the center."

She turned her head like an old, sick woman, and stared without interest at the rabbit then at the man who had caught it.

Something on his face pricked her attention. He was pleased with this kill, and hoped she would be pleased, too.

Like a lover, he offers you his gold and jewels.

What an odd idea. Probably a remnant from long ago when Menoetius called himself Carmanor. The ill-humored warrior named 'Menoetius' was as far from a lover as a man could be.

"Do you think it an omen?" he asked.

"In what way?" She hardly recognized her own voice.

"The villagers said snow fell earlier than it ever has before. They say it is deeper in the mountains than even old women can remember, and it has driven away the game. They blame the Destruction. They say that since that night, Athene has placed her hand between the sun and us and cut off its warmth. But rabbits wouldn't be here unless there was food. See? Look at its belly. It has found enough."

Any caution Aridela might feel was buried beneath abrupt flaming fury. "Why hasn't Selene come for us? I want to go home, to fight Harpalycus, to find my consort. I want to see for myself if he is alive or dead. Curse you for speaking to me of rabbits. I would rather die than live another day in this cowardly fashion."

His eyelashes lowered. The familiar scowl reappeared and he laid the rabbit at the edge of the fire pit. "I told you Selene doesn't know where we are. Chrysaleon is dead. I would not lie to you."

"We have to go to Labyrinthos." She fought to make herself sound rational and convincing though inside, she heard herself shrieking. "Now, Menoetius. What is worth fighting for, if not love and freedom? Your disloyalty sickens me."

"Do you think Harpalycus has stopped searching for you? No. He seems to care more about finding you than holding Crete, and has stretched his men thin. Yesterday, I watched ten of them not half a day from here. They were using a local man to track us. When no one was looking, he wiped away a footprint I had carelessly left in the snow."

His warning swept past her, unheeded. She knew his reason for speaking them. They would be the basis for his insistence that she remain in this cave another day, another month. An eternity.

"The Erinyes tear the skin from my bones." Her voice sounded like an old woman's. "They care nothing for your fears and hesitation." She scratched at her arms; the scars beneath her nails brought back the pain of the burns. "You take revenge by keeping me from my purpose."

He looked puzzled. "You think I seek revenge…on you?"

"Because I didn't recognize you." She spoke with cold emphasis. "I know you hate me because I remind you of how much you've lost."

Betraying color crept over his face and he broke her gaze. He stared at the floor, hands fisting. It seemed an admission.

"Did Harpalycus command you to imprison me here?" she asked, low but clear. "Out of reach of anyone who would help me? You are his countryman. Has ugliness stretched your hatred so far?"

He lifted his gaze. She saw fury and shame combined. His lips were tight, his jaw clenched.

Her words returned to her mind as though through an underwater tunnel, dark and heavy. Her breath shortened. Her heart skipped and speckles blurred her sight. Who had spoken? She hadn't intended to say such things.

He grabbed his jerkin and shrugged into it. He picked up his bow, quiver, and the hunter's satchel. He crossed to the hole and shoved them through.

"Menoetius," she cried. Uncontrollable shuddering racked her and her stomach cramped. "When you aren't here, the shadows gnaw upon me. Menoetius!" She gagged, unable to vomit because her stomach held nothing but blackness that refused to be evicted. "Soon I will be dead," she whispered.

He didn't turn or pause. He slipped through and was gone.

FOR LONGER THAN YOU CAN IMAGINE...I WILL BE WITH YOU...IN YOU...OF you. Together, we bring forth a new world, and nothing can ever part us.

Strange, to hear the god's words—Chrysaleon's words—when Menoetius filled her thoughts.

Aridela hadn't set out to attack him. In fact, she had never considered the idea that he could be following Harpalycus's orders until the words left her mouth. But now that she'd said them, she couldn't cut them from her mind. They echoed with terrifying possibility.

She must seize the opportunity created by her accusations and make her escape. Shrugging out of the soft tiger skin cloak, she donned the boy's jerkin and leggings. The shadows thickened in her mind, making it difficult to focus, but she saw, again and again, the expression on his face.

Menoetius. Carmanor. She had adored him and hated herself for being too young, beneath the notice of such a strong, virile youth.

The leggings felt odd, scratchy against her skin. She pulled on the boots. The soles were finished, though the outside of one still needed about twenty stitches; a leftover scrap of fur shoved into the split would postpone any problems.

She squeezed through the two clefts and exited the outer cave.

Snow fell in a blinding squall, carried first one direction then another by mercurial winds. Bitter cold stung her face and almost immediately penetrated the jerkin.

Slinging a bow and quiver of arrows over one shoulder, Aridela brushed snow from the trunk of one of the cypresses until she'd cleared a strip all the way around. Barbs of ice lashed her eyes and face as she found what she was looking for, evidence of frozen lichen on what should be the north side. She staggered into the blizzard, hoping she'd successfully determined east, and Knossos.

I do your bidding, Mother. I follow your will. Please, please—

The plea died before it formed. Menoetius would never forgive what she had said. There was no use asking.

Snow fell like a cold white torrent from a darkly overcast sky. All sound was muffled. There was no way to be certain she'd chosen the right direction. If only the sun would come out, just long enough for her to place it.

Menoetius's warning returned. What if this reckless escape sent her straight to Harpalycus's search parties?

Surely they wouldn't be looking for her in such a storm.

Don't you trust me? She fancied a thrum of laughter under Chrysaleon's words. *Don't you know I will protect you?*

She closed her eyes. *Show me the way, my love.*

But there was only the swish of snow eddying in the wind. Only Menoetius's face when she called him ugly.

Then she heard it. The crunch of deliberate steps. She opened her eyes and stared into the face of a large wild goat, its long, arched horns almost invisible under a coating of snow. It stood the length of a half-grown fir tree from her, staring back, perhaps trying to understand the sight of a motionless human transforming into a snow-drenched pillar.

Its meat would provide food for a month. But something stopped her even as her half-frozen fingers felt for the bow. *Athene. Lady of the wild things.*

Losing interest, the ibex turned and lumbered away. Aridela followed, trying to keep a discreet distance.

It came to a steep hill, dotted with mounds of stunted juniper bushes and a few twisted pine trees. The beast climbed effortlessly, crossing beneath a curious rock formation that rose high and curved into an arch, like a doorway. Aridela craned her neck to see the rough crown, half hidden in storm fog. Forced to use her hands as well as her feet, she scrambled then slipped backward, unable to secure footing in the slick snow. Almost immediately, the animal disappeared. "Wait," she cried. "I can't walk as fast as you," but wind and a wall of snow stuffed her words back into her throat.

Eventually she reached the summit. Snow was falling so copiously by now that she couldn't see past the length of her arm. She stumbled along the ridge, calling, "I'm here. Where are you? Come back."

Iphiboë materialized before her, arms extended. "Aridela!"

Shock drew Aridela up short. She tried to blink the snow from her lashes, fighting hope and disbelief. "Iphiboë?"

Before she could begin to accept this miracle, the image disintegrated into the dark, solid form of Menoetius. Snow caked his hair and beard.

He squinted. "What are you doing?" Without waiting for an answer, he picked her up like a twig and flung her over one shoulder. "Two more steps and you would have been over the edge. How much would that help your people, you lying dead at the bottom of this gorge?"

Aridela's will dissolved as suddenly as it had formed. Stricken by futility, the dream-demands silenced, the only thing she felt with any certainty was the howling chill. Melted snow wet her face and mingled with tears as it ran out of her hair.

He struggled down the hill, spouting coarse mainland curses. At the bottom she slid off his shoulder, insisting she would walk on her own. They fought their way to the cave through snow that in places rose to their knees. Wind buffeted them without mercy.

As soon as she was in the cave, he left again without a word. When he returned he was dragging a log, pulling it with the help of thick leather straps. It was so heavy and fat it barely fit through the crawl-space. Breathing heavily, sweating, he still didn't speak as he fetched a wad of leather strapping from his satchel. He bound one end around the log then seized her hands before she understood his intent.

He meant to truss her as Harpalycus had done.

Maddened by scarlet cataracts of rage, Aridela kicked him, sank her teeth into his one of his fingers, and fought to twist free, but she would have been no match for him even when she was strong and healthy. One of his hands was big enough and strong enough to confine both her wrists. His other arm circled her waist, restraining her against his body. She couldn't help but remember the day he had pinned Chrysaleon to the wall outside the villa; Chrysaleon had struggled too, without success.

Exhaustion depleted what little strength she had left and she leaned against him, panting and dizzy, her heart thundering. He dragged her closer to the fire pit where he kept a pile of animal skins. Keeping her wrists secure in his unbreakable grip, he wrapped strips of fur around her hands then covered them with the leather straps, binding them together from wrist to fingertips, which would prevent her from working the strap free of the trunk. When he'd finished, she couldn't move her hands or fingers at all.

"You truly are kin to Harpalycus," she said, dismissing how he inspected his work, making certain her skin wouldn't be chafed or the blood flow hindered.

He made no reply and didn't look at her. The only sign he heard her at all came from the reflexive clenching of his jaw.

"Coward!" she shrieked, her earlier remorse burned away. "Do you know how much I hate you? Keep me tied, because if you turn your back I will kill you. Do you hear me, you spineless traitor? You have no feeling. You are made of stone."

*Stone...stone...stone...*echoed off the stalactites in the depths of the cave.

The shadows leaped from her stomach, engulfing her, thrusting her back in time. She lived again the night when the statue of Velchanos came to life, stepped off his pedestal, and crossed the clearing on Mount Juktas to stand above her.

Stone grated against stone as his head swiveled. The shadows had been there that night, using moonlight to paint beautiful patterns on his face.

My love, he'd whispered, but his mouth didn't move. The words had formed in her head. Sparks of brilliant light played through his marble hair. *Save me, Aridela. Open your heart.*

Calesienda? She had asked through fear and fascination.

He lay upon her, pale stone warming into human flesh, eyes burnishing into a hypnotic combination of blue and silver.

She saw herself say, *Carmanor, why have you come to me through Velchanos?*

As Menoetius bound her to the log, her bewilderment and frustration escaped in a gasping sob.

For longer than you can imagine, I will be with you, in you, of you.

"Selene charged me with your safety." Menoetius's bitter tone scattered the memory like wind through mist. He gave the security of his restraints a final check and leveled a gaze on hers that blazed with fury. "I will do whatever is necessary to keep you alive. Do you understand? I will keep you safe against your own will to die."

8

Moon of Flying Swans

THEMISTE OFFERED CHRYSALEON WHAT SHE HOPED WAS AN ENCOURAGING smile as he entered her private chamber, a small alcove separated from the rest by a curtain made of ibex hide.

He dropped onto a footstool next to her, his expression impatient and restless. Placing her distaff next to the basket of unspun wool and folding her hands on her lap, she prepared for more discomfiting questions.

"Why was Aridela not brought here at once when she was freed from Harpalycus?"

"I wish Selene were here to answer your questions." Themiste gave a helpless shrug. "The messenger she sent had hardly any information. She and Menoetius and a small band succeeded in freeing Aridela. Menoetius took her into the Araden mountains."

"Where they disappeared." Chrysaleon's voice was curt.

"The second messenger said the cave in which they were hiding was abandoned within a matter of days. Selene and others have scoured the mountains but have failed to locate them."

"Why?" Chrysaleon rose and paced, shoving his unruly hair off his forehead in a manner that betrayed his frustration. "Have they been captured? Killed?"

Themiste wondered, not for the first time, whether Menoetius, or as she privately called him—*Menoetius of the few words*—had proved false.

Keeping her tone neutral, she asked, "Could he have given her to Harpalycus for the promised reward?"

Chrysaleon stopped pacing and stared at her. Then he shook his head and snorted. "If they have not been captured or killed, he is protecting her as only he can. Completely."

He dropped back to the footstool. She couldn't help but notice the sallow hue of his skin, how every bone in his face stood out sharply. His shoulders slumped.

"Let me send for wine," Themiste said. "You must eat, my lord, and rest. I promise to tell you as soon as I hear anything more."

This wasn't the complete truth. Selene's first messenger had carried a sealed papyrus that briefly detailed some of what Aridela was rumored to have suffered at Harpalycus's hands. Themiste had burned the missive and kept that information secret.

"No." He stared at the rough rock floor with a heavy sigh. "I must know what happened to her. Would you spare me a few provisions? I will go there myself."

"That is impossible. You're not strong enough. Nor are you familiar with Kaphtor. You'll most certainly be captured. Those mountains are remote; you could get lost. And the weather, my lord. We can only imagine how severe it is there."

"Nevertheless, I will leave before daylight."

She saw his resolve and realized nothing she said would make a difference. "Take one of my men with you."

"Your men are needed here. I am not the weakling you think me, lady."

"I will gather what you need." Themiste felt oddly proud of him. "This is a time for healing, Prince Chrysaleon, and for divine intercession. Some intuition tells me the Lady approves of your decision."

He gave her a tired smile and went off to make preparations.

THEMISTE LEFT THE PROTECTION OF HER STONY CHAMBER, THOUGH THIS caused her personal guard much anxiety. She climbed the hillside above the cave entrance and stood at the highest point where she could view the surrounding landscape. Pink twilight deepened to indigo; the air was still and frosty. It was wonderful to breathe fresh, dry, air.

One of Timandra's oracle log entries came to her.

*For longer than can be dreamed or imagined, mortal lives will hinge
upon the tiniest sliver of chance, of human frailty. The final unfolding
of Earth's destiny remains hidden.*

Was earth's destiny even now being determined, not by those with
wisdom and insight, but by chance and frailty?

So much had happened to thrust the uncommon sphere of Kaphtor
from its delicate balance. The Destruction. Harpalycus and his invasion. The untimely deaths of Helice and Iphiboë. The capture and
torture of Aridela, which, if she still lived, must have changed her in
ways that could never be measured.

Now Chrysaleon, the 'Gold Lion of Mycenae,' had proclaimed
himself the thinara king. The prophecies stated this king would bring
the death of all that went before. He heralded a new world, a new way.
Themiste had studied every mention of the great-year-king, but never
felt she understood the subtleties. Would this 'new way' be terrible or
wondrous? The predictions gave no clear answers.

Timandra had written about the thinara king.

*The child must separate from the intoxication in which she willingly
drowns. If she becomes pure, utterly clear, the thinara king and his
disciples will give her their allegiance. If she does not, every living
thing will languish and the end will come.*

Bleeding profusely, near to death, Aridela had said something
about the thinara king when she was only ten years old. Clutching
Themiste's necklace, she pulled her close and spoke, her voice shaking
with dread. Whatever the child saw, in that fearsome place between
life and oblivion, she was terrified of it.

*Death cannot stop the thinara king. He will follow. He will slay me
until time is worn out.*

What if Chrysaleon was, in truth, the thinara king? What did that
mean for Aridela? She loved him so much. How could he be the thing
she also feared so much?

The confusion of it all sent Themiste's mind down another path, the
one that held Aridela's magical dream on the summit of Mount Juktas.
Velchanos had come to Kaphtor's princess, and he had taken on

Chrysaleon's face. In no way had he frightened her, but he had promised to stay with her, to create a new world at her side.

Themiste placed her hand on the trunk of a cypress tree. This tree, from the look of the aged, gnarled bark, had sprouted in Earth's infancy. Through the intervening uncountable years, it had survived. When the rain of fire and ash, the disappearance of sunlight, and the onslaught of frost descended upon Kaphtor, this tree did not succumb. Although alive, the tree didn't grow straight and tall but twisted close to the ground, branched almost like a shrub. She liked to sit with her back against the trunk, breathing its spicy scent, looking westward towards Knossos.

This tree had observed Aridela, Iphiboë, and Selene on the night of Iphiboë's dedication. It witnessed Iphiboë's untimely fall and the injury of her knee. It listened when Iphiboë begged Aridela to serve as her proxy. It watched the arrival of two foreign warriors, and later, a third.

Themiste fancied she heard the young women's voices, at first excited, then anxious when Iphiboë hurt herself. She imagined Chrysaleon and Menoetius tying their horses then slipping toward the black mouth of the cave, not knowing what they would encounter inside.

The decisions made that night took Kaphtor off its course. More, she realized. Those three women may have unwittingly thrown many other societies into the confluence of Kaphtor's destiny.

None could ever now know what would have unfolded if Chrysaleon had become Iphiboë's lover—if Aridela had remained in her bedchamber as she was ordered.

Chrysaleon, as Velchanos, had promised Aridela a love that would transcend death.

Chrysaleon, the thinara king, would slay her until the end of time.

How could these two images of the Mycenaean prince, one adoring, one terrifying, be reconciled?

For the briefest instant, no more than a flash, Themiste's mind opened. She saw into the future, but it was a jumble of incomprehensible images, of men and women she did not recognize, of hatred and jealousy, a desperate competition for power and love, all snarled to the point where none of it could be deciphered.

"Themiste?"

The unexpected voice emanating from the night made her jump in fright, but she recovered as she rose, keeping one hand on the cypress, and smiled at Chrysaleon as he climbed up to her.

"I am leaving before the sun rises," he said. "I came to say goodbye."

"I feel success is at hand, my lord." Themiste bowed her head. "The omens suggest it. Our spies, too, bring happy news, that Harpalycus is continually drunk and has lost the respect of his men. Apparently he has stretched his forces too thinly. I've been told that Kydonia will soon be ours again. We will pray and make offerings. Perhaps they will help guide you to Aridela. I, too, cannot sleep for worry over her."

Silence stretched. He plucked a lock of hair off her shoulder and ran his fingers underneath, allowing it to slip free. "In my dream your hair was lighter."

As his gaze lifted, all desire to speak evaporated. She felt as though her obsessive efforts to translate the prophecies were as useless as grasping at clouds. She swallowed the sensation of her heart rising into her throat, and tried to steady her breathing.

He bent and kissed her on the mouth, then turned and strode down the hill, sliding a bit on the scree.

What had they shared in his death-dream?

She blinked away tears as his figure disappeared into the gloom.

I pray Mycenae's prince has dreamed the key to Kaphtor's freedom.

9

Moon of Flying Swans

Storm after storm blanketed the Araden mountains in treacherous snowdrifts. Warmth and light abandoned Kaphtor and took with them the spirit of Aridela.

She tried to bolster herself with memories of the day she'd leapt the bull. The crowd roared her name. Chrysaleon lifted his dagger in awed salute. Sometimes she managed an instant of triumph, but it was always crushed in the next by painful truth.

He is dead. You will never see him again. He will never touch you. If he were alive, he would turn from you in disgust. He wouldn't care that Harpalycus bound you or that you were unwilling. The proud warriors from Argolis can only see your ruin.

She wept into the furs on her pallet.

When she succumbed to hopelessness, she knew Menoetius had discerned her hidden truth. *I will keep you safe against your own will to die,* he'd said. She didn't think she would ever forget the fury in his eyes when he spoke those words. But she would defeat him. No more barbarians would inflict their will upon her.

Menoetius couldn't force food down her throat. Soon her shade would rise between the stalactites and fly away to Athene's paradise, dragging the infant inside her along.

Her country, her people, her mother, her sister, and her lover—all were gone. Not even her dog was spared. Her pride had been stripped from her like fish scales, her body used like a crude clay cup, leaving nothing but putrid, helpless rage and memories of Harpalycus's rapes, no detail of which faded, no matter how much time passed. His cruel laughter. His vow that she would bear his offspring.

One evening he had stretched out beside her and stroked her stomach. He told her how he would kill the baby if she had one growing in her, since there was no way of knowing whose it was. He described with relish how he would let some of his most loyal men enjoy her if she was pregnant. Then, he said, after, he would keep her all to himself so there would be no doubt about who fathered the next one.

The beautiful palace of Labyrinthos, the bull dances, festivals and harvests, the mead-making and lively competitions between contenders for king—all grew indistinct. Even the need for vengeance dimmed.

She heard the echoing rasp of Menoetius's boots before he reached the inner cavern. Although that meant her hands would be untied and she could enjoy some small freedom, her jaw involuntarily clenched.

"The sun is out."

He crossed to her pallet, holding by the ears the limp bodies of two rabbits. Rabbits were their main source of meat, but often they made do with dried fruit and nuts, for when storms struck, every creature vanished into hiding.

"Were you sleeping?"

She made an effort to soften her frown. "No."

"The sun is setting, but the clouds are gone. There's time enough to enjoy the sunset and I've seen no sign of search parties in many days. Would you like to look at stars again?"

His gaze was uncomfortably intent. She felt him trying to judge how far her will had flown. No doubt he could see the evidence of recent weeping. Perhaps he could tell she was pregnant. No matter. When she died, he would be free. He could return to Selene.

But because she was unbearably lonely, desperately weary of her own thoughts, and because he'd penetrated the long, cold silence between them to invite her outside with such courtesy, she decided to be civil.

"Yes," she said. "I would like to see stars."

They emerged, blinking, into dazzling light. The first thing Aridela saw were two ravens playing in the sky, their harsh cries offering a subtle promise of warmth and coming spring.

Ice clung to the banks of the stream, but the center ran clear and cold. Twisted cypress and hardy pine trees lent hints of green to the otherwise white, formless landscape.

Aridela, bundled in leggings and jerkin as well as furry boots, followed Menoetius up the nearest cliffs and into a bowl between three severe mountain summits that offered protection from the worst of the wind. She drew mosaic patterns in the snow with a sticky pine branch, reveling at the feel of sun-warmth on her bare head.

Menoetius squatted, his back against a boulder that must have tumbled, along with several others, from the rock-choked southern summit. "I went into Araden," he said.

"What did you find?"

"Sprouting grains. The villagers have renewed hope that their crops will survive. Life returns to Crete. If we—"

"How can you say that?" She leaped to her feet, flinging the branch away. "With Harpalycus ruling in my palace? My mother and consort murdered?"

He frowned and looked away. "I thought you would be happy to hear there are surviving crops. It means food, at least for some. Fewer will starve."

Suffocating despair fell over her. She rubbed her wool-covered arms. "If I could be there, with them, I could see for myself. I could share this hope."

He was silent. She felt the intrusive invasion of his eyes, slicing her mind open like a pomegranate, fingering every humiliation forced upon her by Harpalycus and the eunuch, each fearful conviction that the child of Chrysaleon's murderer grew in her belly. His gaze shaved truth from lies, forcing her to face what had become indisputable.

If I could be there, with them. Even from herself, she tried to hide. Beneath Menoetius's discerning gaze, the lie disintegrated.

She no longer wanted to return to the people of Kaphtor. Seeing their pity and disgust. What she wanted was an end to breathing and memories. They could find another queen, one with a soul. One not devoured by shadow.

"It's getting dark," was all he said. "I'll make a fire, if I can find enough wood."

He attempted to distract her by pointing to the sky and teaching her what his people called the colors made by fading light upon wisps of cloud. He made her repeat the words; she told him with some acerbity that he reminded her of her tutors.

As the stars became visible, she showed him the Cretan sky-bull,

Tauros, and beside it, the Hunter. Then, clearer in the south than it had ever been in the lowlands, the star that, for her, had special meaning.

"See?" She pointed. "The bright white star, just above that summit."

"Yes."

"That is Iphiboë's star. So I would know she watches over us." On their climb up, Menoetius had pointed out the cliff she had nearly fallen over during her escape attempt half a month ago. The drop to a bottom strewn with jagged boulders made her dizzy and faint, and brought back the blurred, snow-fashioned image of her sister, arms outstretched, ordering her to stop. The memory had become vague and suspect with the passage of time.

"She was the bravest of women," he said. Silence stretched again but for the hiss of burning wood. Then Menoetius said, "You believe that after we die, there is something left?"

Startled and wary, she asked, "Do you not?"

"I did, when I was young."

"You are young still, Menoetius."

He shrugged.

"Chrysaleon told me you lost your faith," she ventured.

He picked up a branch he'd been using to stoke the fire and stabbed the earth as though wounding an invisible foe. The act brought a faint smile as Aridela remembered him doing the same thing during his first visit to Kaphtor, so long ago. Such an insignificant act, yet it instantly carried her back to happier, simpler times, and how she had adored him.

For a long while he stared at the flames.

"Menoetius?" she asked.

"I wonder if my father is dead."

Compassion flooded her with unexpected force. She hadn't once thought of his kin, so obsessed had she been with the fate of her own. "Tell me about him. You said he is one of King Idómeneus's warriors?"

"No. That was a lie. Idómeneus is my father."

"The High King…is your father?"

He nodded.

"Then you are—Chrysaleon's brother. His true brother." Her mind delved backward, and she added, "I remember. You said you had a brother, half a breath younger than you."

"We didn't share mothers. Mine was a slave, and his the queen."

She searched for any resemblance in the glow of the fire. They had the same straight, dominating nose. Exactly the same, though Menoetius's bore a scar across the bridge. If not for his scars, so severe and transforming, she might have discerned the likeness long ago. "I should have seen this."

"You weren't meant to."

"As Chrysaleon said, you have lied about many things."

He drew in a deep breath. "Not everything has been a lie."

A lifetime ago, she and Menoetius had eaten fire-charred ibex and watched the sun set on Mount Juktas. He told her a tale of his father, a warrior, and of his ambition to become the captain of King Idómeneus's guard. He described his spoiled, selfish brother, and how they had to be separated for fear one would harm the other. "You are royal," she said, "or would be in my country. Are you the heir, now…."

He tossed the stick in the fire. Flames gnawed at it, spitting out the moisture in the wood. "Heir to what? Has Mycenae survived? All I can say is that the mainland's greatest citadel deserved a leader who would place his country before his pleasure. Idómeneus ordered us not to compete in your Games. Chrysaleon defied him."

For the first time, she realized that Menoetius must have been in on the plot. King Idómeneus had instructed both his sons to search for that weakness which would grant him a way to overthrow Kaphtor. Chrysaleon had admitted to it, but Menoetius kept the secret, even now. Perhaps because he would not have succumbed to love over duty. By his own admission, Menoetius would have kept to the plan. If Harpalycus hadn't outpaced his enemies, she might now be Mycenae's slave.

Fury welled. One betrayal after another from those she trusted. Never…never again would she give her trust. And she would learn. She would embrace cunning and trickery, until the day came when she escaped this tiresome existence. She could lie too—maybe even learn to enjoy it.

Nothing you say is the truth, she wanted to shout. But what was the use of confronting him? He would just lie again.

Old, nagging guilt rose up inside, edging out her anger. *Idómeneus ordered us not to compete in your Games. Chrysaleon defied him.* "Chrysaleon competed because I asked him to. Because he loved me."

"Love? He saw no farther than his lust. You would never be so weak or selfish."

"I pray I would not." His cruel statement burned a blush into her cheeks. Harpalycus had insinuated something similar, that day in the palace garden before attacking her. He'd made it clear Chrysaleon enjoyed the favors of many women and cared for none.

"There is no need for prayer." Menoetius's strong, sure voice scattered her doubts. "Day after day, you want nothing more than to fight and free your country. Harpalycus tried to break your spirit. He failed. You have far more courage than Chrysaleon."

She stared at the fire, shivering. Tears stung her eyes. Though she tried, halfheartedly, to tell herself he was lying, his words wrapped around her like rivers of sunlight, like the arms of a lover. She wanted to run into the darkness and hide even as she wanted to take his hand and speak her gratitude. She couldn't bring herself to do either, so she simply hunched further into her jerkin as if it could provide a bulwark between fear and truth.

She'd believed he saw her as dishonored, blighted, ruined, by what had been done to her. Perhaps she was wrong. A very small spark flared where the old Aridela moldered.

He spoke again. At first she didn't hear him, so deeply had she sunk into her thoughts. Gradually, his words drew her away from examination of the bruised frozen sac into which she had stuffed her will to live.

"—Had Chrysaleon returned to his obligations at Mycenae, I could have remained." The crackle of burning wood and the flowing night breeze nearly drowned out his quiet voice. "Nothing held me to that place."

Cold air crept down the neck of her jerkin.

"Harpalycus probably wouldn't have invaded Crete. It is hatred of Chrysaleon that pushes him to such lengths."

"As hatred towards me pushed Lycus."

Also because of Chrysaleon.

Menoetius plucked another stick from his meager collection. Removing his dagger from its sheath, he whittled at the bark and soon a miniature spear took shape. "After I became my father's captain, I never allowed myself to care about a woman. I feared if I did, it would make me hesitant or cowardly. I have seen it happen in other men."

Iphiboë had said almost the same thing. *I have always known this was my purpose. It's why I couldn't love a man.*

But she said nothing, not wanting to interrupt his thoughts.

He spoke slowly, giving each word careful consideration. "I believed I would die in battle. I wanted such a death. I saw no worth or grace anywhere, in anything." He paused and so did his whittling, then both resumed together. "But now…I am being offered another chance." He stabbed the point of the spear into the snow and carved a long, straight line, angling another through the first to form a cross. "If Chrysaleon had obeyed our father, I could have been your partner in the cave. I could have won the Games and become your consort." He faced her. "Only the gods will ever know what difference it might have made."

That night, in the cave of Velchanos, Aridela had propped herself on her elbows, heart racing, as two beasts dropped off the ledge and approached. The bull-man. The lion. It seemed centuries ago. Sitting beside a fitful, pine-scented fire, deep within steep, glacier-like mountains, she replayed their hostile disagreement. Menoetius, the bull, tried to reach her. If he had, she would have willingly mated with him. But Chrysaleon, the lion, had shown similar determination. Only when Selene intervened, twice inviting the bull to join her, did the fight end.

The bull-man had stared at her before he took Selene's hand and disappeared with her into the gloom.

A pinecone sparked and popped. Aridela returned to the cold night of the present, yet the memory lingered.

Other memories flashed through her mind. Menoetius swathing her in a blanket the night he and Selene rescued her from Harpalycus. The way he'd cradled her against his chest, carrying her through the night to freedom. How he'd cushioned her wrists and hands with fur before binding them. And perhaps most strongly, there was the day she had tried to escape. In such foul weather, he could have just let her go. Not even Selene would have blamed him. But he searched until he found her. She would be dead now if he hadn't.

All this time, perhaps ever since Menoetius and his master found that cave and the women inside, she had misjudged him. She had believed his coldness and reserve were evidence of his contempt. But it wasn't that at all. It was his way of denying love for the woman his brother had claimed for himself. What other choice did he have?

Even as she started to amend her judgment, another collection of memories washed over her.

She saw Chrysaleon's face as he snorted his derision. *Menoetius, devout? Not anymore, my lady. He no longer has any use for such things.* Harpalycus's toadying smile. *Had you been Crete's heir and I the winner of the Games, it would have been a matter of love rather than conquest.* Lycus, his eyes cold with jealousy. *I know he has taken what you once nearly gave me.* And Helice. *I have manipulated many rites during my reign.*

All, including Menoetius, had abandoned truth to achieve their own desires. Every one of them had fooled her, even Harpalycus in the beginning.

The spark within kindled to the slow broil of anger, and licked at the cold armored pod surrounding and suffocating her will. She drew in a deep breath and tasted the air, scented of burning wood and crisp snow.

Menoetius had been watching her. Now he concentrated on the fire, inserting twigs and livening the flames by blowing into the crevices. She suspected he was really trying to back away from what he had revealed. He was trying to reform the mask he'd allowed her to peer through.

"I dare not interpret the will of your gods," she said. "Why did you lie? Why call yourself Carmanor? Why not tell us you were Idómeneus's son?"

His shoulders seemed to bunch around his neck. Firelight pricked at the scar on his face, sending it into sad, sharp relief. "Like a child, I played at being free of my father's demands. And I wanted Helice to believe in me for myself, outside of him."

This she understood. She'd grown so weary of expectations, watchful eyes, and constant tutoring. On the night of the Destruction, she and Chrysaleon had imagined what it would be like to be peasants. In that world, they could live together without care or interference.

"You're shivering. This fire is lamentable. We should go back." He rose, kicked snow over the smoldering twigs, and walked by her side along a ridge drenched in moonlight. She glanced up as they hiked, watching the gibbous orb slip from cloud to cloud. *What does this mean, Mistress? Guide me, I beg you, for I know not what you want of me. I no longer trust my ability to tell.*

They returned to the cave and crept through to the inner cavern, Menoetius's arm warm against hers, the frosty green scent of pine drifting from his clothing.

The cover of darkness gave her the courage to ask, "You don't hate me?"

"Hate you?" His disembodied voice betrayed a hint of laughter. He grew silent and still. Then he said, "I am yours. As lover or slave. I thought you understood that."

Could she believe him? She only knew she wanted to, needed to. "Everyone has lied to me," she said. "Everyone—including you."

He left her to light the lamps and coax renewed vigor into the embers he kept glowing hot beneath a cover of ash. Aridela sank onto the pallet, numb and confused. The wounds within still reached out to the peace and silence death would bring. But for the first time in a month, her suffocated will to live knew a desire to break free of its ice-bound chrysalis.

Light wavered; the chill retreated. The shadows withdrew. Menoetius watched the embers for some time before rising and crossing to her. He knelt and picked up a clay bowl containing a handful of dried figs. He chose one. Lifted it. Touched it to her lips. Watched her mouth as she took the fruit between her teeth.

The faint light softened his scar and turned his eyes black as the furthest depths of the sea, black yet not empty. Not frightening. But she didn't dare trust what she saw. Knowing as she now did how easily she was fooled, how incapable she was of separating truth from lies, she held back.

His fingertips touched the top clasp on her jerkin. She wanted him to unhook it. Astounded at this, she opened her mouth to speak a litany of refusals but could not. She sat, speechless.

He studied her face. Her breath shortened; she bit her lip and tried to hide her weaknesses, but he was Menoetius. He saw everything.

"Believe that I want you to feel joy again," he said.

She must put distance between them. Rudeness would work. She could call him the liar he was. She clenched her hands but before she could speak he covered them with his own.

We have been overly concerned with shallow things, Helice said before she died. *We've cared more about beauty than anything; we forgot how to look beneath it for the substance that matters.*

"You have spoken of hate," he said. "I know hate. I have long suffered the hatred of Mistress Athene."

She must push him away. Now, quickly.

Had Leiriope, the priestess on Callisti, been so weak when wooed by the Great Liar, Harpalycus of Tiryns?

Her consort was murdered. Harpalycus slaughtered innocents for sport. Yet she lay here, contemplating lovemaking with one of the Achaean barbarians, kin to those who had brought her island to this sorry impasse.

Bad enough that her people might see her belly swell up with the cursed child of the Usurper.

Aridela had always been praised for her steadfast will. She had taken that will for granted until Harpalycus flayed it from her. She thought of herself no longer as invincible Aridela, daughter of the Calesienda, half-divine, proud as a lioness, full of wit and talent.

The spark wavered and dimmed.

She pulled her hands free of his and folded them against her stomach. "Such things are unfit, my lord, for these desolate times."

Menoetius stared at her. Aridela thought she detected a shudder run through him, but couldn't be sure. She wanted to beg his forgiveness. Instead, she gritted her teeth and remained silent.

"Your island languishes under Harpalycus," he said. "His purpose is to destroy all that makes your country bright. He has used your desire for peace to overthrow your centers of art and learning. Harpalycus seeks to stamp out your people, but especially you, Aridela. By forcing yourself to suffer and starve, by blaming yourself for what he has done, you help him achieve his aim."

She'd never thought of it that way. It was horrifying. To distract herself as much as him, she said, "You speak of love for me. What of Selene?"

His gaze faltered. He frowned then shook his head. "I love her too," he said. "How could I not? She is your truest friend. But more than that, she offers gifts long lost to me. When she looks at me, I feel whole. I couldn't speak to you this way without the courage she returned to me. Must I destroy what I feel for her in order to love you?"

The spark inside flickered with warmth, bringing a smile to her lips. "No," she said. "I feared you were amusing yourself and cared nothing for her. I'm glad you love her, as I do. Our hearts are not as small as your countrymen want to make them."

He could have lied. But this time, he didn't.

He spoke again, his voice husky. "I know a little of trying to destroy something that cannot be destroyed. I have loved you since the day I carried you out of the shrine. I've tried to slay it, but the only way I could is to rip out my mind."

The shadows left her in an abrupt, shivering torrent. They returned to the corners and cracks; their deranged whispers faded to silence.

Tears blurred her sight. She brought his hand to the clasp on the jerkin even as the frozen husk melted and cast her into the violet light of quickened rebirth.

Aridela of Kaphtor is not dead and will not die.

_10_

Moon of Flying Swans

His beard was not wiry and coarse like Chrysaleon's. It was smooth, soft as down-feathers. She'd wanted to touch it since she was ten years old.

Her fingertip traced the ridge of scar arcing from his eyebrow to the corner of his mouth.

A crescent, like the curve on the cutting edge of a labrys.

It wasn't difficult to sense, or feel, how much he wanted her. But he was patient, to all appearances content, one leg over hers, one finger just touching her own scar, the one at her jaw, waiting for her to initiate or forbid.

She was grateful, for as much as she wanted him in return, she couldn't stop her mind from conjecturing images of Harpalycus. Of atrocities. Of pain.

To blot them out, she said, "Chrysaleon told me about the mauling."

He didn't reply for so long she thought she'd offended him.

"What did he say?" he finally asked.

"That a lioness with cubs attacked you, and he killed her. He told me you shared your blood after, and swore loyalty. That you became blood brothers."

Again he fell silent. The ember-glow subsided so they lay in near darkness. "Forgive me," she said.

"That was how he earned his title, 'Lion killer of Mycenae.'"

She felt his chest expand as he inhaled. "After I met you the first time," he said, so quietly she had to tilt her head to better hear him, "a month after I returned home, he and I slipped away from our chores and lessons, and went off with the intent to kill lion or boar. It was Chrysaleon's idea. We believed we were blessed by gods, and thought ourselves indestructible."

She ran along the scar with the tip of one finger, eyebrow to mouth. Mouth to eyebrow. Then she moved to his temple and stroked his hair.

"Her breath was suffocating," he said. "I remember little else. I can't even tell you how the attack started. I was told she charged out of the cave where we'd tracked her. I was nearest. How she disarmed me, what she did, how I survived—" He shrugged. "Only flashes are left."

Aridela's fingers trailed down his cheek to his chest and followed the path of each scar she found.

"At first, there was pain. She clawed me, bit me, as you can see. But it all goes black when I try to remember more. Chrysaleon jumped on her and stabbed her."

A set of four parallel ridges led from his belly toward his groin.

"He pulled her off after he killed her. I could breathe again. I remember that, how happy I was to breathe."

Scars crisscrossed his palms. Aridela imagined him trying to protect his face from her teeth. She kissed one then the other. In return he seized her cheeks and kissed her on the mouth, long and thoroughly.

"Tell me more," she said when he gave her the chance.

"I do have one memory. It's cloudy, like a dream. I'm walking up a hill. At the top are three women, waiting for me. They turn me back. They say my tasks aren't finished. One of the women promises to wait for me. I don't know what it means or if it even happened. The next clear thing I remember is Chrysaleon binding the worst of my wounds with strips from his tunic. Two slaves were helping him. He forced me to make the vow before he would allow them to carry me home. 'We are sons of Idómeneus the High King,' he said. 'Nothing can separate us but death. Your blood in my veins, mine in yours.' He pressed his wound against mine. Then he cut the heart from the lioness and squeezed her blood into my mouth. He said her power would belong to me."

He pressed his palm flat against hers and interlaced their fingers. "But it was Chrysaleon. His will alone kept me alive."

"I've wondered what I see in your eyes." Aridela returned his grip. "It's her. The lioness. She lives still, inside you."

He kissed the hollow in her throat and ran his tongue up to her earlobe, birthing a shiver that nearly defeated her resistance.

"She attacks you from within," she whispered.

He gave a bitter laugh. "Idómeneus was enraged. Had Chrysaleon not suffered already from so many wounds, he would have been whipped halfway to the land of shadows. I spent half a month on my back fighting fever and the loss of blood."

"You believe Athene caused this attack?" Her heart was still racing. She could scarcely remember what they were talking about. She wanted him to kiss her again, and traced the outline of his lips.

"Yes. To punish me." He slid his palm along her arm, so close to her breast but not touching, still keeping himself in check.

"For what?"

"For leaving you."

Her throat closed and she struggled to speak. "I wanted to die I missed you so much."

They lay, holding hands. Aridela was mesmerized by the rhythmic tangled beating of their hearts, and the way she could feel his voice through her chest. But the unbearable memories weren't yet vanquished. They clotted in her stomach, waiting to spring up in attack.

"I thought many times about the child-princess of Crete during my tiresome recovery. How she tried to hide her tears the day I left, and shared that story about her father and the necklace he'd given her. I thought of her through the years, wondered how she fared, listened for any gossip about Crete. When I returned with Chrysaleon I hoped to glimpse her, but I wasn't sure I wanted her to see me. She might be frightened, or pitying."

"I've had to face my ignorance since you and your brother came here. Much time was wasted, in so many ways."

He made light of it with a careless laugh, yet she felt his muscles constrict.

"Not long after," he said, "Chrysaleon brought the cubs to Mycenae. There were two, both female. As I regained my strength, we fed and cared for them. They're still there, if Mycenae is. The king likes to watch his concubines lead them around on jeweled leashes."

Scarlet ember-light flickered across the rock walls. Menoetius rested one hand on her hip.

"I know what I owe my brother," he said.

His fingers traced between her breasts and over her stomach, his gaze following. "I never thought we would be like this. You were his. I thought this could never happen."

"Kiss me."

The way he kissed her was tender yet lustful, conveying so much of need yet also devotion. Menoetius was a hardened warrior. But when he kissed her, he became Carmanor, the untroubled youth with the easy smile.

She longed to forget that beyond the cave walls lay destruction and overthrow. Murder, betrayal, lies.

An unwanted baby.

But she couldn't. Not quite.

Aridela of Kaphtor, immersed in careless arrogance, thinking herself too keen and clever to ever be fooled, had been manipulated, not only by her own mother and probably Themiste, but also Lycus, Menoetius, and perhaps...perhaps Chrysaleon, who had kissed her with love and devotion too, or so she had believed. Now she wasn't sure. She wasn't sure of anything.

Menoetius could lie when it suited him, and he had reason to undermine her feelings for his brother. She thought back to the night of the Destruction, how Chrysaleon had pulled her from the cracks in the earth and used his body to shield her from the horrors at Phaistos. Menoetius didn't know how that night had changed everything between them, had deepened and honed what had been untested. She wouldn't allow her memories to be spoiled by another man's jealousy. She wouldn't be malleable like Callisti's priestess. From now on, she would maintain control over her emotions and her body. No man would touch her until she found an unassailable method of discerning lies from truth.

Still, knowing how he'd suffered, she wanted to be careful. She had to be, for his sake.

"I am empty as a broken crock," she said softly. "You should have a woman who can return your love, as Selene does. Do not care for me, Menoetius."

He met her gaze, frowning, his mouth reforming into its more familiar tenseness.

"The paradise that was Kaphtor is gone." She swallowed the hurt those words caused. "Vengeance is all that's left of me now."

"That isn't true."

"You cannot turn back the days. Neither of us can change what's been done. Let me go."

His grip squeezed, almost cutting off the blood flow in her hand. "Have you not been listening to me?"

"Yes…but I—"

"I will bind you to this pallet until the day of your death," he said.

The threat was weightless, hollow. She couldn't help an almost tender laugh. "You'll tether me like a goat? That is your image of victory?" She almost added, *My love,* but managed, just, to suppress it.

He lowered his face. Kissed her throat, lingering and ardent, then without warning bit her. His body pressed hard against hers. Her blood rushed like ocean tides in response. It was impossible. She was not strong enough to resist. Her heart thundered, her pulses raced; tears filled her eyes. Her arms crept around his neck as though they had their own will, even as Harpalycus reared in agonizing clarity, blotting out Menoetius, replacing his warm, seductive, beguiling form with one that was cold, hated, and feared.

It was too soon. In truth, she didn't know if love could ever again be separated from torture and humiliation.

She pushed at him, biting her lips to keep the torment hidden.

He seized her hand and brought it to his face. He pressed his mouth to the underside of her wrist, where the burn, shaped like bull's horns, had marred her skin since birth. It tingled at his caress.

"I feel the lie of your words," he said. "The truth your body cannot hide."

His lips upon her skin obliterated conscious thought and the memory of speech. All that remained was the swift, consummating pulse beat, radiating outward from her wrist like the heat of the sun through her skin, muscles, and blood.

He put his mouth close to her ear as she breathed rapidly, almost lost. Almost.

"I will have victory, Aridela," he whispered.

11

Moon of Drenching Rain

THEMISTE'S MEN STOLE A MAINLAND CHARIOT-HORSE FROM HARPALYCUS'S soldiers and offered it to Chrysaleon. He accepted gratefully, knowing his journey would be much hastened.

Neoma provided him with leather boots, a bow and arrows, a dagger, food, and a skin of water, as well as a flood of pleas to return her cousin.

Traveling south and west, he skirted the Ida range along its southern foothills. By edging along the steeper, wilder crevasses and gorges, he disguised his movements from enemy patrols that branched out daily from the ruined palace of Phaistos and Knossos.

Deep snow and ice slowed his pace, though impatience made him long to spur his horse onward. The streams he crossed were frozen solid. Wind blew continually, but accustomed as he was to Mycenae's winters and heated by determination, he hunched deeper into his quilted cloak and continued on.

The death-vision drifted alongside, making him itch with need and resolve. It remained so clear that he fancied if he stopped and looked behind him, he could step back into it. Yet Themiste insisted she never led him beneath the city of Knossos, or rode with him on the backs of gryphons, or swam with him through foamy ocean waves to the green orchards of Hesperia. *Athene's grace may have sent you there*, she had said. *Perhaps to learn some lesson. I, too, have experienced visions of compelling power.*

Yet he recalled with scathing clarity the snake she'd worn like a necklace and the gryphon's rippling muscles between his thighs. He could hear the echoing drip of water in the underground caverns and taste Themiste's sweet flesh in his mouth. The serene, youthful face of Damasen, Aridela's father, remained distinct, along with everything he'd said as the two walked through Hesperia's mossy green glades.

Since Chrysaleon had regained consciousness, he had examined each word, every inflection and expression—no matter how fleeting, in his attempts to determine what course to take.

Damasen had described a future of grim possibilities.

"I see a time when new gods will be fashioned and worship of the Mother will be unknown," the bull-king told him. "Mortals who cling to the old ways will be hounded, slaughtered."

Chrysaleon said nothing, though he thought the god sounded remarkably like his own father.

"The female will be considered the substance of corruption, and every manner of evil toward her will be overlooked. Uninitiated maidens will be defiled in violence, forced to bear offspring against their will. The customs and beliefs of your ancestry, Prince Chrysaleon, will spread. As harsh as they are now, they will be further perverted. No longer will property and name pass from mother to daughter as has always been done, but from father to son. Fertile women will serve as tools to increase the wealth of their fathers. Those too old for child-bearing will be discarded or used as slaves."

A fawn approached, still shaky on delicate long legs. Damasen caressed its ears before returning his attention to Chrysaleon. They walked on, the fawn gamboling behind.

"The deeds and stories of women will vanish. Everything they create or accomplish will be forgotten, and history will listen only to men. If your world chooses this future, wickedness will hold sway. All that has been holy since time began will be devalued. Finally, an age will come when woman will embrace her own degradation. Spring will vanish. The ground will crack and burn. Oceans will rise. Mortals will procreate until forests and fields stagger beneath the weight of human flesh and there will not be a single wild place left anywhere. Water will dry up and crops will fail. Disease will spread. Then, Prince, the earth will be crucified, and you will all die."

Chrysaleon maintained a stoic expression. He fully expected Damasen to bring up his father's secret council, Boreas, the clandestine meetings, the subtle manipulations designed to assist the rise of a future very like the one he described. But his people didn't want disease and starvation. They wanted order, power. What any man craved.

Time passed. The youth remained calm. No accusations were thrown. Though divine in some fashion, apparently he could not see into Chrysaleon's mind, or he would know Chrysaleon had been raised to despise female authority and nurtured to defeat it if he could, by any method or means.

As he worked his way towards the western mountains where he hoped to find Aridela, Chrysaleon's own words, spoken carelessly, returned to his mind.

If the man who wins Iphiboë comes from the Argolid, she'll rank no higher than a slave.

Something else struck Chrysaleon as odd. Damasen spoke as though Chrysaleon would somehow experience this bleak future.

Damasen beckoned to the fawn's shy mother. "This is the path upon which the world is now set. You stand at the junction. Unless the present course is diverted, much suffering will occur."

"My lord?"

Damasen faced him, one fine black brow lifting.

"Why do you speak as if I have any part in these events?"

Damasen's gaze changed then. It turned piercing, filled with understanding and cold insight. Chrysaleon clenched his hands and fought a surge of terror, for he sensed his secrets lying naked and transparent between them.

"Have you not listened to my words? The future is never determined. I tell you the worst I have seen so that you may go forth and construct a new road. The fate I have described need not occur. You are the leavening for change. You, Chrysaleon of Mycenae, can guide the people of your world into paradise, with Aridela at your side."

Chrysaleon gathered his courage and glanced at the bull-king's face. He was surprised to see a faint smile. Damasen walked on, bending to pluck a cluster of lavender, and the uneasy instant passed.

His mind flailed. Even in this infinite place, whether dream or reality, it was difficult to understand such mysteries. Needing to compose his thoughts, he turned away from the king to admire the scenery. To his right, above the tree line, there was a smooth-topped mountain ridge; odd, how rounded the summits were.

He blinked rapidly, doubting his sight. For the slightest instant, he thought the ridge had moved.

His mouth fell open. What he had assumed were high immutable cliffs now undulated. They compressed then stretched. As he turned, half frozen with astonishment, he saw the head of an enormous serpent rise above the trees and peer down at him, its tongue flicking. It was a terrifying sight.

Damasen placed his hand on Chrysaleon's shoulder. "He will not harm you. Ladon watches over the orchard."

"Oh," Chrysaleon stuttered. "Oh."

Damasen smiled and returned to his earlier predictions. "Evil will find its strongest foothold at Athens," he said, holding the aromatic flowers to his nose. "Secret brotherhoods will reshape the character of Lady Athene into a hater of women. Zeus will rise to ascendance. It will be claimed that Zeus existed before Athene and in fact gave birth to her. Athene's true origins will disappear. Her children, Velchanos and Niachero, will seem to vanish. Her name meaning will be rewritten. 'I have come from myself' will turn into 'She who has never known man.' From Athens, change will engulf the world."

"Athens?" Half relieved, Chrysaleon grasped at the familiar name. "We at Mycenae give no thought to that pile of mud hovels. Nothing of moment will ever come from there. Mycenae leads the mainland and always will."

Only after he spoke these rash words did he hear the insult, and the threat, within them. But even as he fashioned a quick lie—*they cannot honor the Lady as a Mycenaean does*—Damasen, with another ambiguous smile, changed the subject.

"I have seen another path for your world, and it can be easily achieved. Search out my daughter, Zagreus. Bind yourself to no other. Together, you and she can strengthen fealty to the Lady and bring peace. In that end, man and woman will live together as they should always have done. There will be no more sacrifices. The days of halcyon will reign."

"Crete's consorts will live out their lives?"

"The king-sacrifice grew from observance of the life and death of seasons and crops, and their rebirth after winter rains. It generated from desire to participate in the ecstasy of the life force, to give homage and become one through imitation. My Lady allows the free will that conceived the sacrifice, and honors these heroes with divinity in their own right, but it was never her requirement." He leveled Chrysaleon with a solemn stare. "You, Zagreus, at the rising of Iakchos, are marked to descend into the labyrinth and die, as I did."

Chrysaleon swallowed a lump of uneasy anger.

"I feared my death as any mortal does," Damasen said. "But it was nothing like what I expected. I swam in warm green seas, surrounded by creatures with the faces and breasts of women and the bodies of seals. I heard the mourning cries of those who loved me. I wanted to reassure them, but could not. I was cleansed of doubts and attachments in moonlight and saltwater. These women led me to a wondrous underwater city carved of seashells and stone that glows like the moon. When I was ready to release your world from my heart, they brought me to this place, Hesperia. Soon, you will know for yourself."

He gave a nod and swept out one hand, prompting Chrysaleon to look up. They had reached Hesperia's legendary apple orchard. Chrysaleon saw fruit of pure, shining gold hanging from white-flowered branches.

A figure stood beside one of the giant trees. Branches and leaves threw filigreed shadows over her face. Even so, Chrysaleon recognized her.

"Lady Iphiboë." He bowed, struck by her straightforward gaze. There was no hint of the timid girl he remembered.

She acknowledged his address with a tilt of the head, the gesture regal yet courteous. In her arms nestled a plump partridge. She placed it on the ground and shooed it forward. It spread its wings and made a short clumsy flight to Damasen.

Chrysaleon peered again into the orchard, but in the instant his attention had been diverted by the bird, Iphiboë had slipped away.

Damasen bent to retrieve what dangled from the bird's beak. Chrysaleon recognized the necklace Aridela had always worn—a gift, he remembered, from this man.

"Return this token to your lover," Damasen said. "Defeat the oppressor. Reunite Aridela with Labyrinthos. Reinstate sovereignty to its rightful guardians." He dropped the necklace into Chrysaleon's palm, waiting until he reacquired Chrysaleon's attention before continuing in a low voice, almost a whisper. "Love for your queen brings infinite pain as well as joy, but if you choose honor and truth, your name will be crowned in glory beyond your comprehension. You will harness the force that brings wondrous change to the world."

The promise rang through Chrysaleon's mind as he rode toward Crete's western mountains. He experienced renewed determination at his first glimpse of the shimmering, iridescent mountain range rising, higher and higher before him, like an oath of victory.

Crowned in glory beyond your comprehension. Chrysaleon envisioned magnificent frescoes, marble statues, bard songs so lovely they would make listeners weep.

Yet Themiste insisted no secret corridors beneath Labyrinthos led to an underground sea. Her brow had formed a bewildered frown at his talk of an ancient war. She stroked his hair soothingly, but nothing had piqued more of a reaction from her than a sympathetic smile until he brought up the great year. It was a calculated risk, declaring that Damasen had named him the thinara king. He hadn't understood the conversation he'd overheard in his cell. If it turned out the great-year-king was Crete's enemy, telling the oracle such a thing could have condemned him to torture or death.

But, remembering his family motto, *Fortune favors the bold*, he had taken the chance and was pleased with the result. Shock obliterated Themiste's usual unreadable composure. She began treating him with subtle awe and a respect he had never seen her show anyone, not even Helice.

Had he walked with Damasen in a land beyond death, or had he experienced nothing more than meaningless visions, fashioned inside a dying mind?

One of the refugees, a goldsmith, had repaired the broken links on Aridela's necklace. Chrysaleon held it up, letting it swing from his fingers. Sunlight reflected against the delicate crescents and scattered from the wavy lines symbolizing their labyrinth. The lapis bead mimicked the frosty blue sky.

Man and woman will live together as they should always have done. There will be no more sacrifices.

If he believed a god had given him this charge, his choice was clear. Who would not want to be recognized as the harbinger of endless peace?

Disjointed segments of his will fantasized about achieving Damasen's obvious desire. Chrysaleon wanted to believe he had the power to usher harmony into the world. From the beginning, he had vowed to end the king-sacrifice. Here was the way. All he had to do was bow to Aridela, to Goddess Athene, and swear subservience to the earth.

You won't do that.

His mind spoke softly. *Damasen offers you glory with death. You want glory with life. Why should you bring eternal paradise to the world if your only reward for doing so is to rot in the ground?*

He didn't know with certainty how the necklace had come into his possession, but he would not bow away his moera to a death-dream, no matter how vivid. The Cretans might have put the trinket around his wrist when he lay unconscious. They might even have used one of their visionary concoctions to sway him to their beliefs. They had done so before. He laughed inwardly. His mind knew what he would do. No amount of excuses and justifications would change a thing.

Chrysaleon, son of Idómeneus, heir to the High King's throne, had been suckled on the might of Poseidon and the death of female dominance. Glory beyond comprehension lay in overthrow, a transformation of all that was. Harpalycus understood this, but he had no elegance. Harpalycus was a boar crashing through underbrush, betraying his location to every hunter.

Had not Damasen stated that the world's destiny wasn't set? He had even admitted he didn't know what might come.

Chrysaleon hadn't shared the revelations of his death-dream with Themiste. At first, fear of ridicule kept him silent. Now, after deliberate consideration of the bull-king's speech, he thought the forewarning it held might be useful to his own ambitions, and the insights he'd been given could provide an advantage over the oracle of Kaphtor, or at least put him on equal footing with her.

Damasen made no promises to end the sacrifice before my time to bleed. He wants me to help Aridela then crawl to my death, my usefulness complete.

I will bring an end to the sacrifice on my own terms. Chrysaleon of Mycenae will not be used to the benefit of women.

TWILIGHT FELL. HE MADE A FIRE FROM DEAD OLIVE BRANCHES. THE LAST glow of the sun transformed grey clouds to scarlet and lavender, with hints of green and yellow. Beneath this magnificence he constructed a pyramid of stones and shot an unwary hawk from the sky. He burned its thighs in offering and knelt beside his cairn, clenching the necklace in his fist.

"Poseidon," he said. "Walk with me. Lead me to Aridela. Make our bond unbreakable. Help me slay Harpalycus and bring an end to the king-sacrifice." He peered into the heavens. "Make me this great-year-king, Horse Tamer, and I will present you with the rich island of Crete. I will cover this land with temples and fill each one with your image."

A sudden gust of wind sent a fan of sparks into the indigo sky.

Taking it for the answer he wanted, he wrapped himself in the cloak Neoma had given him. "Bring Aridela home," she had begged, clutching his arm. "I miss her. I don't think she even knows I'm alive." The stone that struck her during the worst of the Destruction had left a noticeable depression in her forehead, like a large, out-of-place dimple, and ongoing headaches forced her to spend time in darkened seclusion nearly every day.

He stared at his fire, thinking of Aridela, longing for her. A memory crept before him, one he'd forgotten, from his time near death in the cell at Labyrinthos.

In his starved, thirsty mind, he'd experienced a vision of Menoetius transforming into a black bull, the enormous bad-tempered kind Cretans used in their ring. The beast gored him and as he lay gasping, his lifeblood seeping away, Aridela came to stand beside the bull, resting her hand on his neck in an intimate manner. She had looked down upon Chrysaleon without any emotion.

"No," he'd whispered, and he did so again now, fury raging through his blood as he gazed into the cold night sky. "Menoetius won't defeat me."

He fell asleep at last, but during the night's blackest point, he was awakened by the earth shuddering. Small creatures scurried; rocks lurched and tumbled. His horse shied and nickered. Farther away, he heard ominous, eerie echoes as an avalanche of boulders crashed into one of Crete's many precipitous gorges.

He stared into the night towards the mountains, aching to be among them.

I'm coming, Aridela. I will find you.

12

Moon of Drenching Rain

IN THE MOUNTAINS, THE WIND SELDOM DIMINISHED. ICY COLD, IT PULSED through high pine branches, which created a constant hollow whispering. But the sun had again made an appearance. Shafts of light fell between the trees like translucent waterfalls. Aridela stepped inside one, turning her face up and closing her eyes, basking in the faint warmth that waged battle against the bitter wind. How much time had passed since she'd left the cave for more than the time it took to relieve herself? Cold, wind, and snow had draped her mountain home in dismal, exhausting, endless grey for so long she had begun to fear she would forget anything else.

Now everything felt different. Air poured through her lungs with the freshness of new milk. She followed rabbit tracks and drank from a creek, the water so cold it burned her throat and made her cough. Menoetius found her and took her hand, pulling her along imaginary paths. Leaving the tree line, they scrambled up a slippery, wind-scoured, near-vertical ascent onto a rock outcropping suspended over vast reaches of space. Mountain summits swept on every side, ridged and monumental, rising to the clouds, their feet hooked to the center of the earth. For the first time since coming here, the sky's clarity offered a glimpse of the sea, sparkling in sunlight, and even hints of the island off the southern coast.

"It is beautiful," Aridela said. "Like it's all been scrubbed clean."

She stepped closer to the edge, unprepared for the surge of lightheadedness that engulfed her. She pictured herself tumbling or being pushed, falling, no way to stop, dissected by the rocks so far below. She clutched Menoetius's arm like an oar in a stormy sea, ashamed, yet helpless against this cascade of trembling fear.

Menoetius didn't seem to sense her terror. He drew her closer to the precipice. Dislodged pebbles fell. Vanished.

"All this is ours." He spoke low, next to her ear. "No one can find us if I don't want them to."

His words were buried beneath an onslaught of cold, white, icy dread. Never before had Aridela avoided heights. She had perched, exhilarated, on the crumbling cornice of earth at Mount Juktas's holy shrine. She'd stretched out her arms, longing to soar to the moon. But that was before ash, fire, and poison had decimated her land. Before her sister had thrown herself over a cliff much like this one, to sink into the eternal embrace of the sea. Before Helice had perished, lifeblood spurting from her throat. Daring and confidence had resided comfortably within her before Chrysaleon had succumbed, in whatever horrible and unknown fashion, to Harpalycus's evil.

Before Harpalycus had used her like an object without value. Mere soil, as he put it, in which to grow his progeny.

Though she drew in deep breaths, gritted her teeth, and fought to regain control, the fear raged on, making her cling to Menoetius's arm. Her head hummed; a kaleidoscopic barrage of color blurred her sight, and the terrible thunder of her heart seemed to propel her closer to the edge.

The innate courage Iphiboë had so envied was gone. Standing in this place of clear, naked altitude, staring into infinity, she saw her life stretch away, bearing her along like a shred of bark stripped off its tree by fiery stone wind. Tears slipped down her cheeks, hot against her skin, and she felt the old Aridela evaporate like insubstantial mist.

Menoetius frowned as he peered into her face. He pulled her away from the edge, rubbing her arms to warm them and lessen her shivering. Bringing her close, he wrapped his woolen jerkin around her and kissed the spot he said he loved the most—at the collarbone, where throat curved into shoulder.

"Sit," he ordered, pointing at a flat dry spot next to a sturdy boulder. "The sun is warm and the snow melted. You can't see over. You're safe." He added, "You are always safe with me."

She could only nod. Her mouth was as dry as over-baked bread.

They sat cross-legged on the limestone rocks, on equal terms with eagles at the summit of the world.

Menoetius, closer to the edge than she, scooped up a handful of pebbles and dropped them, one by one, over the ledge. "Seeing the sea today brought back something I'd forgotten," he said. "An old, old memory, or a dream. I'm newly born. A woman is holding me—a goddess. She—she's standing on the shore. I can hear the sea. The moon overhead is full and glowing. She kisses me and hands me to a serving woman, who carries me through darkness into a hot chamber. There I am given to Sorcha. There's much anxious talk among the women. They claim I understand what they're saying. And I do. Every word."

"That seems more than a dream," Aridela said. "Could it be a gift of sight from the Moerae?"

He shrugged. "When I was younger, I picked these pictures apart like a jackal with a carcass, but I have never been able to decipher them."

"My nurse used to say that when I was little, Lady Athene spoke to me. People overheard me laughing and calling someone 'Mother.' Someone nobody could see. I do remember believing she watched over me and walked with me."

Menoetius smiled. "I have known the truth of that since the first time I saw you."

"Do you remember when you saved my life in the shrine? I thought you were her—the Lady."

"Of course I remember." His gaze was achingly tender.

"Menoetius, do you know why your mother left you?"

"No."

"Sorcha, from the city of Ys."

"I wonder if it even exists. Alexiare told me that when she came of age, she was sent to a magical place to learn women's mysteries, somewhere on the isle of Albion."

"Kaphtor established ties with Albion long ago, and trades with them. I don't know about Ys, but Albion certainly exists, and so does Avalon, a center of learning. Perhaps that is where your mother was taught her power. I have always thought of us—Kaphtor—as a sister to Avalon, since Kaphtor means *Sea of Apples*, and the name Avalon, I was taught, means *Isle of Apples*.

He stared at her, his expression dumfounded.

"Once a year," she said, "we take silver and bronze to Albion. They give us tin."

He returned to dropping his pebbles, one by one, frowning slightly. Aridela listened, but she didn't hear any strike ground. A nauseating sense of vertigo made her breathing shorten; she rubbed her temples, trying to soothe it away. "Do you remember when we went up Mount Juktas and killed a wild goat?" she asked, to distract herself from the gorge yawning beneath their feet.

"You wouldn't stop asking me questions. Do you intend to do that again?"

She gave a rueful smile. "I wish we could go back to those days. I hated being too young for you to notice. Still, when I think of that time I remember being perfectly happy."

"If we could go back, I would not leave you. I wouldn't return to Mycenae." He stared over the expanse of sky, snow, and summits, his dark hair blowing across his face. "The lioness wouldn't attack. My face wouldn't make children shriek for their mothers."

"I would do things differently too, if I were given another chance."

He sighed and dropped the rest of the pebbles, dusting off his palms. "Since we can't change what's done, shall we make a different pact?"

"We have to."

"That day I carried you from the shrine, a vow came to me, unbidden. It sank into me as I held you. I've thought of this vow many times, and every time I remember the words, I want to do things as they were meant to be done. I want to change the past."

"What was it?"

"For longer than you can imagine, I will be with you—"

"In you, of you," Aridela interrupted.

They stared at each other, Aridela's breathless amazement mirrored on his face. Her heart gave a strange stutter.

He began again. *"Together we—"*

"Bring forth a new world—"

His eyes widened. *"And nothing—"* He stopped.

"Will ever part us."

He sighed before repeating, in a near whisper, "Nothing will ever part us."

He brushed hair out of her eyes, but the wind, capricious and willful, returned it.

Velchanos's promise. But Chrysaleon was the dream-god-lover. He had said those words to her the night Velchanos merged with him on Mount Juktas and brought the statue to life. It seemed so long ago.

Menoetius spoke the vow exactly, word for word. Had she said it aloud in her sleep? Could he be trying to deceive her? Surely what she saw in his eyes was truth. But—she'd been so certain of others, too. "Athene, my Mother. What are you telling me?"

"You've heard it too," he said. It wasn't a question.

She nodded. "The promise came over me like a blessing; I have never forgotten. But it wasn't in the shrine. It was years after you left Kaphtor. I remembered the words as they formed, though—they felt familiar, as though I'd heard them before. As though it wasn't the first time."

Months ago, when Themiste used the mind-link on the cliffs at Natho, she had reminded Aridela that at the beginning of the dream on Mount Juktas, the statue resembled Menoetius, not Chrysaleon. Rage had revived the memory again, in the cave, when Menoetius first bound her to the log.

Somehow, in some way beyond her comprehension, the statue in the dream had been both men. Menoetius and Chrysaleon. And Athene had given a vow to all three, together.

Enchantments swirled; she thought if she took her gaze from him and looked into the sky, it would be filled with rainbows, rainbows that she could dive into and swim in; the enchantments would support her and keep her from falling. Enticing flashes formed at the edge of her vision, holding every tint imaginable. Yet she couldn't look away from Menoetius, not even for an instant.

"I have never seen anything so blue as your eyes," she said.

He blinked. His gaze faltered. "If they please you, then I am glad to possess them."

Was that redness on his face caused from wind or embarrassment? She found herself starting to smile, and pressed her hand to his cold cheek. "But I wish I could see your face…without this beard. And I miss your hair, the way it used to be. It was so long. Do you remember?"

His brows rose. He inhaled sharply as though he'd forgotten to breathe. "Soldiers in my country keep their hair short, for convenience." His hand rose and covered hers. "Your hair too, is different."

She'd nearly forgotten. When had she last looked at her reflection? So long ago.

"When I first met you," he said, "you had only a topknot. You wove silver rings in it."

She laughed.

"After the Destruction, with your hair so short and with such small bones, you could have passed for a boy." He gave a short laugh. "You still could." He moved his hand to her shoulder. "You're no longer pale. That terrified look is gone. All I want is to be with you, for as long as my moera allows. I want to live by your side. Do you trust me yet? Do you know I would do anything to protect you? That if you went over the edge of this cliff, I would follow and break your fall?"

"Yes." She scooted onto his lap and tucked her head under his chin, closing her eyes. "I do know." She loved how he made love to her with his words. Every time he did, it pushed Harpalycus a little further away.

Wind blew over them, clean, crisp, tasting of snow and pine. An eagle cried. Sunlight drenched them in a patchwork of yellow warmth.

He will never leave me.

Believing it changed everything. She forgot all that was, all that would be. For this brief space of time, suspended above the earth on a tremulous rock outcropping, she allowed his love to slip inside and press like healing unguent over her injuries.

"TRY THIS." MENOETIUS HELD OUT A BOWL.

The smile he offered her was one she hadn't seen since she was ten years old, and she knew by it that Carmanor had come back.

The water's purity made her smile, too. It no longer tasted of ash.

"I see Crete recovering." Menoetius squatted next to her pallet, resting one arm alongside her thigh. "As the snow melts, it carries ash into the rivers, then to the sea. Rain removes more. Little by little, the earth again grows fertile."

"I hope you're right." Aridela uncrossed her legs and stretched.

"We'll return to the lowlands and it will be as though none of it ever happened."

"Yes." Fierce, hot desire shot through her.

His eyes missed nothing. "You want to go back now."

"You know I do."

Scowling, he stood up and strode away.

She rose from the pallet, her heart sinking. The time had come.

She'd known for days she had to do something. An end must be made to their mountain idyll, now, before another day passed and it grew harder, she grew weaker, and the child in her womb grew bigger. "I belong to the people of Kaphtor," she said softly. "My life is not my own. If it were, if I weren't queen, I would stay here with you."

He faced her, narrow-eyed, mouth tensed. "Would you?"

"Go with me. Fight beside me. We will kill Harpalycus and rout his warriors." She stretched out her hand, palm up. Hesitantly, he approached and clasped it. "I will make you judge or advisor, and you will be at my side for the rest of my life. Chrysaleon loved and trusted you. Now that my consort is dead, I will have no other man but you, for as long as I am queen."

He frowned, but drew her close.

She put her arms around his neck and stroked his hair. Menoetius possessed the softest hair she'd ever felt. It was thick, smooth, lacking even the slightest wave or curl, almost like the still surface of a lake.

He held her face so she couldn't turn away. "Are you saying you love me?"

Tears burned her eyes and she had to swallow before she could answer. "I do love you." She laid her hand against his crescent scar. Mark of the lion, of Athene. *Mother, I have looked beneath the surface. I see what you wanted me to see. I wish it had not taken so long.*

He saw her tears. He laughed. He crushed her against him, kissing her face, her eyelids, her throat, her mouth.

She knew she had to convince him. Athene again demanded more, so much more. Why couldn't she ever be merely a woman? Her duty seemed more arduous than any other queen's.

Give me strength, Lady, if you want me to follow your will.

But as she tried to form what to say, Menoetius picked her up and laid her on the pallet.

He'd been patient last time, understanding of her confusion, her memories, and grief. Twining his limbs around hers, he'd pulled her cheek to his throat and stroked her hair until she fell asleep. He'd been gone when she woke in the morning.

No more waiting, his kisses now told her.

She wanted him to wait no longer.

The time for decision-making passed; their bodies even now were merging, dissolving into each other like two drops of rain. Another breath and there would be no return. Her resolve disintegrated.

"No, Menoetius," she said, yet her arms kept him close. She kissed the skin next to his eye, feeling his lashes brush against her mouth. One more kiss. Then she would find a way to return to sanity and reason. To loneliness and duty. "Wait."

He opened his eyes, but they lacked comprehension. His hands slid between her thighs, coaxing them around his hips.

"No," she said, but it was faint, and held no weight. She returned his kisses and followed his rhythm, longing for what he sought to give.

He took her earlobe between his teeth. "Why do you tell me 'no'?" His right hand slipped along her ribs, over her drumming heart. His mouth followed. "I need you."

"And I, too…but…I must…we must…."

He stopped her with kisses, leaving no space for anything outside the cave, nothing beyond his love.

She heard a voice. It seemed to come from outside; she didn't know at first it was Athene, speaking through her.

"Take me to Labyrinthos," it said. "There I will give myself to you, freely and with love, every night, every morning." She stroked his beard and kissed the edge of it, where his cheekbone began. "Come with me. Fight with me. When my country is free, no man will take your place. I will change our customs and laws to make it so."

He stared at her. Passion slowly faded.

"You play with me," he said, his voice at once despairing and graveled with rage. "To get what you want. You…rouse me, allow me to touch you, then you say no?" His teeth grated. "You think your 'no' will stop me?"

His hand rose over her face. She cringed away from the blow. But instead he grabbed her wrists and pinned them over her head.

"What is to stop me?" he shouted. "Nothing. Do you think I have never raped a woman?" He shoved his knee between her legs. "Your life belongs to me. I have saved it not once but twice. You gave it to me. I saw it in your eyes that day at the harbor."

"Yes. I did. But as a child. Chrysaleon won our Games—"

"Chrysaleon! If I had been the one with you in the cave—"

Rage and humiliation twisted his mouth. "If I were still that man…." He released her wrists as though they burned.

"I don't mean to trick you. I should not have let this go so far. I should be stronger. If I lie with you I will never leave this mountain. You'll never let me leave. Weakness will be master of us both. It frightens me how much I want to stay." Sobs rose in her throat, manifestations of this desire that wanted its own way, just for one night.

They were like stones, and hurt as she swallowed them. She couldn't lie to herself. If she gave in, it wouldn't be for one night. "Please understand."

She tried to touch his face but he jerked away.

"All that was has been stripped from me. I stood at the overhang and saw my courage, too, die. If we mate, will my resolve go? Will I be nothing but selfish need? Is that what you want, of me and yourself?"

He stared at her. He was an Achaean, a warrior nurtured on pride and conquest, from a land where women were considered property. He'd already given her more than most men raised in such a way ever would.

He still didn't know that within her grew a child. That most likely it was the offspring of Harpalycus. There were ways to stop it, but not here. She needed birthwort and other herbs, which were dried and kept in containers at Labyrinthos, if any still existed, if Rhené, the healer who knew about such things, still lived. There was only so much time before it was too late.

Before the day came when he would see, and there would be no hiding it any longer.

She didn't want him to see.

Nothing can ever part us, promised the vow they somehow, incredibly, shared. Menoetius, knowing Harpalycus, would assume he had raped her, but as long as her belly didn't grow, he could pretend it hadn't happened. Aridela knew, with all her woman's instincts, that their vow couldn't survive Harpalycus's living, expanding seed.

She hardened herself, tensing her muscles, routing her love. Speaking with the clear coldness of a queen who would be obeyed, she said, "You forced me away from my people. You had to bind me to keep me here. You knew I would leave if I could. I belong to Goddess Athene, not to you. I am Goddess-of-Life-in-Death. It is through me that man is made sacred. Rape me, but if you do, I will never give myself to you. You will be forced to rape me, like Harpalycus, until I escape or die, and I will bear no child from your seed."

Shudder after shudder ran through him. His teeth ground audibly. She doubted if he'd even heard her.

"Do you think I don't know what your father ordered you to do? He told you to find a way to destroy us. And you would have, if Harpalycus hadn't done it first."

He stared at her. "You think that? I wouldn't have let it happen. I would have found a way to stop it. Even if it meant my own death. But you won't believe me."

Her heart knew he spoke the truth, but she remained silent. She had to make him want to let her go. She had to kill his ardor, perhaps even his allegiance.

His breathing slowed. The anger in his eyes dulled.

She bit her lips viciously to keep from denying everything she'd just said, to stop from begging him to kiss her again.

He leaped off the pallet and paced, pivoting when forced to by the cave walls. His hands clenched and unclenched. He didn't look at her.

She sat up. "Menoetius."

He didn't respond. "Carmanor," she said, softly.

He stopped but kept his face averted.

"You returned my desire to live. With it came my obligation. If you didn't want me to fight, you should have let me die. My mother tried to warn me many times. The people are my covenant. Everything else comes after."

He spat out something in his language, words she didn't know. He turned then and seized her arms. She struggled, but even using all her strength he overpowered her. He bound her wrists behind her back, then her ankles, and straightened. She couldn't find the Menoetius she knew in those eyes.

He left the cave.

13

Moon of Drenching Rain

THE OIL LAMPS SPUTTERED AND WENT OUT. NO SOUND INTERRUPTED THE stillness in the cave but for the endless echoing drip of water. Though she struggled until her flesh bled, Aridela couldn't loosen the bonds. She grew hungry. Thirsty.

Why do I not feel your death, Chrysaleon?

Menoetius must have decided to leave her to die slowly, of starvation. Maybe it was what she deserved.

At last she heard the scuffing of his boots in the outer cave. He stopped. She heard a faint sound, like a sigh.

"Menoetius," she cried. "Untie me. How can you be so cruel?"

"Aridela?"

She struggled to rise onto her elbows as a swarming hum, like a nest of disturbed bees, erupted in her head. "Who is it?" she said, scarcely able to project the question. Perhaps she had died, for that voice sounded like the one she most desired to hear and knew she never would.

More echoing steps. "Keep speaking," he said, his voice muffled by the rock wall. "Where are you? How do I find you?"

"It cannot be," she said. Louder, she asked, "Velchanos? Have you come to take me to my Mother's land? I must be mad from despair."

"I am neither spirit nor god," came the bodiless reply, tinged with that arrogant amusement she'd always found so compelling. "I am a tired, frozen man who has searched endless days for you." There was an abrupt sound of stumbling, followed by a curse. "Themiste promised the Lady would guide me to you. Speak, Aridela. I cannot see how to get through this wall."

"It's a hole at the floor, in the corner. You'll find it if you get on your knees. My heart is breaking with happiness."

The grate of his boots echoed as he crawled through the opening. One groping hand touched her wrist. The other fumbled over the pallet and ran up her leg.

"Why do you lie here like this, alone in the dark? Are you hurt?"

"He binds me when he leaves. Hurry, Chrysaleon. He's been gone so long. Cut the straps."

His hands examined her face then ran down her arms to the thongs on her wrists. "Who binds you? Menoetius?"

"Hurry," she said. "I'll explain when we're gone from here."

Muttering a colorful string of curses, he slit the tethers with his knife and scooped her into his arms.

Aridela wrapped her arms and legs around him and drew in deep breaths of his chilled skin. "Hurry," she said, though all she wanted was to stay there, pressed against him, without care or thought.

He set her on her feet. They felt their way to the entry hole and shimmied through to the middle chamber, where faint shafts of palest daylight allowed them a dim view of each other.

She threw her arms around him again. "Chrysaleon. Chrysaleon. Chrysaleon." Weeping, laughing, she traced the softness of his brows and lashes, the hardness of his jaw, his wiry, springy beard. "You're alive."

"With Themiste's help."

"Themiste lives?"

"Oh yes. She commands a well-organized rebellion. Given enough time, she and her followers could defeat Harpalycus. She has your cousin Neoma with her. They have charged me to bring you as quickly as possible, as did many others. Selene is here, not far away. She has been searching for you, too. It will give me great pleasure to show her I am the better scout."

Giggles flowed from her throat like spring runoff through a gorge.

Neoma. Selene. Themiste.

"I have much to tell you," he said. "Harpalycus abandoned Natho. He took his men and left for Knossos after losing Themiste then me." Cold contempt rang through his laugh. "Themiste's spies know more about Harpalycus and his invasion than he does, I'd wager. They learned early on that he hasn't near enough soldiers. Rebellions and attacks are making his occupation impossible to maintain. Soon he'll be gone or dead. You will sit upon your throne again, and I will be there beside you."

His news, meant to bolster her, did the opposite. Worry crept through her mind. She knew she should tell him of Harpalycus's boasts about King Eurysthenes and reinforcements from the mainland, but as she gazed into his face, worries and fears were suffocated beneath joy. She dropped to her knees, pulling him down with her. "Chrysaleon...." She pushed at the thick furs he wore, weeping as she leaned into him and pressed her mouth to the side of his neck.

He slipped his hands beneath her tunic and felt her shoulders and arms, putting her slightly away to ask, "What is this? There is no flesh on you, only bones. Has he starved you as well?"

"I will eat now," she said, her voice breaking. "I now have reason to eat. It is good fortune to join inside the womb of the Goddess. Love me, Chrysaleon; I cannot bear to wait."

He had her pressed to the cave floor and her clothing pulled away before she finished her demand. The curved rock walls and stalactites threw back the sounds of their union in satisfying echoes.

"Come," he said, after their need was sated, their breathing had slowed, and they had kissed until their lips were swollen. "Let me take you from here. Labyrinthos needs you."

"Yes," she said. "Take me home, Chrysaleon."

They emerged into the sunlight, holding hands. Aridela knelt and scooped up handfuls of rich, wet earth, the sudden intensity of light making her eyes sting. *Thank you, my Lady. Thank you.*

"By the storms of Hippos, you are skinny," Chrysaleon interrupted. "Anyone would take you for a half-starved peasant boy."

"That is a good plan." She laughed. "I shall travel to Labyrinthos as a boy. Harpalycus himself might not recognize me."

"Could Menoetius find no meat? Have the two of you been starving? Where is he? Why were you lashed like a sacrificial dog?"

"After I was told you were dead, no effort he made could force me to eat. I did not care to go on living. I haven't made things so easy for your brother, Chrysaleon—yes, I know he's your brother. He told me. Menoetius did the best he could. I don't know where he is. I have not seen him for...a long while. Perhaps some misfortune came his way."

Chrysaleon shifted the bow over his shoulder and glanced across the silent, barren summits looming on every side. "I feel an uneasiness here, like a curse. Let us leave this place."

They fled down the slope to the east. Toward home.

THE WATER IN THE CREEK WAS GLACIALLY COLD, BUT IT FELT SO GOOD TO wash away the dust and grit that Aridela didn't care. She splashed her arms, face, and hair, scrubbing until she felt clean. Then she leaned against a boulder drenched in rusty orange light from the setting sun, shivering, combing through her wet hair with her fingers and watching Chrysaleon's horse swish its tail and graze a patch of sweet grass in the protective lee of a fallen pine. Though he'd sworn Harpalycus and his men were long gone, it was hard to relax. She jumped, startled and nervous, at every sound.

Chrysaleon had gone off to hunt their supper. Satisfaction exuded from him; he took great enjoyment in reminding her that he'd only been in the area three days, while Selene and her supporters had been combing the mountains for a month.

If only he had found her sooner. The destructive interlude in the cave wouldn't have happened. Menoetius might be here with them, and she wouldn't be consumed by guilt and regret. Where had he gone? Was he injured? Dead? Without Chrysaleon's presence to distract her, she agonized over her mountain champion's fate. Over and over again, she heard Menoetius's exultant laughter when she confessed she loved him, and the way she had pulled him closer yet denied him. He believed she had coldly, deliberately manipulated him, and she didn't blame him.

He would never know how she had forgotten her resolve even as she clung to it, or how much she had longed for their consummation, and in the time she spent alone in darkness, how bitterly she had wished to go back in time and give him everything he wanted, and more.

Menoetius had returned her desire to live. Menoetius had restored the ability to join with Chrysaleon in the cave without ever once picturing Harpalycus. Menoetius had done that. And this was how she repaid his gift.

She would give much to tell him how sorry she was, though she doubted he would believe it.

If he returned to the cave and found it empty, he would think she had run away again, without any care for the pain it might cause him.

Mistress, why does he have to be hurt? He has always loved you. He is a good man. Why?

She picked up the dagger Chrysaleon had left and rubbed her thumb over the leather-wrapped hilt.

Unease drew her gaze to the edge of the forest. Every leaf and branch lay perfectly still. She fancied something was watching her. If only Chrysaleon would return. She couldn't leave these mountains soon enough. Active planning, reuniting with Selene, would suppress these thoughts, would erase Menoetius's stricken face and the promise he'd made. *I will have victory, Aridela.*

She must concentrate on something, and movement would help warm her. Tossing the jerkin around her shoulders, she set off into the forest to search for edible roots, perhaps a valiant berry or two.

The sunset stained the clouds in the western heavens with effervescent crimson, but where she walked, green shadows reigned. Greenish-blue haze settled over her, as though the Goddess, in her guise of Dictynna, *she who helps fishermen find their catch*, had flung mystical sea nets across the sky.

Aridela found and gathered dusky blue berries and twigs from a juniper tree. She would burn the twigs and sweep their campsite with the smoke. It was well known that juniper smoke cast a veil of protection. The berries she could simmer in water and make an energizing drink. As she carried her finds to their camp, she came across a great old plane tree. Gnarled roots protruded from the snow, creating pockets of rich earth. Using the dagger blade, she dug between them, hoping to find the root of white asphodel, or perhaps, with luck, a few leaves of wild parsley.

"How did you do it this time?"

She scrambled to her feet, pressing her back against the trunk. It was so like Menoetius, to appear when she'd finally managed to stop thinking of him.

A sudden breeze sent the high branches swaying. Only a half-rotted log lay between them.

His eyes betrayed relief, though his mouth told a different story, of anger. Impatience. He reached over the log and clasped her wrist.

Her grip on the dagger loosened. It fell into the snow.

"Why do you have to make everything so difficult?"

"Why did you tell me Chrysaleon was dead?"

His brows rose. She saw him stiffen. His eyes widened almost imperceptibly.

"He is here." She moved away from the tree trunk, pulling her hand free. The forest's breath seemed to catch then a breeze brushed against her, cold enough to raise goose bumps.

"That cannot be." Menoetius frowned.

She retrieved the knife then ran from him back to the stream, her emotions so jumbled she thought she might rend into pieces.

Chrysaleon had returned during her absence. He reclined against the rock where she had dried her hair, sharpening his knife on the edge of a wet stone. When he saw her face, he threw down the stone and jumped to his feet. "What is it?"

The tree canopy gave a drawn-out sigh.

Menoetius stepped clear of the forest, his bow dangling in one hand. Immediately a grin spread across Chrysaleon's face, erasing the frown of concern. He stepped away from Aridela. "Finally," he said.

"I thought you dead, son of Idómeneus."

"Themiste took me out of Harpalycus's prison through secret tunnels. The Cretans know much of healing, and returned me from the land of shadows."

"Did Selene send you here?"

"No, I came on my own. She is nearby, though. She's been searching for you a long while." His eyes narrowed. "Explain why you trussed my queen like a goat."

Menoetius flushed. His gaze dropped. "She was always running away. I couldn't hunt or collect water for worry over what she might try next. Once she nearly went over a cliff. I didn't know what else to do."

Chrysaleon squinted at him, his jaw muscles working. Aridela held her breath.

But he slapped his brother on the back and gave a hearty laugh. "I know well how stubborn and troublesome she can be. She said as much herself." He turned away, adding, "I killed a badger. It was all I could find. Come, share our supper. Tomorrow we will find Selene."

He crossed to his budding fire and laid a few more sticks on the flames. "Aridela told me how she refused to eat, so I hold you blameless, but if we bring her back so skinny, I fear what her people will do to us. Her bones are about to split her skin open."

Aridela remained beside the boulder. She stared at Menoetius. He stared back. She couldn't begin to read his thoughts.

He knew her duty. Yet sickening guilt and loss made her feel she'd done everything wrong.

I didn't want to cheat you, Menoetius, she told him with her eyes. *Forgive me....*

14

Moon of Drenching Rain

From the Oracle Logs
Themiste

Aridela has returned! She sits on a footstool next to me, holding her hands to the hot coals, pretending she is cold so she won't have to spin. All the people feel the power she has brought. They walk straighter. Hope brightens their eyes as though they already see our victory.

Chrysaleon reclines on the cave floor next to her. Since their return they cannot be parted. He touches her constantly in some way or other, and her gaze upon him is transparent with delight. Here in this deep underground place where our people have prayed, danced, sacrificed, and made offerings for time beyond memory, love is strong. Desire is strong. It affects me. I ache for what I alone of all the inhabitants of Kaphtor am denied.

Every day, Harpalycus kills five people, sometimes children. He vows to continue these atrocities until I am returned. His warriors seize women for their master's merciless pleasure. My spies tell me he has grown dependent on our wine, which is far more potent than what they ferment on the plains of Argolis. He staggers, rants, and froths. Sometimes his faithful dog, Proitos, must restrain him. Most nights, I hear, the drink steals his senses and he lies in unconscious stupor.

Men will speak of honor as though it is the most important aspect of their lives. *But I have too often witnessed their inclination to seize advantage of their foe's weakest moment. Brutal earthshakings devastated Kaphtor. Cruel mountains of water destroyed the harbors of Amnisos, Tamara, and Elasa. Blizzards of ash smothered crops and killed animals. Harpalycus chose his time well. With few men he conquered our palaces and cities. He vanquished us in our sleep, during a celebration when guards were few and we thought ourselves safe. Now he locks away the remaining stores of grain and we starve. Will he hold us? My visions give no answers, but as long as I breathe, I will resist.*

Kaphtor's people are courageous, but they cannot endure this suffering much longer.

We have smuggled weapons from Labyrinthos. Aridela and I sift through the growing piles of javelins, swords, spears, arrows, and shields. She and the two men who shadow her, Chrysaleon and Menoetius, describe to me the skills of conquest and warfare, sometimes demonstrating the best way to kill a foe. I see their stark desire to engage, but Chrysaleon has advised us to wait a few more days. "My father will come," he insists. It is hard. Everyone grows restless and impatient.

I see something else as well—between Aridela and Menoetius. Something they pretend isn't there. Something Chrysaleon, in his spoiled arrogance, has not seen. I consider the many days and nights spent in the mountain cave with only each other for company, and I wonder.

Catching how they glance at each other then away, I remember the long-ago morning when Menoetius carried Aridela from the shrine and was thrown into our prison for his trouble. I remember how devastated she was when he left Kaphtor to go back to his home on the mainland.

These warriors from the north, these 'Kindred Kings,' are strong and ruthless. Every year they find new places to conquer, to assert their authority and their gods. It is the same to the east, where countless legions of invading tribes swarm the countryside. Everywhere they go, they crush Mother Goddess and replace her with the war-hungry male gods who support their desire for power. To our south there is Egypt, a strange conglomeration where the female is revered but only males rule. How can our tiny island hold out against these vicious, ever-expanding dynasties? Long have they eyed us with greed and envy. They covet our land, our artisans, and perhaps our women most of all, to enslave and dominate. They want to destroy our glory and replace it with their own.

Again I ponder Damasen's words in the long-ago vision. 'Aridela and her sister are as one. Iphiboë must open the path, so Aridela can walk alone into the dark.'

Was this prophecy fulfilled when Iphiboë died and Aridela suffered alone at the hands of the Usurper?

Prince Chrysaleon lingers in my mind as well. He claims he is the thinara king.

If we triumph in this war, but he remains Aridela's consort…

Will we have defeated our enemy?

"Ships, my lady! They come!"

The messenger fell to his knees. Tears streaked his face.

Aridela jumped off her stool. Apathetically spinning wool when the man entered, she dropped the distaff, paying no attention as it clattered to the floor and rolled away.

"No one sails the seas in the Moon of Drenching Rain," she said. "It's too dangerous."

"I swear it's true," he cried. "Their sails bear the gryphon."

She exchanged a glance with Chrysaleon, then Themiste. She had told them of Harpalycus's boast that King Eurysthenes of Pylos, 'The Gryphon,' had promised many warriors to bolster the invasion. She knew they had argued and bartered. Then winter set in. She had half-believed, half-hoped Eurysthenes wouldn't or couldn't appear for at least another month; not until the rough seas calmed.

"Come," Chrysaleon said. "We will see what is to be seen."

The three armed themselves and left the cave by the secret way, quickly hiking to a vantage point above Amnisos.

A thick wet mist rolling in from the sea prevented Aridela from counting the exact number of battle-ships anchored some distance from land's edge. There seemed to be dozens. As one ship then another floated eerily in and out of the fog, she glimpsed men leaning over the sides, pointing towards land. Every now and then she caught snatches of their shouts.

Indeed, the sails did bear the Pylos gryphon. Chrysaleon scowled his fury.

Phalanxes of men marched into sight on the road from Labyrinthos, armed with spears and carrying ox-hide shields stolen from Kaphtor's weapons reserves. A single chariot ranged in front, followed by four rows of foot soldiers holding smaller, round shields and javelins. Mist and drizzle made determining the numbers of this approaching army hard, but Aridela guessed they were about three hundred.

"Harpalycus is in the chariot." Aridela stared at the man who had tortured her for so long. Hatred made her stomach churn. The soldiers following the Usurper carried their weapons upright, in ceremonial stance. Their plumed helmets rode high. They strode without shouting, haste, or alarm.

The warriors lined up in precise rows on either side of, and behind, the chariot. Harpalycus handed the reins to the man standing next to him and stepped out. He wore no helmet and was dressed in fine Cretan armor, tooled in bronze, a bull's head in front and back, horns curling over the shoulders. He wore a treasure in gold that would dazzle the eye if the sun were shining.

Tenders carried the incoming warriors to shore. These legions scrambled like a nest of uncovered snakes as they disembarked and waded onto dry ground, but they quickly formed into organized units.

Aridela bit her lip, trying not to believe all was lost.

Harpalycus, flanked by one man, walked to the commander of the Pylos army, distinguishable by a crimson cloak and personal guard.

"Eurysthenes," Chrysaleon muttered when the commander removed his ornate helmet and exposed his grizzled hair. "Many times has he been a guest on the citadel. My father and he contracted a union between my sister Bateia and his son." He ground fist against palm and cursed.

"How did Harpalycus gain his support?" Themiste asked.

Chrysaleon shook his head. "He must have promised something very great, especially to bring them in winter."

Eurysthenes' spearmen gathered in thick rows, their long pointed weapons resembling a forest of sharp-tipped trees. More landed, and more again.

Harpalycus's men were forced to back up in order to make room on the beach for the incoming warriors. The two armies faced each other in silence.

Still Harpalycus and Eurysthenes spoke. Harpalycus beckoned his guard forward. The man bowed low and offered a welcoming bowl to Eurysthenes, who accepted it and quaffed the wine.

"What can we do?" Themiste asked. "This might be merely the beginning. What if more ships are landing even now in other harbors? There are so many."

Aridela clasped the oracle's hand. "We will never give up."

Harpalycus gestured toward the partially reconstructed pier. He and Eurysthenes strolled to a pile of rubble and stared at the heavy grey seas. Harpalycus swept out his hand. Perhaps he spoke of the wall of water that had raged against the land, leaving nothing but mud and broken bits of lives, of memories.

His arm faltered. Aridela looked up from him and gasped.

A ship's prow…followed closely by another, broke through mist. Two by two they came, edging around the point. The fog couldn't fully stifle the drummers' beat.

These white sails bore the royal lion head of Mycenae, etched in crimson dye.

Aridela and Themiste glanced at one another, bewildered.

Was Idómeneus coming to help her people, or to rescue his son and conquer the island for himself? He could even be in league with Harpalycus. Helice and the council had suspected Mycenae of duplicity. Their warnings crept through Aridela's mind.

"Chrysaleon?" she asked.

"Look." He pointed.

Eurysthenes had drawn his sword. Harpalycus leaped away from him, fumbling for his own.

The warriors from Labyrinthos began to shuffle. Their meticulous line broke. Helmets swung back and forth as men peered from the arriving ships to the formidable rows of armed men facing them.

Eurysthenes' warriors attacked with a united roar. Spears flew in a whistling cloud of death. Mainland phalanxes pushed Harpalycus's men back. Archers rushed on each side like waves borne on a hurricane. Sword-blades cracked against ox-hide. Arrows hissed. Screams ripped through the air as countless soldiers fell in the initial onslaught.

Aridela seized Chrysaleon's forearm.

He grinned, confident now and easy. "Eurysthenes supports my father. It was a trick." He laughed.

"Quickly, Themiste," Aridela said. "Run back to the cave. Get Menoetius and Selene. Tell our people the time has come. Today, we fight. Today, we rout Harpalycus."

"Yes." Themiste wiped at her tears. "What will you do?"

Aridela faced Chrysaleon, thankful to see the same fierce desire blazing in his eyes that she felt.

He bent his head. They kissed.

Holding hands, they ran down the slope to the sand.

ROCKY HILLS LOOKED DOWN UPON THE FURY OF SHOUTING, CLASH OF blades, and whine of arrows and magnified the noise, making it seem an army of divine proportions fought upon Kaphtor's shore.

Both Chrysaleon and Aridela carried swords and were protected by hard leather armor over linen tunics, but they had brought no helmets, and were soon recognized. Eurysthenes' men called their eager support to Chrysaleon. Someone threw him a spear. Word rippled that the Crown Prince of Mycenae lived and fought with them.

Harpalycus's men also recognized them.

"Kill the Cretan bitch," shouted one, pointing at Aridela, but before he could do or say anything else, he sank to the ground, a spear protruding from his stomach. Aridela looked around and saw Selene. Somber-faced, she held Aridela's gaze for only an instant before turning to fight someone else.

Led to battle by Selene and Menoetius, Kaphtor's survivors poured over the hills in a screaming mass. They were not many, but they fought with the pent-up vengeful rage that had festered for months under Harpalycus's cruel regime.

Aridela never stopped searching for Harpalycus. Finally she glimpsed him, backed up to the water's edge, fending off one of King Eurysthenes' guards. The king himself lay on the ground, unconscious or dead.

She caught Chrysaleon's attention and pointed. He nodded and moved with her. Side by side, they slashed a path to their nemesis.

A youth emerged from the mist near Chrysaleon. His green eyes were made intensely startling and ferocious by a frame of bronzed blood-spattered skin, black brows, and wild, unbound black hair.

"Gelanor," Chrysaleon shouted. They clasped arms then turned simultaneously as three enemy warriors attacked them.

So struck was Aridela by this dark, younger version of her consort that she lost her concentration. One of Harpalycus's soldiers slipped in with a feral yell of victory and punched her in the chest with the butt of his knife.

She fell. For what seemed an eternity, she could do nothing but gasp like a land-bound fish.

The warrior's eyes narrowed. He raised and turned the dagger, starting to grin, until he flew off his feet like a bird taking wing. Chrysaleon and the black-haired youth stood on either side, lifting her attacker by the arms. Selene and Menoetius circled, cutting down any who sought to breach this strange tableau.

Chrysaleon thrust his sword into the warrior's side and dropped him in a convulsing heap. He held out a hand to her and smiled.

Aridela tried to keep any tremble from her return smile as she clasped his hand and let him pull her up. Death had breathed upon her, and it hadn't left her unaffected. She took the dagger from the fallen warrior's hand. It was a Cretan ceremonial knife—the curved obsidian blade flaked to such an edge that the lightest graze split the skin and drew blood. The ivory grip was carved into an exquisite likeness of Athene, standing upon the pillar of life, divinatory owl upon her shoulder.

She gazed coldly down at the dying soldier. "This knife was made for a queen." He stared back, his eyes dulling and his gasps growing fainter. "You sully it with your touch."

The handsome youth who fought with Chrysaleon swiveled to parry a sword-thrust and didn't look her way again.

Aridela lifted her face to the misting rain. "*Ololu, ololu,*" she shouted. Her breath exhaled in clouds from the chill yet she wiped sweat from her eyes. Selene, who seemed determined to remain close, briefly clasped her shoulder.

Kaphtor's warriors echoed the call and cheered as their queen held up the knife.

The press of men thickened as soldiers from Idómeneus's ships landed. Rain clouds gave off a frothy-red tint. Aridela searched again for Harpalycus but couldn't find him.

Chrysaleon seemed impervious to injury, guarded, perhaps by the devotion of his god Poseidon. When an arrow pierced the fleshy backside of his thigh, he broke off the shaft and continued with hardly a limp.

Aridela saw one of the guards who had often dragged her to Harpalycus's bedchamber in Natho. He had watched a few of his master's rapes, and his eyes had held lust. Succumbing to the fire of blood-rage, she lunged away from Chrysaleon, lifting her sword in both hands. He was a big man, with massive shoulders and a jutting brown beard. She saw by his sneer that he recognized her as well. He counter-attacked, sending his blade whistling sideways toward her neck.

She braced, ready to parry his swing, but a third blade slipped between them, grinding and screeching as it halted the thrust of her enemy's.

With the strength of just one arm, Menoetius forced the warrior's sword backward toward the man wielding it.

"Traitor," the guard shouted. He barreled into Menoetius and shoved him. "You should be fighting with us."

Drawing the dagger that had nearly killed her, Aridela stabbed it into the man's neck beneath the edge of his helmet. He fell, his back arching.

She made sure he was dead before she wiped his blood from her face.

As she and Menoetius glanced at each other, she found herself reliving the day they had peered over limitless space at the summit of the world. Looking over the dizzying drop-off left her frozen with terror. She had mourned the loss of her courage, and doubted it would ever return.

As she stood on the battlefield, the blood of the slain warrior staining her flesh and Menoetius's eyes upon her, courage and confidence flooded in a tremendous surge, leaving her tingling. She inwardly pictured the battle won, the people of Kaphtor free and triumphant.

The enemy pressed close. Many wanted to kill Aridela, no doubt hoping to score favor with Harpalycus and demoralize the Cretans. There was no time to give Menoetius anything but the briefest smile. As she turned to engage her next opponent, she hoped the bitterness between them had begun to mend.

Selene's teeth bared like a wolf's as she flew from one warrior to the next, leaving behind a swath of writhing death. Blood covered her face, her arms, and congealed in her hair, but it was mostly the blood of the enemy.

There came an odd pause. Shivers touched the nape of Aridela's neck. The roar of battle ebbed, leaving one sound—Harpalycus's snarl as he cut through the royal guard, his eyes fixed on her consort.

Two enemy warriors had engaged Chrysaleon. His back was turned, his full attention taken as he parried, thrust, and cut.

Desperation transported Aridela through a clot of men. She slashed at them almost absently. Harpalycus engulfed her entire vision. Yet she had fallen some distance behind. Harpalycus's sword-blade rose as he raced closer to Chrysaleon. Screaming, Aridela shot like an arrow through the space that cleared before her.

Harpalycus aimed for the area beneath Chrysaleon's ribs. With such power behind it, the thrust would pierce his armor. So engrossed was the Butcher of Kaphtor that he didn't turn at Aridela's scream. He didn't see her coming. His desire to murder his childhood foe made him deaf to all distractions.

Her entire weight struck him in the back. His sword flew from his hand as his spine bowed. She held onto her sword, but lost the knife and fell off balance, landing hard on the side of her head. Dirt stung her eyes. Her ability to think and act vanished in a deluge of pain.

As she lay gasping, he seized her legs and rolled her over on her back. He straddled her hips, grinning. Pinning her sword hand to the ground, he picked up the dagger she had dropped and without any pause to gloat, stabbed her just above her breast.

The obsidian blade was so sharp it sliced her leather breastplate as though it had no more substance than a cloud. A sonorous hum pushed everything else from her mind. All that remained was Harpalycus's satisfied smile.

His hot breath stole hers as he bent over her face. "My Cretan whore," he said in his own language, knowing she would understand. He had used the title many times.

Despair weighted her bones. The earth pulled at her. Was she going to die here, defeated, slain by the man she most hated?

He released his grip on the dagger, leaving it in her. Still smiling, he straightened. He lifted his arm and motioned to someone.

In one instinctive movement, Aridela extracted the dagger from her flesh with her right hand and thrust it into his throat, into the soft, vulnerable spot to the left of his larynx.

She sliced back and forth then withdrew the blade. Blood gushed over her face.

His eyes widened. He grabbed at the knife, gasping, but as his lifeblood spurted he slumped and rolled to the side. He wasn't yet done, though. One hand seized her thigh. The noxious stench of smoldering ashes made her gag. Her eyes filled with stinging water. For the briefest instant, she thought she saw a blackish-green cloud rise from his torn throat. There was a sickening drag on her senses, reminiscent of Themiste's mind link; she felt her thoughts and experiences being drawn to the surface and for some unknown length of time she merged with Harpalycus, with his hatred and loathing, and she understood what drove him. She saw him creep, naked, into the bedchamber of Iros, his sister, slit the throat of the nurse, and stand by the bed, panting as he drew back the blanket. His eyes showed her the day Lycomedes learned the truth. He flayed Harpalycus with a horsewhip, screaming curses and contempt. She floated within Harpalycus as he descended stone steps to a dank underground chamber where Proitos waited, along with a pile of dead bodies, scurrying shiny black beetles, and vials of a stinking tarry substance. She watched Harpalycus vow revenge upon the priest who had betrayed his misdeeds to his father. She heard him tell Proitos that Iros was to be given to Chrysaleon, and she felt herself suffocating in his rage.

Then a spear, shining and bright white as the face of the moon, thrust between them, and the awful connection snapped. A woman, surrounded by a blaze of glistening light, fury upon her face, shouted, *"Release the child of Velchanos!"*

Harpalycus cringed. His hand fell free but he reached out again with the other, this time clawing at the leg of a soldier who stumbled past.

The blinding specter vanished.

Again there was a stench and black-greenish haze. The man Harpalycus had seized fell, vomiting. He stopped moving and lay as though dead, but then, as Aridela stared, he rose, glanced at her, and ran away, disappearing swiftly into the mist.

Aridela fought the urge to close her eyes, to slip into the quiet peace of death. Instead she dragged herself onto her knees, shuddering, pressing one hand against the puncture in her chest, and crouched over Harpalycus's body.

His mouth hung lax; his head fell to the side. Thick pinkish goo bubbled with the blood at his throat, like rotted fish turned to jelly.

"I will feed your carcass to the sea," she screamed.

He didn't hear.

He was dead.

She retched. Blood flowed between her fingers from the wound above her breast. She felt herself falling into pieces like a broken pot. Her mind detached from her body and disintegrated, washing away in the rain.

"Take me, Athene," she whispered, and sank into an emotionless, unfeeling void.

15

Moon of Drenching Rain

From the Oracle Logs
Themiste

After the battle, we victors returned to Labyrinthos, carrying *Harpalycus's severed head on the tip of a spear. The remainder of the usurper's soldiers have been unearthed and put to the sword. Our cities belong to us again.*

The bodies of Helice and Laodámeia were brought to us. Harpalycus had left them in the cave where he slaughtered them. They were amazingly preserved, perhaps because of the dryness in the cave and the frozen weather. Aridela, though she was weak and had to lean on my arm, waited with me upon the quay as they arrived. She insisted on helping me purify their remains. While I washed Laodámeia, she cleansed her mother's body, arranged her hair, and dressed her in a gown stiff with gold. I set my favorite copper mirror into Laodámeia's hand, and around her throat I fastened a necklace my mother left to me. Her most unique and prized possession, it is shaped to resemble a nautilus shell.

Helice was placed in a sarcophagus decorated with cuckoos and partridges. Aridela made the carriers wait while she leaned down and whispered something in her mother's ear. She remained there, trembling, eyes closed; I stood by, longing to comfort her, thinking of all this child has endured.

Hundreds followed the procession to a site not far from the palace walls.

Our Zagreus and his brothers designed their tombs. In their land, important folk are buried in massive graves such as this, which they call monuments.

The grave lies beneath a shaft dug into the slope of a hill, on a bed of pebbles. The men were careful with the placement, so that the faces of our beloved dead are forever turned toward holy Mount Juktas. After setting the head of a white bull at the grave's entrance, we returned to the city, where Aridela ordered the sacrifice of ten more bulls.

I will sorely miss Laodámeia. She was my friend and confidant. I never fully realized how I depended on her. Her crusty voice woke me each morning as she brought me milk. Laodámeia rubbed my skin with soothing oils when I ached from chewing the laurel leaves. I will miss her astute observations, which she never hesitated to share with me.

Chrysaleon has searched the prisons, trying to find an entrance to the caves in his death-dream. I showed him the secret corridors we used to spirit him away. The old paintings on the stone walls caused much excitement. "I saw these!" he shouted. "This is the way to the land of Velchanos."

I didn't like to crush his hopes. I felt weighted with grief as I led him through every corridor, clear to the exit outside the city.

He examined the walls for cracks that might indicate hidden doorways. Disappointment shadowed his face when at last Aridela convinced him to give up. "Why would we keep such a secret from you?" she asked. "You are Kaphtor's hero. If there were an underground corridor into the land of Velchanos, my love, I would gladly share this knowledge."

"Perhaps," I said, "you saw these paintings as we carried you from your cell. I did think you unconscious, but maybe not. It would explain why they seem familiar."

Chrysaleon has an angry frown. He does not like our answers. Though he is powerfully built, with a man's full beard and massive arms that can wield our heavy shields, I see hints of a sulky child within him.

Something curious happened after our forces defeated Harpalycus on the beach at Amnisos. We converged upon Knossos and the palace. There we found Proitos, Harpalycus's eunuch-slave, fast asleep in his master's bed.

Our soldiers surrounded him, ready to impale this blubbery creature if he so much as twitched. But before orders could be given or anything done, a stooped, grey-headed man, leaning upon a stick, pushed his way into the center of the room. He was dressed in a fine tunic and had his hair styled the way men of Mycenae favor. I took him for an old nobleman, and this notion persisted because he spoke in an authoritative manner, ordering the soldiers to step back from the bed but to keep their weapons ready, and under no circumstances allow Proitos to touch any of them.

This man then turned to me. He introduced himself with a wobbly bow as Alexiare, Chrysaleon's slave. He claimed to be acting on the orders of King Idómeneus, explaining only that this cowering, sweaty man was more dangerous than he seemed. He had no interest in how we dealt with the rest of Harpalycus's men, but insisted no one be allowed near Proitos, and moreover ordered that he be taken out onto the plain and killed by a spearman standing a good distance away.

Other matters demanded my attention, so I left them as they prodded Harpalycus's lackey from the chamber. Later, I interrogated one of the guards who went with them. He told me Alexiare spoke to Proitos. With a puzzled shrug, the guard said Proitos made a mad claim. He told Alexiare that Harpalycus the Butcher is not dead. I made him repeat the words exactly as they were spoken. "You think my lord is dead, but you will see, to your sorrow." Alexiare asked Proitos who Harpalycus had 'consumed,' and promised to show mercy if he told. But Proitos could not, or would not say. Alexiare accused Proitos of conjuring tales to save himself. He informed Proitos that Harpalycus's head now resides on the point of a spear, and asked if he would like to see it for himself. The guard reported that Proitos appeared despondent, but seemed to rally. He lifted his head and stated with surety, "I know my master. He found a way."

I made it to the field as the spearmen took aim. I myself heard Proitos curse Alexiare. He swore he would return and take his vengeance, but Alexiare only shook his head, his expression almost sympathetic. Then Proitos called Alexiare 'Father,' and begged him to hold his hand while he died, but Alexiare would not approach him. Secrets curled around these two like smoke, causing me to feel dizzy.

I might be more concerned about all this, but I have seen Harpalycus's body. He is, without a doubt, dead. And now so is Proitos.

Only later, in the midst of instructing one of my priestesses, did I remember Alexiare. He was the old man who accompanied Menoetius to our island years ago, and passed himself off as that youth's father. That must be why he seemed familiar. He is an aged, unwell man who has much trouble walking and talking, as some injury left him with barely any voice. His demeanor is harmless, respectful, yet he avoids me with youthful alacrity. He never lets me look into his eyes.

He makes me uneasy.

CHRYSALEON WALKED THE DIRT-PACKED ROADS OF KNOSSOS, contemplating the changes inflicted on this once-great island.

Snow covered the ground as far as he could see. Where carts ran and litters were carried, it had decomposed to ugly grey slush. The air was unrelentingly chill. Several days of damp coolness coupled with watery sunlight had encouraged the almond trees to put forth blooms, which then blackened in sudden nighttime freezes.

A contingent of his father's soldiers were collecting the abandoned dead and carrying them into the country to be burned. The majority, he was told, were children.

The peasants he encountered were dirty and pinched. Their eyes followed him. When any approached, begging, he sent them to Labyrinthos with the promise of food. Others seemed too far gone to care. He passed a woman sitting at the edge of a narrow alley, hunched over the body of an infant on her lap. She made no response to his queries.

Idómeneus and Eurysthenes brought more than fighting forces. After the battle was won and order reestablished, the men hauled jars of grain, dried fruit, olives, honey, and wine off the ships. These were transported to Labyrinthos, along with oxen, sheep and goats, piglets, and wickets of quail.

It was Alexiare, apparently, who had conceived the idea that Kaphtor would need such things, and he who persuaded Idómeneus to be generous.

His premonitions about the disarray Harpalycus would leave behind proved farsighted. Aridela's first act upon being restored to her palace was to search for food, but the storage jars that survived the collapse of walls had been used to feed Harpalycus's armies and were depleted. Precious oil and other riches had been shipped away to his father's citadel at Tiryns.

Ash had obliterated the crops in the east. To the west, where the fall of ash was minimal, flourishing barley now withered under pervasive frosts. The future of Crete seemed set for ruin.

Aridela, Themiste, and what remained of the council stood in silence at their first glimpse of the palace storehouses. Once crammed with worked gold and trade goods, they now held little but dust and rat droppings.

Harpalycus hadn't found some of the deeper storerooms, however. When Aridela and her council discovered this, it was cause for rejoicing.

At this time in the wheel of the year, Kaphtor customarily blossomed after a short, invigorating winter. Snow would be confined to mountain summits and higher slopes. Fed by spring rains and snowmelt, almond trees would explode with blooms. Carpets of wildflowers and poppies would glorify the plains from one coast to the other. This was normally the much-anticipated season of Velchanos's rebirth, the prayed-for result of the king sacrifice, and was celebrated with feasting and festivals.

As he explored the barren wynds, Chrysaleon thought back to the day—scarcely seven months ago—that he and Menoetius stepped onto the quay at Amnisos. The shouts of vendors reverberated off the buildings. Sweaty children darted, laughing, all sticky hands and mischievous eyes. Ripe fruit intoxicated the senses. Brightly dyed pennants lined every avenue, while awnings promised cool shade. His mind recreated the heady scents of jasmine, aromatic herbs, and baking bread.

Foreigners had swarmed the streets, dark-bearded men swathed in flowing robes, leading their veiled giggling wives, who paused to admire the myriad wares on display. Nobles, adorned to impress, reclined in litters. There were constant distractions—bull leapings, acrobatics, wagering, dancing and music, and competitions. These made the days before the Games pass quickly. Artisans disrupted the peace with their hammering, the clack of potter's wheels, and ring of bronze being shaped.

Chrysaleon's nostalgic memories faded as he passed a villa he knew had belonged to Lycus, the bull dancer who died trying to rescue Aridela. It stood deserted now, its pennants gone, the walls dirty and flaked. One wall had collapsed. Clay pots, once boasting fragrant flowers, lay shattered or empty, half-buried in slush.

Spotting a Mycenaean soldier near the arch leading into the courtyard, he paused, curious. The warrior, wearing inlaid leather armor over a warm quilted tunic, turned and walked toward him. He had his arm, and most of his cloak, around the shorter figure of a woman, and walked slowly to accommodate her. She leaned against him, allowing him to support her; his attention was so engrossed that he never noticed his prince across the lane, watching.

Though Chrysaleon knew not what lay between these two, he had a sudden, sickening realization. The man might keep her. They might even marry. He looked old enough to satisfy Mycenaean law, which didn't allow common soldiers to wed until they reached their thirties.

If they wished, they could live out their lives together. She appeared ill, but the soldier was probably taking her to his barrack where she would receive food and medicines.

Chrysaleon, Crete's royal beloved prince, who wore the king's signet ring and bore the sacred title of Zagreus, had no such choices. Six more cycles of the moon were all he could look forward to. On the day he'd killed Helice's consort, he experienced a vision of an oak grove, of maddened women, their faces disguised by masks. Perhaps it had been a moera-formed image of his own future death, for he'd learned that when the midsummer moon next grew full, in the month called Moon of White Light, he would meet his successor not in the ruined labyrinth beneath the palace, but in a clearing surrounded by oaks and olive groves. There his blood would be spilled. Women made mad by laurel and the cara mushroom would gorge upon his flesh. Kaphtor's soil would swallow him as though he'd never existed, and Aridela would take his murderer into her bed.

His muscles clenched. Fury ripped through him. He forced himself to wander on.

A few more turns brought him nearer to Labyrinthos and a scene of activity. Servants scurried back and forth, laden with wooden casks, tables, cloth, and clay urns. Builders shouted at laborers. Giant new pillars, some already painted red with bright blue stripes around their capitals, lay on the ground, ready to be hoisted into place.

Slipping past all this, he stepped into the courtyard. He scanned the area, searching for Aridela, and quickly found her. Dressed in heavy warm robes, she sat on a low balcony watching the bustle. Neoma and Selene stood beside her, absorbed in conversation with one of the architects charged with rebuilding. They appeared to be studying something, probably plans for repairs.

The chill, noise, and busyness died away. His resentment evaporated, replaced by quiet. The words Damasen spoke in his death-dream returned.

Love for your queen brings infinite pain as well as joy.

Her lost necklace with the crescent moons and blue lapis bead lay in one hand, a mass of metal warmed by his flesh. Stepping out into clear view, he sent his love flying to her on shafts of invisible arrows. Before long she turned, feeling his gaze as he wanted her to, searching the courtyard until she found him.

His heartbeat quickened; his limbs tingled. Truly, he had never known such passion over a woman, not even the first time he'd experienced the act of love. On the night of the Destruction, he had given Aridela his vow that not even death could part them. He knew now, as he returned her smile, that he'd never uttered words with more deliberate intent. His hands clenched as he repeated the oath.

Not even death.

He walked closer.

She rose, leaned over the balustrade, and tossed a cluster of anemones over the edge. They floated to him as though directed by a god. Where had she found them, in this land where flowers had become rare and precious?

Aridela, with a body nearly as delicate as the blooms she gave, had pulled a dagger from her flesh and used it to slay the warrior Harpalycus. Their glorious victory would be praised in song for as long as the sun rose in the heavens. How perfect she was, this unique, irresistible combination of strength and frailty, cold pride and warm succor, giver of life and divine slayer.

He relived the spilled blood, the sweat and froth of battle. His mind recreated the queen fighting with her people, and that agonizing panic when he saw her slumped over Harpalycus's body. Sending desperate prayers and reckless promises to every god he could think of, he leaped to her side.

The amount of blood flooding from the dagger wound terrified him. Her face was deathly white. He pressed his hands hard against the puncture.

"Is she dead?" Menoetius shouted.

Aridela's eyelids flickered. "Butcher," she whispered.

"No. Not yet." Chrysaleon motioned to Gelanor and several others to carry her to safety.

After that, he could only guess her fate as he, Menoetius, Selene, the Cretans, and the mainland armies finished off the enemy on the beach of Amnisos.

Exhausted, bloody, limping, he sought out the cluster of people surrounding the queen. He shoved them aside and knelt.

Padding fashioned from someone's tunic was wrapped around her torso, thicker where herbs had been packed over the injury. Rhené, her arms slimed with blood to the elbows, bundled the fine bone needles she'd used to stitch the wound.

"She will live." Themiste laid a hand on his forearm. "My Lady did guide the blade into the one spot that would not take her life."

"Are we victorious?" Aridela peered up at him. Harpalycus's blood was still stuck in her hair, smeared on her cheeks and the bridge of her nose. Her voice was small and weak. When he nodded, she stretched out her hand. "I want to see."

Ignoring Rhené's protests, Chrysaleon lifted her into the crook of his arm.

Cheers rose as he carried her across the sand, over the bodies of Kaphtor's enemies. Her people crowded close, reaching out to touch her. She held a spear aloft in her right hand and shouted the call of triumph.

They circled the battlefield three times. Aridela asked for a sword, and when it was brought, she offered it to Chrysaleon. He gladly cut off Harpalycus's head and rammed it onto the end of her spear.

Cheering resounded against the surrounding hills. They called Chrysaleon Kaphtor's greatest hero, and bowed low before him.

The adoration from that day echoed through his head as he stood in the palace courtyard and gazed at Aridela. Just above her left breast, hidden by her robes, lay the reddened, puckering wound where Harpalycus had stabbed her. So close to her heart, yet, guided by Athene, it slipped between the vessels that if severed, would have killed her in a matter of three breaths.

Crete's queen appeared fragile to the uneducated eye, a girl just budding into womanhood.

The cloud cover broke. Shafts of sunlight cartwheeled, transforming the dismal scene into one of heady color.

"Here." He tossed the silver chain. It glinted as it flew to her waiting hands.

"My necklace," she cried. Delight warmed her still-thin, pale face.

He forced thoughts of his grim future out of his head. There would be time tomorrow to think of something. "I'm coming up."

Infinite pain as well as joy. Let today be joy.

THE END

241

Historical Notes

In 1965, not far from Knossos, archaeologists discovered an undisturbed chamber next to a plundered larger tomb. Here they uncovered the remains of a woman, dressed in a lavish amount of gold jewelry. One of the signet rings she wore depicts a female in the traditional fancy skirts of the time. The engraved woman stands between two men; one appears to be dancing in a celebratory fashion around a shrine, holding a tree, some kind of plant, or perhaps bullroarers. The other man is kneeling. In 1975, in a second valuable discovery, yet another lady was found, wearing a gold necklace crafted into the likeness of a paper-nautilus shell. Lying on her side, she faced Mount Juktas and held in her hands a copper mirror.

Christos Tsountas discovered the famous Vapheio cups, which portray the Cretan method of capturing wild bulls.

About the Author

While growing up, Rebecca Lochlann began envisioning an epic story, a new kind of myth, one built upon the foundation of the Greek classics and continuing through the centuries right up into the present and future.

This has become her life's work, though she didn't exactly intend it to be that way when she started.

The Child of the Erinyes series is mythic fantasy, inspired by the Greek tale of Ariadne, Theseus, and the Minotaur. As one reader put it, "Loads of testosterone, slaughter, and crazy magic," with a love story, of course.

Though the story is fiction-fantasy, it still took about fifteen years to research the Bronze Age segments of the series, and encompassed rare historical documents, mythology, archaeology, ancient religions, and volcanology.

The Year-god's Daughter is her debut novel: Book One of *The Child of the Erinyes* series. It has been utilized as a study guide in an American university, named a B.R.A.G. Medallion honoree, and was a finalist in the Chaucer Historical Fiction awards. Book Two, *The Thinara King*, a First Place winner in the Ancient History category of the Chaucer Historical Fiction awards and a Next Generation Indie Book Awards finalist, continues the saga. Book Three, *In the Moon of Asterion*, wraps up the Bronze Age segment of the series and leads into the middle trilogy, set in Scotland. These are: Book Four, *The Moon Casts a Spell*, Book Five, *The Sixth Labyrinth*, and Book Six, *Falcon Blue*, which jumps backward in time to the Early Medieval Era.

The denouement comes in the final three books: *When the Moon Whispers, First and Second Chronicles*, and *Swimming in the Rainbow*.

Rebecca has always believed that certain rare individuals, either blessed or tortured, voluntarily or involuntarily, are woven by fate or the Immortals into the labyrinth of time, and that deities sometimes speak to us through dreams and visions, gently prompting us to tell their lost stories. Who knows? It could make a difference.

Connect with Rebecca at her website, BookBub, Facebook, or in a review at your point of purchase.

Erinyes Press and Rebecca would like to thank you for continuing this journey.

Attributions

My author website has maps, bibliographies, and more: rebeccalochlann.com

Front and back cover design—Rebecca Lochlann, Erinyes Press
    Colorization of necklace—Rebecca Lochlann, Erinyes Press
    Marble head of ancient sculpture: Circumnavigation, Shutterstock
    Doomsday: ortodoxfoto, Depositphotos
    Original title Page image: Kiselev Andrey Valervich, Shutterstock
    Fiery shots of active lava flow: Evan Austen, Shutterstock
    Design Elements: A-R-T-U-R, Depositphotos
    Crescent moon, necklace image, & Erinyes Press logo by Lance Ganey: www.freelanceganey.com
    Labrys Axe graphic © "Labrys-symbol" Licensed under Public domain via Wikimedia Commons http://commons.wikimedia.org/wiki/File:Labrys-symbol.svg#mediaviewer/File:Labrys-symbol.svg
    In the Moon of Asterion cover image: Giovanni Dall'Orto, November 11 2009: File Source: Creative Commons, Attribution License/cropped & colored. Ancient Roman bust of Antinous. Hadrian age ((AD 117-138),National Archaeological Museum in Athens, Room 32. http://commons.wikimedia.org/wiki/File:1642_-_Archaeological_Museum,_Athens_-_Antinous_-_Photo_by_Giovanni_Dall%27Orto,_Nov_11_2009.jpg
    https://creativecommons.org/licenses/by-sa/1.0/deed.en
    Colorized, brightened, cropped, background replaced

Titles in The Child of the Erinyes series

Book One: *The Year-god's Daughter*
Book Two: *The Thinara King*
Book Three: *In the Moon of Asterion*
Book Four: *The Moon Casts a Spell* (a novella)
Book Five: *The Sixth Labyrinth*
Book Six: *Falcon Blue*
Book Seven: *When the Moon Whispers, First Chronicle*
Book Eight: *When the Moon Whispers, Second Chronicle*
Book Nine: *Swimming in the Rainbow*

In the Moon of Asterion
EXCERPT

If you enjoyed *The Thinara King* and would like to see what happens next, please look for the third installment.

There is a beast in the labyrinth...a monster.

The people say he is both man and bull; they call him Asterion.

Of all Crete's citizens, only two dare enter his lair. One bears his child. The other sees the Goddess in his eyes.

Terrifying yet compelling, the beast offers Crete's only hope for redemption.

(*In the Moon of Asterion* concludes the Bronze Age segment of the series.)

Moon of Asphodel and Honeysuckle
REBECCA LOCHLANN

FROM THE ORACLE LOGS
  Themiste

WE ARE FREE!

The Butcher is dead!

Our queen is restored to her throne!

Kaphtor thunders with these shouts. The people make merry day and night.

Though the worst is over, I remain uneasy. I want to return to a time before these barbarians unleashed their disaster upon us. I will not draw an easy breath until the earth swallows the blood of our newest bull-king, Chrysaleon of Mycenae. On that night, I will drink mead and dance in the light of Iakchos. I fear him. I distrust him. None are safe while he lives. Yet, I confess this secret, as I must, to the Oracle Logs...

I am drawn to him as I have never been drawn to any other man.

EVERY ROW OF BENCHES LOOKING DOWN UPON THE FAMED BULLRING at Knossos groaned under the weight of multitudes. Those who couldn't fit inside crowded thick as schools of anchovies across the plain. All wanted to be a part of the triple-tiered festival—Queen Aridela's seventeenth birthday, the annual observance of Velchanos's rebirth, and the feting of their mainland liberators.

Kaphtor was free—to survive, to grow, to recover. Harpalycus, cursed prince of mainland Tiryns, the Usurper and Oppressor of their beloved island, had been defeated in a victory of such glory it would never be forgotten. His head now rotted on the tip of a spear outside the palace of Labyrinthos.

In the underground chambers beneath the ring, Aridela and her friends were nearly finished dressing, ready to begin the much-anticipated celebration. One handmaid adjusted Aridela's diadem while another finished rubbing kohl along her eyelashes.

"Color has returned to your face, Aridela," Neoma said, and slipped between the two women to give the queen a spontaneous hug. "You look well and strong, at last!"

"Freedom and victory have granted us both new life."

"Do you remember how we used to fight and try to outdo each other over petty things? It seems lifetimes ago."

Aridela nodded ruefully. "Yes, we are changed. How could we not be?"

"Was it by design, I wonder?" Neoma touched the shallow dent in her forehead, a permanent reminder of the night when stones had fallen like deadly spears from the sky. "I thought this would make things difficult, but the opposite is true. My lovers are so many I cannot choose between them." Her boisterous laugh echoed off the walls of the chamber. "I suppose it could be because they curry favor with the queen's cousin."

"For some men, that could be a hindrance rather than advantage."

They giggled like they were still ten years old.

Selene, also dressed lavishly, appeared in the doorway from the outer corridor. "I have never seen anything to compare with this crowd —not even your mother could draw crowds like these." She lifted her heavy, elaborately braided and bejeweled cream-colored hair so she could fan her neck. This Phrygian warrior, a princess in her own right, had slaughtered many enemies in the battle to free the island, and she had saved Aridela's life more than once. "They grow impatient, and it is stifling down here. Soon they will break the stands beneath their feet. Are you ready?"

As Aridela turned from Neoma, an eager *yes* on the tip of her tongue, a dizzy spell spiraled in the abrupt, unexpected way it had, leaving her ears humming, her eyesight spackled, and her balance in jeopardy. Such attacks were frequent since Harpalycus had stabbed her, and ending the life of the infant in her womb had made matters more precarious. Rhené, Kaphtor's royal healer, blamed the affliction on an excessive loss of blood, and dosed her patient daily with noxious concoctions of half-raw meat and boiled ox bones in an effort to rebuild her strength.

Usually she either fainted or vomited, but this time, hallucinations flooded—dazzling, terrible flashes from the two months Aridela spent as Harpalycus's captive and personal plaything. She grabbed Neoma's shoulder as a litany raced through her mind of his drunken assaults, the filth of the straw mat in her cell, the cruel eunuch's daily beatings, and the leather thongs biting into her wrists.

Chilling echoes replaced the lively chatter. Deep within, as if dredged from her soul, another voice drowned out everything else.

We will make ourselves barren. No more children. No more love. Not until they all lie dead. Then we will begin again.

The chamber walls melted like wet paint, vanishing into a different scene. One amongst a crowd, Aridela huddled on the side of a steep hill, soaked by cold rain. Above, on the summit where her voice would carry, a woman with long dark hair shouted these words. Some members of the crowd wept. Some were angry. Many raised their fists.

If we are barren, Aridela wanted to ask, *how can we begin again?*

Neoma drew Aridela out of the vision and back to the present by clasping her chin and gazing with alarm into her eyes. "What happened? Is it the wound?"

Selene crossed the space and joined them. "Are you strong enough to do this? You're shaking. You're pale."

Aridela composed her senses in the comforting, familiar scents of dust, wood, sweat, and unguents that for centuries had permeated these walls. Her hand rose to the healing puncture above her heart and pressed; beneath her skin, she felt the steady beat of her heart. Harpalycus had done his best to end her life, yet through Athene's divine intercession, she had survived. In the end, it was Harpalycus who failed, who lost everything, who breathed his last in the blood and gore of battle.

The strange, otherworldly vision made no sense, and this was not a day for somber reflection. "Yes!" She gripped her old friend's hand. "I am strong enough. I'm ready to begin life at last, to see Kaphtor begin again." An exhilarating shiver ran up the back of her neck as she pictured her mother. *Be happy, isoke,* Helice would say if she were here.

Iphiboë felt close as well. Her beloved sister, a nervous, shy girl terrified of lying with a man, had willingly sacrificed herself to calm the Lady's anger and bring mercy to their people, and in doing so, had become Kaphtor's most cherished treasure.

Squaring her shoulders, Aridela managed to push away the nauseating whirl in her head.

Cheering and the deafening stamp of feet vibrated the ground as Aridela followed Selene into the ring. Leaves and flowers fashioned from feathers and cloth rained over them. Aridela held Selene's waist, Neoma held Aridela's, another woman held Neoma's, and so on. Together they formed a long, winding, triumphal line. In imitation of the divine serpent, they would weave through the opened sections of the labyrinth, leaving behind a fresh, clean skin, and later, when night fell, smoke from offerings would be sent into the heavens from every mountain sanctuary.

Though the people cheered, Aridela felt a subtle change in mood. Who could miss how sunlight bounced off amber and obsidian where once it was gold and lapis? Real flowers remained scarce, so these poor substitutes of cloth were thrown. Hunters searched for meat yet found little, and sickness stole more lives every day. The harbors were bereft of Kaphtor's famed fleet; now they were crowded with ships belonging to King Idómeneus, King Eurysthenes, and the defeated Harpalycus.

She, too, careened between despondency and elation. After many tears and arguments, she had convinced Rhené to put an end to her pregnancy, just six days after the battle. The healer couldn't manage the task during Harpalycus's occupation because she had no medicines, and she flatly refused to attempt pricking Aridela's womb with a sharpened instrument, declaring the queen would surely die.

Rhené again balked after the battle because of the near-fatal knife wound above Aridela's heart. She relented only because she couldn't argue with the fact that the longer they waited, the more risky any method would become.

After prodding and poking her, Rhené declared it unlikely the child was Chrysaleon's, claiming a lack of hardness she said would be typical in a woman's third month, but she was forced to speculate, as Aridela could not recall whether her monthly course of blood had ever flowed after Harpalycus made her his prisoner. The royal augurers had no better luck divining an answer from the portents and entrails.

Kaphtor's queen choked down foul-tasting brews and endured a suppository of birthwort. After a day and night of ripping cramps, pain that left her helplessly screaming, and profuse bleeding that Rhené and her attendants all but failed to stop, she lapsed into unconsciousness. While she floated ever closer to the land of the dead and the severing of her moera, the unwanted baby was expelled.

Had she stopped the life of Harpalycus's offspring, or Chrysaleon's? The answer always twined away in a bewildering black maze. One was understandable, even necessary, the other a blistering torment. Only the Immortals would ever know the answer.

As she and her sisters danced around the arena, Aridela waved and blew kisses to the audience. The crowd returned her effort with ringing cheers. Her task as queen was to revive their confidence, no matter what personal grief she suffered. She, Themiste, and Chrysaleon, with the intercession of a mollified Lady Athene, would reinvigorate their island, and they could all start over—perhaps with a new baby.

Harpalycus tried to break your spirit, Menoetius had told her one cold winter night. *He failed. You have far more courage than Chrysaleon.* Her smile brightened as she remembered how his words had helped bring back her will to live. She gave a lively toss of her head, sending her hair flying, and the crowd's cheering intensified.

The women circled the perimeter of the bullring seven times while the spectators made a thundering drumbeat with their feet. Continuing through the wynds of Knossos, the dancers shed layers of their skirts and threw bits of colorful cloth.

They crossed the viaduct and glided through the olive groves, accompanied by swarms of boisterous admirers.

At the palace, they entered the processional corridor and danced their way past newly painted frescoes of smiling youths, their arms filled with rich offerings. On they went, circling columns, spinning across terraces, and marching over balconies draped with bright banners.

Their supporters thronged the courtyard as the cavalcade wove down the steps to the underground, where laborers had cleared rubble and hoisted support pillars to create pathways for them.

Deeper and deeper the women danced, singing songs of purification. They stopped only to put out bowls of milk for the holy snakes.

Up and out they climbed, back through the courtyard to the north gate, past the charging bull fresco, which still bore cracks across its middle.

Tomorrow morning, the foreign kings and their armies would

depart. They had enjoyed half a month as Kaphtor's venerated guests while waiting for King Eurysthenes to recover from his wounds. Tonight they would be feasted. Though the meal might not compare to Kaphtor's feasts of old, even now skilled cooks were roasting ibex, poaching seafood, baking bread from mainland grain, and arranging bowls of dried fruit.

Yesterday, Chrysaleon had announced his intent to accompany his father back to Mycenae, "To settle old affairs," he told Aridela. He also wanted to see what damage had been wrought throughout the islands.

His decision added to Aridela's emotional struggles. The Zagreus was never supposed to leave Kaphtor. They couldn't conceive his child if he was gone. And they had already lost so much time. Now they would lose more. Worse, he'd failed to disguise his eagerness to be away, to engage in a new adventure apart from her. She could hardly blame him.

At the fall of dusk, King Idómeneus was lifted onto the royal dais in the feasting hall. Placing his thin, cold hands over Aridela's and Chrysaleon's, he gave them his blessing.

"Our lands are now joined," he said, his voice weak and quavering. "May your womb be fruitful. May the isle of Kaphtor return to its former glory."

Aridela smiled and bowed as courtesy demanded, though she knew his words were a blatant lie. She and many others had overheard the vicious encounter between Chrysaleon, Menoetius, and their father. The very night of Kaphtor's triumph, with Harpalycus dead, his army in ruins, his surviving warriors hiding in any cranny they could find, Idómeneus had summoned his two sons and proceeded to give them an uninhibited taste of his displeasure. The king's healers had raced past Aridela in the corridor at Labyrinthos, pausing for no more than the briefest salutation.

They mean to slaughter you like a pig, Idómeneus had raged. *Do your vows to me mean nothing? All this for lust of a woman.* To Menoetius he shouted, *You promised me you would protect your brother.*

At Idómeneus's peremptory gesture, Aridela leaned closer and allowed him to kiss one cheek, then the other. His watery eyes remained bitter, yet she felt no animosity. Only compassion, which she tried for his sake to hide.

The scent of death lingered on his flesh. No matter what his healers proclaimed, Aridela felt certain Idómeneus did not have long to live. Chrysaleon had told her of Harpalycus's boast that he'd had the king poisoned with hellebore. The poor man's unhealthy color, palsy, and emaciation gave weight to the claim.

The mainland nobles drummed their cups against the tabletops as she and Chrysaleon stood before them, holding hands. She wondered if any were displaying their true feelings.

Gelanor sat next to Aridela at the high table. His rapt gaze leaped from the dancers to the wall hangings to the tables thick with nobles. Being but three months older than she and fascinated with everything having to do with Kaphtor, Chrysaleon's younger brother had quickly become her friend and confidant.

"My mother named him before she died," Chrysaleon said. "He lives up to her vision, laughing so often, over anything at all, we suspect his mind is weak."

Gelanor sneered and sent his brother a crude gesture.

"And you have a sister?" Aridela asked.

"Bateia. She is betrothed to King Eurysthenes' son."

"My lady." Gelanor leaned on one elbow as he regarded her. "There is a story that Goddess Athene buries the moon in your mountains when it vanishes from the heavens. Is this true?"

The words sent Aridela back to the day she leapt the bull. How long ago it all seemed. Chrysaleon had regaled her with Alexiare's tales. She'd told him of her father, and showed him her prized necklace, the charm she'd thought lost forever.

She touched the silver links at her throat and met Chrysaleon's amused gaze. *Back where it belongs, thanks to you.*

That was the day she had asked him to remain, to fight in Kaphtor's Games and find glory, for one year, as sacred king.

"I believe it is true," she told Gelanor. "Every year hunting parties make their searches, but no mortal has a chance of finding the Lady's hiding place."

Chrysaleon's faint, intimate smile told Aridela he recalled that distant day as well. When life was simple. When she was carefree, happy, newly in love, and quite ignorant of what horrors were about to descend.

Now that he was clean and richly attired, Gelanor bore little resemblance to the blood-spattered warrior she had fought beside on the battlefield. His innocence and naivety were evident, but earlier, during the formal speeches, his face had displayed an ominous frown as he stood next to his father's litter.

She was queen of Kaphtor again because of these men. Honor, gratitude, and gifts were being heaped upon them. Yet in six short months she would reward all they had done by overseeing Chrysaleon's ritual murder.

Aridela lowered her gaze and tried to fight off a sudden queasiness she suspected was caused by guilt rather than a supper swimming in rich sauces.

If only her mother were here. Helice would know how to handle this delicate situation. She would find a way to satisfy Idómeneus, Gelanor, Chrysaleon, and the Immortal Goddess.

Duty and obligation lay heavy as a yoke over her shoulders on this night that had been designed for joy.

She didn't want Chrysaleon to die. Yet she dared not confess her selfish desire to anyone. She could do nothing to save him. Instead, she must stand with her head lifted and her grief hidden as his blood seeped into the earth, as he looked his last upon her, as his manhood was carried to the sea.

Blinking back tears, she turned to her consort. "Are you taking your slave with you to Mycenae, my lord, or leaving him here with me?"

"I cannot leave him here," Chrysaleon said. "That old man is far more trouble than he seems, and loves to interfere in matters beyond his station. Who knows what mischief he would cause while I'm gone? Change your mind and come with me. It will be a short stay—a fortnight, no more." He added, low, "We can use that time to begin a child," and kissed her palm.

They had already discussed the impossibility of this. Rather than restating tired arguments, Aridela said, "Would that not make your many citadel women jealous?"

Startled surprise, followed by a hint of uneasiness, flickered across his face. She turned away, giggling.

Aridela's stewards had scoured the palace and town to obtain suitable offerings for King Idómeneus, King Eurysthenes, Prince Gelanor, their officers, and men. Merchants who had squirreled away their wealth to protect it from Harpalycus donated it now in hopes of gaining favor with the queen. Presented with much fanfare were gifts of golden tripods, carved signet rings portraying full-breasted Athene with lions at her side, miniature bulls carved from crystal and onyx, bolts of Egyptian linen, and delicate quartz jars filled with Cretan oils.

Idómeneus in his turn gave Aridela an exquisite painting made especially for her. It depicted Athene herself, brandishing a spear on the summit of a hill, flanked by two lionesses. The High King told her it was a likeness of the stone carving he'd had constructed for the main gate into his citadel.

The night wore on. Idómeneus was carried off to his bed. Many left for other entertainments and the feasting hall grew quiet. Aridela and Chrysaleon made excuses and slipped away to stroll through the neglected palace garden.

Jeweled rays of lavender offered a new dawn's subtle promise. "I will bring it back," she said, struck with fervor at the beauty in the heavens. "I will make Kaphtor as great—no, greater—than it ever was."

Chrysaleon folded her arm around his. They walked on without speaking, their steps making no sound on the dirt footpaths.

As they detoured around the skeleton of a dead bush, they nearly ran into Menoetius. Leaning against a stone pillar, the last remaining piece of an elaborate arch that had once framed the outer entry into the garden, he was staring into the sky. He straightened at their appearance, obviously as startled as they.

Guilt prompted Aridela to step away from Chrysaleon. She fancied Menoetius noticed, and felt her cheeks flush.

After Chrysaleon took her from the cave in the Araden mountains, Menoetius returned to Selene. He hardly spoke to Aridela. In fact, she'd scarcely seen him since the battle. Obedient as always, he bowed to Chrysaleon's wishes and hers, unspoken though they were.

Chrysaleon cuffed Menoetius on the shoulder, oblivious or dismissive of the tense atmosphere between his consort and half brother. "Where have you been hiding? I can never find you these days. Is that milky Amazon girl roping you to her bed?"

In this brief space before sunrise, the sky deepened from lavender to purple, much like a vast royal robe soaked in the precious dye Crete's fishermen extracted from snails. Such a richness of color made it hard to determine any subtleties, yet Aridela acutely sensed Menoetius's desire to escape.

"Leave off, Chrysaleon," he said. "I don't ask what you do with your time."

"Let every foolish wench on Crete invite you to her bed. Why should I care? I alone possess the queen of women."

"Chrysaleon." Aridela's attempt at criticism was interrupted when he plucked her into his arms and swung her in a dizzying circle. So close were they to Menoetius that her heel struck his shin.

Setting her down and holding her fast, Chrysaleon gave her a long, suffocating kiss, effectively halting her sputtered protests. He lifted his head and shouted, his words bouncing off the crumbling walls. "The queen of Crete is mine!"

"You show me little respect, Zagreus," she said, her face burning.

"My property. My chattel. My slave." Lowering his voice, he added, "My wife, my love, for as long as the pyramids stand in Egypt."

"An earthshaking could bring those down tomorrow. What of you? Are you my property and slave?"

He dropped to one knee and pressed her right hand to his forehead before kissing it. "Command me. I am yours."

Tears stung her eyes as she drew him upright. "Who will make me laugh with you gone?"

Chrysaleon squeezed her hands, but she thought she caught the slightest hint of that anticipation she'd noticed when he first told her he meant to go.

Menoetius stepped away. She swung toward him, startled and guilty.

The bow he offered was rigid and formal. "I leave you to your privacy," he said, and stalked toward the palace, swiftly vanishing into murky violet shadows.

Aridela realized what she'd said and how it must have sounded. She was glad the dim light would disguise this persistent guilty blush.

"Not him." Chrysaleon sent a derisive laugh after his brother. "Women find Menoetius alluring because he frightens them, makes them shiver and feel alive. They fantasize about taming the ugly beast of Mycenae. But when his true nature is revealed, they run away as fast as they can."

He wagged a finger at her. "Stop frowning like that or I will think you are one of those simpleminded females."

"I assure you I am not simpleminded."

He laughed. "Until recently I suspected my father preferred the bastard over his true son. I was ravaged by jealousy. He is older than me, you know, by a few breaths."

"Yes. I know." Menoetius had described how the brothers came into the world almost simultaneously, from different mothers—one the queen of Mycenae, the other a slave.

Tilting his head up, Chrysaleon contemplated the sky. "At last I know differently. My father is angry and must shout his curses, yet I saw his pride. He has disavowed Menoetius, though, for allowing me to compete. Menoetius has become a man with no home. It is me Idómeneus values."

Aridela stiffened. "I will not stand for this. Menoetius has twice saved my life. If your father cannot see his worth, his home will be here, with us."

Chrysaleon kissed her again and guided her backward, into the still-deep shadows behind the ruined arch. As he drew her to the ground, he said, "I suspect you are too soft to be queen. Did I say I was disavowing Menoetius? He is still my brother, as far as I'm concerned. And my father will forgive him when he calms down. He always does."

A small, pale lizard, the kind with bumps that looked like armor, skittered across the pillar. She couldn't help smiling as it paused and seemed to peer at them. She'd caught one when she was little and kept it as a pet, toting it around on her shoulder with a tiny leather leash.

It seemed a good omen.

"I overheard King Idómeneus the night of the battle," she said between his kisses. "He was so angry. I feared for you. I thought he might have you both killed."

"If you knew him better, you would understand." Chrysaleon hiked up her tunic as he nuzzled her throat. "His anger is what made it clear. He wishes Menoetius, not me, was facing death at the midsummer moon. That was the plan, you know. Menoetius was supposed to compete in your Games. My father considered him expendable."

His callous statement brought back the confession Menoetius made when they were living in the Araden mountains. *If Chrysaleon had obeyed our father, I could have been your partner in the cave. I could have won the Games and become your consort. Only the gods will ever know what difference it might have made.*

Chrysaleon lifted his face from hers long enough to add, "Be cheered it was me who fought for you and won." He grinned. "My humorless brother would have made your life as grim as the ash-buried isle of Callisti."

In the Moon of Asterion

Book Three

Available Everywhere in digital and paperback

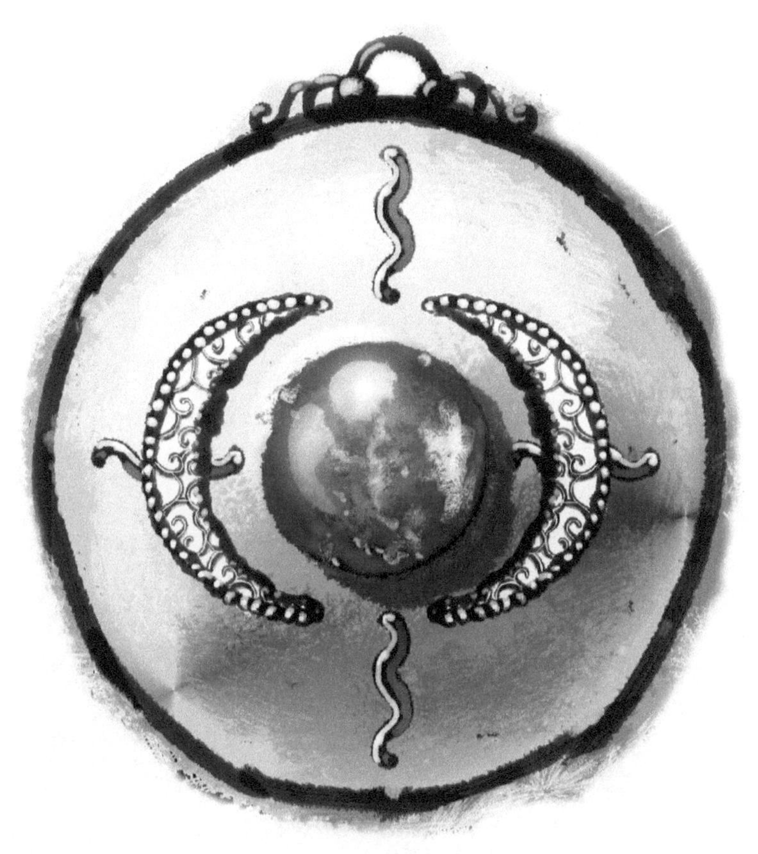